THE
BELIEVING
GAME Eireann Corrigan

SCHOLASTIC PRESS • NEW YORK

Library of Congress Cataloging-in-Publication Data available

ISBN 978-0-545-29983-1

10 9 8 7 6 5 4 3 2 1   12 13 14 15 16

Printed in the U.S.A.   23
First edition, December 2012

The text type was set in Sabon.
Book design by Christopher Stengel

For David Levithan —
who I am proud to call my friend and editor,
and who truly deserves his cult following

ONE

I knew they'd caught me before the store manager came hustling down from the café area, before the checker from the next register over stepped out and blocked my cart with his foot. Maybe I felt the closed-circuit camera zero in on me, the bull's-eye suddenly blazing on my back. Most likely, though, it was that my regular checkout lady wouldn't make eye contact with me. Her name tag read LORNA, and she'd pasted a happy-face sticker on it. Usually she smiled, asked, "How are you?" I always chose her line because she was nice and sort of frazzled. Distracted. Lorna and I were pals. In her version of my life, my single mom worked too hard and made me babysit my siblings far too often. Sometimes I bought diapers so I could say something like, "This flu has just knocked my mom out. My brother's two and he's a real handful!" And she'd laugh and grin and shake her head about what a good kid I was.

But that day Lorna wouldn't even look at me. When the machine spit out my receipt, she pursed her lips and I knew. For a second, I considered bolting. But the exit was a good six aisles away and I'd cornered myself with the cart. By the time the manager motioned for the security guard, I had already lifted my backpack off the items at the bottom of the cart and faked shock. "Oh gosh. I almost forgot all this." Hastily piled my stash of lip glosses, necklaces, sunglasses, personal lubricant, and silky underwear onto the conveyor belt. "So sorry — I'm such a moron!" But Lorna only glanced past me.

I heard the manager first. He wheezed behind me. He had apparently really exerted himself. "Miss." My legs wobbled. He reached over and turned out the light for the checkout station. Aisle twelve was closed for business. "Miss. We're going to need you to come with us."

My face felt suddenly sunburned. Later on, Joshua would teach me, *Shame is just a retreat into weakness.* But then I spoke softly because of the knot in my throat. "I apologized." I snapped open my wallet and whipped my debit card back out. "Seriously." When I slapped the card onto the counter, it sounded desperate. "Just a mix-up. Really, I'm so sorry."

The manager wouldn't cave. "Come with us, please." Lorna studied the buttons on the register. I smiled meekly at the security guy, but he only smoothed out his blue uniform and looped his thumb into his holster. It looked like it held a canister of pepper spray.

If I got through the doors and into the parking lot, they couldn't detain me. Most retailers maintain that policy — I knew that. It's not like Target wanted to deal with a lawsuit from some teenager their overeager rent-a-cop had wrestled to the ground in order to save a helpless tube of mascara.

But the security guard must have noticed me plotting my path to freedom. He clamped on to my shoulder and pushed me forward. "Let's go."

"Take your hands off me." I pleaded toward Lorna. "This is all just a mistake." She simply handed over the bag of items I'd actually paid for: a package of Oreos to surprise my nonexistent little brother and a bottle of Target-brand fabric softener. The manager grabbed the bag in one hand and reached for my backpack with the other.

"That's my stuff," I protested.

"Let's go into the back office and take a look," he told me. By then a little crowd had gathered. Just a bunch of nosy housewives and their mucus-faced kids — all pinched faces and pointing fingers. Joshua would say, *They're not seeing you as you are. They're seeing you as they are.*

"What?" I barked at one of them. Then I turned back to the manager. "My father's an attorney. I don't think you're allowed to detain me in some closed back room." We entered a white hallway that smelled like stale coffee. "I'm a minor." I looked back at the security guard. "It's not legal or appropriate for you to be touching me." His hand dropped down.

"Well, we certainly don't mean to make you uncomfortable," the manager said sarcastically before shuffling over to his desk and sinking into his seat. He picked up the phone and spoke to me as he dialed. "But the truth of the matter is, we've caught you on camera several times now."

He held one finger up for me to wait, as if I was going somewhere. "Frank? Yeah, it's Bob Dennis over at the Sturbridge Target. We have a shoplifting situation. A repeat offender." Bob Dennis took out my fabric softener and studied my receipt. "Right. We'll be pressing charges." Bob Dennis examined my Oreos. "Yup. Thank you kindly. We'll sit tight and wait for you here."

I tried again to negotiate. "Look — I just won't ever come back here, okay? What are you doing? You can't go through my backpack." But Bob Dennis apparently felt totally justified in rifling through my personal property. And pulling out my cell phone. "That's my phone. You won't find any stolen property."

Bob Dennis didn't respond. He just scrolled through my numbers, then picked up his phone and dialed again. "Mrs. Cannon? This is Bob Dennis at the Sturbridge Promenade Target Greatland. I'm sorry to tell you that we're holding your daughter here." He flipped open my wallet and peered at my driver's license. "Greer Cannon?" For a second, I wondered if maybe my mom might deny knowing me. "Yes, for shoplifting. I take it this is a recurrent issue, then?" *Thanks for that, Mom.* "Well, I have already contacted the authorities." He held the receiver slightly away from his ear, presumably to distance himself from the shrieking. "Mrs. Cannon, I'm very sorry, but we need to follow company protocol. You understand." Bob Dennis sneered into the phone. "I think it's a good idea for you to come down here too." He turned to me and smiled widely. "Perhaps you'll arrive before the police, but unfortunately we have consistent company practices to protect both our employees and our customers." I felt sorry for Lorna. I'd let her down, and here she had such a douchebag boss. "Either way, of course I'm happy to discuss restitution, Mrs. Cannon. I imagine that's a necessity at this point. We'll see you soon."

So that's what I ended up doing one afternoon in late August, the summer before my junior year in high school. Waiting in a musty office, dreading the arrival of my mom, praying she didn't just abandon me. It was the third time I'd been caught.

Somewhere, in places I'd never seen, people I didn't know were watching their own lives similarly unravel. Maybe this was the night that Addison drank himself into a stupor and kicked some kid until he bled from his mouth. Maybe as I sat there, Sophie started cutting again, and her sister told her parents. And a girl named Hannah Green found even more creative ways to hurt herself.

And all the while, Joshua Stern hovered off in the distance, waiting for each one of us to disintegrate. He held court in the coffee shop or in the Stop & Shop parking lot. He ran the Narcotics Anonymous meetings in the church basement. While my mom tore through the Target with her checkbook and pointed out that I hadn't actually stolen anything, while she hauled me out to the car and told me that she could no longer stand to look at my face, while I waited for my parents to stop bickering and decide what to do to me, maybe Joshua sat beside a sad girl in a diner booth and carefully explained how she underestimated the power of her own person. Or he trolled the self-help section of the local bookstore, the almost empty Laundromat, combing through the wreckage.

Later on, he would claim he felt us all out there. Like a storm gathering — that kind of crackling energy. Joshua told us that in the ancient world, followers often wandered into pilgrimage. The wise men followed the North Star without knowing for certain who they would kneel to once they arrived.

It was the rest of the world who considered us aimless. Joshua knew we were just finding our way home.

CHAPTER
TWO

Even if it were scripture, it wouldn't start with Joshua. Joshua might claim that, but he came after. Maybe it started with Addison, or with McCracken Hill. It probably started way before McCracken Hill because it's not like I ended up there by chance. I made choices.

All anyone at McCracken talked about were choices. Life was a series of decisions and we had whiffed most of them. We'd been sent there to learn how to make smart choices, informed choices, positive choices that displayed proper judgment and an understanding of our role in society. That was the steadfast message of the staff and it was stenciled on our walls, carved in the massive mahogany classroom tables, even etched into the unbreakable glass of the vending machines outside the dining hall.

Those snack machines were stocked with granola bars and popcorn, vitamin water and organic juice, so it's not like anyone actually trusted our sense of self-control. Dorm lights functioned on a timer — they snapped off at ten and blinked back on at six in the morning. When I toured McCracken with my parents, I noticed that none of the rooms we visited looked like real people lived in them. There weren't any posters. No drawings on the walls. No clothes thrown across chairs, no laptops or phones, or even chargers left plugged into the electrical outlets. Each room had two beds with the same navy blue blanket stretched tightly across each mattress. Two identical piles of books stacked carefully on each wood desk. And the dorms all had their own self-help names: Discipline House, Self-Discovery Hall.

I say *tour*, but it was less of a tour than a display. We'd gone to visit colleges two years before, during my older sister's senior year. Back then we ate in the dining halls. Eliza sat through classes. She stayed overnight a couple of times and when we retrieved her the next morning, she'd always have some new mannerism — a word I'd never heard her pronounce before or a gesture that looked too dramatic, too large for her arms. Once, after she visited NYU, we picked her up at the train station and she had a long, pink strand running through her hair. My mom freaked and then Eliza reached up and unclipped her barrette. The whole offending piece came away in her hands. My sister would never have done anything permanently bad.

And this place wasn't NYU — we were in Shitstain, Pennsylvania, in the middle of nowhere. McCracken Hill was not a top-tier university or even an unranked community college. It probably landed somewhere between boarding school and rehab. Closer to rehab.

Mom didn't even ride along in the car to drop me off. She didn't iron my clothes before I packed them all up or take me anywhere for toiletries. In a way, that was a relief — neither of us pretended it was camp. In the days leading up to my departure, Mom didn't actually talk to me much. I thought then that she felt guilty, that my dad had pushed her into the decision. She'd meant the pamphlets as a warning, but Dad had made her follow through.

In the end, I didn't need the toiletries. When we got to the admissions office, a biology teacher named Ms. Crane went through my bag. She sorted out my shampoo, conditioner, even my contact lens solution.

"I'm assuming you wear eyeglasses?" she asked.

"I wear contacts." I swiveled toward my dad. This was crazy.

"Not here. Not yet. Contacts are a privilege."

"Seeing? My sight is a privilege?" My eyes watered in spite of themselves and my dad cleared his throat. For a second, it seemed like he was going to speak up. But then Ms. Crane's fingers clamped down on my eyeglass case. She snapped it open.

"There!" she announced triumphantly. "Do you want to go to the ladies' room to switch?"

"No." I felt that old ache at the back of my throat and couldn't believe I was about to cry so soon. That they'd broken me already.

My dad cleared his throat again, but before he actually spoke, Ms. Crane tapped one long nail against the laminated pamphlet on top of my pile of books. "I'm sorry — our handbook states our policy very clearly. Students must lay some groundwork of trust before earning the allowance of liquids in their rooms."

"How am I supposed to shower?" I asked. In response, Ms. Crane set a generic bar of soap on top of my bag. "What about my hair?"

"Soap works just as well. You'll find there's a lot we categorize as 'needs' that we should really consider 'wants.'"

"Well, I *want* to know why you smell like Pantene, then." Ms. Crane's smile didn't waver; she just kept digging through my bag, then handed me my contacts case.

"That's a very stylish pair of eyeglasses," she said. The smile deepened spitefully. My glasses had thick lenses and puke-colored tortoiseshell rims and I only ever wore them in cases of pinkeye. I even slept with my contacts in. I knew I wasn't supposed to, but I hated waking up and finding everything blurry.

My dad valiantly forced words out. "I don't see this as necessary — Greer's hygiene —"

"This has nothing to do with hygiene, Mr. Cannon." Ms. Crane's voice rose and then plateaued back to even-keel territory again. "I'm sure it won't surprise you that some of our students struggle with substance abuse issues. In the interest of maintaining an alcohol-free environment, we monitor liquids very carefully, especially containers coming from off campus."

My dad rubbed at his temples. "Can't you just sniff it?" I could tell he was wishing he had just put me on a train. That's what the admissions team had recommended. "Greer — there's nothing in —" He turned to confirm that I hadn't yet resorted to smuggling vodka in Bausch & Lomb bottles. I didn't bother to answer. He had already remembered that I wasn't to be trusted.

If Ms. Crane hadn't taken such obvious glee in the whole process, I would have laughed at McCracken Hill's ridiculous liquid policy. But I met most of my classmates wearing my Army of Dorkness glasses, with the residue of cheap soap caking my hair.

I told myself it didn't matter what I looked like. And it didn't, at least not for a few weeks.

I suffered through a full month of classes and counseling to get to the point where the team designated me fit for shampoo and other bottled fluids. My treatment team consisted of my four academic instructors, the principal, vice principal, and my counselor. Because I struggled with "self-destructive eating patterns," I also had to meet with a nutritionist. Some kids went to Narcotics Anonymous and others went to AA instead, and twice a month the school even bused a bunch of kids to Philadelphia for a Gamblers Anonymous meeting. They sent my lab partner, Dale, there and he said the kids spent most of the ride trying to bribe the driver to take them to Mohegan Sun.

I'd never been on parole — nothing had ever gotten that serious. Even still, I imagined a parole board review would feel cozier than a McCracken treatment team session. First of all, sessions took place in one of three conference rooms, all named for dead kids. There was a framed picture in each room and a plaque. And so you sat there under a photograph of a dead kid, surrounded by the adults who judged you every day. No one ever explained how the kids had died.

Under the dead kid's watchful eyes, you sat there and reviewed your choices. Each member of the team brought a file, so you got to explain why you chose to turn in your last lit essay late, why you decided to sneak out of peer tutoring. You sat there while they dissected you and it really felt like that — a series of slices across your belly. You realized how exposed you were when you listened to all of the tiny, stupid, little decisions that you didn't even realize you were making. They wrote them all down. In that room, at least, it seemed like they noticed everything.

No one asked me about stealing. I hadn't stepped off campus since I'd arrived, so maybe they figured it was a non-issue. And I'd landed a single, so no roommates to pilfer from. Instead they pointed out that I hadn't yet joined a club. "Extracurriculars give us the chance to focus our energies on our passions," the principal told me. I recognized the language from the student handbook and wondered if that meant he'd written it or just memorized it.

Greer, are you happy? No one asked this. We sat around and measured how productive I'd been, how cooperative. I waited for someone to point out that I hadn't yet made a single friend. I planned to blame the glasses — but no one mentioned it. Making friends wasn't the point; it's not like any of us were gunning for reform school homecoming queen. It took me that little bit to get used to McCracken. Keeping focused, holding myself accountable, all of those buzzwords pretty much made the idea of "happy" obsolete. That's what I left that first treatment session knowing. No one really cared. But at least they gave me back liquids.

I washed my hair twice that night. Swirled Listerine around my mouth and slipped in my contacts and felt so absurdly euphoric about it that I almost knocked on the other doors lining the girls' corridor of Empowerment Hall. I nearly asked the dorm counselor if I could sign out my cell phone and call home to share my renewed appreciation for leave-in conditioner.

But I didn't do either of those things. I finally felt clean and decided not to ruin that by reaching out to someone who'd most likely disappoint me. I ambled from the hall bathroom to my single, with my plastic bucket of irreproachable toiletries knocking hopefully against my leg. That night, my bare room seemed more pure than forlorn, like a monk's cell. I remember feeling like I was readying myself for something miraculous, something life altering.

Or someone. Right after that, Addison showed up. It turned out I'd been preparing myself for him.

CHAPTER
THREE

Maybe in real life, Addison and I wouldn't have registered on each other's radar. For one thing, he was muscular. Some girls appreciate that, but not me. Addison was built the way cartoon superheroes are built. Bulging. Cabled. His shirts strained across his chest; veins pulsed along his thick arms. The first thing you understood about him was that Addison could hurt someone. His hair was clipped so short, you couldn't make out its color. He always wore jeans — not thug-saggy or painted on. Just regular jeans, along with white or black T-shirts and work boots. When he first showed up in the middle of English class, I guessed he worked on the maintenance crew. And when he sat down, it surprised me that he didn't slump. Dr. Rennie asked him to read a passage on the handout aloud and I braced myself. Part of me expected that he would stumble over the words, that he wouldn't be able to read.

Now I understand how ignorant that assumption was. Joshua would call it *shaping the world to fit the hole in my heart*. Addison read the poem like it was a script he'd already memorized. It was the Browning poem about the duke who kills his wife, and he didn't even hesitate on the foreign names. It also made the poem creepier — hearing it read by the Incredible Hulk.

I noticed him. And then he noticed me back.

It surprised me. He didn't look like someone who would look at me. But he did. A lot. Mostly because his seat at the seminar table faced mine. It wasn't that my face was that supremely magnetic or anything. They gave me back shampoo. They didn't airbrush me.

But that first day, I felt Addison's eyes on me like tiny needles, embroidering my face with his gaze. He read the poem, then answered Dr. Rennie's questions with his clear, even voice. Dr. Rennie droned on, prodding us to psychoanalyze a fictional character from the nineteenth century. "Sir," Addison said, "I'm not convinced the poet wants us to empathize with the speaker here." Everyone in the room knew something was going on, that the new kid was trying out for something. It wasn't until the third time that he answered and then slid his eyes in my direction that I let myself believe it: Addison was auditioning for me.

Dr. Rennie held him back afterward, supposedly to check his books, but really to remind us all that he could. I paused in the doorway, but Addison didn't turn. I remember feeling myself carried out into the hallway, in the wave of everyone else around me. Already I was thinking about him. Already I felt his presence tugging me in the opposite direction.

My profound and unwavering appreciation for the penis certainly factored into my parents' decision to ship me off to McCracken Hill. They never said so, but I knew it anyway.

Ancient pagans used sex as a form of ritual worship, but I didn't mention that to Ms. Crane or Ms. Ling or any of the other perky women in polar fleece who had been recruited to teach me to keep my legs crossed. I dutifully picked at my cuticles and pretended to be embarrassed. When they said, "Sometimes it's easy to trick ourselves into feeling powerful when we give up that gift," I wanted to offer them techniques, because if they'd never felt mighty like that, then they weren't doing it right. One night, when Todd Gibbons and I had snuck into the botanical gardens back home, he'd taken a step ahead of me on the wooden, slatted path and I'd stopped and pulled my dress right over my head. I'd stood there in heels with nothing else on and watched his knees buckle when he turned back.

Todd Gibbons was shorter than me and talked too much about obscure bands. I hadn't even expected to go out with him again, but I could have watched him stumble over and over. I wanted to tell Ms. Ling that I was the one who'd caught him and tugged him to the patch of moss off to the side of the walk. And afterward it was me who hadn't called back. *Sometimes it's like that,* I wanted to say. Sometimes seeing your own bare limbs soaked in moonlight is sacred. Sometimes you need to know you can make someone else shake and sigh.

Both Ms. Crane and Ms. Ling could run the abstinence script by me all they wanted, but I noticed they both went still anytime Addison entered a room. Lots of girls did. He never made any kind of sly comment or stood up any straighter. Even when the female teachers would lapse into a beat of silence and then restart — more loudly, with their hands fluttering around their hair, the top buttons of their blouses — Addison just kept going, like he was used to having that kind of influence.

Early on, he let me see him notice. At McCracken, you were privileged with the choice of table for breakfast and lunch. But for dinner, they assigned you tables each week.

Everyone rotated. It was supposed to prevent cliques but mostly it meant eating a lot of meals in silence. A member of the faculty lorded over each of the tables, and conversations went something like this:

Ms. Crane: "Wow — Mondays, right? They can be tiring, but they're also an opportunity for a whole new beginning each week."

Us: Silence.

Ms. Crane: "What are we all planning for this week?"

Us: Silence.

That time, Ms. Crane told us, "I'm looking forward to Friday's movie night. The film club has chosen an inspiring selection about a marathon runner who loses his leg after drinking and driving. It's intense, but it has an incredible message. What do you all have planned? Why don't we just go around the table so everyone has the chance to share — Hannah, why don't you begin?"

Hannah Green was looking forward to huffing the Scotchgard she'd lifted off the cleaning woman's cart. Her eyes darted back and forth; her mouth opened and closed. "Hannah." Ms. Crane spoke firmly and slowly. "Please share your plans with the group." A slight wheeze escaped Hannah's lips. She sounded like a deflating tire. I don't know why I decided to help. Maybe it was because Addison was there. Maybe it was my turn to audition.

"Hannah and I were going to sign out some board games from the rec room on Friday."

"That's lovely, Greer. But I'm sure Hannah will tell me all about it." Hannah's tongue darted across her lips. She looked tweaked out. Ms. Crane's pen hovered over her conversational scorecard. "Game night sounds like fun, Hannah. What do you like to play?"

Hannah reached out for her glass of water. I watched the liquid slosh toward the cup's lip, realizing I'd never heard her speak. Most of the kids at McCracken seemed hardened, not weak. It was just like Ms. Crane to zero in on one of the few who wouldn't fight back.

Addison reached across and laid his hand over Ms. Crane's. She looked down at it and her skin reddened — the blush first blossomed up her neck, then her whole face. "That movie sounds really compelling, Ms. Crane. Sometimes I think about the stupid mistakes I made, you know — back when I was drinking. Any night of the week, I could have destroyed my life. Or someone else's."

She tore her eyes from the sight of his hand resting on her own. Ms. Crane didn't seem to see anyone else at the table. She just drank him in. That might have counted as the first time I saw a guy execute my moves. I pictured Ms. Crane's evaluations: *Addison takes initiative. Addison has a keen understanding of anatomy.*

Addison flickered his gaze up to me and I willed my eyes to ice over. *Go for it, whiskey dick.* When the clock hand clawed over to 6:30 P.M., Hannah skittered from her seat and I pretended to be concerned so I could chase her.

"Hey, Hannah — slow down, speed freak." I hoped he heard me being a good person. I hoped he laughed at my effortless addiction punnery. Hannah Green was not amused.

"Enough, okay?" But she stopped at the dining hall's little footbridge. She waited for me to convince her I cared.

I didn't. "Sure thing." I pronounced it in two clipped syllables, like my mom does when she won't entertain a tantrum. Hannah Green had to hold on to the railing, I strode by her that fast. I hurtled over the stone paths until I could close myself in my stark room and remember the minutes when I made myself matter.

I knew it was him knocking. Recognized the three short raps, even though I'd never heard them before. They sounded like Addison. I remember sitting straight up in the bed and glaring through the door. And when I swung it open, he stood there with his head bowed and pressed to the door frame. He looked guilty, which made it worse.

"Listen," I said, "we had historic eye contact. That's it. You don't have to explain yourself to me." I used my best assassin voice.

"Can I come in?"

Addison moved forward, but I stepped out around him, pulled the door shut behind me.

"Are you kidding?" I checked the length of the hallway. No Ms. Crane. Maybe he'd applied for a restraining order in the fifteen minutes after dinner. "If someone sees you here . . ."

He didn't care. And neither, really, did I.

"Do you not hear the bedsprings squeaking up and down the hall?" he asked.

"People are doing sit-ups, right? Working off dinner calories?"

"No — I mean — wait, you're just screwing with me, right?" Addison rocked back on his heels and grinned, and I felt my whole face flush hot. My right leg actually shook, and suddenly I developed a tiny shred of empathy for Ms. Crane. Miniscule, but there. And then Addison reached out. He rubbed his thumb across my cheekbone, like he was marking me. I half-expected to go back in the room and find a bruise of war paint across my face. "Greer Cannon. You might be the most well-behaved delinquent here."

The metal door cooled my back. I wondered if Addison's eyes would widen if I reached behind me and turned the knob, drew him into the room and onto the narrow bed. But then I remembered how Ms. Crane's eyes had glittered, tracing the movement of his lips when he spoke. I thought about all the girls straightening up in their seats when he first strode into a classroom. Any of them would pull Addison into bed.

I wasn't just anyone.

So I headed for the dorm doors. I heard Addison's steps, even before he gathered himself up to call after me. "Greer! Wait." I paused at the vestibule for a few seconds. It was just dusk and I could see the barest outline of Addison's reflection behind mine in the window's glass. He asked, "Where are we going?" as if it were totally up to me.

That night, I learned it's possible to walk for hours around the same grassy quad and still see a fresh view on each pass. Addison listened to me. He looked at me too. But not the head-to-toe checking out that I'd grown used to. Addison considered me in the same careful way we considered the McCracken Hill scenery, finding something new every time. Sometimes you're just living your life and suddenly there's a moment that hits you harder than others. You think that flash will go on glimmering for the rest of your days. You'll always look back and remember it.

Addison made every moment feel like that.

We looped around the school grounds, sticking mostly to the stone paths between buildings. Most of McCracken Hill was fenced in wrought iron. I kept reaching out and grabbing at it as we walked by. We didn't actually go anywhere. Even still, we traveled closer and closer to each other.

"How often do you go off campus?" he asked.

I shrugged. I didn't go off campus. I'd thought the gilded cage was the point.

"You don't ever just walk to town?" Addison looked at me incredulously. You had to ask for a treatment session in order to request village privileges. I pictured sitting at the vast conference table, arguing that I needed fresh air. Dad and I had bypassed the town on the way in. But I knew there was a Rite Aid nearby. A 7-Eleven. A Starbucks. Rite Aids usually use electronic surveillance devices on valuable items. Most 7-Elevens use closed-circuit TVs.

"I haven't really needed anything." When you left campus, you had to return through the ornate gates near the administrative building. Security guards checked through your things. You signed a ledger book when you left and when you came back to campus.

"What do you do here all the time?"

I shrugged, thought of the journal full of scribbled letters that I kept. The hundreds of times I'd written Always, Greer at the bottom of pages I'd never send. "I study a lot" is all I managed to come up with. And then, because that sounded so pitiful, "I write a lot of letters home."

"Do you miss it?"

I didn't. But the sympathetic tilt in his voice suggested that family was a big deal for Addison Bradley. For him, home meant sitting around the kitchen table late at night, shooting the shit with his dad, or maybe a brother. His mom stood at the stove, flipping pancakes and laughing at their stories. Or maybe he had a little sister who he picked up and threw over his shoulder every time she mouthed off to their parents. He shook her until she dropped the attitude and finally smiled. Addison looked like he raked leaves, took out the trash, carried in groceries from the car.

"I miss them," I said. I let him think I meant my family, but really I meant the phantom folks in his family portrait. I missed the Bradleys, whoever they were.

Except they couldn't have been too perfect. Addison had landed at McCracken.

Mostly we talked about school. What was bullshit. What made sense. Addison was better at picking out what made sense. Even with Ms. Crane. When I shook my head, he reached out and stopped me, held my chin between his thumb and finger. I thought he would tilt my head to kiss me, but he just said, "When you nod your head, you're so beautiful. Because you're accepting possibility."

Accepting possibility. I had never thought of things in those terms. Mostly because no one had ever offered them to me that way.

Addison told me that even if Ms. Crane's motives were flawed, they had to stem from kindness. "You don't sign up to work at a place like this just for money."

"Maybe she's building her resume."

"No — seriously," he said. I'd meant it seriously. But Addison kept going. "At least someone spoke to Hannah Green today, right? How often does that happen?"

I remembered barreling past Hannah outside the dorms. How stricken she'd looked when I'd said, "Sure thing." Like a door was shutting in her face.

"What are you thinking?" he asked me. It felt like he knew what I was thinking.

I said it aloud anyway. "It'll happen more often. Hannah Green talking. I'll make sure." Still I felt compelled to add, "But that's not because of Ms. Crane."

"No." Addison said it solemnly. "That's your goodness. I spend a lot of time thinking about goodness because there's a lot I have to make up for. You would hate me if I were drinking."

"How would you know?"

"Because I hate me when I'm drinking."

Addison told me that when he drank, he threw punches. At door frames. Through windows. At people. "Who?" I asked.

He rubbed his face with his hands. "Anyone." He must have seen my eyes widen. "Not girls." He looked past me, like he was actually putting together a list of people he'd hit before. "At parties, mostly." Once he put a kid in the hospital. "I sucker punched him and when he went down, I kicked the kid again and again. I was so out of it, Greer. I degraded myself. And then, well, you know, there's my brother."

He wasn't the brother I had imagined for Addison. His name was Chuckie; he was two years older; he could drink Addison under the table. It sounded like that's what they did. They sat around in their family room and drank and sometimes smoked weed or took pills. Then Chuckie had moved up the substance abuse food chain. Mixed with whatever they were drinking, that meant that sometimes Chuckie slept so hard, Addison thought he was dead. Sometimes, he tackled Addison and slammed him into the wall.

"But he couldn't hurt you —" I stopped speaking, wondering if that's why Addison worked out so hard.

"We're both pretty huge. Like two bears wrestling down in the rec room."

"So why are you here and not Chuckie?" I asked and then a wave of dread washed over me. *Oh God,* I thought. *His brother's dead.*

But Addison only said, "He's home. Chuckie needs my mom and dad more."

So they sent Addison away and brought in an in-home counselor for his brother. "Really?" I tried to imagine the self-empowerment exercises and quacky language of McCracken distilled into one person's constant presence. "I'd go crazy," I said. I'd turn to pills.

"Yeah. Pretty much." Addison shook his head slowly like he was sad. Then more quickly to shake himself out of it.

There was nothing fragile about him. Even when he was revealing his vulnerabilities, there was a sturdiness there that I admired. Nothing seemed to rattle Addison. We swapped arrest stories and shared our disastrous paths to reform school and he never suddenly went all squirrelly with lack of eye contact. He never backed away from me and I remember thinking, *This is a person who could really know me.* I hadn't felt that way in ages. Since long before McCracken Hill.

The wrought-iron fence didn't matter. We covered a lot of ground that night.

Addison felt it too. As the night reached for sleep and our curfew loomed, he told me, "This is the first time in months I haven't felt like a monster. It's enough to make me glad I'm here for the duration."

It took a moment to figure it out. "Not just until you get better."

He finished my thought. "Until Chuckie and I both get better." Addison smiled and enveloped my shoulder in one of his sturdy arms. "You too. I'll wait for you to get better too." It would be poor form to argue right then that nothing was actually wrong with me besides my tendency to get caught in fairly spectacular ways. Instead I nodded and let Addison think it was a small step toward healing. A tiny breakthrough.

I was still nodding when he told me, "There's someone I really need you to meet." And then stopped nodding abruptly because I thought he meant his brother. I didn't want to meet a larger version of Addison — a beast rattling his cage in the Bradleys' living room.

But Addison didn't mean his brother. Addison was talking about Joshua then.

CHAPTER
FOUR

Tucked into the basement of Liberty House, the main administrative center at McCracken Hill, is a narrow office lined entirely with hanging files. I gained access once and almost got high off the scent of manila folders. The Office of Student Records holds all of our secrets — each McCracken alum's entire journey of self-discovery condensed into a two-pocket folder of progress charts, teacher evaluations, and psych reports.

There's no receptionist or anything. Maybe no one actually ever looks at the files. They just keep them in case there's a school shooting and the administration needs a paper trail to slowly release to the media. I never went back for my chart. Later on it didn't seem to matter. Back then I never wanted them to think I cared.

Mostly I lied in my sessions — lies of omission. I let them think they were the ones helping me, bringing me back into the world of eye contact and positive thinking. Otherwise, they wouldn't have counted it. No one would have believed how connected I suddenly felt. How when I walked into a room, I knew without even looking whether or not it contained Addison.

It felt weird to move closer and closer to someone without all the usual ways of communicating. Within weeks, Addison had earned back his phone, but mine still sat in the lockbox in admissions. I wasn't allowed any e-mail besides the weekly therapist-approved messages I sent to our family account. And my last Facebook status had been updated as *Grounded — to the extreme* almost a month before. So instead of posting on my wall, he slipped notes under my door. Once he folded a napkin into a flower in the cafeteria.

McCracken had rules against "exclusive relationships," but I didn't care. Addison, though, said he did.

"Why?" I asked him, while we trudged between class and dinner.

"It makes a great deal of sense, actually." I glared at him then. Sometimes Addison lectured. You had to wait until the fake patience soaked out of his voice. "Before, maybe I drank or smoked weed because I needed a distraction." He crossed one arm across his chest, stretched. "They don't want you to find a person to stand in for a bottle."

"I'm a distraction." I recognized the flat tone in my voice and tried to imagine getting through McCracken without Addison's pencil sketches, his sly sideways looks in class.

He stretched his other arm. "Well, yeah, you are." He grinned. "You're telling me that I don't distract you?"

It felt like everything else was a distraction. But that's not the kind of thing you say out loud to people. I settled for, "You don't just distract me," and waited for his arm to snake around my shoulders.

Sure enough. "Oh, dearly Greerly." Addison squeezed and sighed.

I heard the voice of my old tennis coach flicker in my ear, as he wrapped his arms around me and said, *Greer, Greer — with legs up to here.*

"C'mon. Are you really mad?" Addison widened his eyes. "At least give me a chance to make you mad with my own words." For a second, I thought he'd actually heard Coach Hendrikson's lechy voice too. But Addison didn't know about all that. He only meant that I'd been putting words in his mouth. He told me, "I never said *just*. That was you."

"It's fine." But I said it in the chick voice that means it's not really fine. I hated falling into that voice. It made me sound like my sister. In individual therapy, Dr. Saggurti had been nagging me to "make I statements." I tried it. "When you say that, I feel like a bad element, something damaging."

"But that's not it." Addison stopped walking. He turned to face me. "Really. It's the opposite, even. But you can't just pick and choose the steps that seem easiest to you. It's a formula, you know? It's worked for millions of people. I can't pretend I'm different from every other drunk. That's when you end up passed out on a park bench somewhere."

"So then, what is this?" God. I wanted to crouch down right there on the pebbled path, punch myself in the stomach again and again. It seemed like something to ask after months or years, not weeks.

"Between us?"

"Yeah." Even that one syllable sounded needy.

"You're the only person I want to talk to." Acceptable. Maybe. I thought Addison might kiss me then. I glanced from side to side. Delinquents and dorm counselors surrounded us. But I saw him look at my lips before he looked up and met my eyes. "You're my best reason for staying sober."

I felt a thrill even as I pictured Dr. Saggurti arching her meticulously shaped eyebrows. "Greer, Greer — better than beer?" I asked him.

Addison laughed. "Exactly."

At the dining commons, we moved through the food line together. I pushed my tray along right behind Addison's, watched him load up on beef chow fun and some pitiful-looking egg rolls. I ladled some of the broth from the wonton soup into a bowl, grabbed a whole wheat bagel.

"No Chinese food?"

"The egg rolls freak me out."

Addison lifted his and waved it at me. "Scary food. Fried food."

"Not that, brainiac." We hadn't ever talked about my eating disorder. I wasn't about to start right then. "Their egg rolls look exactly like their burritos. I think that's questionable." When I left him, he was still standing at the salad bar, examining his dinner with a stricken look.

The only reason we knew our relationship, whatever it was, had registered on the radar of the McCracken administration was that our seating assignments for dinner had shifted. Now Addison and I were rarely directed to the same table. In some ways, that was excruciating. Invariably, they placed me next to one of the kids too zoned out on lithium to hold a conversation. I'd sit there salting and salting my food, and see some ponytailed head bent toward Addison's like a secret.

It felt like every female body on campus experienced the Addison Bradley animal magnetism. But he didn't like me to mention that. On break from assembly, we stood in line at the watercooler, waiting for a Dixie cup of whatever doped-up liquid McCracken called water. Theodora Garrow narrowed her eyes at me, then widened them toward Addison. I watched her look him up and down.

"Do you see something you like?" I asked.

"Settle down, tiger," he said, with a laugh. But when Theodora swung her hips in another direction, Addison's voice pivoted too. "Don't do that again." His voice sounded calm, but grim. And when I tried to defend myself, he said, "I felt like a piece of meat."

"That was Theodora —"

"She's never going to have the chance to affect how I feel." And I understood the rest of his logic. I had that chance. Addison expected me to be more careful with it.

Joshua Stern was not who I expected he'd be. I knew he'd be older than us. After all, he mentored Addison through the twelve steps, and that meant he needed a few years of sobriety behind him. But Addison had called him his best friend, so I'd pictured someone older than us by only a few years.

At the pizza place, when the door's jingle signaled a new customer, it didn't even register that the silver-haired, black-skinned man in sweatpants might be Addison's sponsor. He had to be forty, at least. Maybe even fifty. But he stepped forward and Addison stood to be engulfed in his embrace. "There he is," the man murmured, as if he'd been the one waiting for us to arrive. "Hmmmm." The man held Addison by the shoulders and seemed to search his face.

He turned to me. "So this is she." I felt myself blush like an idiot. "He said you were beautiful, but he didn't say *gorgeous*." The man shot Addison an accusing look. "You should have said *gorgeous*." I tried not to show it mattered, that Addison had called me beautiful. I tried to concentrate really hard on the metal napkin dispenser so that I didn't meet anyone's gaze straight on.

"Joshua, you're embarrassing me." But when I looked up, Addison just looked proud. "Sit down," Addison told him. "I'll get you something to eat."

28

"And a Sprite, please. Remember about the ice, now," Joshua called after him. Addison bounded to the counter.

I rose to follow, calling, "Let me help."

But Joshua covered my hand with his. "He means for me to have some time with you." He looked at me steadily. "He's kept you a secret long enough." Joshua let go of my hand and sat back in the booth. "Greer." I waited, expecting him to ask me how I ended up at McCracken. *What's a pretty girl like you* . . . But he only asked, "What's your middle name, Greer?"

Maybe he was planning a background check. "Elizabeth."

"Does anyone call you Elizabeth?" I craned my neck to see Addison. He was chatting with the guys behind the counter. "Addison doesn't call you Elizabeth?"

"No. People call me Greer." *Because that's my name, Uncle Crazypants.*

Joshua nodded. "Well, I would like to call you Elizabeth. Not always. Not even often. But it's important to me that there's a name that only I use. Would that be all right with you?" I nodded. It didn't seem like such a big deal then. Joshua tugged out one of the paper napkins and tucked it into his shirt like it was a bib. "I'm glad that's settled."

"Spaghetti with meatballs and sausage," Addison announced. He turned to me. "What's settled?"

Joshua didn't acknowledge the question. He gestured to the plate of pasta in front of him and waved his hand up at Addison. "He loves to take care of me." Addison, despite his broad body and the scruff on his cheeks, looked like a little kid. He glowed. Joshua coughed a few times and then searched the table.

Addison clapped his hand over his mouth. "The Sprite! I'll be right back." He pretty much scampered back to the counter. I looked at Joshua. Joshua looked at me. I didn't ask why he couldn't just go get his own soda, but I could tell he knew I wanted to.

"Are you two going to eat?" Joshua dug into the plate of pasta, just as Addison returned with a brimming plastic cup. I felt Addison's eyes on me.

"We ate earlier."

"Go get yourself a slice of pizza." There was no mistaking the command in Joshua's voice. He added, "And for Greer too."

"I'm okay," I said. And then again, to Addison, "I'm fine." Except for that bereft feeling when he left the table once more.

I watched Joshua twirl strands of spaghetti onto his fork.

"So you're one of those beautiful girls who don't eat."

"No, sir, we ate earlier."

"Don't call me *sir*." The gentleness in Joshua's voice had evaporated. "Save that for your counselors."

I wanted to tell him to leave the menu interrogation to my counselors. But nothing came out of my mouth.

He said it for me. "I'm not your counselor. But I care. Do you know why I care?" Joshua sounded furious. He nodded back toward the counter. "I care about you because he does."

This time when Addison sat down, he didn't ask what we were talking about. He just came back raving about the pizza. "Joshua, you should see what they have me eating at the dining hall."

"Rabbit food?"

"It's criminal. It's all steamed or tofued or bok choyed or whatever."

"They have plenty of coffee for you there?"

"Actually, no, but some of the teachers let us use the pots in the faculty lounge."

Joshua nodded to himself. "The female teachers." He told me, "They want his sex. Everywhere this kid goes, women demand fucking." He kind of smacked his lips a little and grunted.

If I'd been eating, I would have choked. I managed something lame like, "Is that so?" Maybe it achieved the intended sly tone. Joshua might not have noticed I was shocked, but Addison did.

"I'm sorry." Addison gave him a stern look. "Joshua sometimes forgets to be a gentleman."

"Don't apologize for me." Joshua's voice was laughing, but his eyes weren't. "Talk to me about being a gentleman — I have fished you out of more shit and vomit than I care to discuss. I don't need to apologize. Greer knows I'm speaking the truth. She doesn't want us to talk any different because she's here. Greer doesn't want you to hide yourself. Isn't that right?"

"No." I didn't want Addison to hide anything.

"See? My Elizabeth and I have an understanding."

Afterward, after pie and coffee and hugs outside on the street, Addison and I headed back to campus. When we got to the foot of McCracken Hill, he finally reached for my hand. His skin felt rough against mine and I felt his thumb press itself into the center of my palm. "So your middle name is Elizabeth."

"Yep. He must pull that routine on all your girls." That time I managed the sly tone flawlessly.

"Once in a while." Addison pulled me closer. "Sometimes Joshua makes people uncomfortable." I heard the question in his voice.

"Not at all."

"Really?"

"He cares about you, that's all. I'm sure he was testing me a little because of that."

"Well, you passed."

"Yeah?"

"I could tell. I can always tell." We walked a little ways. "Did he surprise you?"

"Because he said *fuck*? Seriously?" But I already thought I knew what Addison meant. I was just buying some time.

"Or because he's older?" Addison asked it carefully, so I considered my answer carefully.

"How old is he?"

"He doesn't really believe in age in terms of numbers. He thinks it's bigger than that. I'm one of the oldest people he knows." Addison shrugged. "Maybe you were surprised he's black?"

"He just wasn't how I pictured him," I said. Addison swung our clasped hands out, held them up to look at them. How many times had I said the wrong thing and ruined the perfect moment? "For one thing, I thought he was Jewish. Because of his last name."

"Joshua *is* Jewish." Addison squeezed my hand as if he were about to let it go. I held harder. "African Americans can be Jewish, you know."

"I — I didn't know that, actually."

"Greer, honestly? That's so ignorant." I felt sick to my stomach. The gabled buildings of McCracken Hill rose up against the dusky sky. We were almost back to campus. I prepared myself to tightrope walk the rest of the way. Addison said, "Judaism is a religion. A member of any race can practice any religion. We only limit ourselves."

"I don't know what I was thinking," I murmured. "I'm sorry."

"When I first met Joshua, everything about him blew my mind. It's okay to have questions." Addison wrapped his other arm around me. "We should all have so many questions for each other."

I had questions. *What are we? If I were to write a letter home to a friend I no longer have, what would I call you?* I wanted to pull him close by the collar of his shirt and ask him before he dropped me off at the door.

He bent his head toward me, but he didn't kiss me. "Greer, Greer — have no fear."

"Never," I said, in the voice of the kind of girl who meant it. "Thank you for introducing me to Joshua," I told him. "Good night," I said and turned quickly inside, glad that I had said it first.

CHAPTER
FIVE

We got to have a routine. Addison usually got to breakfast much earlier than me, since he worked out in the mornings. So we'd see each other first in class. We stared at each other a lot, but not always. The thing about Addison was that he never made me feel embarrassed about the notes I was taking. I knew when I answered a question, he'd be listening and nodding, not rolling his eyes. It was different from back home.

Ten minutes to walk across the building, down two flights of steps, and then across the hall into the dining commons. Maybe five minutes in line for food. Twenty-five minutes to sit at a table together for lunch. Another walk. Another class. Then separate counseling. Afterward we'd meet at the bottom of the hill by the gate. We'd walk to town and meet Joshua. Each day, I signed out and penciled in fresh air in the space left to write my destination. Addison never signed out. "What can they do if they catch me?" Apparently the Bradleys had some kind of court order for Addison to be at McCracken. It even meant they got to write the institution a smaller check.

I knew I'd be staying the school year. "Right now the transcript's looking good, Greer," my father's voice boomed in the hearty way that was meant to convince me. "We just don't want to uproot you when it seems like you're making some progress."

It didn't matter. It didn't matter that he didn't even bother with the pretense of putting the phone on speaker. We all knew my mother would have nothing to say on the subject. I was making progress. Each day, the minute we walked through the ornate iron gates at the bottom of the hill, Addison reached for my hand. Clockwork.

And Joshua officially approved of me. We'd get to Sal's or the Boston Market and he'd scoot out of the booth so that I could sit down. Then he'd sit beside me. The first time he did it, he pointed at Addison and said, "I want him to be able to look at you."

But usually it was Joshua looking at me. "You are one lucky bastard." He'd say it to Addison, but he'd be staring at me. "Does Chuckie know how he got the Shit. End. Of. The. Stick. I mean, really. What does he get to look at all day? Oprah? Your poor, suffering mother? And you got this?"

"This has a name, Joshua," I chided him once.

But he said, "Don't even pretend you feel objectified. I know you've been treated like a thing to be owned. No man will ever treat you better than this young man right here. And do you know where he learned how to treat a woman?" Joshua clapped Addison on the back. "What taught you?"

"You did." Addison laughed.

But then Joshua followed up with, "It wasn't your father running around on your poor mother, right? Leaving her to clean up after her two drunk sons while he spent the night in hotels with pharmaceutical sales reps? It wasn't him, right?"

Addison had stopped laughing. I craned my neck, but he wouldn't meet my gaze. He'd always described his parents as so loving — to him, to each other. Even to Chuckie, who needed his stomach pumped every other week. My teeth clenched with embarrassment for him and then a protective rage. I turned to Joshua, who hadn't yet looked at my face but still said, "Don't look at me like that. You don't get to judge me. If you're surprised about this, it's because Addison was dishonest with you. I thought we'd all decided not to lie to each other."

When did we decide that? I wanted to ask. Instead I sat there, waiting for someone to decide how to move on from the moment.

"It's okay." Addison finally spoke. "I don't think I lied to you. It's just not something that really comes up."

But Joshua wasn't going to let it go. "It doesn't come up? The two of you are lying around in bed together and it never occurs to you to examine the relationships you've grown up watching? You don't mention those when you're declaring yourselves the great love affair of the century?"

If I'd felt my cheeks at that moment, they might have seared my hand. My face went that warm, with embarrassment.

"Stop." Addison said it quietly.

"I'm sorry if I am *challenging* you." Joshua sounded so angry. I tried to think back to the past few minutes. How had we made him this furious?

"Man, you don't know what you're talking about." Addison's voice had a serrated edge.

"I know what counts as intimacy. And it's not just blow jobs." Then my face went full-on scarlet. I didn't know if I felt embarrassed for us or for him.

"It's not like that." Addison measured his words out carefully. "We don't have chances like that, to spend time alone."

"You're telling me you're not fucking?" Joshua was incredulous. I considered getting up from the table. Across the way, a lady glared over at us from under her perm.

"That's enough." Addison sounded like a stern dad.

Joshua's giggle was as high-pitched as a little kid's. "You two." He pointed back and forth between us. I counted out how many steps it would take to cross to the door. "Start preparing yourselves now, because it is going to be amazing." Joshua sighed and grunted. He crossed his arms on the table and leaned in to talk to me. "I don't know if you're playing some kind of game with him, but you're only hurting yourself. This boy drives women crazy. Insane. Addison, you should play her some of those voicemails. Seriously, Elizabeth, honey, you didn't strike me as the type to fall for that born-again virgin propaganda."

"My name is Greer."

"Now don't get hurt."

"This isn't any of your business."

"See, that's where you're wrong. The happiness between you two — I have made that my business. There are plenty of beautiful things in this world. Relationships. Amazing love stories. And sometimes the love between you? It doesn't count for shit. Because no one's standing by, protecting it. But I'm there for you two. That's my vocation. Do you know what a vocation is?"

I could see the wind pick up, a few stray leaves straggle along the sidewalk outside. "A job," I told him, with the same flat voice I usually saved for bad classes.

"Almost," Joshua corrected. "A vocation is a calling." He gazed over at Addison lovingly. I wanted Addison to stand up, grab my hand, and stride toward the door. "Everyone is called to something in this world. I was called in service to him." Addison bowed his head. "I'm truly sorry if I offended you, Greer Elizabeth. I just want to make sure that you have every joy possible in this life. Especially with him."

I looked from Joshua to Addison. For the first fraction of a second, I expected Addison to give me the slight nod saying we'd stand up together and leave. But who was I? The least devoted person to him at the table. I mean, he was the most crucial person in my life, but I hadn't heard a message from God about serving him. Addison looked at me with a slight, sheepish smile. As if he was asking, *Is this so bad?*

It wasn't like I was going to tell him yes.

Had our days always revolved around the cluster of me, Addison Bradley, and Addison Bradley's spiritual guru, I might have objected. But Joshua wasn't the only person Addison had carried into my life. It embarrassed me, since I'd been at McCracken longer, but Add had more friends. And good ones, who were funny and smart and made me laugh even when we sat at dinner tables away from Addison. In a matter of weeks, he had forged a following. Like the girl with the parade of rings marching across her right eyebrow, who always walked him right out the door of the bio lab. She'd see me and veer off toward Self-Respect Hall.

"Did you know Sophie before?" I finally asked him.

"Sophie's from somewhere on the Main Line, I think. She's always talking about almost getting shot in Philly. Why?"

"You just seem really close."

"There nothing going on between me and Sophie."

"I know that," I said. "I just meant . . ."

"Seriously, Greer? Are you worried about this?"

It took me a few starts and stops to explain. Addison has this ease with people. This wasn't something he'd understand. Finally I just blurted out, "I don't know how to talk to people."

"God, you're crazy. You just have to be a little warmer. You know, smile a little."

This was the problem. "But I'm not like that . . . naturally. I panic, blank out on what to talk about. And then people think I'm cold. A bitch."

"You don't like to be uncomfortable, but no one does. Would you rather they're uncomfortable?"

"I never thought of it as an either/or scenario."

"Well, it is, you know? The only reason Sophie thinks you're a bitch is that you never talk to her."

"She said that?"

Addison shrugged. "Well, yeah."

"And what did you say?"

"We were eating lunch. I probably said, 'Please pass the salt substitute.' Greer, I'm not your press agent."

"I'm not asking you to —"

"You are, though. I know you have plenty to say. But listen, you can't come at Sophie now, all angry and offended. That's only living up to her mistake about you."

"So what am I supposed to talk to her about?"

The pathetic part was that I started most conversations with Addison. I'd ask, "Have you seen Addison?" Or "You're in Addison's Latin class, right?" It took a week and a half of practice before I tracked down Sophie and said, "I'm planning a surprise for Addison's birthday."

"I don't do threesomes."

"What?" Things were not going according to plan. "No, we're going bowling."

She raised her eyebrow and the metal rings caught the light. "Sounds kinky."

I forced myself to breathe deeply. I warmed my voice. "I asked permission from the dean of students, and Ms. Ling agreed to chaperone already." Sophie grimaced and I said, "I know. But it was the only way. I got them to think of it as a practice for Addison to be out and about on his own."

"Therapeutic."

"Exactly."

"Okay."

"Yeah?" I must have sounded too excited. She shrugged. "Can you help me figure out who else to ask?" She looked dubious. "I just don't want to miss anyone." She reached out for the list I'd scrawled out during nutrition.

"So are you guys together? Officially? This is very wifely of you, Greer." I felt the few licks of anger flame up.

"I'm crazy about him." It's all I said. And then held my breath and waited. It was my last try, I told myself. After that, I could rip the rings out of her face.

"Yeah, that's apparent." I looked up, ready to unleash. But Sophie kept talking. "He's crazy about you too."

"Yeah?"

"Yeah, it's pretty adorable." She laughed. "Revolting. But adorable. You guys are like the two-headed kitten of campus."

We talked for a while then, first about Addison, and then about home. Sophie had found McCracken Hill on her own, after she'd gotten tossed out of her Quaker Friends school for failing three drug tests. "It was this or military school," she told me. "I chose to serve my time with the broken people."

I didn't argue, and later that week, on Friday, when we all had gathered at the far lane of the Strike & Spare to wait for Addison to show, I realized Sophie was right — we were a collection of damaged goods. Teenaged angsters and addicts. Disordered borderline personalities. Almost fatalities. But Hannah Green showed up. She'd even baked cupcakes into ice-cream cones. Addison's roommate, Wes, was there, along with the bench-press bros he worked out with each morning. We totaled twelve people, counting Ms. Ling; considering not all of us were usually even allowed off campus, it qualified as a good showing.

When Addison walked in and looked around for me, the guy who ran the lanes made all the computer scoreboards flash, SURPRISE! HAPPY BIRTHDAY, ADDISON!

He scooped me up and swung me around and whispered, "I can't believe you," into my neck. And then he made his way around, grabbing hands and hugs. We'd almost bowled a full game when he called over, "Hey, when's Joshua coming?"

I'd been standing at the ball drop, waiting for the lightweight, lavender one to come hurtling up to the surface. Addison grabbed at my sleeve. "He doesn't usually get off work until nine on Fridays." I must have just opened and closed my mouth. "Greer, you told him, right?"

"I didn't. When would I have asked him?"

"I don't know. Maybe during the four times a week we see him."

Wes looked over from Addison's tense face to mine. "Hey, what's with the dick tone? Greer set this whole thing up for you."

"Yeah, it's great, but she forgot something." Two lanes down, an old guy must have gotten a strike. I could hear all the pins crash down. Addison looked at me for a second and then turned away. "Hey, Ms. Ling, may I use your cell phone, please? My sponsor loves to bowl. It would be so great if he could celebrate with me."

"Are you struggling with your sobriety right now? There's no shame in us heading back to campus, you know." She smiled apologetically at him. "Maybe we might have chosen a leisure activity that wasn't so steeped in the alcoholic lifestyle."

I wished the lavender bowling ball were heavier. I would have hurled it at Ms. Ling's teeth. Sophie sidled up to me. I told her, "It never occurred to me —"

"Don't be stupid," Sophie broke in. "Of course it wouldn't."

Addison said, "I'm fine. It would make it perfect if Joshua were here to see how well I'm handling things."

Ms. Ling handed over her cell to Addison and shot me a disapproving look.

"The hell?" I murmured. We were at a bowling alley. It's not like I'd hired a girl to jump out of a keg or something.

"Let it go," Sophie counseled.

"No. I should have known about Joshua."

"Enough, wifey. There's no major breach of protocol here."

There was, though. Addison moved back to his game and didn't speak to me. I concentrated on whipping the ball down the lane. One time, I took down seven pins in one shot. I heard a hoot behind me. "That's my girl. Greer Elizabeth!" I turned to see Joshua standing in the center of the crowd, grasping Hannah Green's left wrist. He tugged her toward the lane. "Let's go, cupcake. Let's see what you can do." And Hannah shrieked with laughter. She rolled the ball out, grandma-style, and knelt down to watch its slow progress down the wooden lane. "Get out of the gutter, you turkey!" Joshua called as Hannah shook with giggles. The ball swerved center. It chucked three pins down. "There you go!" Hannah's face practically split open with her smile.

Addison grinned over at me. He raised his hands up, as if to say, *You see?* I fidgeted with the scoreboard, felt him beside me seconds later.

"I'm sorry if I seemed ungrateful," he said.

"Seemed?"

"I'm not ungrateful." I used the computer to dock a point from his score. He didn't look up. He gestured to his friends, gathered around the stacked pizza boxes. "This makes me so happy. But it wouldn't have happened if I'd never met Joshua. How could he not be here to share it?"

"I don't know," I said softly. "Maybe we would have a really fun night and you could have told him about the great time you had with a bunch of kids your own age?"

"That's the issue? He's too old?"

"I don't have an issue. It didn't occur to me to invite your sponsor to your birthday party. You got angry. That's your issue."

Addison finally looked up. I'd changed his score from 168 to 2. "I still get to keep two points?"

"You're really good-looking."

He smiled. The really good kind of smile that spread slowly across his face. "You're right."

"But . . ." I waited for the excuses.

"But nothing. You're completely in the right. I was barbaric."

"Barbaric?"

"That's pretty bad, right? But you know what?"

"What?"

Addison wrapped his arms around me. I could feel the eyes of the others. Ms. Ling was probably outlining her next abstinence lecture. He drew me closer. "It's still my birthday."

Addison kissed me in the middle of the bowling alley. I could hear the bells and whistles of the arcade ringing. His lips tasted like buttercream frosting as his fingers sifted through my hair. I lined my whole body up against his and leaned in. It felt like I'd been designed to fit right there.

It could have been a full minute before I blinked and glimpsed Wes lifting his hand to conduct. Even the guys behind the shoe counter had chimed in to serenade Addison with "Happy Birthday." I stepped back to sing too. I really belted it out, the way you do when you're a little kid, just so happy to have been invited to the party. Sophie winked at me, bookended by the bench-press bros. Hannah closed her eyes and swayed. Ms. Ling looked more human than lizard just then. I felt myself looking around frantically, trying to memorize every sliver of that moment. Maybe that's why I noticed that Joshua was the only one not singing along.

The birthday party solidified some things. Addison and me, for one. It meant we both had to sit through sessions with the dean of students. "You've been making such progress, Greer." She tapped her pen against her desk as she spoke. "Are you certain you're not throwing that away?"

We'd reviewed our answers together. "Addison is such a good influence," I told her.

"I feel inspired to stay sober" was his line.

And both of us: "We've agreed it's nothing serious." I can't imagine we fooled anyone, but we still tried. We kept up a hands-off policy on campus and never argued with dinner table assignments. I signed out each day as usual and he met me at the bottom of the hill. Sometimes we snuck into one of the movie-viewing cubicles in the library. Or sat on the curb between two parked cars so that we could kiss and kiss without being seen. It never went further than that. "I don't want all of this at once," he told me, looking embarrassed. "A little at a time." I found myself thinking, *This must be what it feels like to be good.*

The pictures Addison slipped under my door suddenly had lines written along the margins. Nothing insanely saccharine. *I carry you in my heart,* he wrote once. Another time: *This matters to me.*

Since bowling, we formed what Sophie called *our elitist clique*, but she was only half-joking. It felt as if that night had counted as some kind of induction. I felt close to everyone who'd been there. Sophie claimed it was Add and me. "People like to be part of a secret." She spoke with her usual authority. "You two are easily the best cause on campus. And then there's Joshua." She said it like it embarrassed her.

"What about Joshua?" I felt something tighten, like the air around us got thicker.

"He just has a way with people." We were in the common space of the dorm. Sophie had boosted herself up on the beige Formica of the kitchenette. She picked at the edge of the counter, where it lined up against the wall. "Joshua has a way of talking to people."

He'd been to campus, it turned out. A couple of times when Add and I were holed up in the library or walking into town. "How is that allowed?" I asked when Sophie paused for a breath.

"He's running some kind of group session with the NA kids. Ms. Ling came back from the bowling alley raving about him."

It ended up that I was the last to know. When I confronted Addison about it as we walked back from Sal's that night, he acted like it was no big deal. "The dean had this idea for a group," he said. "So Joshua's leading it. Working."

"Oh." I felt myself deflate.

Addison looked at me with sad eyes. "We need to figure out your deal with Joshua. Seriously."

"There is no deal with Joshua."

"Yeah, there's something."

I wanted to tell him that there was something, an uneasy feeling I got watching Joshua watch us. That I felt like if I told anyone that my boyfriend's best friend was a middle-aged Narcotics Anonymous sponsor, they'd at least look askance at me, if not declare it was, in fact, a deal.

"Look," Addison said. There was no anger in his voice. If there had been, I would have fought back, claws out. Instead, Addison spoke so sincerely that I couldn't just shut down. He said, "It makes me feel weird that Joshua's made room for you and you're still trying to force him aside."

"Where has Joshua made room for me?" I asked.

"In my life."

"How can he do that?" I wanted to ask, *Are you listening to yourself?*

"We talked about this at the very start. This" — Addison gestured to the space between us — "isn't supposed to be happening. But Joshua recognizes how rare you are. That's what he said to me — that you were some kind of comet. Miraculously passing by. Do you get that? He's going against everything he believes in because he believes in you. And all you do is attack him."

I opened my mouth, but there was nothing to say. He kept his hands deep in his pockets, but he nuzzled against me, so that we were both a little off balance. It felt like we were stumbling down the street. "It's not just that it makes it hard for me, Greer." Addison's voice coaxed its way over to me. "He could help you. Joshua's the best gift I could give anyone. And you keep refusing that gift."

It was pointless to argue that I didn't want help. McCracken Hill loomed above us. I was there, wasn't I? And it felt better to be there, so obviously something had been wrong with me in the first place. I could tell the truth, that I only saw myself accepting help from Addison, but that would have had him backing away faster than the dean of students could proclaim "codependent relationship." So I found myself saying, "I want that gift," with the appropriate halting vulnerability lining my voice. "Maybe Joshua and I could sit down together and talk things through."

Addison was so happy with that answer. And what can I say? That seemed like enough to make me happy too.

Joshua picked me up the next day at Westlands Gate. He signed me out and everything. "I didn't know that was allowed," I told him. "My parents —"

"I spoke to your father earlier this afternoon."

"My father?" We hadn't driven a full mile, but I already felt carsick.

"I cleared it with Dean Edwards first. She felt it was appropriate in my capacity as a counselor."

"Where are we headed?" I asked, as trees blurred by the window.

"Where would you like to go? Where will you eat something, Greer?"

I kept my face as placid as possible. "Wherever you prefer." A few minutes later, he coerced the car into a tiny spot in front of a coffee shop. I was still getting my bearings when he hopped around the side and opened the door up for me. A gentleman.

Joshua stopped for a second by the driver's-side front tire. He slipped a little metal box out of the wheel well and tucked the car key in there.

"You don't carry keys?" I asked him.

"I lose physical objects," he told me unapologetically. "I can't train my human self to find them important." While he hid the box, I studied the building. It wasn't a Starbucks or a

Dunkin' Donuts, but a real coffee shop, with hand-lettered signs in the window and living room furniture scattered in groupings inside. Someone had painted a deer on the front window. It looked like a real deer, paused in the center of some leafy trees. From the outside, it looked like it was studying us. When we walked inside, the eye still seemed like it was tracking me. It creeped me out.

I moved toward the counter. "We'll sit down," Joshua said. He guided me toward an overstuffed couch in the corner. "Holly will take care of us." I sat down on one end of the couch and he sat back on the other. I shifted a little to face him and made sure to keep my arms at my sides. When I crossed them in front of me, Dr. Saggurti claimed my body language was closed. Joshua seemed like the kind of person who'd buy into the Saggurti School of Interpreting Positions Chosen Solely For Comfort as Passive-Aggressive Statements.

"Elizabeth," Joshua said, and at first it didn't register that he was talking to me. "Do you know the meaning of the name *Elizabeth*?" I shook my head. "It means God is my oath." Joshua's face was very solemn. "I'm going to make an oath to you right now, okay, Elizabeth?" *Go for it, Uncle Crazypants.* "I promise I will always be honest with you. I promise you will always have me on your side." The first part I wasn't particularly interested in. Honesty is overrated. But the second — I knew it was my duty as a responsible, reasonably intelligent young adult to be skeeved out by the way Joshua leaned into me, by the slow way he spoke as if he was reading rehearsed lines. But I didn't have a whole lot of people on my side. I had Addison. And it had already been made clear to me that Addison came with some stipulations.

Holly, the waitress, arrived with two oversized white mugs.

"That's lovely, Holly. Thank you so much. How's life, Holly?"

Holly grinned. "Life's good, Joshua."

He said, "That it is." I got the feeling this was a familiar routine.

Joshua turned his focus back to me and nodded sagely before he explained his oath. "This is not a reciprocal interaction. You don't have to be on my side." He shifted over and closed the distance between us. "You just have to be on your own side. That's the magical thing about faith — because I believe in you, because I'm taking this oath to fight for you, we'll be on the same side together."

I felt like I was missing something. But Joshua didn't explain what we were fighting for, who we'd be fighting against. "How did you meet Addison?" I asked.

"Do you see what you just did there?" Joshua sat back in his seat. "You're putting him between us. That's not love, Greer. That's what the gunman does with his hostage — he holds the body in front of him as he makes his exit." I thought about my troubled cousin Parker waving a handgun over the dish of cranberry sauce at Thanksgiving. But I'd never told Addison about that particular holiday memory. And it wasn't the kind of thing my parents would have put in my file. Joshua kept talking. "Addison shouldn't be your bulletproof vest. He shouldn't be your umbrella in the storm."

I told myself Joshua was just spewing metaphors, searching for an image that would stick. I clutched at the one that didn't involve handguns. "We can't shelter each other."

"That's right," Joshua said. "What are you most afraid of?"

"Being invisible." It came out before I even had the chance to wonder if it was weird. But Joshua just nodded to himself.

"Addison and I met once in a parking lot, but he doesn't remember. I used to buy him liquor. Has he told you that?" I shook my head. "He doesn't believe it." Joshua shrugged. "I was a drunk, spent most nights on the curb, waiting for kids to show up at the store to buy booze. I'd drink my fee." Joshua expected me to look surprised so I raised my eyebrows. "It must have been two, three years later. I'm in the basement of Our Lady of the Sea parish. By then I'm going to daily meetings, but Sunday night was show-time. That's when the rest of the drunks and drug addicts showed up. And in slouches this kid. He's taller. And worse for wear. But it's one of my old regulars. It's Addison. Do you know how these meetings work?" Joshua peered over his mug of coffee.

"Just what's in the movies: 'My name is Greer and I'm an alcoho —'"

"Yeah, yeah. That's part of it. Usually you say that to wrap it up, after you share your story. That night, I spoke up and told my story. And this kid stared off into space the whole time. I mean, I was watching him out of the corner of my eye. He looked like he was sitting in front of the Game Show Network or something. So I wrote him off. I felt guilty and all, but you know, ef him, right? Coming to a meeting and not even listening. That's my life story, right?"

Joshua was getting all worked up. I really thought he was still angry about it, but then he smiled widely. "You know where this is going, right?" They were inseparable now, so I figured it got better. I nodded. Joshua asked, "Have you ever known Addison to not be listening? He's got that stealth brain. He looks like he's zoning out, but the whole time, he's just taking everything in." I thought of Addison in class, his careful way of talking, his deliberate notes. "He came up to me afterward, you know what he said to me? Has he told you this story?"

"No." I should have asked about it, though. Somehow it felt like I'd let Addison down not asking about it. The look on Joshua's face said he thought so too.

But at least he got to tell the story. "He told me — this giant of a kid, with the skinhead haircut — he said, 'I think we're a lot alike.' I said, 'Yeah?' He said he felt drawn to me. I didn't tell him for months that was the drunk talking."

"What do you mean?"

"You're not seeing it, Elizabeth. It's right there in front of you. Addison wasn't drawn to my story. He remembered me as an access to alcohol. His body remembered me, even if his brain didn't. Isn't that amazing?"

I didn't think it was amazing. I thought it was sad.

"Addison says you saved his life."

"I did. But I also helped ruin it." Joshua sipped from his mug. "Who ruined you, Elizabeth?"

The tea scalded my tongue. I wasn't ruined. And I felt inexplicably hurt that Joshua thought that. But I shrugged and said, "I don't know."

"Why are you at McCracken?"

"How did you save him?"

Joshua paused and I thought that maybe he wasn't going to answer until I did. But then he said, "I just cared. You think you know what that feels like but it's possible that no one's ever cared for you before. Not your last boyfriend. Not your mother. We give each other so little. Maybe your mother was a little more than indifferent to you. Maybe your boyfriend cared about you. But they didn't care for you."

"That was it? You cared for him?"

"See, that's how I know you've never been cared for," Joshua said. "You would never say that if you knew the feeling." We sat in silence for a minute or two. I sipped my tea, touched the burned place on my tongue to the roof of my mouth.

"I take things." I looked Joshua in the eye. "I like to steal."

"And you got caught?"

"A few times."

"And they didn't put a rich, white girl like you in jail? Imagine that." Joshua shook his head.

"I also like men." I looked at Joshua and clarified. "Boys. I mean, I like sex."

Joshua nodded like it was no big deal. I felt like an amateur. But he said, "Yeah, that's a kind of stealing too."

We sat for a while and then Joshua stood, stretched, and told me he'd go warm the car. "You skinny girls. I know you're always so cold." Holly dropped the check off after he left, and I stopped her.

"This is wrong, I think." I looked at the scrawled list of items: three muffins, four cookies, a bag of organic chips. "We just had tea and coffee."

"No, he wants it to go." She handed over a paper grocery sack. "His usual." I looked out the window, past the painted deer. Joshua had pulled up to the door. He tapped lightly on the horn. I dug into my wallet and handed Holly a twenty-dollar bill. "Thanks!" she said brightly. "I'm sure I'll see you again."

When I climbed into the car, Joshua took the bag of snacks. "Thank you, Elizabeth." He reached back to toss it on the backseat. I heard the chips crunch. We drove in silence for a little until he said, "You might be a master thief. You won't be able to steal him."

There it was. "I'm not trying to." I smiled. I couldn't decide if it was a lie or not. Joshua smiled too. Like we were just being friendly, two jokers joking.

He slowed the car and stopped at the curb outside of the campus's iron gate.

"You're not going to sign me in?"

"No, just go straight back to your dorm."

"But —"

"It's all right, Elizabeth. It's cleared with the dean." I stood with my hand on the car door, considering. "You have a lot to think about. Go back to your room and think about my promise. I would like you to know how it feels to be cared for."

My room seemed even colder than usual. The standard navy blanket. Schoolbooks stacked on my desk. On the inside of one of my wardrobe doors, I had taped up the drawings and writings that Addison had given me. That was my secret gallery. There weren't any family pictures on my walls or stuffed animals perched on the bed. If I shut the door to the wardrobe, it looked like a robot lived there — a zombie. Someone unloved, who didn't care for anything at all.

CHAPTER
SEVEN

Three weeks later, Joshua asked to sleep in my bed.

Addison was there at the table. When Joshua brought it up, he straightened his back, set down his fork, and chewed his food slowly. The two of them were eating spaghetti and meatballs. I waited for Addison to say something.

He smiled. "I think Greer is going to need a little more information."

"It's not a sex thing." I just sat there, looking from Joshua to Addison. Joshua kept going. "This is what I do for those in the circle. You might think of it as a ceremony. It's an exercise in trust."

I watched Joshua twirl the pasta on his fork. "I don't get it."

"I know what it sounds like." Joshua looked steadily at me. "It must trip all those alarms society has built around your body. You're a young girl — white, upper-middle class. That's one well-guarded body. And I'm the enemy they've warned you about. Older. A stranger. A black man, no less. Parents used to lock up their daughters, you know. And I mean in attics and cellars, not ritzy rehabs like McCracken Hill. Well, now we lock daughters up in different ways. We teach them fear. We teach them to loathe their bodies."

I decided to skip the first part. "I don't loathe my body."

"Then where's the rest of it?"

"Joshua," Addison warned.

"This is sick," I said.

"It's not at all sick." Joshua's voice crackled. "Your interpretation of an innocent request shows your illness. The word is *depravity*, actually. It shows that you are depraved."

I sighed. "Well, we knew that." I turned to face Addison. "How is it an exercise in trust?"

But it was Joshua who answered. "When you sleep, you are vulnerable. That will be hard for you. I don't think I've ever seen you with your guard down."

"So you just sleep next to me?"

"It's most important that you sleep."

"I'll bet. Do we wear clothes?"

"I'm not interested in being insulted." Joshua's jaw set. His eyes shifted from mine and moved to focus on some space past my shoulder.

Addison reached his hand across the table. "Greer. It's okay if you're uncomfortable with the idea. But try to be respectful, okay?" I nodded and he looked relieved.

But then I asked, "When did Joshua spend the night in your bed?"

"That's not how it works." *Of course not.* I tried to keep the smirk off my face.

When Joshua pushed himself up, the plates rattled. "I don't want to sit at this table right now. I'm sickened."

I kept my eyes on Addison. When the door slammed, he bit his lip. "Are you going to go after him?" I asked.

"No. Joshua and I can talk later. It's okay if you're not comfortable with this." But Addison's voice was hollow. We both knew that was just how the script read. That's what the good guy was supposed to say.

"I don't even sneak you into my room."

"This is more important."

"If I get caught . . ."

"You won't." He was pleading just a little.

"It wouldn't just be bad for me, you know —"

"No, it would be much worse for him," Addison told me. "Joshua knows that. I hope you understand that. He's still offering this."

"Okay." I don't know why I said it. Because it was late and I was tired of smelling marinara sauce. We'd miss our sign-in, and that would bring its own kind of trouble. Really I just wanted Addison to stop looking at me in that disappointed way. He reached out, held my face in his one hand, like he did when we had just met and he hadn't kissed me yet.

"But listen," I said. "If I do this, I'm doing this for you. You can't expect me to also be thankful for the honor of hosting Joshua in my bed. It's weird. You know it's weird."

"It's about trusting people, though."

"Well, for me it's about trusting you. That's all." Addison didn't say anything. I pressed harder. "Can you take that? I mean, is that enough?"

"Yeah." Addison's voice sounded rough at the edges. "That's plenty."

Sophie's red Chucks were the first things I spotted when I got back to my hallway. She'd parked herself right outside my door. She had on black leggings with a black leotard, so she looked like a skinny little insect wearing red sneakers.

"It's our very own cheer squad — Sophie Delia." My voice boomed through the corridor, announcing.

"Shut up — I hated those bitches."

"You were totally on cheer squad."

"We called it *dance team*. And I still hated it. Where have you been?"

"Same old." She looked blankly up at me. "Sal's."

"You're late even for you, though," she said. I shrugged. "Did you get in a fight?" Another shrug. "A big one?"

"Do you want to come in?" I nodded toward the room four doors down and across the hall. "Or do you want Jenn Sharpe to blog about this?"

"God — is she still writing that shit?" Sophie shouted toward Jenn's door. "Someone needs to learn the definition of *the spirit of confidentiality*. This is a THERAPEUTIC environment."

Jenn started screaming back even before the door fully swung open. "Relax, Sophie — you're not interesting enough to write about. And our day-to-day lives aren't supposed to be confidential."

"You're a parasite," Sophie hissed theatrically.

I poked her in the back. "Get inside there, Sophia Maria."

"She's a tabloid."

"Fuck you, Sophie," Jenn said. "People find recovery memoirs inspiring." I closed the door on her.

Sophie opened it a crack to say, "Shut up, Sharpe. No one wants to see you recover."

"Sophie, seriously." I closed the door.

"Fine. What happened with the creatine prince?"

"It's Joshua. Again," I said. "He wants to sleep with me."

"Well, yeah, I mean, isn't that already happening?" Sophie crinkled her face into a question.

"What?" I shrieked loudly enough to put Jenn Sharpe on high alert.

"Wait — who?" Sophie asked. "Addison?"

"No. We're talking about Joshua. JOSHUA."

"Wants to sleep with you?"

"It's an experiment in trust."

"Wait — sleep with you?"

"Yeah, but just sleep." I felt awkward then, because I hadn't really meant to tell Sophie. I could already see Addison in my head: the sad, quick shake of his head, as if I had confirmed some misgiving he'd felt. This wasn't something he'd want left open to Sophie's analysis. My voice scurried, trying to fix it. "He would just stay the night. The idea is to spend time together and prove that I'm comfortable enough to fall asleep. You know, like an experiment —"

"In trust?" Sophie sounded more than dubious.

"Right."

"So the dean cleared this?" My eyebrows lifted up into their are-you-crazy? position. Sophie said, "Of course not. Because it's bonkers. Capital *B* bonkers." I felt my chest ease up. Maybe I shouldn't have told her, but it was a relief to hear Sophie agree with me. She kept going, "And you'd sneak him in here?"

"Addison said he'd take care of it."

"And he didn't say anything else? Like 'Hey, guru, paws off my lady friend'? Jesus. You can't do this, Greer." She sounded so definitive. And then she saw my face. "You're kidding, right? You're going to do it?"

"I know it's nuts."

"Yeah, exact —"

"It actually helps to hear you say it's nuts. Because sitting at Sal's, I felt like maybe I was crazy. Or mistrustful. You know?" Sophie nodded. "It's really important to Addison, though. Like I'm not sure..." I didn't want to finish, but Sophie nodded again like, *Go on.* And so I finished, "We might be done if I don't do this."

Sophie sat forward a little. "Greer, honey, did you ever go to summer camp?"

"Like Girl Scout camp?"

"Or any kind of camp."

"I went to Girl Scout camp."

Sophie sighed. "So this might be new for you, then. But I am a summer-camp veteran. From fourth grade to freshman year, I went to one every summer. Horseback riding camp, hot-air ballooning camp, theatre camp...you name it. And every year, around week five of the six weeks, I'd decide some brace-face kid was going to be my boyfriend and we'd sneak off behind the cabin or the boat dock or whatever and make out and we loved each other and wore each other's lanyards or something. And when it was time to board separate buses at the end of the whole thing, we'd promise to write and visit. And I'd cry the whole way home and maybe we'd send e-mails or something. Or I'd even bake cookies and mail them, but by the end of September, the rest of my life started back up again. And real life wasn't camp. And I was busy picking out a new camp anyway. Do you get it?"

"It's hard to get past the idea of hot-air balloon camp, frankly."

Sophie exploded in giggles. "Shut up, judger." But then she got serious again. "Maybe this isn't real life." Sophie waved her hand around my sparse little dorm room. She must have seen me back away from that because she rushed to say, "I know that it feels real. The system and the treatment team and all the serious talks we're having. But eventually we're all going to have to go home. And God, I hope you and Addison stay close and he drives out to see you. I hope your frosty-pants parents love him and you go apply to the same colleges or move to Seattle together or whatever you crazy kids have planned. Whatever you want, Greer, I wish it for you. But maybe you'll get home and want something different. So maybe you shouldn't jump through so many hoops for him now. These are some serious hoops, you know?" She sat back. I felt myself exhale. "I'm sorry."

"No, it's okay." My eyes felt hot and shiny, though. I couldn't make myself imagine home. That word didn't even really fit anymore. Addison. He was where I lived now. That's how it felt.

"You're still going to do it, though." Sophie sounded resigned but not in a bad way. I realized then that I didn't like thinking of home without Sophie there too.

I told her a little while later, after the lights had blinked on and off, three times in quick succession — *Lights-out. Bedtime. Moving on.* — I said, "If we met at camp, you would have been my best friend and I would have e-mailed you every single day afterward."

"No way." Sophie stood up and tossed her hair back. "I would have been too busy making out with my camp boyfriend to even learn your name." I threw my one lonely pillow at her. She slipped out and the door clicked closed behind her.

My toothbrush and its accompanying liquid privileges sat in their plastic bucket on my dresser. I ran my tongue over my teeth and considered making a run for the bathroom to wash up. But the lights blinked again. Warning. I didn't want to risk an infraction for something as stupid as brushing my teeth. Curfew needed to be as uneventful as possible for the next few days.

EIGHT

The night Joshua actually stayed over, I felt almost like my old self. We'd decided on a Tuesday, since he ran a campus group then anyway. Besides, it's not like floor faculty would expect any weekend hijinks so early in the week. Addison told me not to worry about it. Sophie said, "But how is he getting in?"

"I dunno." I slid her a look. "I'm not gonna worry about it."

"Okay, then." She held up a deck of cards. "Want to play Set?" We played two or three rounds before Sophie noticed me checking the clock. "Any idea when this shit goes down?"

"Nope."

"It's like we're waiting for Santa."

That made me laugh. "That's what I used to say every Christmas Eve. When I was a sweet little girl, I'd be hanging out in my feetie pajamas, looking up at the chimney, and I'd ask, 'When does this shit go down?'"

"I bet you did." Sophie grinned and then got serious. "Listen. Anything weird, anything that makes you feel uncomfortable, just yell."

"Yeah?" It felt good to think that Sophie had my back on this.

But she said, "Yep. You just yell really loudly and then Jenn Sharpe will bust in to blog about it."

"I feel loads better now."

Sophie took my chin in her hand and made sure I was looking her in the eye. "Okay, for real now. Fuck curfew. I am going to be patrolling this hall like Ms. Ling on meth. I won't sleep all night. And if I hear so much as a whimper from you, I am going to start pounding — first on the door, then on him. You understand?"

I nodded. Sophie slipped across the hall to pace.

About forty-five minutes or so after lights-out, I heard a soft rap on my door. I might have missed it if I hadn't been listening so hard. And for a few seconds, I considered pretending I was asleep. But then I heard Addison's quick whisper. "Greer, Greer — it's late and we're here." I opened the door. He ducked into the room and Joshua followed.

"You're such a cheese ball," I chided.

"He loves to make a hymn out of your name." Joshua stood with his hands clasped in the center of the room. I gritted my teeth. The little rhymes that Addison made with my name were just stupid little things, but they were ours — a joke between us. I didn't need Joshua to make them holy.

"Are you staying?" I tried to keep the hope from my voice.

"Nah, I just figured I'd check in on you." Addison searched my face. "You okay?"

"Sure. No one saw you?"

"We're clear."

"You guys must have superpowers."

"People see what they're looking for." Joshua sounded solemn, but he smiled warmly. "Elizabeth, give me a hug.

Are you all right with this? Truly? Addison felt you were ready for this step, but the last thing I'd want is to make you uncomfortable."

I looked at Addison and then Joshua. "No, of course not. I'm happy you're here."

"Good. I'm glad to hear you say that."

"Me too." Addison wrapped me in his arms and squeezed. "I better sneak out." He kissed my neck, right below my ear. "You'll take good care of my lady?"

"Of course. She's your treasure." Spending the night with Addison's spiritual adviser might be awkward, but at least I got to enjoy all the possessive pronouns flying around the room.

Addison put his finger to his lips, shushing us as he opened the door. He was there for a second, silhouetted in the doorway. I could just barely make out his smile in the low fluorescence of the hall lights.

And then the door shut. Joshua stepped closer to examine the reading lamps clipped on to my bed. "So the lights-out policy is just a saying."

"Well, no. All the overhead lights go off at the same time. After a while, they let us have little ones, for reading."

"You have to earn that?"

I nodded. "It's part of the patented McCracken privilege system."

Joshua smiled again. He motioned to the bed. "May I?"

"Umm . . . yeah. Sure."

"Do you feel like you've had a lot of privilege?"

It was apparently time to discuss my spoiled upbringing.

"My parents are sort of wealthy."

"That wasn't my question." His voice wasn't mean, just firm.

I thought of our stately brick house, standing at attention at the top of Hillside Lane. "Some people would say I grew up very privileged."

Joshua still smiled, but his voice didn't waver either. "I didn't ask what some people would say. Would you call yourself privileged?"

"Yes."

"Because?"

"I always had enough to eat. We have a nice house. With running water —"

"One second, please." Joshua held up his index finger. "Did you just say you had running water?" I bit my lip. "That's what you can come up with when I ask if you've led a privileged life?"

"Well, some people don't. I never went to bed cold or hungry. I was educated. Not everyone on this planet can say that."

"Well, all right, Saint Greer, I hear you. But tell me this, did you feel loved?" I felt my eyes roll. "Well?" I looked at Joshua and saw him watching me steadily.

"No. Not always?" It came out as a question.

"More often than not?" He asked it like the nurse at the doctor's office would, filling out a questionnaire.

And at first I went to answer yes. But that wasn't true. It felt like a scab coming loose, to look at someone and confide, "No. I don't think I've felt loved since I was little, really little."

Joshua nodded. His smiled faded, but it didn't completely disappear. "Well, Elizabeth, then I'd say that you must have often gone to bed cold and hungry. Right?"

"You mean psychologically?"

"I mean, your heart also needs to be warm and well fed." I nodded. That made sense. "Do you normally sleep with the light on?"

"Yes." I would have lied even if I didn't. That light was going to stay on.

"Why?" After I shrugged, Joshua asked, "What are you afraid of?"

"Tonight?"

Joshua chuckled. "How about any night?"

"Nothing."

"Are you going to be able to lay down with me and rest?"

"You're not going to buy me dinner first or anything?" As soon as I cracked the joke, though, I wished I could take it back. Joshua noticed. He waited. "I'm sorry," I told him. He kept waiting. "Sometimes I make fun of things because — well, because I'm not sure —"

"Most jokes come from a place of fear." I sat down on the bed next to him. It didn't feel skeevy or anything like that. "Well then, Elizabeth. I've been here ten minutes. Look at how much we've already accomplished."

"My therapeutic team should watch out. You'll put them out of business." We sat for a minute. "That came from a place of humor."

"Addison has told me how much you make him laugh. That was one of the first pieces of you he shared with me." I knew Joshua was an expert on addiction. The health and well-being seminars I'd taken at McCracken were intra-mural sports compared to his junkie Olympics. Joshua could probably see the pleasure centers of my brain light up every time he passed along another detail about how Addison loved me.

"But he's talked like that about other girls, right? Like Heather?" Heather was the girlfriend who'd left for college and stopped calling after Thanksgiving. She'd broken things off with a status update. Addison had said he was too drunk to care. "I think that was her name, right?" I pretended that I hadn't googled her obsessively when I was supposed to be using library time to research the possible sentencing for theft and larceny convictions.

"Ah, Elizabeth." Joshua said my name in such a kindly way I knew I was about to feel embarrassed. "You're too good for that." A shiver of shame stiffened my shoulders. I braced against it and then threw myself down on the bed. Lay on my side and tried to avoid scooting all the way against the wall. I kept my eyes from sliding to see how Joshua settled down on the twin cot. Back home, I had a full bed all to myself. That might have been more conducive to trust exercises. When Joshua murmured, "Let me assure you that I don't forget those questions you avoid," his breath brushed against my ear.

It felt like a test. "You asked me what I was afraid of."

"That's right." Aces.

"Nothing." The room filled with heavy silence. It felt like I'd deliberately failed a test. Turned a quiz in blank or something. "I'm afraid of disappointing Addison." The quiet stretched on. "I guess I'm afraid of losing him." Still nothing. "Or something happening to him. An accident or even a relapse, you know?" Joshua still didn't answer, so I turned toward him. "Is that crazy?" Joshua just gazed at me, not like he was angry, just like he was waiting for something. "You think it is?" I heard panic edge under my voice.

Joshua spoke slowly, calmly. "It's a little crazy that we're still talking about Addison." It was my turn to wait in silence.

I kept my eyes steady. Joshua asked me, "What would happen if Addison disappeared next week?" I refused to blink. He made it more real. "What if his parents decided to send him away, to get him farther away from Chuckie? What would you fear then?"

"That I'd never see him again."

Joshua shook his head. "Don't me make wipe that boy off the face of the earth. Neither of us wants to imagine that." I bit my lip. Joshua asked, "What are you most afraid of?"

"That I'm unlovable." I blurted it out without thinking, but it sounded right. And Joshua nodded so I knew it sounded right to him too.

"Think back to the time in your life when you were most afraid. Were you unlovable?" I heard my heart tick between us like a metronome. Steady. Steady. I never talked about Parker and the gun. No one told me to keep quiet about it. At least no one said it outright. It was more like an unspoken understanding. The next year we all went out for dinner on Thanksgiving and since then that became the tradition. I'd hear my mother gaily laughing about her inability to wrestle a twenty-pound bird into the oven. It took a while before I even connected the two, considered that maybe my parents had been afraid — truly afraid — also.

"No." Back then I was eminently lovable — the youngest cousin. Perched on my uncle Brady's lap and singing a song I'd learned at school when Parker raised the gun up, quivering. When he pointed it at his father, the muzzle was directed at me too.

"So, who were you then?"

"I was the littlest. Because of that, Parker and I would get to snap the wishbone."

"Explain that for me."

"You know — the wishbone? When the turkey's done, you dry out the wishbone. Then you tug on it and whoever gets the bigger piece wins."

"Wins what?"

"Your wish. It's just a kids' game. Usually the two youngest get the honors. In my family, it was me and Parker."

"Parker is how much older than you?"

"Two years."

I remember when Parker raised the gun in his hand. I thought it was a toy. I figured he was about to get in trouble for bringing a toy to the dinner table and then his mom shrieked, "Parker!" She must have said, "Parker — my God!" Or something like that because everything got very serious all of a sudden. And then she said, "He has a gun, Brady," really urgently. But that was unnecessary. Because Uncle Brady knew that. The gun, after all, was pointing at him. Us.

"So you and your cousin did the wishbone tradition — what did you wish for?"

"We didn't. Not that year." Ordinarily we'd play a superstitious game with a bird carcass, but that night Parker went straight for the gunplay. I giggled, a quick blurt that seemed even louder in the hushed room.

"Why are you laughing? Is that a joke?" Joshua's stern look was back in place.

"I'm sorry." It wasn't my real laugh. It meant, *This sounds bad, but it ended up being okay — no worries, right?* Or *I know — my family is certifiable.* "I get nervous when I talk about it," I explained.

"What's making you nervous?"

"It's not really something we talk about."

"Where is Parker now?"

"I don't know. He was in a residential program for years and then came home for a few months after he turned sixteen. He was on parole or something, I think, because at first he couldn't leave the state, but then he moved out. He lives on his own. In Colorado, I think."

Parker liked to ski. I hoped he was out in Colorado. Working as an instructor or something. Maybe Joshua read my thoughts, because he asked, "You're not afraid of Parker."

"Not anymore." I thought hard about that. "I don't think I was ever afraid of Parker. It was more . . ." I shrugged my shoulders and felt Joshua's hand settle on my neck.

"Go on."

I tried not to bristle and to find the right words for it.

"He had this really desperate look when he raised the gun." I remembered it as wild. Like someone had called, "Ready or not!" in hide-and-go-seek and Parker hadn't yet found a spot.

"Who got the gun away from him?"

"My dad."

"Wow." Joshua looked impressed. "Really? That surprises me."

He didn't even know my father. "Why would that surprise you?" And then, "You haven't even met my father."

But Joshua only shrugged. "It just doesn't fit with what you've told me about your father."

"I never told you anything about my dad."

"I got the impression of a very nice, hapless guy." Joshua paused. "Not a hero." It didn't seem particularly heroic. My mother actually did more that day. She stepped away from the table, casually retrieving the second crock of mashed potatoes — something like that. She called 911, passed along our info, and then returned to the table with the dish. No biggie.

Through the dining room windows, we saw three squad cars pull right up on the lawn, lights flashing. I remember the red and blue lights spilling into the room, the wide O of Parker's mouth, and then my father simply reached over and closed his hand over the pistol. Parker kept sobbing and trembling, even as the kindly policeman led him away. It was all so pitiful.

I told Joshua this. Then, to fill in the blanks, I told him the rest.

"And he claimed it was because his father whipped him?" Joshua sounded doubtful.

"Parker was telling the truth."

"Did you see it?" No. I heard later, from my mother's whispered phone conversations with my aunt Shelby, that it was true. The police took pictures of the marks on his back at the station. But I would have known anyway. My father's brother is a callous ass. When his son pointed a gun at us, I'd been sitting on Uncle Brady's lap. And he held me there, even shifted position so that I blocked his chest.

Joshua let out a low whistle. "And that was the worst part?" he asked. "Realizing that?"

"More like realizing that it didn't matter. No one ever called him on it." It killed me that Parker got sent away, but my dad still golfed with Uncle Brady on the third Saturday of each month. My parents went to dinner with Brady and Shelby. My mom commiserated when my aunt moaned about Parker's latest setback. His setback, I wanted to shout into the receiver, was having that dad.

"You felt betrayed by them."

"Not personally. It was more like it taught me that the world wasn't fair." We lay there quiet for a few minutes. I realized, to mild shock, that I hadn't thought of Addison for the past few minutes. And it felt easier between Joshua and me.

And then Joshua said, "It makes sense to me now." He sounded happy, excited.

"What does?"

"What would you say if I told you that was it?"

"What was it?"

"Greer, you have to open yourself up to the idea. It's not an easy one to conquer."

Oh God, I thought to myself. *This is when he asks me for a blow job.* But instead he asked, "You were how old?"

"Ten."

"Ten! See? On the cusp of womanhood." That was a little younger than the cusp of womanhood, I wanted to point out. But Joshua continued, undeterred, "That was the gateway."

"I'm sorry — I'm not following you."

"What would you say if I told you that you never left that room?"

"But I did leave the room." As soon as they'd cuffed Parker, my uncle had leapt to his feet. I might have even slid to the ground. There was shouting — "You little shit!" my uncle had hollered.

My mother had bellowed, "That's enough!" and hustled Eliza and me into her and Dad's bedroom in the back of the house, while my aunt Shelby followed her around, whimpering apologies. "Shelby, for God's sake —" my mother had said. "Go see to your child!"

"What if you didn't?"

"You mean what if I had died there?"

"Did you believe you were going to die?"

I thought back. The gun had looked oversized and clumsy in Parker's hands. Not like a toy. When he pointed it, I stared at it, into it. Maybe I was adding this to the memory — the sense that the muzzle was full of a deep nothingness and I could stare right into it.

Most likely, though, that was my own sense of melodrama warping it. I searched and searched and all I could remember is feeling pinned against Uncle Brady's chest — trapped, unable to breathe or scream. My scalp felt wet and cold. Maybe I was sweating.

"Yes." As soon as I said it, I felt certain of it. A flash of memory — I had pictured my entire fifth-grade class assembled. Would the principal solemnly inform them? I figured they would gather around my empty desk at school. No one would sit there for the rest of the year. "Yes," I repeated. Swiveled my head to try to search out Joshua's eyes in the almost dark.

"That's right," he told me softly, like he had known all along and I'd just confirmed it for him. "What if that was all it took to change the arrangement of the universe?"

"I'm sorry?" We had veered into a weird turn. Joshua sat up to explain. Clearly that signified the seriousness of the matter.

"You were very young. Too young to imagine your own death, to experience something that horrific. So, yes, your father swooped in for the gun. Your uncle released you. That happened in one piece of the universe. But maybe in some other fragment — you stopped growing right there, right where you imagined your life cut off. You never left that room."

"That doesn't make any sense —"

"But it does, Elizabeth. Think about the methods of self-destruction you've selected: men — like all the men in the room who failed you. Theft — as if to make up for all that life that was stolen from you."

It was elegant, but untrue. I knew that, but Joshua's fervor could be contagious. And anyway, wouldn't it help to have one afternoon to blame all my screwups on? I thought of the long hours in one-on-one therapy, trying to thaw the remote frost of our family. Or the hours I'd spent trying to verbalize the plain fact that I'd never be good enough to rival Eliza, to even vaguely satisfy my mother.

"What does that mean, then?" Meaning: *What do I have to do?*

"It means you are one of the most fortunate, the most blessed, Elizabeth. You don't have to answer for your time. According to the universe, it's all extra. Isn't that freeing?"

Kind of. But also creepy. "Because I'm dead in a room?"

"Because part of you is. It's okay if you haven't fully processed this possibility — it's a lot to comprehend. Take some time to allow yourself room for faith and we'll talk about it more in the coming days. For now you should rest. You should sleep." Joshua's words seemed to drag over me slowly. I hadn't planned to doze at all. But right then, without even feeling self-conscious, I sank into sleep.

CHAPTER NINE

I slept through my alarm. And through Joshua's exit. When I made the bed, I found a scrap of paper under my pillow. Joshua's shaky handwriting: *ELIZABETH — YOU ARE LIKE A STAR, UNAWARE OF ITS OWN BRILLIANCE.* I folded it in thirds and stuck it behind one of Addison's sketches. So now Joshua was like my own bizarre, New Age tooth fairy.

I heard Sophie's familiar rap against the door, followed by her voice, concerned, calling my name. I shouted to her that I was fine, and that I was alone, and that she should go ahead without me.

I slipped into statistics class right as the soft tone sounded over the loudspeaker. I shot a quick smile toward Addison, who looked worried. I didn't feel like reassuring him, though. *Focus on the numbers,* I told myself. I worked through each of the problems in the chapter review without allowing my mind to drift to alternate realms or the meaning of life. Afterward he hung back like I knew he would, and I made sure to keep my voice even. Open. I didn't even understand why I was angry with him.

He picked up his pace to keep up with me. "You okay?"

"I'm fine. Overslept."

"Late night?"

Um, yeah. You know that. But I just said, "Yes."

"Joshua said you did a great job listening. To him and yourself." It wasn't even ten o'clock yet. Addison had already checked in with him. I refused to comment. "Maybe we can bring lunch out to the quad? After lit class? Talk about it then?"

This was a gift. I preferred eating outside. You could put together a salad in a plastic case or make a quick sandwich and then be done with it. You didn't have to sit in a room smelling of all different kinds of food. Reeking of bacon.

But. For whatever reason, I wasn't ready to accept any grand gestures from Addison.

"Nah," I said. He looked confused. "I had to skip breakfast. I might want seconds."

"I don't know, Greer. Joshua doesn't usually work miracles." On another day, it might have been funny. I mean, even if it wasn't exactly hilarious to me, I could see why someone else might find that comment funny. Unexpected.

I tried to keep my voice easy. No big deal. "When you say that, it makes me feel as if it would be wrong for me to eat more food. Like I should feel embarrassed to be hungry." Dr. Saggurti would be proud. Cause-and-effect statement. Accurate description of my emotional state.

"Greer — it was a joke." Addison's brow furrowed in a way that I ordinarily found compelling. "You know that was a joke."

"Yeah, I get it. But I thought you'd want to know how that joke makes me feel." I shrugged again. No big deal. Never a big deal.

"What is your problem? You said you were okay last night. Did something happen? Joshua said —"

"I don't care what Joshua said." Ahead of us, Sophie and Hannah swung around to gawk at us. I lowered my voice. "Did it maybe occur to you to check in with me before Joshua? To ask me how I thought it went, instead of awarding me the gold star of Joshua Stern's approval? I mean, Jesus Christ."

"I *tried* to check in with you. This morning, at breakfast. I skipped lifting to try to catch up with you before class." And I could tell by the way he said it that it was supposed to count for something huge — he missed time at the gym. I slept with his guru breathing down my neck, but Addison had skipped his morning meathead session so we were pretty much even.

He held open his hand to me, bewildered. This was the kind of crap I did. He'd asked if I was okay with last night. I'd said yes. And the truth was, the whole thing wasn't half as bad as I'd thought it would be. I hadn't been molested or caught or thrown out of school. Maybe Joshua had even provided insight. Completely bizarre insight. But it was something. A glimpse. I'd overslept and rushed around, but none of that was Addison's fault.

I saw his hand. *All you have to do is reach for it,* I thought to myself. I willed myself to do it the way I sometimes had to will myself to reach for a piece of bread at the salad bar when I knew the monitoring teacher was watching. It felt like that — like accepting something meant giving something else up.

I reached out and tapped the inside of his palm with my index finger.

"Greer, Greer — I just want you near," Addison sang softly. He walked me to government class. "I'll meet you at lunch? Um . . . in the dining hall?"

"I'll show up more normal," I swore.

"Promises, promises." But he grinned, relieved. And so was I. It felt like I had narrowly escaped some grave disaster. He was one of the kindest people I'd ever met. The whole time Mr. Lanre lectured on the idea of separation of powers, I kept reminding myself of that.

Lunchtime was kind of a tug-of-war. Addison obviously felt owed some kind of reassurance from me, but Sophie had stayed up most of the night, patrolling. She wanted details. "I can't explain it." I said it to her, but I was talking to both of them. "Nothing really happened, but I feel like what we talked about should be private."

They both looked hurt, but Addison recovered faster. "Makes sense."

Sophie snorted. "What is this guy now — your priest?"

"Enough with the interrogation — what are we doing tonight?"

"It's Wednesday. You're going to group," Sophie said. "Unless you tell them Father Joshua Stern has miraculously healed you. Then we can watch *Top Chef.*"

"I skip eating disorder group so that we can watch a cooking show?"

"Sounds right to me."

Addison said carefully, "It could be worse — when's *The Biggest Loser* on?"

"See? That's funny."

"As long as you say so. I don't want to come off as insensitive." Sophie and I laughed. "I'm serious." Addison started stacking up all his wrappers and crap onto his tray. He could eat so much in a single sitting. It amazed me sometimes.

"I know you're serious."

Sophie cackled. "Addison Bradley, that's pathetic. You are easily the standard for sensitive men everywhere."

"Not always." He shook his head, gazing at me. "I try pretty hard, but not always."

That night in group, I probably spoke more than I had in the entire first three months of weekly meetings. This time, I showed up with a checklist of questions I wanted answered. Dr. Saggurti looked like she wanted to award me the Most Improved Anorexic Award.

"Speaking hypothetically," I hedged my bets, "let's say you experience a traumatic event while eating a meal — a memorable meal. Could that imprint somehow?" I tried to make myself clear. "Could that give you an eating disorder?"

"That's a fascinating question, Greer." Dr. Saggurti practically glowed. "The short answer is yes. For instance, many cases of anorexia have been documented in children who'd recently had some kind of choking episode. The child associates food with fear and then that grows into a disorder very similar to the disease of an older sufferer. It just has its root in a different kind of source."

"But say it wasn't choking? What if you wrecked your car going through the McDonald's drive-through or something?" Dr. Saggurti wrinkled her nose at me. "I'm serious." I tried again. "What if you're little and a meal you had associated with fun or comfort suddenly seemed really scary and dangerous?"

"Well, I suppose it would make sense for one to develop emotional issues around food and eating." Dr. Saggurti chose her words carefully.

So did I. "So maybe if a person were to talk through his or her issues, the symptoms might disappear?"

"Well, that's the best-case scenario. An individual might wander into eating disordered behavior through some sort of trauma. But then patients often discover that they can use their behavior with food as a kind of coping mechanism. The benefits of the coping mechanism quickly overshadow the rest. And, of course, many eating disorder cases have nothing to do with an initial trauma."

I filed away the info for later on, to talk over with Joshua, and spent the rest of the hour attentively listening to people discuss their fear foods and body dysmorphia. I caught Dr. Saggurti studying me thoughtfully at least twice and had to talk myself down from a blind panic that she might contact my parents for background about a possibly traumatic meal lodged somewhere in my psyche. The parental figures would not be cool with that. They'd refer to it as "making excuses."

The next day at Sal's, Joshua called it progress. "I'm so relieved that you found our time together productive," he practically cooed. "When you invest time in yourself, you reap huge rewards. You become more of who you are."

Joshua and Addison were sharing a pizza as I nursed my usual Diet Coke. I'd discovered a useful trick. As long as I thoughtfully examined my "disordered behavior" at the table, Joshua reserved his comments on my food. Or the lack of it. I didn't even have to order my usual halfhearted salad to sit around and make vague promises of self-improvement.

"We need to go on a retreat," Joshua proclaimed. Addison smiled and nodded, as if this was a tradition. Joshua gazed at me. "It's the perfect time. It will capitalize on your breakthrough."

"What's a retreat?" I meant for people like us. My dad had been on plenty of corporate retreats. I understood people went away and did bonding exercises and discussed productivity. They roasted marshmallows in a fireplace and sometimes drank too much. I knew this much from my mother, who enjoyed making passive-aggressive comments about my father's corporate retreats in front of their friends.

"Sometimes you need to journey together to clarify a shared perspective," Joshua explained. I looked to Addison for a translation.

"We go off somewhere. We spend time together, talk a lot, live as a family. It's nice."

I eyed both of them. Were they crazy? McCracken was not the kind of place that allowed students to plan their own school trips.

"Where would we go?" Joshua asked Addison.

Addison played with the saltshaker. He turned to me, as if suddenly struck by an idea. "Sophie has a place somewhere, right? In the Poconos?"

"*Her parents* have a place," I corrected him.

"That would be perfect," Addison said. "I'll bet it's a cabin, right? In the woods? As long as there's a working kitchen, we can cook our own meals. Build a fire in the fireplace. Play cards, watch movies —"

"We can have very thorough times of talk and self-reflection." Joshua's voice was firm. He started drumming his fingers on the table. "Elizabeth, where's your notebook? It would help if you wrote down these plans."

I had one hand in my backpack, tugging my Moleskine out before I tried to stop the madness. "Aren't we getting ahead of ourselves here? It's kind of presumptuous. We don't actually know her parents." Both Addison and Joshua just looked at me. "And how would we swing permission for this?"

"Greer —" Addison started to speak.

Joshua held up one hand to stop him. *"Elizabeth,"* he said, like he was correcting Addison. "You need to learn to play the believing game."

"The what?"

"Nothing good in this world happens without faith. If you don't believe it into being, the dream just dies unrealized."

"We're talking about a road trip. S'mores and Pictionary, right?" I want to press it, to say, *Not everything has to be so goddamn lofty.* But the two of them had launched a new mission. I played the dutiful secretary. I took notes and tried to keep the dubious look off my face.

"This will be a retreat focused on self-esteem and inner peace," Joshua announced solemnly. "I will explain the need to the dean. We'll request the presence of you and Greer. Jared Polomsky. Everett Wesley."

I looked to Addison. "Wes," he explained.

Joshua listed, "Sophia, of course. Hannah Green."

My pen paused. "Why Hannah?"

"Why not Hannah?"

Because I thought she was too fragile to deal with Joshua. Because I thought she couldn't deflect his philosophical onslaught. I said, "I'm just not sure she'd want to spend so much time with us. You know, she's not always so comfortable with people."

"What would you say if I told you that Hannah Green is the loneliest person you've ever met?"

"That wouldn't actually be a shocking revelation, Joshua." He sat back as if astonished and seemed to study me. "What?"

"You know that about Hannah?"

I tried to keep my tone matter-of-fact. No big deal. "Most people know that about Hannah. She has . . . she kind of has this wounded bird quality."

"Well, I find it hard to stomach that you could know that and not support alleviating her suffering. That's not like you, Elizabeth."

"It's not that —"

"Do you feel threatened by Hannah Green?" Joshua asked.

I swung my head to look at Addison. "Seriously?"

"Joshua —" Addison only sort of halfheartedly interrupted.

"What else does it look like? Be honest. Maybe Addison looks a little too long at Hannah? And it makes you uncomfortable? That's on Addison, then. It's his job to make you feel loved and secure." Joshua added a scolding tone to his voice. "My man, you're not doing your job."

"That's not his job!" I shouted.

Addison shot me a hurt look. "Why wouldn't that be my job?"

"That's no one's job." I still sounded borderline hysterical. I muttered, "It shouldn't be a job."

"Hannah needs this. I would even hazard to claim that she is our sole reason for planning a trip together. It will be a family trip. And Hannah needs a family."

Somehow it seemed to me that the only person who ever won the believing game was Joshua. But Addison looked so excited and hopeful. That's what I should have been noticing: the incredible guy across from me who wanted to play house. Who now bent his head forward toward me and asked, "Will you ask Sophie?" I hesitated. Addison went on, "Joshua's going to speak to the dean. I'll handle the rest of the logistics. You two have grown so close — I figure it would be weird for me to ask."

"Yeah, sure." I tried to ignore the sinking feeling beneath my ribs — the lingering sense that something was wrong. That some of this had all been scripted ahead of time, but only Addison and Joshua had cue cards.

"That's great, Greer." Addison sat back and beamed. "I knew she would," he told Joshua. And then said to me, "This is going to be an amazing time for us."

After dinner, when Addison was dropping me off, I tipped my head back to kiss him and he said, "I know it's not supposed to be the point of a retreat, but I'd love to just have one night when I don't have to take you back to your dorm. Won't that be incredible? I just want to watch you sleep." Which was decidedly less creepy than Joshua saying it.

And if Addison could make my time in adolescent lockdown feel like a vacation, what could he do with an overnight in the country? I let myself imagine us outside the confines of the academy for a whole two days. The luxury of falling asleep next to him in front of a television. Time away. Time together. Yes, Joshua would be there. But I could handle that drawback. The upside was a weekend with my friends. With Addison. After those first lonely weeks at McCracken, I felt like I'd earned it.

It took some time to convince Sophie.

"I can't call my dad and ask to host my new friends from rehab at the family lake house," she said. "Seriously, Greer."

"It's asking a lot of you." I was inadvertently channeling Joshua's way — acknowledging the obvious problem and waiting for the other person to find a way to overcome it. He'd call it *readying the path for goodness* or something flake-tastic like that.

"Too much. And honestly, it's asking something of the parental figures. Asking them for anything is too much right now."

"What if you didn't ask?"

"Meaning?"

"Do you have a key?"

"No," Sophie said. Then, shaking her head, she told me, "But I know where it is." And I knew I had her on board.

.

Over the next week, Joshua continued to work his magic. I kept waiting for someone in one of the plush offices of Westlands Hall to notice that this middle-aged man had managed to insert himself into the daily schedules of so many McCracken students. But they didn't. Instead, they lent him a van and allowed him to take us off campus.

He told them we were going to build houses for Habitat for Humanity. To build character.

Joshua assigned me the task of inviting Hannah Green.

"Why should I be the one to ask her?" We were sitting on the steps of the Walcott building. Lately I'd started waiting there until Addison and Joshua wrapped up the NA group.

Joshua said, "It will make her happiest to know that you want her there."

"See, that just shows how little you understand about girls. I'm the last person she cares about. Addison should ask her —"

"Hannah, like all the other young ladies at McCracken Hill, knows very well that Addison is taken." Joshua thought that kind of bullshit line worked on me. That was supposed to get me all preening and pleased. Then I'd be so distracted panting over Addison that I'd just follow Joshua's instructions. Okay, so those lines had worked in the past. But as soon as I realized it, I started working on it. Amending my vanity.

I pointed out, "There's Jared. And Wes. She'd be happier to be invited by them."

"False. You presume that other young women value each other as little as you do, Elizabeth."

"That's not true."

"Which isn't true?"

I hadn't heard a choice in the question. But I picked the point most important to me. "I value other women." I looked back and forth between them. Addison said nothing. Joshua said less. "There are plenty of women who I admire. And if I'm such a terrible female, Joshua, why pick me to ask Hannah? I might influence her in some way."

Joshua stood up and looked out toward the parking lot. "Because I'm hoping she'll influence you."

I didn't want to keep arguing, so I agreed to do it. I showed up at Hannah's door as she was leaving for breakfast the next morning. When she heard me call out for her, she stopped in her tracks and darted her eyes around.

"Has anyone talked to you about this weekend?" I asked. "You know — Addison or Sophie or anyone?"

"Is there another party?" Hannah asked as if that would be the only reason people would get together and hang out. She was probably that kid who only saw the inside of other kids' houses when the entire class was invited for birthday parties.

"It's no one's birthday, but it's going to be a great week-end. We're going away, on a retreat."

"A retreat from what?"

I waved my arm, gestured toward the length of the corridor. "Well . . . from this."

Now I had her interest. "How will you do that?"

"We actually have permission from the dean and everything. We'll stay at a cabin in the Poconos from next Friday night until Sunday evening curfew."

"Who?"

"Well, I'm going." Hannah did not seem impressed. I wish Joshua could have seen her blank look. "Sophie's going. Addison. Jared Polomsky. Wes."

"Three boys, three girls. How'd you get the dean to allow that?" I hadn't even noticed how coupled up we sounded. Hannah was right. It sounded a little insane that the dean would give us the go-ahead. Maybe Joshua could work miracles after all.

"Joshua is taking us." She looked confused. "You know, Joshua Stern? Addison's friend. He runs a group on campus."

"The old guy?" I swallowed a snicker. "He runs a Narcotics Anonymous group."

"He does."

"I'm not a drug addict."

"Okay." I kept trying. "It's not that kind of retreat, though. I mean, it is, but not necessarily for drug addictions. We all have ways in which we're not living up to our potential." Hannah just kept staring at me. She certainly wasn't acting as if she'd been sitting in her room, pining after inclusion in our little circle.

"Do I have to join a club?"

"No. We like to think of ourselves as an elitist clique, but there's no sign-up sheet or anything." Hannah didn't even crack a smile. "I'm in charge of figuring out a menu for the weekend. Any requests?" Hannah shook her head. "Are you a vegetarian? Or do you have any allergies or anything?"

"I'm a vegan. And I'm allergic to wheat."

"Oh wow, really? Okay. Okay, I'm glad I asked."

"Do you still want me to come?"

"What? Yeah, of course."

Hannah smirked a little and started down the hall. She called over her shoulder, "Really?"

"Yeah, sure."

Hannah stopped walking and broke into laughter. "I lied," she told me.

Maybe I needed a translator. Someone who spoke crazy. "Hannah, I don't get it. I don't understand."

"It was just a joke. I'm not really vegan or allergic to wheat."

"You're seriously so strange." Joshua wouldn't approve of that comment, but it's not like Hannah argued with me. She still agreed to come.

CHAPTER
TEN

When we finally piled into the van, I realized it would be my first night away since climbing out of my dad's SUV three months before. I felt giddy about the prospect of deciding for myself when to turn out the lights and couldn't even comprehend the possibility that Addison might be there beside me at bedtime. We'd loaded the bags into the back and Joshua had called for me to ride shotgun up front. Sophie just shrugged and handed up the directions. About forty-five minutes into the trip, we pulled into a Pathmark and Joshua sent Hannah and Sophie in with me to do the shopping.

"Is that because it's women's work?" Sophie was laughing, but I knew her well enough to know she meant the question.

Joshua simply said, "Your words."

The three of us had hopped down into the lot when Jared called out, "Wait!" and handed two twenties up to the front.

"Hey, thanks for thinking of that." I meant it. "You want anything special?"

He exhaled. "I've been craving root beer. I haven't had a root beer in six months."

Sophie laughed. "Jared's living dangerously," she said.

"Anyone else want to kick in?" I called out and studiously avoided looking at Joshua. Nothing. Crickets. "Okay. Let's do this."

Hannah pushed the cart. I worked through the list and sent Sophie to pick up the things I didn't find just glancing through aisles. "Why do you need two gallons of vegetable oil?" Hannah hauled an oversized jug off the shelf.

"Dunno. Joshua added that."

"What's it for — some weird sex thing?"

Hannah Green: showing signs of life. I laughed. "We can only hope, right?" And laughed again to make sure she knew I was kidding. At the checkout, the lady at the register raised her eyebrows at the volume of food: six cases of soda, four boxes of Cheerios, five pounds of chicken. "Family vacation," I said. Sophie chose that moment to show up with a pack of condoms.

"Don't say no." She answered my raised eyebrows. "It's just in case. You don't know what'll happen when we're all feeling cozy in front of the fire."

The checkout lady read the total without looking at me. I whipped out the credit card and ran it through, adding sixty dollars in cash back. With Jared's forty, that gave us a hundred dollars in an emergency.

It took both Hannah and me pushing to get the cart moving again and Sophie helped guide us out the door. As soon as we reached the fresh air, Hannah erupted in giggles. She looked really pretty, with her head thrown back, laughing.

"Thanks so much for that moment of supreme awkwardness, Sophie."

"What? The condoms? I'm just looking out for you, sister." In the distance, the van doors rolled open and the boys rushed to help us load up. Joshua rolled down his window and nodded at our haul.

"You've embraced abundance, Elizabeth. I'm proud of you."

We got everything into the back of the van and strapped on seat belts. Joshua backed out of the space.

Wes rummaged through the bags. "Tell me you bought cookies." He landed on a bag of flour. "Or maybe stuff to bake cookies?"

"Don't get your hopes up," Sophie informed him forlornly. "I saw a lot of vegetables." Jared groaned but in the way I always imagined my hypothetical big brother might groan when my mom said the whole family had to go to my dance recital. A sitcom-big-brother kind of groan.

"Whose genius move was it to put the anorexic in charge of food for the weekend?" Sophie bellowed from the backseat, and for a second or two, no one said a word.

At McCracken Hill, we didn't really use that term. We called the NA kids addicts. And the AA kids alcoholics. Girls like me had "boundary problems," but I'm not sure if they meant the sex or the stealing. But the eating thing was different. For one thing, if we'd been really sick, there were other places for us to go. Hospitals. Care facilities. I'd never been that sick. That thin. That would have required a kind of concentration I hadn't yet demonstrated. Instead, I fucked up in little ways across the board. So we didn't say *anorexic* or *bulimic*, we said *disordered*. Maybe for insurance reasons. Maybe for morale?

"Elizabeth is not anorexic," Joshua declared without even looking away from the road. "Elizabeth is stubborn."

"That's right," I said. "And Addison was just thirsty." I turned up the volume on the stereo and we drove on. When we exited I-80 the route got complicated enough that Sophie needed to switch seats with me in order to navigate. She climbed over all the legs and tumbled into the front. I scooted back and Addison pulled me into his lap.

"You having fun yet?" he murmured in my ear. I leaned into him and let my eyes close. The sun warmed my face and some man crooned over the radio.

"As soon as we left the parking lot," I told him. "Best weekend of my life as soon as we left." The strip malls and fast-food huts thinned out on the side of the road until finally we saw a shuttered gas station and Sophie's hand pointed right.

"Turn here." Tall pines lined the patchy asphalt. "It switches to gravel partway up," she said. "So don't slow down up the hill. We've gotten stuck before and that's a mess." I saw the nerves kick in. "It's not like we could even call someone for help." Sophie craned her neck back.

I reached out to pat her shoulder. "Relax. Just breathe. We won't get stuck."

"Listen to that positivity," Joshua crowed. "That's the radiance that's going to lift us all up."

Ahead of us, the pointed roof of the cabin stretched to the sky like a steeple. "This is really the place?" I asked, incredulous. The way Sophie had talked, I'd pictured a cute little cabin. This was a bit more imposing. All glass peaks and wood beams, with skylights and solar panels glinting on the sides of the roof. "Dude. I just got replaced as resident rich girl. Just so you know."

"Shut up." Sophie looked mortified.

Hannah said, "But we all come from money, right?"

Sophie said, "Maybe can we please just stop talking about this?"

"No, really." Apparently, Hannah was now determined to solidify the group. "McCracken Hill's a pricey place. And I can't imagine you get scholarships to schools for" — she searched for a McCracken-approved euphemism — "challenging students like us. So all of us must come from comfortable homes, right? That's one way we all have common ground."

"Okay, but there are different kinds of comfortable," Wes said, with an awkward glance at Addison.

The inside of the house was that rich kind of rustic. As Joshua explored the place, the rest of us unpacked the groceries in the kitchen, and Hannah stopped at a family photo. Young Sophie sat there, her wide smiled encased in braces.

"Your sister is gorgeous." Hannah gasped. At first, I rolled my eyes, but then I actually snuck a peek at Josie Delia. Holy smokes. Talk about fraternal-twin inferiority complex. The boys craned to see. Sophie concentrated hard on organizing cans of soup in the cupboard.

"Wow. That's Josie?" I searched her face for a reaction. Nothing. Just an intense interest in the main ingredients of Cheerios.

"That's Josie, all right."

"And that's your brother?" Hannah breathed. He too was beautiful. He had Sophie's big grin and Josie's dark curls. Obviously older, he had his arms spread around both girls. He smiled directly at the camera. Josie seemed to gaze slightly off into the distance. Sophie's eyes seemed to be fixed on him. She squinted through the sun.

"I didn't even know you had a brother," I said.

"I don't." Five heads swiveled to look at her, including mine. "He's dead." She said it simply, with no inflection in her voice at all.

The floorboards began creaking all at once. All of us shifting our stances, trying to figure out what to say next. After a few beats of silence, Joshua called out from the living room, "When we're settled, I'd request your attendance at a family meeting, please." He sat in a big leather chair next to the hearth.

We drifted toward him, but I reached back to squeeze Sophie's hand. I wanted to tell her I was sorry, because when I'd said, *I didn't even know you had a brother*, my tone had been hard, offended that she hadn't told me.

Sophie stepped forward to sit on the brick ledge by the fireplace. "It's really no big deal," she said.

Joshua asked, "Elizabeth, do you still feel comfortable preparing the meals for us?"

"Yeah, I mean, anyone can help, but I can handle it." We'd covered this, I felt like telling him. Several times.

"I'm going to request that no one offer help." Joshua clasped his hands under his chin. "Do you understand these instructions? Can you comprehend why I've made this decision?"

"I'm assuming it's a food thing," I said.

"That's an unfortunate assumption." The others stared at me as if I'd answered wrong in math class. Joshua said soberly, "I'm assigning you the responsibility of preparing our meals because since ancient times we have given that role to the most honored of women. Why would that be the case?"

"Because the most honored of men busied themselves golfing or something?" I said. No one laughed.

"Addison. Please explain the reason behind this history."

"Well, only the most trustworthy of women were given the task of handling food. You know, to prevent poisoning."

"You are beloved to me," Joshua said. "This request demonstrates that."

"Thank you, Joshua. Should I start preparing a supper?"

Joshua smiled and nodded. "That sounds excellent." I stood up and Addison grabbed my hand. He opened my palm and kissed it. As I walked away, I shut my fist tightly as if I could hold on to that moment.

Honor or not, leaving the group behind and starting work in the kitchen felt odd. I could hear splinters of the conversation in the next room as I washed and chopped vegetables. Joshua assigned sleeping quarters. Sophie told everyone where to find extra towels and blankets. I heard the boys get rowdy at one point, but couldn't make out what they were saying. Hannah murmured something but it got drowned out in the sizzle of the sauté pan. I found a big pot, put rice on to boil, and when I looked up, Hannah stood there, waiting for directions. "Joshua sent me to set the table."

Like I was the mom or something. "I don't know where anything is."

"Do we have paper plates?"

"You could just open up the cupboards. Look around a little. Or ask Sophie." I went back to the two enormous frying pans on the stove.

"Are you mad about something?" The front pan seethed and I added the chicken. "I'm sorry no one's helping you, but Joshua said —"

"I heard Joshua, Hannah." And then because it had come out so harshly, I added, "I was right there."

Hannah opened and closed the rows of cupboards. "I feel weird just nosing through someone's stuff." I kept stirring. "You didn't know about Sophie's brother?" I shook my head. "That's weird. Maybe we should have picked another place to stay, you know?" I stared intently into the steam rising from the pan. "Joshua had asked how much longer. He sent the boys out to collect firewood."

"How very gender-appropriate." I hadn't looked up, but I felt Hannah's presence still in the doorway.

She just stood there. Finally, "How much longer?"

"Maybe ten minutes." My voice sounded flat. I felt an inexplicable lump in my throat and the urge to go home — all the way home, not just back to my sparse room in Empowerment Hall.

"Great!" Hannah sounded like a stir-fry cheer squad. "It smells incredible!"

"Thanks!"

Once we were all settled around the table, I felt better about everything. Sophie must have brought out a table-cloth and candles. Joshua sat at the head and we had just enough room to crowd around. He'd asked Addison to say grace before we ate, and we all grabbed hands before we bowed our heads. Like it was natural. As if we always did that.

"Bless us, Lord, with your bounty," Addison intoned. "Thank you for the food and the family. For the opportunity to each play our part. Teach us to walk in your light."

"Amen." Joshua said it first, setting off a chorus around the table. "Why don't you serve supper now, Elizabeth?" It felt like a test I should have studied for. I passed his plate to him first — that was a no-brainer. Then Addison's. Then I figured I should serve the rest of the boys because it might seem strange to skip over them. I filled Hannah's plate before Sophie's because Sophie was the closest we had to a host. Then I served myself.

When I sat down, Joshua picked up his fork. Then the others all started eating too.

"So good, Greer," Wes told me, avoiding the chicken but eating the rest. Jared nodded. The truth was we all ate together all the time in the dining hall, but it felt different to gather around a table in an actual home. As nervous as I was, maybe the others felt unsure of themselves too. Usually, in the cafeteria, by the time I sorted out my plate and drinks, Wes had started in on his third helping, but sitting down in Sophie's dining room, we were all on our best behavior.

"When we're through here, I expect the gentlemen to clean up so that Elizabeth can rest." Joshua smiled at me from across the table.

"Of course," Jared said. "You dry, Addison."

Joshua scraped a last forkful from his plate. "Wonderful nourishment, Elizabeth."

"So this weekend away, is she Elizabeth or is she Greer? I mean, what should we call her?" Wes pushed back his chair. "I'm just confused. I'm not trying to be a prick or anything."

"I'm sorry." Joshua did not sound a bit sorry. "Does the uncertainty bother you?" I recognized the look on Joshua's face as the one he got when facing down a challenge.

"No, man, it doesn't bother me. I just don't get it."

"Elizabeth is Greer's second name."

"Her middle name?"

I nodded at Wes.

Joshua explained, "I call her Elizabeth because that is the name she has chosen. That's how she'll be addressed in the next life. It's the name she chose for herself. I use it because she is so valuable to me."

"It's her middle name," Wes said. "She didn't choose it any more than I chose Lawrence."

"It's also my confirmation name." I spoke up then, trying to explain it clearly. "When you're Catholic and you get confirmed, you choose a name. I just chose the middle name I already had." Wes looked up at me. "Some people do that."

"Does that meet with your approval?" Joshua asked him.

"It didn't need to meet with my approval. I just wanted to understand."

"Well then, are there any other questions you've been holding on to? Are you happy being addressed as Wes?"

"Yeah, for now. Unless you're willing to call me King."

"You'd have to first demonstrate a willingness to act kingly."

Wes laughed a little. "Ahhh, very tricky. Is Joshua your first name or your middle name?"

"It's my given name, my first name. Do you know the meaning of the name Joshua?" He looked all around the table as if indicating it was a question open to any of us to answer.

Hannah squeaked out, "Joshua fought a battle." Go, Hannah Green, biblical scholar.

"Indeed he did. And the etymology — the root — of the name Joshua means *salvation*. So that allows me to offer salvation."

"My name means wisdom, but it's not like I necessarily think I'm that smart," Sophie piped up, scraping her bowl with a chopstick.

"But that's the most foolish thing you've ever said," Joshua offered. "It might be the only foolish thing. You exude intelligence, Sophia. You have extremely wise eyes." Sophie set down her bowl and gave him a withering look. "What makes me sad is seeing wariness replace that wisdom. I hope we will change that."

Apparently Jared and Wes were less interested in the meanings of their names. They got to work, carrying stacks of dishes into the kitchen. I rose to help them, but Joshua said, "I meant what I said about resting." He turned to Addison.

"Yeah, yeah. I'll go."

"Why don't you stoke the fire first? The ladies and I will gather and talk."

Addison knelt by the fireplace and started picking out fatwood from the pile. Sophie nudged me and I giggled. In jeans and his plaid flannel shirt, he looked like a lumberjack or some kind of porno actor.

"What's so funny?" Joshua asked.

"Go on — tell him," Sophie teased me.

Addison looked up. I explained, "It's just — well, you look like one of those dudes on the cover of romance paperbacks, you know?"

He laughed and blushed. "No. I don't know. But I'll take it."

"Oh come on, Add — you've probably got a collection of those. *A Wintry Love* or *Safe from the Storm*." Sophie's laugh rang out through the room. Joshua laughed too.

"Brother, brother. She just devoured you with her eyes. Tell you one thing, I don't want the room next to yours tonight." I made myself keep laughing, but I hated when Joshua referred to Addison's and my sex life. Or our not-quite sex life. When we'd planned the weekend, my first thought had been that we might seal the deal. But I didn't want to do it knowing other people were in the house listening to every squeaky spring or soft moan. "Is that fire roaring? That fire needs to be roaring. I'm going to sit down with the ladies and we're going to discuss unity while you boys get that kitchen clean. You know how to clean dishes, correct?"

"Sure thing, Joshua."

"Good. 'Cause I'm not setting loose any cavemen onto this planet. The world has enough cavemen, am I right about that?"

I nodded.

Joshua sank into the sofa and patted the squares on either side of him. "You want to see a caveman, you should have seen Addison when I first met him."

"I've always known how to do dishes, Joshua," Addison called back over his shoulder.

"The only suds you were handling when I met you were the ones at the bottom of a keg, brother. You might have known how to do dishes, but you weren't demonstrating that knowledge in any way. There's no shame in growth, right, Elizabeth? Let me tell you, this young lady couldn't look at you with more adoration in her eyes. It would be illegal. Hannah, what's the first word you'd use to describe Greer? Just say it — don't think about it." Joshua switched gears so fast, I was still stuck staring at Addison's flannel back, a dish towel thrown over his shoulder. I turned, surprised, to face Hannah.

She said, "Pretty."

"That's the bare fact about Greer, isn't it? Do you think that's the first thing people notice about her?"

"Yeah. Yes."

"Do you know that about yourself, Greer?" He turned to Hannah and then Sophie. "Even if I ask her that, though, what can she say? She won't admit that, right? What would it mean to admit that?"

"It's not a question of admitting anything." I looked at each of them. "It's not true. People think all sorts of things about me."

"Of course it's true. Why would Hannah lie? What's the first word you'd use to describe Hannah, Greer?" I hesitated. "Go on," Joshua coaxed. Hannah nodded.

"Weird." I apologized with my eyes, but she didn't even blink.

"Sophia? What's the first word you'd use?"

"Maybe *strange*?"

"And for Greer?"

"Pretty."

Joshua held my eyes. "Now do you believe me? How would you describe Sophia?" But I shook my head, crossed my arms across my chest. "Hannah —" He prodded.

"Sad."

"Wonderful. You're only saying that because of my brother." Sophie rolled her eyes.

"Greer? What's the one word you would use?" Joshua asked.

"*Sad,*" I said and turned to look her in the eye. "I've always thought that deep down you might be really sad."

"Not that deep down, apparently." Joshua sat back. "Feel that fire. That's a good, comforting warmth. Elizabeth, you look like you're mulling over something. Do you want to share something with me?" I didn't say anything at first. "Maybe express some anger?"

"No anger." I was almost able to stop myself from talking. Almost. I couldn't let it stand, and that's probably what Joshua was counting on. "I just thought this weekend was about coming together, connecting. And that kind of question seems designed to split us apart."

"I find your reaction very curious."

Where was Addison anyway? How long did it take for three guys to wash about twenty dishes? "Somehow I knew you would."

"Yours especially. The words you thought of for Hannah and Sophia were *weird* and *sad*, respectively."

"I told you whatever popped into my head first. Neither of those are the only words I'd choose to describe either of them."

"No one has forgotten the parameters of this activity. You don't even see where I'm headed. Do either of you?" He studied Hannah and Sophie. "Hannah? Could you help illuminate Greer?"

I didn't think it was possible for Hannah's voice to get smaller. "I'd give almost anything if the first word people thought of when they saw me was *pretty*." Joshua nodded and Sophie sat up a little. Hannah's voice grew a tiny, tiny bit. "You act like it's nothing. But it's an advantage."

Joshua leaned into me. "Can you listen to this?"

"I'm listening." The fire crackled and hissed. I heard the guys horsing around in the kitchen. Hannah watched me with her saucer eyes. "How am I supposed to respond to this?"

"Honestly," Joshua said. "I'd like some cocoa. Is there a kettle?" When Sophie nodded, he said, "I'll look forward to that when we're complete here. Why did the word *pretty* insult you?"

"It implies certain things."

"That's all you're going to give us? You're going to sit there, pouting, but not provide any more by way of an explanation?"

"I'm not pouting. The implication is vapid. *Pretty* is all about the surface. That implies that there isn't anything beneath the surface."

"But no one said that."

"That's usually what *implication* means. No one says it outright. That doesn't make it less true. At least *weird* suggests interesting."

"Is that how you feel about the word *weird*, Hannah?" Sophie asked. "Does it make you feel like you're more fascinating than the next person?"

"Et tu, Sophie?" I said.

Joshua jumped in. "We're just discussing first impressions here. I'd hoped we wouldn't take these words so personally." He looked puzzled, but I didn't buy it. It felt as if I'd walked into a trap and, in trying to claw out, ended up covering myself in dirt. "I apologize."

"There's no need to apologize just because Greer doesn't enjoy hearing that she's pretty." Sophie stood up. "I'll put on the kettle."

We watched her walk away. "Do you understand why other women might be impatient with you, Greer?" I held my hand out in front of me, moving my fingers. Maybe it looked like I was playing an invisible piano, but really I was counting the number of girls I'd ever trusted. Definitely not my sister. Maybe Trina, the girl who lived three doors down from us until she moved away in the sixth grade. Two girls in middle school who I thought were my best friends until they decided I was a slut the summer before high school. And, yep. That's pretty much the sum total. An hour earlier, I might have named Sophie until she turned out to have a previously unmentioned dead brother, an obvious family trauma, and an unmistakable chip on her shoulder because I didn't enjoy being referred to as merely pretty. So I could really care less if other girls were impatient with me. I was feeling pretty freaking impatient with them.

But I wanted it to end. So Sophie turned out to be like any other girl. I could survive that disappointment. And it's not like I'd expected me and Hannah to enter into some sisterhood of the unraveling rants or anything. She could be crazy all by herself. I wanted a cozy weekend in the woods with my sensitive, muscular boyfriend.

"Wow," I murmured, as if enlightenment were just dawning on me. "I'd never tried to see it from someone else's perspective. Sometimes people write you off, though, for all kinds of reasons. I guess I'm just sensitive about that."

"Do you see how your looks can be a privilege?"

I made sure to pause before I nodded, so that it looked as if I was carefully considering it. "I do."

"Who's privileged?" Addison strutted in, drying his hands on his jeans.

"You are all privileged," Joshua answered. "I've taken on the challenge of showing you how."

"Uh-oh — have you started the white-power lecture yet?" Addison looked at Hannah and me. "A little advice, ladies. Just admit you noticed that he's black." Addison laughed.

"Don't make it easy on them. I hadn't even gotten there yet." Joshua smiled, but his eyes narrowed.

Sophie came back with the kettle and a tray of mugs, tea bags, and cocoa packets. "Who's black? Besides you and Wes, I mean."

"Who's the happy homemaker, here?" Joshua started giggling. "I'm not black, Sophia D. I am hot cocoa."

"Jeez," Addison groaned. But he smiled and nuzzled my neck. I shifted on the sofa and let him move in between Joshua and me. Maybe he knew enough to sit strategically. We reached for mugs. I concentrated fiercely on my tea and hoped we'd move on to talk more about hot beverages than identity politics.

Jared and Wes stuck their heads in the room. "Hey, Sophie, it's probably not okay to smoke in the house, right?"

"Probably not! But thanks for asking," Sophie called out gaily.

"Since when do you guys smoke?" Addison sounded personally wounded.

"Since we crossed the property limits of McCracken Hill."

"C'mon, guys, there's no reason we can't continue a fitness regime up here. We've got logs to lift out back. And Sophie says there's trails to run."

"Or we could just relax and enjoy two days off of the self-improvement reservation." Wes grabbed a pack of Marlboros out of his backpack.

Addison turned to Joshua for backup, but Joshua said, "Let them have their vices."

"Says the addiction specialist. Jesus. What happened to work the steps or walk the plank?"

Wes shook his head. "Whatever, Add. You've got your vice sitting right there on your lap."

"Okay, now settle down," Joshua said. "I'm sure that Greer would appreciate being seen as a loving and giving person, not some kind of bad habit. Right, Greer?"

"Not even a pretty bad habit."

At least Jared had the decency to look a little chastened. "Greer, you know we're just jealous, right? I'm sorry if we're using you to give Superman over there a hard time."

"However I can be of service," I called out as Jared and Wes headed out the door.

"Hope not." Addison grinned.

"Shut up." I slapped him and laughed until I caught Sophie rolling her eyes. "I didn't mean it like that." Somehow it felt like I was apologizing to her.

Joshua stirred his cocoa. "You got those mini marshmallows?" Sophie shook her head. "It's a shame to have hot chocolate without marshmallows. Do you know why, Addison?"

"I can only guess."

"That's right, because you need the light with the dark,

isn't that right? Greer, what did you expect when you met me? Did it shock you that this skinhead was hanging out with a black man?"

"Yeah." I said it simply.

"Look at you, Greer Elizabeth, just embracing honesty."

"Why were you so shocked?" Addison turned to me. "You'd seen me with Wes, right? Did you really think I was some kind of racist?" He sounded a little bit wounded. "What, because of my hair?"

"It didn't have anything to do with your hair. Or even you, really. Especially the skinhead thing — when you'd told me about him, I'd figured Joshua was Jewish."

Hannah almost choked on her cocoa. "Exactly!"

"Honestly, right?"

"Because I have a Jewish name." Joshua seemed peeved that we ruined his big, important discussion on race. "Sure, yes. *Stern* is traditionally a Jewish surname. I mean, I'm Jewish —"

Hannah said, "I assumed that too."

"That's lovely for you, Hannah, that you can be our resident expert in Judaism."

"Well, I didn't mean to imply I was an expert." Hannah's voice shrunk back into its shell.

"While you're all busy congratulating yourselves, try to realize that you are still making assumptions based on the color of my skin. Which is prejudice, no matter what you want to dress it up as."

Addison's face looked like granite. He sat perfectly still, as if he'd checked out and left the rest of us behind to defend ourselves. I could tell he knew what Joshua meant. He didn't speak up, though.

So I did. "I'm sorry if we said something to offend you."

Hannah nodded next to me. "Could you explain what I said that was hurtful?" Dr. Saggurti would be proud of my conflict-resolution skills.

Joshua sat still and silent. Sophie said, "I assumed that because you're black, you couldn't also be Jewish." Joshua snapped his fingers and pointed at her. He nodded. She nodded. Addison nodded. Hannah and I just looked at each other.

"Don't question my faith because of the color of my skin. All of you white boys and girls have grown up as members of a majority population." He raised up his hand to ward off an objection that Addison hadn't had the chance to voice. "And don't you talk to me about your African American roommate. Wes has grown up with every advantage too. None of you are aware of the assumptions you make." Hannah pursed her lips like she had something to say. I wished I could will her into speaking up. But she didn't. She sat there and I sat there and we all listened to Joshua tell us how important his Judaism was to him. Addison squeezed my hand between us. And just as the silence stretched into something painful, Jared and Wes tumbled in through the kitchen.

"God, it is so beautiful here. We should go out for a hike."

"We need to be a little careful," Sophie said. "I'm sorry — I just don't know who my dad has checking up on the place."

"Well, you know if someone called the cops, they'd haul my ass in first," Joshua said.

Wes laughed. "Because you're black or because you're old? I'm sure I'd be right behind you, Joshua."

He stood up. "I might not appreciate your complete and utter insensitivity, but you happen to be the only honest individual in this room. I commend you for that. Now if you'll all excuse me, I'd like some time to reflect before we gather together for an evening session." Joshua started up the stairs. "Don't worry, brother," he called down to Addison. "I will leave the master suite for you and Greer."

Out of the corner of my eye, I saw Sophie grimace. "That's not necessary," I said.

"Leave it be," Addison said. "He's just making a point."

"But that's Sophie's parents' room. We're not staying at some random bed-and-breakfast."

Sophie started clearing the mugs and spoons. "It's really not a big deal."

"Sophie —"

But she cut me off. "My mom and dad are pretty much separated. It's a perfectly nice bed. Someone should fuck in it."

"Jesus. Why is it that I always catch the tail end of these conversations?" Wes propped his feet on the steamer trunk in front of the sofa. "Is that the kind of session Joshua was talking about? Count me in."

"You're such a perv," Hannah muttered. "You okay, Greer?"

Sometimes people surprise you. Hannah actually seemed like she cared. "Oh, I'm good. We're all just having fun, right?" My voice sounded hollow even to me. "If it's okay, though, I'm going to lie down. If you want to pile the mugs and stuff in the sink, I'll clean up."

Sophie seemed to soften a little. "It's fine." She looked up. "Dinner was really great. I had no idea you could actually cook."

I unwrapped Addison's fingers from my hand. "Neither did I." If I didn't ask him, I knew Addison wouldn't follow me upstairs. He wasn't like that. Especially after all the stupid sex comments, Addison would know enough to give me some space. Still, I cringed a little when the old wooden steps creaked below my feet. I just wanted to find my room and lie down. I didn't want to risk Joshua stopping by for a private talk.

Mr. and Mrs. Delia's room was easy to pick out: right at the top of the stairs. It had a peaked roof and an enormous iron bed. It must have been directly above the den downstairs, because there was a second version of the stone fireplace in the middle of the room. When I closed the door, I could barely make out the voices below. Someone laughed and dishes clattered into the sink. The party went on without me. Or Joshua.

When I look back, maybe that's the first time I felt like something was truly wrong. Not even Addison's mood swings or Joshua's sleepover had sounded whatever personal alarm system of instinct was wired up my spine. But in that grand house, surrounded by my friends, I didn't feel safe. I locked the bedroom door.

ELEVEN

When I first woke up, I'd forgotten where we were. The bed stretched a lot wider than the narrow dorm cot at school. I knew that much. The quilt felt soft and fresh. The sun had eased down and streaked the sky with pink. I could still see the feathery silhouettes of the pine trees outside, though. My eyes adjusted and I remembered the room.

Even half-asleep, I knew Addison was with me. Somewhere, under that beamed roof. We were linked like that. It took a few seconds to remember that Joshua was there too and that we'd made him so angry. I lay back on the big bed and dreaded the next few hours. I consoled myself with the idea that afterward, after whatever sharing and caring Joshua had orchestrated for that night, Addison and I would climb the spiral staircase up to this room and I'd finally have the chance to fall asleep with him right there.

I peed, threw some water on my face, and brushed my teeth. I stood at the top of the stairs and, for a little bit, I got to just look down and watch everyone. Jared, Wes, and Addison had found some old video-game thing and plugged it in. Hannah sat in the corner, in a pile of pillows. She bent over her leather journal, writing. Sophie and Joshua sat at the breakfast bar in the kitchen. Their heads bent close together, deep in discussion about something. There was a bowl between them catching peanut shells, but at first, I thought they were dropping tiny shreds of brown paper there. When I had to explain it, I figured they were writing wishes on little scraps of paper. That seemed like the kind of activity Joshua would have planned for us.

Joshua looked up first, held my eyes for a second. He cracked a nut between his teeth and called up, "Hello, beauty." He smiled. It's not like he looked like a jackal or something. He looked like a friendly uncle or a patient chaperone. Sophie looked up and smiled. Addison shot up and bounded up the steps.

"You're awake." He grabbed me around the waist and twirled me down the last few steps.

"God, you two are obnoxious." It was Sophie, but when I turned to face her, she was smiling again — same old Sophie, no trace of the bitterness that seemed to have puckered everything when we first arrived at the house. She even tousled my hair. "You actually slept — how was the room?"

"The room's amazing. Sophie. Are you sure it's okay for us to be up there?"

"Yeah, it's fine. Joshua's in my grandparents' room —"

"Tell her where we are." Hannah set down her book. She rose and stretched. "Greer, you might want to trade."

Jared cackled. "Greer, you have to see this. You're going to feel like you and Add won the bedroom lottery."

"Guys, it's not that bad. I'm telling you, it's actually kind of fun." Sophie laughed.

I peeked into their room and saw the four sets of bunk beds — eight little mattresses topped with alternating blue and red comforters. On my right, a steel set of lockers gleamed against the wall. The kids' room.

"So we can push all these beds together later on, right?" Jared reached up to pat one of the upper bunks. "Or we'll just drag all the mattresses into the center of the room and build a love nest."

"I think you should just reserve the far bunk by the window," Addison suggested. "That way, if you start acting up, the girls can just shove you out." He picked up the duffel Jared had dropped on the blue bunk closer to us.

Before he moved it, Sophie blurted out, "Just leave that bed, okay?" Addison turned back and looked at me with wide eyes. We didn't need to be detectives to figure out whose bed he'd been headed toward. Sophie must have seen his look of horror because she pretty much just flung herself toward Jared. "I'll have to find a way to fight him off somehow." She smiled brightly, moving us all on from the moment.

Jared bent to nibble on her ear, happy to oblige. She pretended to karate chop him in the solar plexus.

"I think it's time that we regroup in a room that might be less distracting," Joshua announced. "The beds seem to have sidetracked young Jared's concentration."

Jared raised his hands up, like he was a suspect emerging from a bank robbery. He backed his way through the kitchen and we followed him toward the great room.

Addison hung back with me in the kitchen and shot me a worried look. "It's okay," I told him.

"I feel awful." He shook his head. "What happened? What if she hasn't been back here since —"

I had thought about that. "If that's true — and we don't know it's true — maybe that's what she needed. She didn't have to say yes to this." He looked dubiously at me. "It might have felt like she had to agree, but Sophie's not a sucker, you know. She does what she wants to. Maybe this is how she wanted to come back here."

"Addison. Elizabeth." Joshua had apparently realized that we'd hung back. He did not sound happy about it.

"I'll try to get her alone and talk about it," I said. "But you didn't know — you can't beat yourself up over not knowing which bed —"

Addison looked miserable. "Christ. I break everything I touch."

I craned my head to kiss his cheek. "You're seriously the most gentle person I know." He bent to kiss me, leaned in, and pressed me against the wall. I heard myself gasp.

And then I heard someone cough. "Ummm . . . Joshua asked if you would join the group." Hannah looked like she wanted to sink into the floor. "I'm sorry if it seems like I'm always the one to have to fetch you." She trailed off and looked back, as if worried that Joshua would yell again.

Addison kept one arm around me, but wrapped the other around Hannah. "No way, Hannah — that's on us." He stepped ahead of both of us. "Can I get you ladies a root beer? Or other nonalcoholic cocktail beverage?"

Hannah giggled and blushed. She turned around, looked back over her shoulder. "It's okay," Addison reassured her. "He'll wait as long as he knows I'm being a gentleman." He reached into the fridge. "We're just gathering some drinks. Can I get anyone anything?"

"Water would be nice," Joshua called out. "Have Elizabeth bring me some water, please." I heard him tell Sophie to sit down. "You don't have to play hostess every second. Is there anything you want to talk to me about?"

Hannah, Addison, and I exchanged looks. Addison handed me a glass of ice water and a can of Diet Coke.

"Go see what's going on in there."

There was not much going on. Sophie looked like she was in self-preservation mode. She sat cross-legged in one of the enormous reclining chairs. Jared sat on the floor next to her. Wes sat next to Joshua on the couch. For the most part, the room was silent, except for the crackling fire. "Sophie, you okay?" She looked up. "I mean, did you want something to drink?"

"I'm okay. Thanks." But she wrapped her arms back around herself. I did notice one of her knees resting on Jared's shoulder.

"Anything?"

"Greer, we'd just like you to join us. That's all the refreshment we need." Joshua said it between sips of the water I'd just brought him. He patted the sofa. "You know where you should sit." He gestured to Wes. "That might actually be Hannah's spot. We'll see how she feels."

Wes mumbled and dove into the other recliner. "Joshua, you just like to surround yourself with the ladies. That's how I feel."

"Are we already talking about feelings?" Addison handed out the cans of soda he'd been juggling. Hannah stood on the edge of the room until Joshua motioned her to sit near him. I watched her eyes move around the group, taking stock of everyone's positions and expressions. I wondered if she read the room at the same temperature as I had. "What feeling are we focusing on first, Joshua?" Addison draped himself across the love seat. Sometimes it shocked me how giant he looked. He filled up the sofa like it was a chair. He cracked open the soda and raised it up to the group. "To feelings!" he said.

"I thought that we would discuss defensiveness first."

Addison grimaced. "Well, I don't want to toast to defensiveness."

"That surprises me a bit. It seems to be a feeling that many people close to you embrace."

Sophie looked up and met my eyes, as if to say, *here we go*.

Wes spoke first. "Well, Joshua, I don't mean any disrespect, but I don't really consider that a feeling we should focus on."

"Is that so?" Joshua asked, in his bored voice.

"Defensiveness isn't really a feeling, you know. Being defensive is an action. Right? It's a behavior. Maybe we should try to pinpoint a feeling that's at the root of defensiveness."

"You all speak like such frauds."

"Hey —" Addison set down his drink. "That's a little unnecessary."

"No, it's absolutely vital. Do you hear yourselves? Do you hear the people you've surrounded yourself with? I'm trying to confront you about your inability to discuss matters in any real or true way and you're feeding me this self-help crap they've been spooning down your throats at your rich-kid rehab. I'm tired of wasting my time."

It's not like it was the first time I'd thought of it. But I really wanted to ask at that moment: What was the rest of Joshua's life like? Had he been married? Didn't he have family that would miss him over the weekend? Friends his age? How could his whole life revolve around Addison?

But then again, mine did. "Joshua, we're sorry," I said. "You get used to talking a certain way, you know." Addison looked at me gratefully.

"I expect you to be stronger than that, Elizabeth." But the edge on his voice had softened a little. "Maybe we need to shift the room."

"What does that even mean?" Wes asked. He sounded done with the whole thing. Over it already. I caught Addison motioning slightly with his hand. *Back it up. Calm down.*

I tried to help, asking, "How can we do that?"

"Candles. We'll shut the lights and use candles."

I looked to Sophie, who said, "Okay, we just have to be careful, you know —"

"No one's going to move once we light the candles," Joshua commanded, and so Sophie pretty much leapt up for the kitchen cupboard. Jared's eyes shifted around the room, first following her and then appearing to yearn for the front door. Someone in Sophie's family must have owned stock in Yankee Candle. Maybe that's where they got all their money. By the time she finished lighting the jars, the tapers, and the little tea lights on saucers, we must have had fifteen or sixteen flickering wicks. And because they all had different fruity scents, it smelled like we'd bombed a produce stand.

As soon as we got all the candles lit, Joshua reached out and shut the lamp. He motioned for Addison to switch off the kitchen lights and he did. We were doused in shadows. It sounded as if everyone exhaled at once. I expected all of the flames to waver because of it.

"Now." Joshua had adjusted his voice to his slow groove. "Why don't we try this again? I want you all to sit back. You've arrived with a lot of secrets bundled up. We're going to unpack them. There are some of you in this room" — I watched him zero in on Wes — "who don't seem to understand that you have obviously faltered. But we must acknowledge the fact that this faltering has led you to this moment. I would never have had the opportunity to meet you if you'd been living your life at its highest capacity for success and fulfillment. Is that understood?"

I saw heads slowly nod across the room. "There are others of you in this room who see yourselves as flawed." Hannah looked down at her lap. Addison's eyes slid toward me. That stung a tiny bit. Did he see me as damaged? Or did he just think that's how I viewed myself? I had this urge to reach out to him, to burrow in. But Joshua seemed to sense that and I felt his papery hand touch my arm instead. "Let the burdens fall away. That's all I'm asking right now." Joshua's hand brushed down my wrist. He laced his fingers in mine. "I'm going to challenge you to sit for five minutes of silence."

It sounded simple enough, but those minutes crawled. I kept my eyes closed for the first bit, and when I eased them open and peeked, everyone else sat with eyes shut. Except Wes, whose eyes flicked around the room. When they met mine, he winked. He was trying to make the best of things, but I worried about him. It wasn't easy to exist in Joshua's harsh glare. I knew why I put up with it, but probably Wes wasn't in love with Addison, so I wondered a little.

"Addison, does everyone know what your life was like before you saved yourself?"

"Yes," I said. "We've talked a lot about that." I didn't want to hear any more about what a brute Addison had once been.

Joshua spoke coldly. "Elizabeth. Please don't interfere with Addison's ability to be truthful. If you want to coddle yourself, that's fine. Let him be the warrior he is." I heard choking coming from the far corner.

Wes waved off our concern. "I'm fine. Sorry, sorry." He held up his root beer. "Went down the wrong pipe."

"Addison," Joshua ordered. We sat in silence for another full minute before he spoke.

"It wasn't just that I was lost. I felt like there was a darkness. But not just around me — inside of me. I felt eaten up by it. Devoured. When I drank or smoked weed or took pills, I could look away from it. I remember feeling so alone. And then so angry. I guess I drank to move from loneliness to rage."

"Why aim for the rage? Why was that preferable?"

Addison didn't hesitate. It almost sounded like he saw the question coming. "I guess rage felt less vulnerable." I heard his low, wry chuckle. "When I was swinging away at someone, at least I was connecting."

"Why did you sober up?"

"It was at a party. You know, just a bunch of townies getting together. Someone's parents had left for the weekend. The kid — the kid whose house it was — I'd played Little League with him way back. But the only reason I know that" — Addison paused, inhaled. Exhaled — "His parents faced a bunch of lawsuits afterward. For providing alcohol. Unsafe environment. They lost their house." He'd never shared that part of the story with me.

"I couldn't even tell you what pissed me off. I remember the kid's face before." He stopped for a second. "And I remember it after." While Addison talked, I made sure not to look away from him. He kept his eyes on the fire. He said, "I guess the damage I did — the serious head injury — that was the curb. The kid went down. I remember kicking him. You know, in the ribs. He curled up and for some reason, that made me mad, so I bent down and grabbed him by the hair." It seemed like it had been ten minutes since anyone in the room had breathed. Addison kept going. "I slammed his face into the curb. His teeth shattered. I just kept banging. Chuckie was wasted too. So it took him a while to get to me. You know, to pull me off. By that time . . ." His voice faded and he finally tore his eyes away from the fireplace. Addison looked around at all of us. "I sobered up in the holding cell, I guess."

"One of the twelve steps involves making amends for our mistakes," Joshua explained to us. Then he asked Addison, "Could you do that with this boy that you hurt?" It was another question Joshua knew the answer to. I knew it too and it hurt to hear.

Addison said, "I couldn't. Not fully. I wrote a letter to his parents. He goes to a special school now. That's what I did to him. My dad — he's probably not like your dads —" Addison looked at Sophie and me. "But he's got his own kind of pull around our town. I know a lot of people in the community stepped up and wrote letters to the judge on my behalf. You know — I was such a great kid. This kind of episode was completely out of character. Bullshit like that. They did it for my dad. So I ended up serving some time in this halfway house. Summertime, nothing major. And then they gave me two hundred hours of community service."

"What else, Addison?" Joshua asked. I watched my own fists clench. What more could there be?

Addison's head swiveled to Joshua. For the first time, he seemed surprised by the question.

"What other burdens are you carrying? Who else do you feel responsible for?"

I shut my eyes and prayed he didn't name me. But instead, Addison said, "Chuckie," in a strangled way that made it seem like he was trying desperately not to cry. His voice strengthened as he explained. "Maybe seeing what happened that night did it. My brother lost it. He just . . . I had to pull it together, right? That was basically court ordered. But the more I got myself together, the more Chuckie fell apart."

"Addison, you're so hard on yourself," Sophie said. I sent her a silent thanks. If I had said it, Joshua would have scolded me for interrupting. He didn't even motion her to stop, though, when she added, "Chuckie's choices are his. You can't take those on too."

We all nodded sagely, as if any of us knew what the hell we were talking about. He said, "It's not that so much. My parents pulled whatever kind of strings they could so that I avoided serious jail time. You know, people thought of us as a good family. Everyone saw what happened as a fluke thing. When your dad's a union guy and your mom's a nurse and your family sits in the first few rows at church every Sunday, people just figure you messed up. Some kids do that. And then everyone steps in to help them straighten out. But when Chuckie" — he searched for the word — "disintegrated, that made two of us. Two fuckups in one family. That's no fluke, right? That's what people think. So no one stepped in for Chuckie. And he was two years late. So Chuckie did time. Like real time. When he came home — I don't know what happened to him in there. But he wouldn't have landed there if I hadn't started falling first."

When Addison stopped talking, he searched out Joshua. He looked at him as if to say, *Enough*. Joshua nodded and took over the talking. "Whenever we fall, we take down people with us. Sometimes it's the people we love most. Sometimes we don't even know who we've hurt along the way. Addison couldn't have predicted what his actions would cost his family."

I couldn't stop myself. "Yeah, but that's discounting a major part of Addison's life. It's not looking at why he was

121

drinking or doing drugs in the first place." I looked to Addison. "You even said it — Chuckie was too loaded that night to break up the fight right away. Don't you ever ask yourself why you were both so set on getting out of your heads like that?" In the corner, Wes nodded to himself, and that bolstered me a little.

"Maybe it's simplistic to blame all of that on someone's family, but your family couldn't have been perfect, or you and Chuckie wouldn't have been chugging whole bottles of vodka at a high school party. You wouldn't have developed a drug habit or even known how to hurt someone like that."

"Elizabeth, that's too easy. Addison doesn't need you to let him off the hook." Joshua didn't sound mad. More like weary. He was tired of me. "When we blame our mistakes on our families, we give away our power. That's the cowardly route."

Addison nodded. "It's not like I was abused or unloved or anything. Most people might not like admitting it, but sometimes people get fucked up because they enjoy the feeling of being fucked up." I'd spent hours leaning against Addison and listening to him talk about his dad's affairs, the coldness that had settled over his house after his mom discovered the cheating. But that wasn't the story Addison and Joshua had decided to tell that night. So I kept my mouth shut.

Jared spoke up then. "But genetics play a part in drug use, right?" He cleared his throat. "I don't think my parents were particularly shocked when I tested positive for coke."

Hannah shot him a quizzical look. "What do you mean?"

"For cocaine, Hannah. I failed a drug test."

He sounded angry and Hannah looked stricken and Joshua stepped in then, saying, "Okay, now, let's show each other patience," in his low, calm voice. He sat up and leaned toward Jared. "Did your parents also struggle with drugs?"

"Yeah." At first, I thought that's all Jared would say. But he explained, "I wouldn't say *struggled*. My dad went to law school in the eighties. When my test came back, the school freaked out and my mom got all weepy, but he didn't even seem to consider it a big deal."

"Is he still using?" Joshua asked matter-of-factly.

"I don't think so. They sat me down and gave me the talk. The disappointment talk." Nods around the room. We'd all heard the disappointment lecture. "But my dad — it seemed like he was going through the motions. It was more about figuring out how to keep it off my transcript. I just wondered. He fell into it and then twenty-five years later, I did too. What does that mean?"

"Was it hard to stop using?" Sophie asked him. "You don't talk about it like you miss it."

"Yeah, no." He looked apologetically at Addison. "I'm not working the twelve steps. I go to the meetings because that's what the treatment team assigned, but the rhetoric just doesn't feel useful to me. I got caught and sent away and so I stopped."

"Why do you think they sent you to McCracken Hill, then?" Joshua wasn't challenging, just asking.

"I think they just wanted someone else to deal with it."

"Maybe your father worried about his own recovery?" Addison asked. I could almost see the wheels turning in his head, thinking about him and Chuckie needing to split up to get better.

"I just don't know that we're wired like that. That's why I asked about genetics," Jared said. "My dad never went to rehab. He must have just stopped."

"You believe he stopped," Joshua corrected.

"Listen, my dad does not do coke." Jared seemed embarrassed to hear his voice rise. He said, "Sorry. But maybe Addison and Chuckie have some genetic disposition that I lucked out and don't have. This just isn't that hard for me."

"Is anything hard for you?" Joshua asked. I waited for Jared to lash out. It was the kind of Joshua question that seemed designed to infuriate.

But Jared stayed calm. He tipped his head to the side. "Yes." I waited for the rest, for him to explain. We all waited.

Jared didn't say anything else. He stretched his arms and folded them behind his head. "Yes." He looked at Joshua. "When did you get clean?"

Joshua smiled. "Brother" — he paused and smiled even more widely — "thank you for asking me for my story. But this weekend is our time to learn your stories. We have plenty of time to rehash my old life." Joshua looked down at my hand and petted it. It seemed like out of all the people crowded into the room, he was only talking to me. "I'm an old man, so it's an old life. Remnants from a long time ago. Right, Elizabeth?" He laid his hand fully over my own. It rested heavily there, like his voice in the room. "Let's talk about those remnants of our old lives. Those scraps of pain. Maybe you didn't pack them in your knapsacks, but they're here with you. You all know what I'm talking about. There is a darkness following each one of you. Something has interfered with your radiance. It's standing in the way of your life. So we need to take it down."

My eyelids felt heavy. I was relieved we were sitting down because my knees shook a little. I got the idea that if I'd stood, they'd be too weak to hold me up. Joshua lifted his hand off mine and that helped me feel less stifled.

"Elizabeth is very sensitive to this kind of episode." I felt eyes turn to me. The staring smothered me. "What do you need to unpack, Elizabeth?" And then, maybe because I didn't answer right away, "Greer?"

My gut instinct told me to keep my mouth shut. I hadn't told anyone in the room besides Joshua what had happened. Maybe I had a valid reason for that. And it would hurt at least Addison and Sophie that I'd confided something like that to Joshua before either of them.

There was something in the room, though. Pressing me forward. So I told the story as quickly as possible. "My terror sometimes stands in my way. When I was ten, my cousin Parker held our family hostage on Thanksgiving. He accused my uncle of abusing him. He had a gun." No one in the room spoke. I filled the silence. "We all were fine. It's not like he shot anyone. So no one really talked about it. But I was little and it really frightened me. I think it probably changed how I see some things."

I sat still on the sofa, next to Joshua. I bit my lip and willed my eyes not to slide toward Addison. He'd have to decide whether or not to be angry that I'd hid something so major from him. But Addison didn't really hesitate. He moved from his seat to the floor and wrapped his arm around my leg. "Is this okay?" Addison looked up and then down to where he'd shackled my ankle in his grip.

"Yeah." I nodded. "Are you okay?" Meaning: *Does knowing that hurt you?*

"I'm good. You feel lighter, I bet, with that off your chest. Right?"

"Almost weightless." I let myself smile at him before looking up at Sophie, but she didn't actually seem angry at all. She held her hand up, making an L shape with her thumb.

and index finger. Her pinkie stuck out too. Sign language for *I love you.*

"Was it sexual abuse?" Hannah spoke in a rush.

"What?" And then because my voice came out sounding sharper than I'd meant it, I asked more carefully, "What do you mean?"

Hannah fidgeted in her seat. "You said your cousin accused your uncle of abuse. I just wondered what kind. Sorry." She looked like she wanted to sink into the couch cushions. "It doesn't matter."

Sophie and I exchanged looks. It seemed like maybe we could guess at the secret standing in Hannah's way. "It matters. I mean, what matters most is that my cousin Parker was a child and he felt that hurt and helpless, right? He was physically abused. I don't think it was sexual."

"What happened to him? Afterward?" Wes asked.

"I don't know." It sounded awful now. Until McCracken Hill, I'd never thought about how my family pretty much turned away from Parker. It's not like my parents took Uncle Brady's side. But they didn't stand up for Parker either. And I never questioned that. "He went away to a bunch of different schools."

"Like McCracken Hill?" Jared asked, sort of half-smiling.

"A little like that, I guess. Maybe more intense."

"What does your uncle do for a living, Elizabeth?" Joshua asked.

The question startled me. "He's a clerk. He works at a law firm."

"He's not a lawyer?"

"No. There's some tension about that. My dad's always been more successful."

"Places like McCracken Hill are expensive."

"I believe we've covered that topic already," Addison said wryly.

Joshua studied me. I was beginning to see where this was headed. "I don't think my uncle Brady makes enough money to send a kid to that kind of school. Not for years anyway."

"So, then, what do you think happened?" Joshua asked, but I still didn't connect all the dots. "I think if you looked into your father's bank account, you'd see years of tuition checks." As soon as he said it, I knew it was true. I remembered my dad driving me up the hill to school that morning, how he'd even gotten teary when Ms. Crane searched through my stuff. I wondered if he'd been the one to deliver Parker to his new school. I'd figured I had put him through something he'd never pictured. But maybe my dad was an expert in sending away Cannon-family bad seeds.

"Elizabeth?" Joshua's voice broke through. "Where are you in this?"

"I'm here. I'm dealing." Addison's grasp tightened around my leg.

"Let us in. What are you dealing with?"

"I feel like Parker. Like we're just problems that my dad paid someone to take off his hands." I saw nods around the room. "But I'm almost an adult, you know. I'm sixteen. McCracken might suck sometimes, but I met you all. Parker was a little kid. How do you just send a little kid away?"

Hannah opened her mouth, shut it, and looked down to her lap. Joshua told her, "Go on. Hannah, tell us."

She craned her neck past Joshua to see me. When she spoke out, she pronounced every word really carefully, like she was building a wall. Or tearing one down, brick by brick. "Maybe you send the kid away because it's all you can do to keep him safe."

It felt like something had punctured my lung. Like, inside, I was deflating. I couldn't breathe. It made me sad for Parker — that even the adults in our family felt like leaving was his only option. And it hurt to realize what I'd assumed about my father. I'd grown so accustomed to thinking he was doing the cowardly thing. Lastly, I ached for Hannah, since she sounded like an expert in something so awful.

"I hadn't thought of it that way. Thanks, Hannah."

"What are you thanking Hannah for? Be clear."

"Greer, Greer — make sure you're clear," Addison sang softly below me. It made me laugh. And as soon as I laughed, I started to cry.

"Thank you for giving me the chance to see my dad as —" I couldn't find the right word.

"As a hero?" Joshua asked.

"Probably *hero* is too strong a word, right?" Joshua refused to give me the answer. I said to Hannah, "At least heroic."

"I think it counts as heroic," she told me.

"Who else has a burden we need to unpack?" Joshua asked.

I reached down to squeeze Addison's arm, relieved that the spotlight had moved away from us for a while.

"Hannah? Is there anything you'd like to tell us?" he asked over a current of another thought: *You've already started.*

Hannah stared off into space. We all fidgeted, getting ready to listen. But she seemed to make a decision. She said, "No, thank you. I think I need to keep my suitcase zippered for right now."

I thought Joshua was going to press it. He would have forced any of the rest of us to talk. We collectively wished he would back down. And he did. He said, "We are ready to listen and waiting for you to share." But then that left Sophie and Wes. Stalemate. We all sat in silence.

Joshua cleared his throat. "I'm going to take us back to Brother Jared's question. But I'm not going to tell you why I got clean. That's a story for another day. I'd like us to go further back, tell you why I started using in the first place. Some of you might know that I spent a night in Elizabeth's room last week."

Wes's and Jared's reaction made it clear that Addison had not shared that development. "Can I ask why?" Jared asked Addison.

Joshua looked steadily at Jared and told him, "Elizabeth needed to know that she could trust me. She needed to prove to herself that trusting someone would not result in harm." He reached over then and took my hand again. "She never had to be afraid of me. I am probably the last person who would hurt her, who'd betray that trust. Do you know why?"

Wes grinned. "Because Addison's ginormous?" Addison snickered, but Joshua just refused to acknowledge Wes all over again. I watched him kind of fade into the background of the room. He might claim he didn't care, but I hurt for him.

Joshua just kept going. "When I was a child, I was sexually abused. Repeatedly. Almost since birth. I grew up feeling filthy." He stroked my hand. "I hate touching people. Every time I reach out and offer one of you my touch, it costs me. I find it to be excruciating."

He could stop at any time. That's what I wanted to tell Joshua. But I sat there and stayed quiet. "Later on, I was also physically abused. Beaten. Burned. Scalded. The worst case you hear about on the news — that was me. The courts removed me from that home and then I bounced from foster home to foster home. Predators. They all housed predators." Addison was listening attentively. Hannah hung on every word. Sophie seemed a little twitchy, though, and Wes had pretty much zoned out. I couldn't get a read on Jared.

Sophie broke the silence first. "How do you even move on from something like that?" Joshua shut his eyes. A beatific smile spread over his face and he started rocking a little in his seat. The whole sofa moved like a cradle.

Just when we started to freak out, Joshua's eyes opened. "This way." He spread his arms out, as if to encompass us all. "I serve as an instrument of peace. I play the believing game."

It's hard to admit, because you're not supposed to doubt stories like that. But if Joshua was playing the believing game, I'd have been sidelined. I didn't buy it. It felt unkind to doubt him, but Joshua didn't approach the world like someone who'd been beaten down by it. He reached out to people. He even took advantage of them.

Something just felt wrong to me. When I looked around the room, though, I saw rapt faces. It's not like Addison would ever question him. And even Jared and Wes looked sold. So I played along. I made sure to have an adoring look on my face and reached for Joshua's hand on my shoulder. "I'm really happy you're here."

"You don't know how happy I am that you're here, Elizabeth." Joshua spoke softly. "Listen carefully — you will deliver us all." He looked around at the others. "Did you hear me?" Solemn nods all around. "There's more to explain, and I'll share that with you, but there are powerful forces blocking our progress. Heavy weights holding us back." He narrowed his eyes at Sophie and she wrapped her arms around her knees.

She started speaking almost immediately. "My brother's name was Nicholas. He was two years older than Josie and me. He wrecked his car and he died. Not too far from here on the highway. Usually we stopped on the way, but we'd gotten a late start. So we got here and he went out later on that night. For breakfast stuff, I guess."

I felt my eyes well up. Sophie met my gaze and gave me a little smile. Like she was apologizing for not telling me sooner. *Oh, Sophie.* Joshua said, "I find your wording interesting, Sophia. And I wonder if it doesn't reveal more about the circumstances of your brother's death." I sucked in my breath. He needed to leave her alone. I looked down to Addison, but he only tightened his hold on my ankle, like some kind of leg iron, locking me into place.

Sophie blinked. Joshua kept going. "You didn't say he died in a car accident. You said he wrecked his car." She just rested her chin on her knees. "Did he usually need to drive on the highway to get to the supermarket? That seems odd to me. Couldn't Nicholas have stopped in town?"

Jared interrupted. "Joshua, I don't know that we need to play detective." Sophie shot him a grateful look. He said to her, "I'm really sorry for your family's loss."

"We're not trying to unravel the mystery of the accident." Joshua wasn't going to let the two of them have any kind of moment. He told us, "Sophia has already done that. We're trying to shed the shroud of language she uses. Do you understand what I mean by that, Sophia?"

She nodded miserably.

"Was it a single-car accident, Sophia?"

She leveled her gaze at him. "Yes."

"What does that mean?" I really didn't get it. No one answered me. I ducked down to whisper in Addison's ear.

But it was Sophie who answered. "He drove into a pole on the side of a highway. In clear weather." I must have still looked lost, because she said, "It didn't seem like an accident." But then Sophie straightened up in her seat. She planted her feet on the floor. "To some people."

"What about to you?"

She tilted up her chin. "He was also a new driver. It's easy to get lost on these roads and people drive like assholes. Maybe someone was tailgating. Or blinded him with their high beams. We're never going to know."

"Has anyone ever discussed the warning signs of suicide with you, Sophia?" Sophie's face crumpled. Joshua spoke softly and slowly. "I'm going to guess that you recognized some of those signs afterward?"

"After that night . . ." Sophie started and stopped. She tried again. "Afterward, we packed up the house and went back home for Nick's funeral. We haven't come up here since. If it's okay — I think there are pieces of this I need to keep private."

She looked up at him. I swore I could see her trembling from across the room. Joshua said, "Of course. For now." She sighed, a long exhale, and looked toward the collection of family portraits.

"Are you okay?" Hannah asked. "Can I get you some water or something?"

Sophie gave her a small smile. "I'm fine. Thanks, though."

Joshua clasped his hands behind his head. I could feel the weight around my shoulders lift when he took his arms away. "It certainly is kind of Hannah to show her concern, but make no mistake — she's longing for the kitchen right now. Isn't that so, Hannah?"

Hannah Green actually flinched. But when she spoke, she did so clearly. "I'm not ready for this, Joshua."

"I'm not convinced you're capable of knowing that." She said nothing. She just waited, bracing herself. "That's your default mechanism, isn't it? You're not ready? Doesn't that make things easier?" As Joshua's voice rose, I expected Hannah to cringe more. That maybe she would even buckle.

But Hannah surprised me. Hannah kept surprising us all. "I'm here." She looked around the room. "I thought I wasn't ready for that. But you challenged me and I stepped up. This . . . confessional stuff isn't right for me. Not right now. But I'll let you know when I'm ready."

Addison let loose a low whistle and grinned. Joshua recovered quickly. He nodded and smiled. I watched Addison watch Hannah and thought that if I hadn't come on the trip, someone else would be sleeping in the master bedroom with Addison. That much seemed pretty obvious, at least to me, for that second.

I might have let his spiritual adviser sleep in my bed, but Hannah knew how to actually handle Joshua. I watched Addison's fingers loosen from my ankle. He didn't even realize he was letting go. He was mesmerized.

"How do you feel about that, Elizabeth?" Joshua's question surprised me. I thought I was finally off the hot seat. Addison tore his eyes from Hannah and smiled up at me, clueless.

Sophie shot me a warning look. She knew me. I must have been radiating *jealous bitch* and Sophie had picked up the signal. "It's really tough to make yourself vulnerable." I searched for more words that Addison would recognize. That he might appreciate. "I understand if Hannah's not ready for that yet." *Because she's a freakazoid maniac.* But I kept that last part to myself. Instead I put on my best supportive smile. "Just so you know — I'm here if you need to talk about anything. We all are, right?"

Sophie nodded along with me. As soon as Addison nodded too, she spoke up and said, "It especially helps to have girlfriends to confide in, right, Greer? No offense to you guys, but sometimes you just need your girls." Sometimes it made me really happy that Sophie was on my team.

Hannah seemed to glow. Joshua said, "Well, we've moved some boulders out of the way. I feel grateful for that. Our way is less obstructed now. Do you all see that?"

We nodded, but I felt hollowed out and shaky.

Joshua said, "Let's bring the circle closer." And we all drew in, leaned forward, and prepared to listen closely. "Let's welcome our own spirits. I thank you for your courage and your resilience. You've all struggled so much and you've come this far. And it's only because of your struggle that you've managed to find me. And the others, those powerful people sitting close to you." Addison's grip tightened around my ankle again. "Don't be frightened." I realized that usually I started to get scared whenever Joshua advised us not to be. "We're not the only ones in the room." He gave us time to look up. "That's right. We have souls circling the room, eager to bolster our courage. But they are also demanding to be recognized."

Like clockwork, I felt myself begin to shut down. My eyelids grew as heavy as they always did when Joshua made me really uncomfortable. Now we were talking about ghosts in Sophie's vacation home. Right after he'd tried to make her admit that her older brother committed suicide. It was more than I could take. Either Joshua's voice got softer or I stopped listening so closely. "Don't back away, Elizabeth." His voice rose as he warned me.

"Sorry," I mumbled. Joshua waited, made sure my eyes were wide open. I blinked a few times and even pinched my thigh to wake myself up. "It won't happen again."

"There is a young boy in the room," Joshua announced and Sophie's breath caught loudly. It sounded like fabric tearing. I wanted to reach out and wrap my arms around her. We'd just head out right that minute. I'd bundle her up and lead her away. We'd hike to the highway and someone would pick us up, shuttle us far away from Joshua and his sick games.

That's how angry it made me, to think after everything, he was going to use Nicholas's death right there. I didn't get up and start packing our bags. Instead I prepared myself to watch him break Sophie down right in front of me.

"I'm sorry," Joshua said. "My statement lacked clarity. It's not a teenaged boy among us. This boy has a lot of growing to do. He feels very lonely. He sees himself as abandoned." I'd been so preoccupied with plotting Sophie's escape that I hadn't been listening closely. It took Wes's caring look from across the circle to jolt me into realizing that it might be my own life Joshua was mining.

But Parker wasn't dead. He might very well feel lost and abandoned. I could certainly understand that, especially since recently feeling similarly discarded by the Cannon family dynasty. Someone would have told me that Parker died, though, for no other reason than that would have tied the tidiest knot on the cautionary tale that was my cousin. "Joshua, Parker can't be a ghost if he's still living." I kept my voice even.

"No one mentioned your cousin Parker. Do you hear yourself at all? I'm asking you to bring your best self out for us. And that might mean realizing that we cannot focus on your needs all the time. Our collective story cannot always star Greer."

God. Shame broiled me. I looked down, but Addison wouldn't even make eye contact. I probably could have stared a hole right into the back of his head. Tears behind my eyes threatened to pour, but I didn't want to give anyone else in the room that victory. Even Wes. For all of his meaningful looks, he hadn't spoken up for me either. We must have just sat there for a few full seconds and I tried not to sob.

"Forgive me, Elizabeth." Joshua grabbed my hand. "I'm just feeling overwhelmed by the pain of this spirit. I understand — I'm sure we all understand why you might have leapt to make the connection with your cousin. Who among us doesn't see the world through the lens of our own self?"

It made me hate myself a little that I felt so grateful to him.

Wes spoke up then. "Listen, this is creepy. I didn't sign up for a séance." Jared nodded and Sophie stood up. It felt like we were all scattering, like maybe someone had finally broken the spell.

But then Joshua blurted out, "An infant. It's an infant, and he's demanding to know why we have forsaken him."

If I could have stepped outside of myself, I would have seen my head do the WTF swivel. Later on, Sophie would go through this phase of replaying my reaction over and over. She called it one of the most hilarious cult moments ever.

Joshua would be the first person to point out that I could never step out of myself, though. We were, for good or bad, anchored to our own bodies, doomed to egotistically view the world, even if we strove for something better. So it took me a minute to process his claim that there was a spirit of a baby there with us in the warm, wood-paneled room.

And it took even longer to figure out that the high-pitched wail was not some kind of siren going off in my own head. Someone in the circle was wailing. It was Hannah and she pushed past me as she ran for the door.

CHAPTER
TWELVE

For a second or two, no one moved. We watched Hannah blur by and then the door slammed so hard, the chandelier swung back and forth. By the time Jared hit the switch, it still swung. It cast shadows on the room that moved along with the iron candelabras.

"What the hell is going on here?" Wes practically bellowed. He moved before any of us and swung open the front door. "Hannah?" And then louder: "HANNAH?" He stepped in and reached for his jacket on a hook. "I can hear her crying."

Sophie said, "Let Greer and me go." She looked toward Joshua and worked it further. "Hannah needs women with her now, right?"

Joshua sat on the couch by himself. He appeared completely untroubled. "I'd like some tea," he said. "Hannah will return to us."

Wes had stopped right by the front door. "Are you going or not?"

I said, "We'll go. Sophie's right. It'll be better if she has girls."

"Well, go, then," Wes ordered shortly. "Seriously." He looked around the room. "I cannot believe this shit."

It was cold and I realized we should have thought to bring along Hannah's coat with us. The wind whipped through my hair and every time we called out her name, we just heard the whistle of the weather in response.

We walked closer to the road and found her huddled against a fallen tree. She looked so small, curled into a ball, and sobbing so hard, her whole body shook.

"Hannah, what the hell?" Sophie had her tough voice on. "We scheduled the stargazing hike for tomorrow night, too-tie." No reaction. Nothing penetrated the trembling cocoon of the girl cowered against a mossy log. Sophie's voice was firm and even. "Let's go back inside and figure this out."

Hannah mumbled something behind the sheet of her hair. I crouched down. "We can't hear you, kiddo." I moved to brush the blond cascade out of her face.

"Get your hands off me!" she screamed so loudly, I almost fell back.

"Jesus Christ, Hannah," I said. But Sophie placed her hand on my shoulder, shutting me up.

"Okay, then," Sophie said. "We won't touch you. But we won't leave you either. We're in the sticks up here, Hannah. You can't imagine the characters that drive by on this road." The highway stretched empty for miles. Sophie said, "We need to go inside. You don't have to talk to any of us." Silence. "We can leave first thing in the morning if you want."

Hannah sat still. I'm not sure when she stopped trembling. "I can't go back in there. I can't do it."

"When were you pregnant?" Sophie asked so calmly. I knew that meant I needed to stay composed too.

"Right before."

"Right before McCracken?"

Hannah nodded. Once. Quickly.

"Did your parents make you get an abortion?" I swung my head to look at Sophie, but her eyes were fixed on Hannah.

Hannah said, "My mom said if my dad knew, it would kill him."

Sophie nodded sagely, shrugging off her jacket and wrapping it around Hannah. "Did you do the counseling afterward or anything?" We watched Hannah shake her head no.

Sophie made a face as if to say, *Of course not.* "Not even at McCracken?"

"My mom said — well, she basically said, 'What's the point, right?' I had plenty of other things to work on."

"You never talked about a boyfriend," I said. Sophie shot me a warning look.

"It's not really something I want to get into." Hannah's voice sounded frosty. "It wouldn't matter to him. Let's put it that way." I looked up at Sophie and wondered if we'd maybe gotten in over our heads, but Hannah kept talking. Maybe she did want to talk about it. She just didn't know it. "He was in college. One of my mom's students. I thought . . ." Her voice faded. "God, he was the center of everything." She gave us a wry smile. "You know, for the whole two months we hooked up. I found out after . . . there were a lot of other people. You know, he was making the most of his college experience."

"Who told you that?" I tried to make my voice as gentle as Sophie's.

"My mom. On the way to the clinic."

"Oh, Hannah. I'm so sorry." I meant it too. Hannah's mom and my mom sounded like maybe they played tennis together or something. I wished we could smack them both with rackets. "So when Joshua said —"

"What else could he be talking about?" Hannah broke in.

"I don't know." Sophie drew a line in the dirt with a twig as if she could figure it out right there. "But I feel like Joshua throws a lot against the wall, just to see what will stick, you know?" She looked like she was considering telling us something. And then she decided. "Josie — my sister — she had an abortion when we were fifteen. The guy who got her pregnant was older — her field-hockey coach — and he pretty obviously took advantage of her. He used her and then just discarded her. She felt . . . I guess she just felt worthless for a long time afterward. We made her go to counseling and stuff. It was actually kind of an open thing, maybe only in our family, but we talked about it. I know that might not be how most families work." Hannah was rapt. I listened to her too and tried to figure out how I could have possibly felt like I'd known everything about someone as complicated as Sophie Delia.

She told us, "I knew from the get-go and then Josie and I decided to tell Nick. He's the one who convinced her to tell my parents. And then made them really listen, instead of just judging her. That's the kind of brother he was to us." Hannah bit her lip and looked like she was about to start weeping all over again.

Sophie said quickly, "I'm sorry if you didn't have anyone like that then. But you do now. You have us."

Hannah smiled a tiny, tiny smile. But then it disappeared. She said, "I don't mean to freak you out."

"We're sitting on a log in the freezing cold, Hannah. We are beyond being freaked out." Sometimes I had trouble keeping my voice on the gentle end of the spectrum.

"Well, maybe the ghost is Josie's baby. You know? This place is your family's place so maybe —"

"Josie didn't have a baby, Hannah." Sophie spoke like a strict teacher. "She had a fetus. Just like you did."

"Yeah, but its spirit —"

"I don't believe in spirits." Sophie cut her off again.

"You did when you thought it was Nick's." As soon as Hannah said it, her finger flew to her mouth. "I'm so sorry. I didn't mean it to come out like that."

But Sophie shook it off. "No, you're absolutely right. I just — people use different words, especially about pregnancy." She looked to me for help. "Do you know what I mean?"

"Yeah," I said. "Sometimes people choose specific language to inspire guilt."

"It is a baby, though, right?" Hannah sounded insistent.

"It's going to be a baby. Just like one day it's going to be an eight-year-old." Sophie looked up and half-grinned at me. "What?"

"Nothing. It's just pretty impressive logic."

"Well, it's going to be a baby sooner," Hannah told us.

I sighed. "That is also pretty good logic. Can we go inside now?" Sophie and I stood up and each took one of Hannah's hands. The three of us stood there, in a huddle. For the first time in a while, I couldn't care less about anything with a dick.

Hannah relented. "Okay. But I don't care what he says. This isn't something I share with people. No one else knows. And I'm not going to sit there and dissect it in that room."

"You did a really good job of making that clear before, Hannah," I said.

She turned to me. "Yeah?"

"Oh yeah. If you feel uncomfortable with anything in there, just speak up again, like you did before. And we'll have your back, right, Sophie?"

She said, "Exactly. We'll all have each other's back."

By the time we walked back into the house, our arms were linked. The guys looked at us like we were insane. Jared recovered first. "Helloooo, ladies." Hannah smiled at him. She perched on the bar stool in the kitchen.

Joshua called from the couch, "Hannah, would you come to sit beside me again? Please?" Sophie and I glanced first at each other and then at Hannah. She looked like she was preparing to be yelled at.

"Let's all relax, Joshua," I said. "We need to just warm up for a second."

"Thank you for that insight, Greer. Hannah can warm up with me. By the fire."

She sat on the brick hearth. I could hear him whispering to her, but couldn't make out his words. At one point, Hannah said, "I know, I know." But she didn't sound defensive. Instead she sounded like someone who felt silly, who maybe was apologizing.

"Everything okay?" Addison chucked me on the shoulder. "I was starting to worry there."

"Just girl talk."

"It's good to see you have girl talk." I rolled my eyes. "What? Why is that bad — me saying that?"

Wes just sat at the bar, eating ice cream from the carton and watching us argue. "We must be mesmerizing," I told him.

He shrugged. "You are." Something crackled between us, but I recognized it as the same old electricity that had flickered between me and half the teenaged male population of Sturbridge.

It seemed like Addison recognized it too. "Greer, Greer — look back here," he said, half-joking. I turned to Addison and Wes turned back to his ice cream and the moment passed by. I felt relieved, like I'd aced some kind of test.

"I don't ever look away. Not really," I told Addison. And I meant it.

Joshua and Hannah both stood up. "We're going to turn in," Joshua announced. Hannah stood next to him, shifting her weight from one foot to the other. Just in case we didn't get it, Joshua clarified, "Hannah will be sleeping upstairs with me."

I thought Sophie was going to tackle her. She rushed to say, "You don't have to. We'll quiet down. I don't know about anyone else, but I'm ready to hit the sack. Big day tomorrow, right?"

Joshua held up his hand, palm facing out. He stood there like a crossing guard signaling traffic to stop. "It's not necessary." And then, "Hannah has decided she'd like to demonstrate her trust."

My skin crawled. Sophie's face read the same way, but I turned to Addison and he stood there, smiling over at Hannah and Joshua. "We'll be right down the hall, in case you need anything."

"Thank you, Addison. Brother, you are always my rock. That's a good man, Elizabeth. He's a man to hold on to."

I nodded. And then just stood there, watching them climb the steps.

"What the fuck?" Wes said.

"Shut your mouth," Addison barked at him. "Seriously."

"Seriously? C'mon, man — you're not crazy. You can't tell me that's normal."

Addison lunged forward. "No. It's not normal. We don't strive to be normal. We strive to achieve the extraordinary. What exactly are you doubting? Greer, tell them."

I sank down onto the arm of the sofa. "Tell them what?"

"Did Joshua touch you the night he stayed in your room?" I hesitated. "Was he in any way inappropriate?" I still hesitated. I didn't know anymore what was appropriate.

"No." I said what I believed was the honest thing. I met Wes's eyes and then Sophie's. "Seriously. He really respected the boundaries I set up."

"But you're not Hannah," Wes told me.

"How am I supposed to take that?"

He just shrugged and said, "I'm going to bed." Jared followed him.

After a second or two, Addison muttered, "Jesus Christ." He reached out and squeezed my shoulder. "I'll be back, okay?"

I nodded.

But he asked again, "Okay?"

"Yeah." The night had somehow derailed. "Yeah, go. Of course." He headed to the kids' room and Sophie went to put another log on the fire.

She said, "I'm not sure if I should just let it die or what?"

"Someone will be awake." That didn't reassure her. I asked, "Do you want to go back and talk it through with the guys?" I watched her gaze slide up to the top of the iron banister. She turned back to me. "I should just sleep. I'm going to wash up. Is there anything you need?"

"No," I said. "It's so wonderful to be in a home again. Right? No dorm bathrooms. No curfew." And then because Sophie was still looking at me like I was some kind of monster, I said, "I'm sure she's okay. We could go up and knock. See if they need anything."

"Doesn't that violate protocol?" Sophie asked.

"Probably. But what the hell, right?" For a second, it looked like Sophie was going to say yes. And maybe had we knocked on the door or crowded into the room with Hannah and Joshua, things would have turned out differently. Hannah would have known she wasn't alone. Joshua would have understood that he'd succeeded — we were strong girls who would support one another. No matter what.

But Sophie said, "No." She went on, "I just feel really drained. I'm probably overthinking things."

"We didn't know how much pain she was in. The baby thing — it explains a lot, right?" I sounded like my mom did on the phone, clucking over a neighbor's divorce or something. Sympathetic, but secretly thrilled.

Sophie nodded. She'd headed toward the bathroom and turned on the tap, before spinning back around. "Greer!"

I had already given the door to the kids' room a quick rap. Really, I just wanted Addison to carry me to bed.

I turned around to look at her. "Yeah?"

"Hannah said she kept it a secret. From everyone."

"What are you saying?"

Sophie looked at me like she wished my brain worked just a little bit faster. "How did Joshua even know?"

Addison and I raced to the bedroom as fast as we could without stomping on the stairs. When we stepped inside, he picked me up and placed me carefully on the bed. "There. Now it's the best room in the house."

"Should we check on Joshua and Hannah?"

A cloud passed over his face, briefly. "I'm sure they're asleep."

"But we can just tap on the door. Really lightly."

Addison stretched out across the bed and wrapped his hands around my waist. "Do you want to spend another half hour talking to the rest of the people in this house? Because I don't want to use up a single minute. There's a lot I want to do, but hearing about the problems of Hannah's traumatic past or Joshua's brilliant solutions to them isn't one of them."

I guessed that meant sex trumped crazy cult leader. Good to know. Except. "I don't want to have sex tonight." I blurted it out, shut my eyes, and waited for Addison to write me off.

"With me? Should I send Wes up here?" Addison deadpanned. When I opened my eyes, he was smiling up at the ceiling.

I sat up. "You don't mind?"

"A little. You'd probably mind if I didn't mind at all, right?" Right. I nodded. Exhaled. "I don't want to sound sinister or anything. We've had enough premonitions tonight — I get that. But I have this strong feeling. . . ." He tapped his index finger on his own chest. "It's rooted, you know?" I didn't know. I waited for Addison to explain. He turned then and looked right at me. "I believe that you and I have plenty of time, Greer." He kissed me then and pulled back to add, "And I'm really happy about that."

"Me too," I said, wrapping my arms and legs around him.

"Are you going to torment me all night?"

"Yup."

Addison slipped one hand under my shirt and trailed it along the waistband of my jeans. "All right. But then I get to torment you too."

Addison taught me that there didn't have to be an either/ or. We could lie in bed laughing, but that didn't mean our feelings weren't serious. He made my heart race with giddy happiness, but I also felt settled into this serene and simple joy.

That night, in the big iron bed, I told him, "You're such a giant. You make me feel dainty."

"What the heck does that mean?"

"That's a good thing."

"It doesn't sound particularly empowered."

I leveled my gaze to him. "You do empower me. I mean it. I've learned so much since we met. About you and relationships and myself. Mostly it's from this — us figuring stuff out together. Learning. Three months ago, I was so screwed up, Add. And I'm still not perfect. But I'm better because of you."

He cradled me close to him. "I think that you're a little bit perfect." He kissed my forehead, my nose, my lips. "But I would also request that you should show me exactly how empowered you are." I giggled and the sound seemed to bounce off the walls.

We kept laughing. And we kept learning. "I want my hands to memorize you," he said.

We made our way to sleep like that, and it was just right. No rush and no doubts.

We weren't the only ones who'd had an eventful night. At breakfast, it was clear something had happened between Sophie and Jared. They refused to look at each other. Instead Sophie smiled at her plate of eggs and Jared grinned stupidly at Joshua.

Joshua seemed normal. He didn't stride down the stairs with Hannah's severed head or anything. She came down for breakfast a little bit after everyone else got going, but I figured she just wanted to jump in the shower before we all started fighting over the hot water. Addison was superclingy, playing grab-ass the whole time I cooked up omelets. That earned some raised eyebrows and elbows from Wes and Jared, but that wasn't anything new.

Once Hannah came down and we all settled around the table, Joshua asked me to say grace. "I've never said grace for breakfast," I protested.

"That's a shame, then. You've never thanked a day for its possibility."

Addison winked at me as we all bowed our heads. "Thank you for the sunrise and for the sunset. And for all the moments we'll share today in between." I moved to let go of Addison's and Joshua's hands, but Joshua held on. That meant I needed to keep talking. "We're grateful for the chance to spend time together and to share our lives with honesty and openness."

Another squeeze. "Um . . . in order to achieve self-acceptance and wisdom."

Then Joshua finally let me drop hands. "Another talent is revealed. She can do it all, can't she, Addison?"

Wes pretended to choke on his eggs. "What all can she do, Add?"

Joshua took a bite of breakfast and said, "Hmmm. That's what I'm talking about. Hell of a cook too. Have I told you yet today — Elizabeth is the perfect woman. You'd be a fool to ever fuck this up."

"You hadn't mentioned it yet, but it's only eight thirty." Addison yawned.

"Well, consider it said." Joshua reached over and squeezed my wrist. "I tell him every day. How often do I tell you that?"

"Every day," Addison repeated dutifully.

"He listens to me," Joshua confided. "But it probably wouldn't matter. He's too smart not to notice for himself." He dropped his voice. "Did he give you the night you deserved?"

I felt myself blush and shrank closer to Addison. "She's not raving about you, brother," Joshua said. I kneed Addison. *Make him stop. Make him stop.* But Addison didn't speak up. He stood and asked Joshua, "You want more breakfast?"

Joshua raised his plate. "Yessir, brother."

"Then you have to be nice. You need to be respectful."

"I apologize, Greer. I was not aware you were such a delicate flower. What other delicate flowers we got growing in this sunlight?" Joshua studied each of us carefully. "Sophia, how was your first night back under this roof?"

Sophie considered her words carefully. "A little tough, Joshua. Thank you for asking. But it helped to be surrounded by friends."

We all paused and sat in silence until Wes cracked, "I'll bet you were surrounded."

She laughed at him. "What does that even mean? At least make sure the innuendo makes sense."

"What are we doing today?" I started stacking plates.

"The gentlemen will clean up," Joshua said. "Do we have the big jug of oil?"

"We do," I said, hoping Joshua wouldn't make me drink it to prove I wasn't afraid to eat fats.

"We'll sit on the porch, then. We'll need a basin of warm water and some towels."

Sophie said, "Sure thing. What's up?"

But Joshua wouldn't tell us until we were out on the deck. That's when he ordered me to wash his feet.

"Hannah's going to stay beside me until it's time to dry off my legs with the towel." Joshua sat on a deck chair and rolled his pants up to his knees. I noticed ridiculous things — his leg hair was pretty sparse; it looked like he'd recently trimmed his toenails. Sophie knelt in front of me to set down the plastic tub. "It that warm water? I don't want to be scalded now." Joshua actually looked fearful.

And Sophie looked absolutely flabbergasted. "It's warm. I didn't want to freeze you out either."

"Do you know how mothers check their babies' bathwater?" Joshua asked Sophie, and then when she didn't respond, he said, "Elizabeth?"

"I don't know." I'd never bathed a baby.

"Dip your elbow in. Or the inside of your wrist. Roll up your sleeve. Is it too hot?"

I shook my head no.

"Well, then it's safe to put someone else in there. How old

are you both — seventeen, sixteen? No one's taught you this? What do you do when you babysit?"

It didn't seem like the best time to remind Joshua that none of us had been considered trustworthy enough to care for small children. He set his feet in the tub and splayed his toes. "Did you bring out a cloth or a sponge?"

Sophie dunked the washcloth and soaped it up. I crouched down with her and poured more warm water from the pitcher into the basin over his toes. I wanted to giggle and also to retch at the same time. Feet disgust me, for one thing. But the whole scene felt creepy. Joshua must have noticed my discomfort. He told us, "My feet are actually quite clean. This is more symbolic than any kind of actual hygienic exercise." I noticed he was holding Hannah's hand. "Washing a leader's feet signals deep love and respect." Joshua leaned back and closed his eyes. "When you wash the feet, you support the journey — do you hear what I am saying?" None of us answered. The steam made wisps of my hair stick to my face. Joshua kept shifting and we'd filled the tub too high, so the water kept splashing. "Hannah?" His voice emerged forcefully.

"We hear you, Joshua," she said. I glanced up and saw adoration stamped on her face. Part of me felt relieved. She'd previously reserved that look for Addison. But then the ick factor sunk in.

Joshua stretched and perched the soles of his feet on the edges of the basin. He nodded to Hannah to dry them and she knelt to do so. Sophie and I sat back and listened to Joshua tell us, "In the Gospel of John, we learn that Mary of Bethany washed the feet of Jesus and dried them with her hair. And Luke tells of a woman who was a sinner of Nain who bathed his feet in her tears. By *sinner*, Luke most likely means 'prostitute.'" Sophie bit her lip. "Of course I don't mean to imply that any of you ladies are prostitutes." Joshua paused to think. "Although you'd have to admit you've all acted with serious disregard of the precious gift of your bodies."

"Joshua, I don't get that." It came out before I had the chance to rein myself back in. Joshua looked pleased at least to have inspired a reaction. "You talk about sex stuff with Addison and me a lot. You obviously support a physical relationship between us. You assigned us to sleep in a room together. Maybe I'm wrong, but I read into that."

"You shouldn't read into things."

"If I didn't, you'd accuse me of being too literal."

"Of course I support a sex life between you and Addison." I blushed. How very badass of me. "You love each other." I nodded, awash in the glow of hearing someone else acknowledge that Addison loved me. "That differs from the open-for-business sign you hung above your twat before you met him." It felt like he'd slapped me. He looked to Hannah and Sophie. "Am I wrong?" I waited for them to say yes. Or even just *gross*. But Hannah kept perfectly still. Sophie said, "It's made me happy to watch the two of them fall for each other because it seems so rare and special." A very diplomatic dodge.

Joshua went on as if nothing happened. "According to the ritual, once the feet are washed, they must be rubbed with oil."

"That's what the Wesson is for?" I would have laughed if I wasn't choking down my own vomit.

"Do you feel that touching my feet is beneath you?"

"Joshua, it's vegetable oil — you really want that on your feet? Couldn't it cause an infection?" Maybe there was a hospital staff, orderlies on some psych ward, searching all over the place for their escaped patient. And I was in the mountains of Pennsylvania, greasing up his toes.

"Myrrh would be difficult to locate at the Stop & Shop."

"Well, that's practical." I held out my hands and Sophie opened the jug of vegetable oil. She tipped it to spill over my hands. The rest of it pooled in the basin, forming a slick puddle on the surface of the water. When my hands looked glossy, I took a deep breath and then started rubbing Joshua's feet. I made sure to work oil into the crevices on his heels. I kept my face still and blandly pleasant.

"Thank you, Elizabeth, for treating a ritual that holds importance for me with respect. Why would John tell us that the whore washed the feet of Christ?"

Sophie cocked her head. "Well, John didn't say that. You said Luke did. According to John, it was the sister of Lazarus."

"Tell Hannah who Lazarus was."

"Lazarus was one of Jesus Christ's first miracles. Jesus raised him from the dead."

Hannah asked innocently, "So maybe Sophie should do it?"

I sucked in my breath a little and said, "It's okay. Out of the three of us, I bet I've come closest to Luke's lady."

Sophie had heard, though. She could have nailed down Hannah with her glare. "Because that's going to be our afternoon activity. Joshua's going to resurrect Nick? Maybe then we'll all play a game of Scrabble?"

"I meant metaphorically. He's already got you thinking about your brother more."

"Hannah —" I tried to position myself between the two of them, in case Sophie decided it would be easier to just choke her to death right there.

"He's got me talking about Nick more. There hasn't been a moment when I've forgotten about my brother."

"Okay." Hannah didn't sound convinced. She also didn't seem to understand how close she was to being drowned in vegetable oil.

"Seriously. That's a really crappy thing to even imply."

"I wasn't implying anything. Perhaps I drew the wrong conclusion."

"Hey." I'd had enough of the squabbling. "None of us are actually biblical figures. That would be helpful to remember, right?" I looked up to Joshua, to see if my message had sunk in. I didn't need a savior. He needed to understand that. Joshua had tipped his face to the sky. He looked like he was soaking up the bright sun and enjoying the foot rub. He also seemed to relish watching us turn on one another.

I patted his feet and squeezed the pads of his two big toes. "That's it, little piggies."

"Don't belittle yourself, Greer." Sometimes I wished the twelve steps included a line about maintaining a sense of humor. "Sophia should clean the basin."

"Thank you, sir," Sophie snarked.

"Did you know who also knelt down to wash feet, according to the Gospel?"

I was ready to place a bet on Cain. We looked up to Joshua and waited for him to tell us. "Jesus Christ himself washed the feet of the apostles at the Last Supper." Joshua looked meaningfully at us.

"That's okay. We're good."

"Part of following sometimes means accepting the gift of wisdom in all its forms." Hannah nodded solemnly.

"I don't mean to be contrary —" I began.

"You do," Joshua interrupted.

"I don't." I paused and waited for him to stop me. "But yesterday we talked about how important your Jewish faith was to you, right?"

"I said I was angry that you had made assumptions about me."

"Right, and I'm sorry for that. It's just — a lot of this . . ." I pointed at the basin, his feet glistening on the towel. "Well, it's rooted in Christian tradition, right? So doesn't that interfere with your beliefs?"

"I appreciate that question. That is an Elizabeth question." Joshua's voice boomed his approval. "That's the kind of holy questioning I'm talking about." Joshua smiled at me. I waited for his answer. "You know why."

"I don't."

"Try. Think critically."

"Well, those beliefs might overlap."

"Because?"

"Don't you want to provide the big, revelatory moment? I don't want to rob you of that."

He grinned at me. "Jesus was a Jew."

"Right."

"And the world underestimated him. Misunderstood him. His followers were not plenty. And some of them even joined him from the far outskirts of their society. But they were loyal and faithful. He told them the meek would inherit the earth." Joshua gazed up at Hannah. "And I believe that is true."

"But you're not comparing —" Sophie started stammering and rubbed her face with her hands. "I mean, that's just —"

"Arrogant? Impudent?"

"Well, yeah. I think it's that. I'm sorry. But you've asked us to speak honestly."

"I recognize that. Your reaction is not surprising. It's just more typical than I'd expect from you. Because, Sophia, I view you as an extraordinary young woman. Greer is smart and strong. She carries the gift. And Hannah is resilient. But you are our visionary. I wish you would understand. I'm not claiming to be God any more than I claimed I could resurrect Nicholas." Sophie winced at her brother's name.

Silently I willed her to just let it go. We weren't going to win at this. And at least if we nodded, we could go inside and maybe watch a movie, snuggled against two lovely specimens of young men who were clearly and maybe miraculously interested in us. That was a remnant from our old lives that I intended to enjoy this weekend.

Sophie met me halfway. "I'll think on that," she told Joshua.

His smile broke across his face and he said, "That's excellent, then. That's all I ask." Sophie dumped the warm, soapy water out onto the dirt and we paraded back inside, Joshua carrying his beat-up sneakers in his hand.

The boys sat around the dining room table, playing poker. So they got card games and we got to bathe the master's feet. Addison looked up. "Everything okay?"

"Peachy." The boys had already broken out a box of brownies I'd picked up at the store the day before. "What's with the sugar rush before ten in the morning?"

Wes dealt a new hand. "Second breakfast."

"You guys amaze me." Sometimes I watched Add eat and wondered what it might feel like to eat like a guy. Whatever tasted good. No worries. Sometimes, at the dining hall, I had seen him throw out a whole half of his sandwich. Not to prove some point about how little he could eat. He felt full. No more sandwich. The wonder of it being a nonissue killed me.

Not all guys ate like that. I knew that. Jared made a lot of jokes about his fat ass, for one. He wore jeans he probably had to lie down to zip and usually chose salads at lunch. But Wes, Addison, Joshua — they all ate thoughtlessly. I wondered what I'd fill my brain with if I hadn't packed it up with hundreds of thoughts about food and fat all day. Poker, I guess. Probably porn.

Wes dropped his voice so only I could hear. "I'm sorry. Were the brownies reserved for anything?" I couldn't help smiling. "What?" he asked. "What's funny?"

"You're so careful to make sure the whole room doesn't know you actually care about people. God forbid anyone know you're not a complete dick."

He muttered, "I don't want to ruin it for Joshua. He needs a villain, right?"

"He needs a Judas." I said it under my breath. "We were washing his feet."

"Whose feet? What?"

"Joshua called it a ritual. We went outside and washed his feet and then rubbed oil on them." The whole time we talked, I watched Addison out of the corner of my eye. He was laughing about gambling crap with Joshua.

"Are you for real? You realize we're now treading the edge of true insanity?"

"How come you're playing poker?" It had just occurred to me. I hadn't meant to ambush him.

But Wes's eyes slid away from me.

I tried to tease it out of him. "What's happened to the Gambling Anonymous poster boy?"

158

That backfired. "Listen. If it's not something that anyone takes seriously, then it's not something I feel the need to answer for."

"Wait —"

But he held up his hand. "Stop." He spoke the rest over his back as he sauntered into the living room. We'd been talking so quietly, but Wes meant for the others to hear his parting shot. "I'm sorry you had such an awful morning. We just sat back and relaxed a little. I didn't win too much bank from your broke-ass man."

"Hey, now!" Jared spoke up and Joshua's head whipped toward me. I plastered an I-don't-know-what-the-hell-just-happened look on my face and shrugged my shoulders. "What's up, Wes?" Jared wrapped one arm around him.

"I'm sick of all the sanctimonious bullshit — that's what's up. Who suggested the poker game, Jared? Why don't you clue Greer in? Who pulled out the cards?"

"I don't remember. You know, I'm sorry I wasn't thinking in terms of gambling stuff, you know. It was just us guys playing."

"To you, it's just guys playing," Joshua said sagely. "To an addict, it's a step off a steep cliff."

"Let's get one thing straight — there's no cliff," Wes said. "It's a bad habit. I'm not worried about falling into it again. I go to meetings and I talk the talk to try to make up to my parents because they're good people and I blew through my college fund."

Most of us just stood there, watching Wes unravel. Joshua said, "That is your burden."

"Yeah, you knew that was my burden. Because Addison knew that. Who brought the cards out, Jared? Do you remember yet?"

"We were just playing for Cheerios, for Christ's sake —"

"Who brought out the cards?"

"Addison." Jared said it and then glanced over to Add, an apology in his eyes.

Wes faced me. "So, yeah, don't ask me about it with that self-righteous look. Okay?" But his anger was quickly fading. He looked more embarrassed.

"Okay. I'm really sorry."

And I meant it. He mumbled, "Going for a walk." When he slammed the door on his way out, I felt bereft, as if I'd lost the one other person in the cabin who was asking the questions I was thinking in my head.

The silence in the room seemed to stretch on. Addison turned toward the fridge to grab the carton of milk. "What the hell was that all about?"

"He doesn't feel supported by us," I said. "Maybe he has a point. I mean, how would you feel if Wes brought up a keg in the van with us?"

"It's not the same thing."

"It kind of is, though."

Addison poured a glass of milk and downed the whole thing before he deigned to answer me. I watched him wipe the pale, little mustache off his face. "I'm sorry." Except he didn't sound sorry. "I had no idea you were so concerned with Wes's struggle to stop gambling. I'll try to be more vigilant to make sure he doesn't blackjack himself to death."

"I don't get this — this hostility. You wanted me to buy in. I'm here. I'm in." We'd dropped our voices but I still had the idea that the whole room was watching. We were entertaining certain people in particular. When Joshua headed toward us, I inwardly groaned, but he turned out to be the only one able to talk sense into Addison.

"Brother, don't mistake feeling guilty with feeling attacked. You messed up. Sometimes we treat others' burdens carelessly. Don't compound that by pushing Greer away. She's trying to lead you to goodness."

I heard Addison say, "I don't need —"

Joshua stopped him. "Brother." He spoke deliberately. "She is leading you —"

"Okay. Okay. I'm sorry." Joshua held his eyes. Addison turned to me and repeated, "I am sorry. I overreacted."

"It's okay." I stepped into his open arms and buried my face in his chest, trying to shake loose the glacier look in his eyes, his dead tone. He smelled good. Woodsy, like smoke and pine, and I tried to focus on that instead of the sinking feeling spreading across my chest.

Addison gently separated himself from me. "I need to go find him and try to make things right."

I watched him go and stood there in the kitchen, feeling helpless. Everything was falling apart. "Anyone want lunch?" I asked brightly.

Hannah lifted up her eyes from her book. "It's too early." I resisted the urge to hurl a wooden spoon at her. Sophie and Jared had snuck off, probably to have the kind of morning I had hoped for me and Addison.

When Addison and Wes came in, they did so joking and laughing. Addison made a huge production of kneeling in front of me. "I'm sorry."

"I know. You said that."

He laughed. "But this time I mean it. Should I beg for forgiveness?"

"No. It was over the first time you apologized. Whether you meant it or not." I felt Wes's eyes on me and smiled. "So everything's okay now?"

"It's all good," he said. Nothing more earth-shattering. I nodded and looked sideways in time to catch Joshua watching me holding eye contact with Wes. I looked at my feet for a while then. "So what's the word? Have Jared and Sophie eloped yet?" Wes asked. I heard the leather recliner squeak as he leaned back.

"How about we have some shut-up sandwiches for lunch, ladies and gentlemen?" Jared called out from the kids' room. "Stop talking smack and start making some hoagies."

I giggled and sighed. "Back to the kitchen."

Addison laughed. "That's right, woman." But when I sent him a withering look, he tacked on, "I'll help out."

Sophie followed Jared in, with three or four DVDs in her hand. "Can we have a film viewing after a belly filling? We have an assortment. Sappy rom com? Political thriller? Prom night slasher?"

"Rom com," Wes called out and we all gaped at him. "Don't judge — I'm a sensitive guy."

I set out a bunch of bread and lunch meat and cheese and mayo and mustard and we crowded into the kitchen, building sandwiches. I looked over at one point to see Jared feeding Sophie a pickle. Addison wriggled his eyebrows at me, and I laughed and shook my head at him. Let them be. Let us all be. No one gave me any crap for rolling up turkey and cheese and not eating it on bread. It felt good. It felt like family again.

Except my mom would never have let us eat in the living room. Addison's mom might have been sitting and looking out the window, waiting for his dad to pull into the drive. Sophie's parents would have been too focused on Josie the Genius. I don't know for sure about the others. But I can't imagine family movie time was a barrel of laughs in any of their original addresses. Otherwise they would still be there.

We tumbled onto the sofa and the easy chairs. Some of us even sank into laps and settled in to watch a movie together. At that moment, I believed Joshua when he said he could create love and safety out of the air. That's what it felt like. Like we had created our own version of family ourselves.

CHAPTER
FOURTEEN

By the time we circled up that night, we'd watched a movie, hiked down the back trail, eaten dinner, and even had nap time. The house hummed with happiness. Hannah seemed quiet, but I remembered how much I had to think about the morning after Joshua and I had stayed up talking. Sophie and Jared were obviously sitting in a tree, and I was happy for her. I just worried it left them vulnerable to Joshua's interpretation. At that point, though, Sophie would have said I was acting paranoid. So I shut my mouth and savored the perfect day at Camp Contentment.

I hid in the upstairs bedroom for an hour or so after dinner. The guys washed the dinner dishes. Sophie and Hannah dressed up and did each other's hair. I heard squealing and, at first, I didn't recognize the voice. Then I realized it was Hannah, sounding giddy and girly.

Once we gathered in front of the fire, Joshua asked us to study all the faces around the room. "We've spent a full day distancing ourselves from McCracken Hill, from your old selves. Look and see how relaxed you all are. Tension has fled. Worry lines have eased." None of us were old enough for Botox yet, but I saw what Joshua meant. With her makeup done and her hair curled, Hannah looked like a different person. Older, but less haunted. Jared and Sophie seemed drunk on each other. And Addison looked like the same old comfortable-in-my-skin-and-maybe-yours Addison. Except even more so. He looked like a better version of himself.

"I've given over much of the past night and day to reflection. Some of you have noticed me challenging you. That has caused some discomfort. For that, I apologize." It occurred to me that Wes didn't seem any more relaxed. He had that trapped look, like he would just sit there in a comfortable chair until the weekend passed and he could climb into the van to return home. Joshua announced, "I feel such optimism about tonight and hope you share that with me."

Hannah asked the question we were all thinking. "What's tonight, Joshua?"

"Tonight we're going to talk about our role in defending the world."

"You're joking?" Wes rubbed his hand over his face.

Sophie corrected him. "No, it's a symbol." She nodded to Jared.

"It's not a symbol," I told her. "He's speaking metaphorically."

Sophie looked puzzled. "That's not the same thing?"

"There is no joke. There's no symbol and there is certainly no metaphor." Joshua's voice rose and boomed. Some of us flinched. All of us focused. "Not every generation has the good fortune of hearing a calling, and I offer it to you. You must listen closely to the universe for it. It speaks to you now. Stand as a cadre of warriors together and hear it. Historically, that's the way. Youth must rise up and take on the worthy wars. It's not your parents who will rise up — they have careers and children. Mortgages and country club memberships. Your older siblings are consumed" — he looked at Addison and then Sophie — "by one thing or the other." Joshua slammed his fist into his thigh so hard, I knew a bruise would blossom there. "You are the ones left to stand and defend us."

I swung my head to check in with Addison, figuring he'd chuckle and slap Joshua's shoulder and we'd all have a good laugh. Then we'd put back on the lights and maybe watch the political thriller. Call it a night. But Addison looked as serious as I've ever seen him. His chiseled face, his shaved head. He stood at attention like the kind of soldier Joshua was ranting about needing for the front lines.

"None of you will have to fight right away," Joshua assured us. "We have time, not a significant amount, but we do have time for you to train. When we get back to campus, that's going to take some creativity. Because you know the strictures they place on you. They are afraid of your potential. Rightly so. The weekend has given us the gift of a head start. Before they even look up, we will have begun preparations for the battle on the horizon." Joshua dropped his voice down low. "Do you all hear me?" He searched each of our faces. "Do you all trust each other?" He sat back and crossed one leg over the other. "We're it, for a while. This isn't information you should share with anyone else."

"I feel like I missed something major." Jared spoke tentatively. "Maybe when Sophie and I — you know, we spent a good amount of time alone together. But I don't remember discussing a conflict besides the private ones we talked about yesterday." Jared looked around frantically for help. I tried to formulate words and failed.

Addison spoke then. I thought, *He knows this has gone*

far enough. Addison will put a stop to it. But instead he said, "Maybe you should tell everyone a bit more about the situation we're facing."

"Thank you, brother. Again, I need to stress that you might not have even considered the looming danger. That's all right. That's not your job. Your job is to answer the call. It's my job to be the conduit for the call. Do you understand what I mean by *conduit*?" He turned to Hannah.

She looked puzzled. "Usually you use it to describe electricity."

"That's right." Joshua lifted in his seat. "Exactly right. I am the channel for that electricity — that fire, that inspiration. I carry the message to the chosen few. And we've spent the past hours uncovering how each of you was chosen. The burdens that have already tested you. The paths that led you right to this place."

"Who chose us, Joshua?" Sophie asked.

"See, you want me to say God, because that would give you an excuse to dismiss me. If I claim that God talks to me, then I am a kook. I lose my credibility. So I will say the universe chose you. I will say that confidently and leave it at that."

Addison whispered to him, "We all feel chosen." When he said that, I panicked for a second, that Add would only make the whole thing worse. But then I thought, *Okay, it's true that we all chose each other in some way. Maybe that's what Addison means. Maybe he's just trying to break down the metaphor for us.*

"You're telling me to tell them about the war." Joshua's voice grew grim. Addison issued a curt nod. It wasn't difficult to picture him saluting next.

Joshua cleared his throat. "In less than two decades, we will be fighting a war against the militant vegan movement."

I blinked.

Sophie mouthed one word, "Wow," and didn't manage to close her mouth again.

"Jesus Christ. You take that much issue with the fact that I'm a vegetarian?" Wes sounded pained. "Greer, seriously — has it caused that much inconvenience to make meatless meals? I haven't made any kind of fuss. I'm not vegan, for Christ's sake."

"This isn't about you." Joshua spoke before I had the chance to tell Wes to stop worrying about that. To remind him that I kind of understood the idea of dietary needs. Or to mention that Joshua had just announced we would be fighting a war against vegans and that was kind of outrageous. Joshua went on, "Think of what history has taught us. Wars are fought when the poor go hungry, when resources run dry. Haven't you heard of vandals destroying SUVs, picketing new industry? Ecoterrorism. That's the first wave. When food starts to run out, when we start to change the way we eat, then the conflict between omnivores and herbivores will turn bloody. Just like the dinosaurs."

"Wait. What?" Jared's eyes bugged out a little. "You're saying the dinosaurs killed each other off over food?"

"What, does a random meteor make more sense to you? When resources run low, animals turn on each other. Make no mistake — we are animals!" Joshua's face contorted as he spoke.

Tears washed over Hannah's face. "I don't understand what we're talking about. Joshua, you're scaring me."

"You should be scared. We need to capitalize on our own fear and fight back. Your families have already cast you out.

You are disposable to them. But in this group, each of you has a very specific function. You contribute a piece to the machine. I'm telling you, it's as if the force of the universe delivered you to me. Don't turn away from that, I beg you, for the sake of the future."

Addison said, "Maybe if you show them how — like you explained it to me."

"No one resents your vegetarian diet, Wes. It provides insight. It teaches us about the enemy. Jared and Addison have been training so hard as athletes. They have already developed the bodies of warriors. And they can testify to the importance of the omnivore diet. We need them to sway the masses if it comes down to that."

Wes threw up his hands. "So now I'm not built enough to be a warrior. On top of all the other ways I'm a loser. This has been a terrific weekend. Thanks for inviting me. Really."

My mouth tasted sour with fear. Joshua turned to Sophie. "Sophia, your name means wisdom and we need your intellect. I'm one of the four smartest people I know, but you are the first. Do you hear me?"

Sophie bit her lip and nodded. I tried to make eye contact, but her gaze stayed on Joshua. "There's more, though. You know there's more." Sophie nodded and swallowed. Joshua said, "Tell me."

"Money." She said it miserably.

"I know it sounds crude, but it will cost us money to arm ourselves." An audible gasp blew through the room. He held up his hand again. "Not now. There will come a time, but not now. We still need to train. We need headquarters off the grid, where we won't be disturbed. You take care of the access here. I will find a way to ensure that McCracken Hill allows, encourages, our field trips. They just will not know that we consider them field ops."

Sophie looked sick. Joshua asked gently, "Can you make that happen?"

"Maybe. Yes."

I tried to shake my head with my eyes. I wanted to send her a message telepathically. *I'm sorry I got you into this.* I followed Sophie's eyes around the room. They stopped by her family pictures. The last time she'd been up here was the week she'd lost her brother. Now we were talking about turning it into home base for the meat-eating militia.

"Why me, Joshua?" Hannah's voice sounded shaky and small.

He turned to her with one of his enormous, bursting-with-pride smiles. "You didn't think I'd forgotten you. What have I told you, Hannah Rose? What do I keep promising?"

As if auditioning for the part, Hannah spoke in the smallest voice possible. "The meek will inherit the earth."

"That's correct. Maybe your brothers and sisters can explain why your presence will be so valuable. What happens when others meet Hannah? Sophia?"

"They want to help her."

"Exactly. The myth of Hannah's fragility will be our strength. Do you all see that? Hannah, you inspire empathy. We'll need your talent for drawing in others when it's time to swell our ranks."

This was about the time I remember wanting to stand up and call bullshit. I sat there and listened to the news about the impending vegan invasion, the dinosaur cage fight, but the idea of Hannah working a crowd counted as the most unbelievable part of the plan. It wasn't just that she was awkward.

She usually managed to say the most wrong thing at the worst possible time. She did not appear to understand the complexities of human emotion. She veered between aloof and needy, apparently depending on whether or not she had a good book to enjoy. She could not have served as the ambassador to a ham sandwich, let alone help inspire a world revolution.

While I ranted in my head, the room had grown quiet. Everyone stared at me and for a second, I worried my Hannah Green rant had come out main mix. "Elizabeth," Joshua said.

"What?"

I must have sounded superdefensive because Addison sang lightly, "Greer, Greer — you need to hear." He took my hand in his. I waited. Joshua kept me waiting even longer.

He stood up and stretched. We all watched him pace around the room. He bounced a little, like a boxer headed into the ring. My hand felt sweaty. When I moved to wipe it on my pant leg, Addison just squeezed harder and said, "Greer, Greer — no need to fear."

Joshua sat down and leaned forward. "Some force has selected all of you to serve as warriors." His eyes shot arrows at Wes. "Even those of you who continue to doubt your own calling — the universe has chosen all of you." We nodded, maybe because we had grown used to nodding. "Except you, Elizabeth."

So once again I was cut from the team? Honestly, that was the first thought that popped in my head. Who will I sit with in the dining hall when everyone else is avenging Oscar Mayer? "Elizabeth, you only think you are a warrior. You fight everything. You fight your parents, your teachers. You fight me.

You fight love. You fight your own physical form. Would you like me to tell you why?"

Go for it, guru. I nodded.

He said, "I need you to vocalize it."

"Yes. Please tell me why I fight everything." He kept staring at me, so I added, "Even my own physical form."

"Because you shouldn't have one." Here we go. The same old Greer-Cannon-actually-died-as-a-ten-year-old argument. Hannah seemed baffled. Sophie looked troubled. Addison appeared prepared. Jared and Wes looked as if they were hoping we could break for some kind of snack.

Joshua clapped his hands loudly and we all snapped to attention. He looked around at the gathered group, at everyone except me. Then he proclaimed, "Elizabeth is an angel, sent by God to protect us from our enemies."

Jackpot. I got to be the angel. No going to the gym, no ponying up cash. No infiltrating the mysterious vegan underground. Surely I'd make eye contact with someone and then we'd all start giggling. The jig would be up but at least I could savor this moment while it lasted.

But that's not what happened. Instead we all hushed and sat there, studying our own hands. Joshua kept pressing. "How does hearing that make you feel, Elizabeth?"

I went with, "Confused."

"I understand that. And shocked?"

For whatever reason, I didn't want to give Joshua any sense that he'd caught me by surprise. "No." That's all I said. We sat staring at each other.

"How about you, Addison?"

Part of me hoped that the fact that Addison had spent time with his hands in my pants would preclude him from believing that I was actually an otherworldly being.

"I know in my heart that it's true. I feel this emanating power when I'm in her presence. Since we first saw each other — we were in class together and I recognized her as the source of so much comfort. She keeps me safe and strong." Addison's voice sounded choked. He was saying all the right things, for all the wrong reasons.

"You're speaking this to me. And I thank you for trusting me. But, brother, I noticed this lightness wash over you as soon as you first mentioned her to me. Why not tell Elizabeth about it?"

I could have sworn I heard his head creak as Addison turned to face me. Maybe Joshua would next announce that Addison fulfilled the necessary cyborg component of our team. When Addison stared into my eyes, he looked very much human, though. I saw tears. He meant all of it.

He looked at me just like I'd dreamed of him looking at me. This was simply a different context. When he spoke up, I expected the usual singsong, but instead he used Joshua's name for me. "Elizabeth, you have my complete faith."

I guess *Elizabeth* was more challenging to rhyme. I couldn't tell if he was trying or not. "Feel free to respond, Elizabeth," Joshua prodded, and I wished someone would tell him to cram it. I felt my eyes well up too, but it wasn't this outpouring of joy. Joshua had invaded us. That's what I wanted to tell Addison.

The way we felt about each other had been good because it had been real. I couldn't stop myself from looking away, but managed at least to look down at our entwined hands. Staring at them, I thought, *All I have to do is play Joshua's stupid believing game. Addison is the prize I win.* Right then he still seemed worth it. Even now I'd swear he was worth it.

So I squeezed his hands back and looked in his eyes and told him, "Addison, you have my complete faith, as well."

Joshua meant for it to seem like a wedding. I knew that. He meant us to feel as if we were making vows. So I made mine. It probably counted as the first time I looked at Addison and lied.

FIFTEEN

Joshua never declared, "You may kiss the bride," but Addison still leaned in and kissed me. It felt crass, like I'd been displayed.

Joshua kept talking. "You all resemble shell-shocked soldiers. We haven't even yet begun to fight. We need a rest. I know it's early, but I'm not sure we can follow up such a pivotal moment with board games.

"You have all truly surprised me. Impressed me. Listen to my careful warning, however. In the morning, we'll all feel the instinct to distance ourselves from the power of this circle. We might reexamine this in the harsh light of day and find it easier to dismiss the truths we have uncovered here. I urge you not to take that easy route. I believe in each and every one of you. We will talk further." We all stood up at once, like the bell had just rung at the end of the creepiest class ever.

Joshua called out, "Wait." We stopped, trained well. "From here on out, all discussions about our calling are reserved for the entire circle. Is that clear?" Silence.

"Addison, make that clear to the others."

"Guys, we shouldn't talk about this unless everyone's there to participate in the conversation. Once you start talking in pairs and stuff, your team fragments and the mission could suffer. That includes Joshua. He needs to be with us too when we make any more plans."

"Sure thing." Jared actually seemed relieved.

"Do we all agree on this?" Joshua asked. "I'd prefer to hear actual voices acknowledge my question."

We all spoke out in the affirmative. We stood and stretched. Wes made a beeline for the kitchen and started digging around for the last of the brownies. Joshua headed to the stairs and then stopped. He held on to the banister as if he needed it for support. "Hannah, this has exhausted me. I would ask that I not be alone tonight." She'd moved into the kitchen with Wes and, for a second, I saw a jolt of disappointment wrench through her.

Joshua had said we needed to invite her because she needed more experience forging friendships. More normality. Fun. This hardly counted. But Hannah smiled obediently and called out, "Of course." She even rushed over to help him up the stairs.

"Hannah, your hair looks really nice curled around your face." It was Wes who thought to tell her that. He yelled it across the room and when we all turned to gape at him, he got embarrassed. He ducked his head a little and then defended himself. "She does, right? It looks lovely, Hannah. You should wear it that way more often. You know — if you feel like it."

Hannah patted her hair down a little, as if she was checking to make sure it was still there. "Thanks. I think I will." She and Joshua shuffled up the stairs.

I turned to see Addison watching their slow progress. He said, "He just uses himself up on us, you know?"

"Yeah. I see that."

"I'm so glad. I'm not gonna lie. You worried me for a while there, Greer. You have this spark."

"Yeah, and that's a bad thing?" I dared him to say yes.

"Never. That's not what I meant. But."

"But what?" I poked his chest.

"Greer, Greer — you're hard to steer."

I laughed — a real, true laugh. "You bet I'm hard to steer."

"I'd like to steer you upstairs now, if that's okay." By all rights, it should have been creepy, but it was way less alarming than Joshua's whole I-might-die-in-my-sleep-because-of-our-emotional-conversation-about-impending-vegetarian-doom routine.

"That should be fine." I called out to the kitchen crew, "Does anyone mind if we turn in?"

Wes didn't even look up. "Knock yourself out." Sophie nodded too. Wes cocked his head at Sophie. "Ten minutes 'til she and Jared push together the bunk beds in the back room anyway."

Sophie squealed, "Absolutely not true."

Jared turned to her. "I thought that was accurate. Did I misunderstand the bat signal?"

"I can't believe you!"

"Sophie, I'd rather know now than go to sleep in the bunk next to the two of you. That couch is comfy. I have a typically misogynistic horror film. And two more brownies," Wes said.

"Were we that bad?"

"Let's just say I almost just begged to demonstrate my trust in Joshua upstairs."

"Wes, that's not funny."

Addison had already started backing me up the steps. "Okay, then. Night, kids. You all amaze me. In good ways." He paused. "Seriously, I feel so close to all of you right now."

Wes stopped him from turning on the waterworks again. "Go feel close to your girlfriend."

When we got upstairs, Addison stood in front of our overnight bags. "Hey, we should change into our pajamas." I froze and studied him for a minute or two. "What?" he asked. "What did you bring to sleep in?"

"Just flannel pants and an old T-shirt."

"Perfect." I stared at him. "Seriously, Greer. Don't you ever wonder —" He stopped and then tried again. "I just want to know what you look like when you go to bed, on just any old night. We're on that campus and sometimes I'm lying in bed thinking, *She's right in the next building. In a bed just like this one.*"

"That's the sweetest thing I've ever heard."

"I know, right? Is it working on you?"

"Some people would also consider it a red flag of your creeper status." He nodded and I toppled back onto the giant mattress. "I didn't bring anything fancy or lacy."

"Well, of course not. I wouldn't expect you to pack up your Victoria's Secret for your stint at reform school."

I sat up quickly. "That's kind of judgey. What if I did do that?"

Addison threw his body across the bed. The springs creaked. "But you didn't." He leaned into me and breathed against my collarbone. "Don't pick a fight, Greer. We have one night, right? Who knows when Joshua will swing another one of these weekends for us?"

Back to Joshua. Always, always back to Joshua and our profound gratefulness. "Let's leave," I found myself saying.

"Let's start over somewhere. We can leave right now. I don't even care — we can just walk until we find a bus station. We can buy a ticket to some random town that sounds good just because of its name. Or even New York. We can go there."

"I don't care how much allowance you've stashed — we won't be able to afford living in New York City."

"Then we won't. We'll go to Michigan. We'll find jobs and live in a motel and cook canned food on a hot plate. If we run into trouble, Sophie will send us money — I know she will. Or I can write my aunt Tracy."

"Greer, stop."

"People live in motels all the time. I've seen it in episodes of *Intervention*." He still didn't say anything. "It means shelving some dreams for a little bit. College. But we'll still get there. It'll just take longer. And in the meantime, we'll be together. We can apply for jobs at Macy's or something. Or wait tables. I'd make an excellent waitress, right?"

"Stop." He whispered it, so I pretended I hadn't heard him.

"As soon as we're safely settled in somewhere, we can write our families and let them know we're okay. And after a while, if we miss them — we can come home. But we'll have established ourselves as adults first and then they won't have the right to decide for us —"

"GREER, STOP." He seemed to have surprised himself with his own raised voice. "I'm sorry, but this doesn't help. None of it will actually happen."

"It can, though. We can even just walk to the road and hitchhike." It would probably be safe to hitchhike with him. What deranged killer would pick up a muscular beast like Addison Bradley?

He lay still on his back, his arms folded behind his head, propping it up. "You're not thinking straight. And you'd regret it. We'd start getting on each other's nerves on the bus ride. Then what? We'd step off in some miserable midwestern town and you'd hate me. You'd look around at that shabby motel and that minimum-wage job and remember the chances you blew when you chose me. Give it three days before the excitement wore off and you'd start to blame me."

"Psshhht." I had sat up to listen, but plopped back down to stretch out perpendicular to him. "Look who's playing the unbelieving game." He didn't respond. He just lay there, twitching his foot back and forth. "What chances are those exactly?"

"Don't be stupid. You know what I mean. College. Summertime tours of Europe. Your dad's McMansion. Whatever's waiting for you once your parents get tired of grounding you at the esteemed McCracken Hill."

"You haven't listened to me at all. Hey." I said it sharply, but he didn't even flinch. He just sat there, waiting for me to get the tantrum out of my system. "Listen." I tried to word it really carefully. "Maybe you're right and I've wasted a lot of opportunities. But I'm not making those choices anymore. I can't take them back or reverse them. This isn't just a time-out, you know. They sent me to McCracken, knowing it would screw up any chance I had at a decent school." He opened his mouth to argue but I said, "Wait, let me finish. I take responsibility for that. You say I had every advantage. I admit I blew them. But it's not like I'm looking at a welcome-home party and early admission to Columbia."

He watched me carefully. But he listened at least. Telling him was the first time I let myself really imagine what the next few years might be like. It turned out my vision of the future sucked ass.

"My mom and dad will probably let me finish up at McCracken, so they won't have to deal with me for a little while. Then I'll go home and turn eighteen right after. They'll tell me that technically I'm an adult and I should be out on my own. But they'll say they're willing to provide me with a safe and wonderful place to live as long as I continue to make progress." The more I spoke, the more I saw the whole crappy future laid out. "I'll get some shit job in order to pay car insurance and expenses. Probably also some kind of rent. It won't be a lot, but my dad will say that I need to contribute like an adult. I'll go to community college when I'm not working at the PetSmart or, if I'm lucky, my dad will get me a job working as a receptionist at a friend's firm or something.

"None of that is terrible," I admitted. "You know, it's not superexciting, but eventually I'll save money and move into a little apartment. Maybe eventually I'll end up transferring to UConn. But for the first few years, I'm not going to have anything for myself. My grounding continues when I get home."

He still didn't say anything. So I went on. "I know if we ran away, it would be harder to somehow make it, starting from scratch. But it just takes fighting harder. I'd rather fight hard if it meant fighting with you."

I meant all of it. I leaned in to kiss him and he kissed back, and for as long as that kiss lasted, I thought I'd convinced him. We could pack up right then, and tread so quietly down the stairs. We'd slip out the door and walk miles and miles until we found a place to start over.

But when he pulled his face away and brushed the loose strands of my hair from my eyes, he said, "Yeah, we can't do that. They need us. We don't know how quickly this thing is going to move. And if we just disappeared. God. Can you imagine what they'd do to Joshua?"

"So we wait and leave from McCracken. On one of our sign-outs. I don't want Joshua to get in any kind of trouble —"

"*Greer,*" Addison scolded my name. "He just got done explaining everything to us. I understand if you're afraid, but you have to fight the instinct to run."

"You mean the war with the vegans?"

I hoped hearing me say it out loud would reveal its position on the upper echelon of Planet Crazy. But Addison just looked nervously at the closed door. "We made a promise not to discuss that without the whole group."

"Yeah," I said, feeling defeated. "Yeah, you're right."

He leaned in to kiss me again, this time lightly. "If you want to talk about this, the next time we gather as a circle, I'll support you. I'll stand by you. But you do understand, it will probably hurt them."

"I don't want to hurt anyone."

"I know. I love you for that." He kissed each of my eyelids. "We'll have our time, Greer. You and I will have so many adventures." He chuckled and kissed my neck. "Greer, Greer — we'll brave the frontier."

But I wasn't ready to joke about it. "Should I knock and see if Joshua or Hannah needs anything?" I stood up.

"No. They might be asleep by now. Where are you going?"

I grabbed the bundle of my sleep clothes out of my backpack. "To change."

"Seriously? You can't just change in front of me?"

"It's important to maintain the mystery."

"Yeah, who taught you that?"

"Your mom."

He pelted me with a pillow. "We could just sleep naked."

I stood straight in front of him and gave him the opportunity to imagine me that way. "No, that's not how you picture me, right? Lying on your bed, after lights-out? You conjure me up in flannel old-man pajamas. So sexy."

"Sometimes. But also sometimes naked. If we're aiming for fulfilling fantasies . . ." He spoke pleadingly, but I knew Addison well enough by now — this was just part of the dance. He'd meant what he had asked for before. And maybe it counted as one last-ditch effort to show him what it would be like to sleep together every night. I could make old-man pajamas sexy. Especially if the future of the omnivore universe depended on it.

I slipped out the door and padded down the hallway to the bath. A light glowed under the guest-room door. I stood there for a second or two, but I didn't hear the low mumble of voices that I'd expected. In the bathroom, I changed quickly and decided to skip the underwear. I found some decent makeup in a bag under the sink and put on some lip gloss and a little blush. I dabbed a little bit of perfume on my wrists and neck, then stared at myself in the mirror.

It wasn't the first time I'd considered going to bed with a guy as a declaration of war. But usually, as Dr. Saggurti had painstakingly explained to me, those qualified as hostile acts toward my parents. Not my boyfriend's delusional Narcotics Anonymous sponsor.

Joshua had a two-year head start on me. He brandished twelve steps, meetings up the wazoo, and a shared fondness for obliterating himself with dangerous substances. Joshua also operated under the banner of a legend that he had created for Addison, in which he could exist as a superhuman warrior. I'm not going to pretend I wasn't intimidated. And because I'd already sworn that the self I gave to Addison would be a better one, I felt a little let down.

But also determined. I looked at myself in the mirror and promised it would be the last time I'd use sex to try to convince someone of my own worth. Once Addison understood and I got him away from all of Joshua's psycho brainwashing, then I would figure out the rest. I wouldn't be able to have a do-over, but I'd find a way to make it special somehow.

On the way back to our room, I heard Hannah Green crying in the guest room. I did. It stopped me and I listened to make sure. And then I decided that I needed to focus on Addison. I didn't barrel in or knock on the door or call out. When I stepped forward, my foot even creaked on the floorboards. So she might have known I was right outside the door and didn't care enough to check or help. That's what I have to live with.

When I got to the room, Addison had turned off the lights and lit candles. I remember worrying about the fact that we were in a log cabin and wondering about the good sense of that and then thinking: *What a way to go.* And then I thought, *That's exactly how my life works — waiting so long to have sex with him and then dying in a burning bed.*

When you think about it, sex shouldn't mean so much. It's just one part of his body touching one part of your body. You don't freak out about the first time someone shakes your hand. Or sticks his tongue in your mouth. Except you do. I remember the first time Addison touched my shoulder in class and the first time he grabbed my hand. I certainly recall our first kiss and the first time I showed him how I could pull down a zipper gently, with my teeth.

And I remember every second of that night. When I tucked into the bed and he wrapped the blanket around us. When the wind blew against the house and knocked at the window's thick glass. When Addison knelt over me and pinned down my hands and kissed my ear. I remember when he realized what clothes I was wearing and what clothes I wasn't and the sharp gasp that felt like a burst of warm air on my neck. I remember all of it and I remember thinking in the back of my mind how crushed Addison would be if he knew I was trying to show him what life could be like, every night, every minute, if he would only give up Joshua.

I have to live with that too.

CHAPTER
SIXTEEN

The next morning, I woke before everyone and made breakfast. I found an old can of oatmeal in the back of a cupboard and mixed it with brown sugar and raisins to try to jazz it up. We'd brought up mix for pancakes, but I didn't feel like standing in front of the griddle like a short-order cook. If Joshua complained, I figured I'd tell him that oatmeal seemed more like army food to me.

Wes slept sort of half-on, half-off the sofa. He'd wrapped a down comforter around himself and arms and legs dangled out. He snored and his head lolled sort of adorably. But the night with Addison had broken the Attractive Asshole spell that Wes had cast over me. I might have meant for it to give Addison a preview of what life might be like waking up next to me each morning, but I also managed to sell myself on the idea. So I stood there in the state-of-the-art kitchen of Sophie's lavish home, fantasizing about seedy motel rooms.

Sophie wandered in first, with her hair sticking out in all directions. She'd clearly packed her supply of fancy nighties. She wore a long ivory gown with this frothy, floor-length robe. It looked like a Tennessee Williams episode of *Bridezillas*. "Good morning, darling. Coffee?"

"I'm working on it."

She nodded grumpily, saw me examining the silk getup. "It's not mine."

"A whole new side of Jared, then?"

Sophie climbed up onto one of the kitchen stools. "From Mommie Dearest's closet upstairs."

"Wow. What would Dr. Saggurti say?"

"Probably between this and me giving you and Addison my parents' bed, she would have a lot to say."

I put on my best pompous professor voice. "When we feel hostility, our actions display hostility, even if we believe we are presenting a different attitude. Resentment seeps through."

"Do you buy into that yet?"

"That *yet* sounds ominous." I felt like saying, *Next you'll tell me that Dr. Saggurti tried to convince you I'm an angel sent down by God.* Instead I said, "So you and Jared . . . ?"

She nodded, then opened a cupboard door to hide behind. "Yeah. Is that crazy? Or utterly predictable?"

"Neither. It's perfect. Maybe inevitable, but only because I think he might have come up here just for you."

"Not at all."

"Quite possible."

"Hmmm." Sophie seemed to consider it. "I'm pretty hot, after all." She spun around on the stool. "I'm very flexible."

"Downright bendy," I agreed, and we both giggled geek-ily. "Serious confession, though." I figured it was the best time as any to come clean about it. "When I first sought you out . . . well . . . a lot of it had to do with Addison —"

She cut me off. "Yeah, I know."

"I mean, he told me how great you were, so I wanted to get to know you, but I also worried and figured that, this way, maybe I could head you off." It came out all wrong.

"You are so not slick."

"You knew?" I hadn't meant to earn a nomination for the Awkward Awards, but it appeared I was in the running.

Sophie laughed. "I think everyone within a five-mile radius knew what you were up to."

"I'm sorry." I looked her in the eye. Her smile never wavered. "If it's worth anything, I'm so glad. Even if things between Addison and me didn't work out, I'd still be glad."

"Me too." Sophie spun again. It's like she found it impossible to handle anything without absolute class. She stopped herself with her palms on the counter and told me, "You weren't wrong. I was gunning for Addison."

My mouth must have gaped open. "I knew you were! See, I didn't make it up. Joshua says that I make it a practice of preemptively making enemies."

"Does he say that like it's a bad thing? I don't think it counts as paranoia if you're accurate in your read of the situation. Of course I harbored a secret yearning for Addison — I think most of the female population at McCracken do. Students. Faculty. Lunch ladies. Still, you don't have anything to worry about."

"Thanks." I said it simply and went back to stirring the oatmeal.

Joshua's voice rang out as he descended the stairs. "Why are we wasting this day with our sleep?" He tweaked Wes's big toe as he shuffled past the sofa. Joshua wore socks and I worried we'd have to wash his feet again.

Jared stumbled out of the back room next and Addison bounded down the stairs. "Why are you yelling, brother?" Jared asked.

Joshua grinned at us. "That's the first time Jared Polomsky has called me *brother*. We have achieved another breakthrough."

" 'Cause I'm going to kill you, brother."

"Cain speaks." Joshua laughed and then grew serious. "What happened to Cain after he killed his brother Abel?"

Wes groaned from under the covers. "Cain went back to bed."

"The opposite, actually. God doomed him to wander all over the world, and wherever he tried to lay down roots, the people around him learned of what he'd done. He never found another moment of peace. Instead the brother he betrayed haunted him for the rest of his days." I swore that Joshua was looking at me as he told us.

"I made oatmeal," I said. Brilliant diversion tactic.

Wes sat up on the sofa. "That doesn't really count as cooking, Greer. That's boiling water. I vote Greer has to do the dishes this time."

"No, it's not instant. I made it with brown sugar and crushed walnuts and raisins."

"I was promised pancakes." Addison started bringing down bowls from the cupboard.

"You got plenty of pancakes last night," Wes muttered.

"We didn't eat pancakes."

"I was using *pancakes* as a euphemism for sex."

"How about cocoa?" Sophie spoke up shrilly. "Let me boil the water for cocoa. Cocoa and marshmallows. Warm and sweet." She sounded like a maniac.

It was too late. Joshua had already gone and embraced Addison. I watched him whisper something in his ear. Addison smiled at him and then at me. I turned away. Good thing we finally had a sex life. Now he had something else to share with Joshua.

"How are you, Elizabeth?" Joshua stepped close to me and spoke softly in my ear. I felt like slapping Wes for starting the whole thing.

"I'm good, thank you. Excited for another day."

"Do you and Addison need more time to yourselves upstairs?" He was trying to get me to react, and then he'd attack me for being embarrassed of my sexuality. I could see a map of the ensuing argument laid out right in front of me.

I tried to step around it. I smiled brightly at Joshua and then the whole rest of the room and said, "Addison and I can always find time for each other."

"Did we buy this oatmeal? At the supermarket?" At first, I thought that Sophie was just saving me with another distraction. But she'd fished the empty cardboard carton out of the garbage and held it up. That seemed like a lot of effort just to switch the topic. When I saw the look on her face, I knew something was wrong.

"I found it in the cupboard — is that okay?" I asked, even though it was pretty obvious it was anything but okay. "Will someone miss it?"

She struggled to hold it together. "No, it's fine." We all stared, waiting. Sophie brushed tears from her eyes. "Jeez, guys. Sorry about the melodrama." But even as she said that, she kind of petted the carton and laid it down gently on top of the garbage bin. I had a pretty good idea of what was wrong, and I felt awful.

I waited until Joshua had focused back on Addison, and then asked her, "It was Nick's?"

She nodded. "It's stupid to make such a big deal of it." Sophie rolled her eyes at herself. "He'd launched this crazy cholesterol kick, though. He made a list of old-man foods and that's what he'd eat up here. Steel-cut oats. He spent the whole last grocery run lecturing Josie and me about the heart benefits of steel-cut oats." She stopped. "I mean, on our last trip up before — not the very last weekend. I'm being ridiculous."

"You're not. It's a sweet story. I'm sorry — I should have asked."

"No, what are we going to do, enshrine a carton of oatmeal?"

Joshua spoke to her from across the kitchen. "Nick's care with his health — doesn't that change our interpretation of events, Sophia?"

Her eyes still shimmered a little with tears. "I'm sorry?"

"Well, you don't normally hear about the health kicks of suicides."

"Holy shit." Wes seemed to sum up my thoughts exactly. It felt as if Joshua had just tossed a grenade into the breakfast nook.

Jared took a step closer to Sophie. "All right, that's not necessary right now."

Joshua held up his hands. "I am truly sorry. I didn't mean to upset you, Sophia. Rather, one would expect this kind of news to hold some comfort."

"I never said I thought my brother killed himself." Sophie's voice sounded like a thin razor wire.

"Oh no, you just implied it when you mentioned that others had drawn that conclusion."

"Actually, you brought up that possibility, Joshua. I sat in our living room and listened to you guess about why Nick took the highway that night." Sophie spoke in lashes. "You asked me why Nick didn't go to town instead. You asked those questions. I never thought Nickie left us on purpose."

"I'm so sorry for your pain." Joshua reached for her hand. "I just remember our conversation differently."

Sophie snapped back her hand like he had physically hurt her. "I'm going to go straighten up the back bedroom." She headed out without even looking back and we heard the door in the back of the house slam seconds later.

Joshua shook his head slowly and looked at Jared. "I would have thought that Sophia had a better night than that." I waited for Jared to haul out and hit him. At least call him an epic asshole. But Jared just took slow breaths, inhaled then exhaled, like he needed to count to ten slowly a few times to calm down. Not the kind of heroics I knew Sophie would expect. More along the lines of Addison's helpless cooperation, actually. Maybe it was contagious. Even Wes concentrated fiercely on his mug of cocoa instead of calling out Joshua on his cruel bullshit.

We were all afraid he'd start picking at our own freshly healed wounds next. Joshua fixed his gaze on me. "Sophia's usually so tough. That just doesn't seem normal for her — dissolving over a carton of oatmeal. That's not typical."

"Sophie's grieving."

I heard the threat in Joshua's voice when he told me, "It's really hard to lose people."

I lost my appetite. It was the first time I'd had a problem with food all weekend. I sat there on a bar stool, with Addison on one side of me and Joshua on the other, struggling to eat a dead kid's oatmeal. "Where's Hannah, Joshua?" I asked him, preparing myself to hear him say something like, *Dismembered in the bathtub.*

"She asked to sleep longer. Hannah has experienced so much growth this weekend, but it has sapped her energy. She's truly blossoming with your friendship." He looked around the room. "I'm glad to have a moment to address this with the group, actually. Jared, bring Sophia back."

I straightened up, ready to point out that maybe Sophie's energy was pretty sapped also, but Addison stopped me with his hand on my arm. Jared looked miserable, but he still went to fetch her. She stood in the doorway, rigidly.

"Thank you, Sophia. I just wanted to remind everyone how very fragile Hannah is. For some reason" — he seemed to single out Sophie and me for this part — "she doesn't feel completely accepted. She's also worried she's inadvertently offended others here with her honest assessments. We all need to stop being so sensitive." He stared right at Sophie until she looked down at her feet. "We must begin to support a source of much strength and potential for all of us. If a single member of our circle feels alone, then we have already failed. Is that understood?"

Joshua turned to Addison. "I have something else to share with you. Forgive me. Brother, I have held my own burden." Addison glanced up toward the top of the staircase, as if to ask if he should wake Hannah. "She knows," Joshua told him. Addison's brow furrowed, but he didn't question him.

"You may have noticed my weakening state. I've asked for more than I usually do; you've all been so generous to care for me." I searched the room for reactions, but everyone stayed very still. Addison's face had drained of color. Sophie had folded her arms in front of her chest. Otherwise, no one moved or spoke. Joshua continued, "I'm sorry for withholding news so important from you. But I valued this weekend. And if this is all the time we have together, then I know we spent it the right way. And I know I've prepared you all to support each other in our future battles. You don't actually need me anymore. And if my condition deteriorates to the point that I become a distraction or a hindrance to our cause, then I will take the steps that I see fit to remedy that situation." As he announced that last part, Joshua straightened up and bellowed as if arguing against questions we hadn't asked. Then he faltered a little and reached out to steady himself on Sophie.

She propped him up. "Joshua?" He went limp. "Joshua, are you okay?" Sophie braced against his full weight and Jared leapt forward to help her. They dragged Joshua into the living room and settled him into a chair.

"Sophia, I am sorry. But it's so cold in here."

"Let me get a blanket." Wes handed over the comforter he had wrapped around him and stood there in boxers and a T-shirt.

I looked at him and he shrugged. "It's actually pretty warm. I was just preserving my modesty." He padded off to put on clothes.

Addison sat on the stool, with tears running down his face. Joshua said, "Brother, don't waste your time on anger." Addison shook his head. "Or hurt." Joshua pointed up. "Last night, I experienced trouble breathing. I fear my fate most at night, in the darkness. In a moment of shaken faith, I confided in Hannah. She tended to me." Addison brushed the tears from his face. "I would have rather sat you down and shared this with you first. But you've had other things on your mind." Addison looked down. I waited for him to meet my gaze, but he didn't. "That's certainly no reason to feel guilty," Joshua said in a way that seemed to imply that Addison ought to feel extremely guilty. "Life happens when we are busy enjoying it."

"What is it? Is it cancer?"

"We'll meet with the doctors when we go back. They've urged me to bring you in so they can explain it all. I told them that my son" — Joshua's voice rang out clearly on the word *son* and Addison started weeping all over again — "I said that my son is so smart. He'll be able to understand all the lingo that I'm too ignorant to absorb. I'll need that from you." Addison nodded.

Joshua looked around. "I have struggled my whole life, been beaten and scarred. Tread on. But I have also inflicted damage on myself. With alcohol. Narcotics." Joshua enunciated each syllable of the word so that it sounded like *nar-COT-ics*. "And now my body has turned on me. My blood platelets are attacking healthy cells."

"That sounds like leukemia," I said.

"Elizabeth, you are so powerful, but you are not a doctor."

"Of course not, I'm sorry." Addison still wouldn't look at me. "What can we do to help? I mean, logistical stuff?"

"Look at what a gift she is to me." He beckoned me and I knelt by the chair. "Addison will help by meeting with my team of doctors. I will work as long as I can, but there may come a time when my body just gives out. It embarrasses me to ask, but —"

"Anything you need, man," Jared spoke up. "We've got a lot of resources to pool between us. We'll take care of you."

"That's the kind of love that stuns me." Joshua closed his eyes and nodded to himself. "That's it. I don't know why I thought for a second that you all would abandon me." He sobbed into his own hand. "I apologize for my doubts. You know, people see how much I support you all. The hours and hours, the immense energy . . ." Addison nodded tearfully. "I tell them — these kids are my heart. They are my children. We sustain each other. No one else is willing to play the believing game for you all. This, this outpouring would shame them. Your generosity would silence them."

I rose and took stock of the room. We all seemed to be standing up straighter. Addison had finally come forward, but he bypassed me and moved right to Joshua's side. I remember chastising myself for noticing that. Telling myself that it wasn't the time to selfishly wonder if my boyfriend was mad at me.

And Joshua wouldn't be the only one who needed me in all this. Addison faced the prospect of losing the most important person in his life. I promised myself to support him no matter what. I heard them whispering behind me.

"Tell me more about these doctors," Addison prodded.

I moved away then and went to work cleaning up the kitchen. A few hours before, I'd been trying to convince Addison to skip town and maybe send a letter later. Had he listened to me, we would have snuck off without knowing about Joshua's condition. "Someone should check on Hannah," I announced to the room, but what I really meant was *Look at me, Addison, I'm trying to be that best version of myself for you.*

Hannah didn't answer when I knocked, but the door pushed open when I leaned on it. She'd already showered and combed out her hair. It seemed a little odd that we hadn't heard her walking around. When I stepped into the room then, I realized it had its own bath. I could still see the steam. She must have just gotten dressed.

"I didn't realize this room had a bath," I said. Hannah sat in a little rocking chair by the window. She turned to me as if I'd made the most inane comment she'd heard. In light of everything, it might have been. "Usually the master has the bath." Silence. "I don't mean to say that we should have had this room — our room is lovely. Not that your room shouldn't be lovely." Hannah Green kept staring at me. "I'm sorry," I said, trying to start over. "Joshua told us."

That earned a gasp. I went on. "I feel so awful that you had to deal with that on your own. I wish I'd have known. I would have helped. Even just moral support." The more I talked, the more uncomfortable Hannah looked. "We're all going to help from here on out. Once we get back to McCracken Hill, we'll work out a schedule or something so that he's taken care of." Hannah slowly stopped rocking. "We'll take turns."

"What are you talking about, Greer?"

I figured that maybe she knew more of the details. Maybe she was in shock.

"Joshua told us about his illness." She pursed her lips together. "He said he had some kind of episode last night and you took care of him." Hannah seemed to consider that carefully and then she nodded. She went back to rocking in the chair. "It must have been really scary."

"I thought it was just an asthma attack or allergies." She looked down at her hands. "But Joshua said it's much more serious."

"It sounds like it."

"Do you think he's dying?" she asked in her strange, flat voice. As if she didn't care about the outcome either way.

"I guess we'll get more information soon. Addison's going to meet with his doctors. I thought it sounded like leukemia, but I guess not?" I looked at Hannah, waiting for her to volunteer an opinion. "The two of them are having a powwow down there now. Joshua told us you needed your rest. But are you hungry? Do you want breakfast?"

"Why do you like to feed everyone so much?" Hannah asked in her abrupt way.

"You know, when we got here, Joshua gave us all jobs. I get to be cook." I said it in a joking way, but Hannah didn't laugh or even smile. "I guess I took it kind of seriously."

"I think you like to feed us because that helps you feel like you deserve to eat too." I made sure not to grimace, remembering what Joshua had said about Hannah's blunt way of talking. If Sophie had said it, I wouldn't have gotten angry.

"Maybe. That makes sense."

"It doesn't really." God. Hannah certainly didn't make it easy.

"I meant that your interpretation makes sense to me. I see how that could be true."

"What's my job this weekend?"

Acting really bizarre and making everyone feel uncomfortable.

But I didn't say that. Instead I said, "It seems like your job has been comforting Joshua."

She snorted a little. Like some kind of dainty, wild pony. "Yeah. That makes sense."

"Hannah, are you angry at me about something?"

"Why would you even ask that?"

"You just seem . . . I don't know. You've kind of had your own thing going on this weekend. But I hope you haven't felt like I've been excluding you from anything. Addison and I . . . well — this weekend was special to us. I mean, it was supposed to be. I'm just sorry that we didn't all get a chance to spend more time together."

Hannah stopped rocking again. She stared up at me and her tiniest smile emerged. "You really love him."

"Yeah." I wasn't quite sure how Addison felt about me right then but I didn't say that. "I didn't mean for this whole weekend to be about that, though."

"No, we did a lot. We learned a lot." Hannah's voice kind of cracked then.

"Are you sure you're okay?"

"What's it going to be like back at school?"

"After this? I'm not sure. Probably a little intense. But we'll have each other, you know? We'll all have to remember that and reach out when we need something." She nodded and turned her gaze out the window. Outside the pine trees stretched high up against the mountains. "Come on downstairs so that I can feed you, okay? It'll improve my self-worth."

I made Hannah a cheese-and-toast and scrubbed the rest of the dishes. "Sophie, should we strip the beds?"

"Will we have enough time to run a load of laundry?"

I looked back at Joshua and Addison, still deep in conversation by the fire. "I think so. We're not due back on campus until dinner."

She handled the sheets from the beds she and Jared had pushed together. And I went upstairs to her parents' room. I was just rolling all our linens up into a big ball, when I heard her calling quietly, but frantically, "Greer! Greer!"

I found her in the guest room. "What?"

She had pulled back the quilt from the bed. Beneath lay a bare, tufted mattress. I didn't get it. "What's the problem?"

Sophie stared at me. "Where are the sheets?"

"Well, don't go all crazy about it. I'm sure if he was so uncomfortable, he would have mentioned it."

"No, there were sheets. I checked."

"Sophie, relax." I stepped out onto the landing. "Hey, Hannah." She looked up. "Where are the sheets?"

"What sheets?"

"From the bed? Upstairs."

Hannah paused. She looked toward Joshua. He appeared riveted by whatever Addison was saying. He didn't even raise his eyes. Hannah said, "I washed them."

"Oh. Are they in the machine?"

"I washed them in the tub."

"What?" Sophie went back to check the bathroom. "You didn't have to do that, Hannah. That must have taken forever." She emerged carrying the wet linens.

Hannah had rushed toward the stairs. "I'm so sorry. I didn't know you had a washer." She looked panicked. "If I've ruined them, I'll replace them."

Joshua finally glanced up. Addison shot me a look, like *Seriously?* I lowered my voice to a whisper. "I'm sure it's fine. Let's just get everything in the wash so that they can dry together." Hannah looked like she was edging toward tears. I put my hand on her shoulder. "It's really no big deal."

Sophie laughed. "You're making Greer look bad, though. She's trying to show off her housewife skills and here you are, playing pioneer woman." She showed us the laundry room and Hannah loaded everything into the washer. Sophie stood in front of a closet, staring at shelves of flannel sheets.

"Maybe we should just make the beds now?"

"Yeah, but what if your parents make the trip up? Won't your mom notice the difference?"

Sophie just said, "No. They're not coming back here."

"We might not either," Hannah volunteered. We looked at her. "If Joshua dies."

It wasn't until we were packing up that Addison and I had a moment alone together. I was putting the sheets back on our bed when he popped his head into the doorway to ask if I'd seen his phone.

I couldn't stop myself. "So you're speaking to me now?" I said. "Because you can't find something?"

He stepped back. "Greer — seriously. Please don't fight with me now."

"You haven't spoken to me. All morning. Since I came downstairs and started prepping breakfast, all happy that we'd —" I didn't know how to put it. And I didn't want to embarrass myself any more than I already had by whining. *We just had sex and now you're ignoring me.* It was, after all, the same old story.

So I tried to maintain some dignity. "I'm sorry if I pushed earlier. I wasn't thinking clearly. But I also didn't expect that as soon as we actually slept together . . ."

"Of course not." Addison spoke in his same old earnest way. "Jesus, Greer. I'm the asshole. Seriously. That's not what I meant." He stepped closer to me and reached out his arms, but I ducked away. "I'm sorry." I watched him warily. "I wish we'd never come downstairs this morning, but when we did. Well, when I did, I just —" Addison choked back sobs again. "I had no idea he was sick, Greer. And I don't know what I'd do without him."

I'm not a monster. By then Addison was full-on crying. Huge, wracking sobs that shook his whole body. I wrapped my arms around him and whispered in his ear that Joshua would be okay, we'd figure it out. I told him I knew he had to devote himself to helping Joshua get well and I'd help in any way I could. And in the meantime, I'd wait for him. We'd found something incredible between us. Miraculous. Nothing would interfere with us. But right now we had other obligations. And we wouldn't let something amazing like finding each other interfere with fulfilling those either.

Slowly, Addison went from weeping in my arms to nuzzling at my neck. I kissed his eyes and his face before his mouth. And then, once we got really swept up in kissing and pressing and craning toward each other, we tangled up the sheets of the bed I'd just made.

We treated each other less gently in the morning. Maybe because the sunlight streamed in through the gauzy curtains and there was no point in acting bashful about our bodies. Maybe because the whole house was awake, creaking with footsteps. We heard doors slamming and occasional laughter.

I guess I was trying to console him. But there was something else. At some point, Addison whispered, "We should try to be quiet." And I nodded and then pretended to find that impossible to manage. Just a little. And I resolved to make sure that Addison needed to yell out also. I could make him forget for a few minutes. Just like earlier that morning, when Joshua had fixed it so that Addison hardly recalled how he felt about me. I could work my own miracles. Or maybe we would call it *creating a circle of belief.* If anyone called us on inappropriate timing, I'd argue that Addison and I chose a life-affirming activity. So I threw back my head and celebrated. Loudly. And I remember hoping that, down the hall, Joshua would hear.

CHAPTER
SEVENTEEN

At about quarter after two, we loaded up the car and bid farewell to the site of what Jared called *our first summit of strange superpowers*. He said it as he climbed in the van, and Joshua responded by saying, "If you're going to mock our calling, you're welcome to take a thousand sarcastic steps home."

"What?" Poor Jared looked genuinely confused. "No. I just — I thought we needed something catchy. No joke, Joshua. Brother," he tried.

Joshua surprised me by saying, "Brothers, sisters — I seek your forgiveness. I made myself vulnerable to you this morning and that's difficult for me. This might have been one of the best weekends of my life. I can't think of another time that I've felt less alone. That's saying a lot, considering what I'm about to face. Each one of you is beautiful. Each of you has a superpower. You're absolutely right about that, Brother Jared."

Jared looked up, but didn't speak. Wes called out from the seat in the way back. "Where did we go anyway? What town will we say? You know, for Habitat for Humanity?"

Joshua had already prepped answers. It turns out that we had worked on a one-story, three-bedroom house for a single mom in Milford, Pennsylvania, named Charlene Ebberts. We felt as if the experience really bonded us, and we hoped to return to the area, both to check on Ms. Ebberts and her two little boys and to help with other projects in the area. Addison and Jared had really excelled at drywall work, but next time, they hoped to help install the kitchen.

As we coasted down the highway and rehearsed our cover story, I started to feel the first flickers of nervousness. Not for the first time, it occurred to me that Joshua's grip on reality was tenuous at best. No one actually saw him talk to the dean. He pulled up the van. We all climbed in and left. What if he'd never said anything at all? I pictured bed checks, then search parties, tense phone calls with my parents. We'd been gone two full days, so if McCracken Hill had sounded the alarm, my parents — my father at least — had probably driven up by now.

Addison kept turning around in his seat, smiling at me. He was trying at least. It's not like I'd have to do the walk of shame back to my dorm, feeling completely used and discarded. He didn't seem worried, but Addison didn't worry about what most people thought. Just Joshua.

Wes stared out the window. He stayed quiet after pressing us to get our stories straight, as if he didn't know any of us at all.

Sophie lay down in the seat behind me, dozing, with her head on Jared's lap. Hannah sat next to me but felt farthest away. She held her book on her lap, but kept it closed. Once in a while, I caught her eyes wandering out the window, but mostly she sat there, staring at the back of Joshua's headrest.

"Elizabeth, I feel your restlessness." When Joshua noticed, it only made me more antsy. Like maybe he knew I had a reason to worry.

"I don't want to go back."

"Where? Connecticut? Or McCracken Hill?"

I thought about it for second. "Neither. I'd rather start off somewhere completely new." Addison looked over his shoulder at me, reached back behind his armrest, and grabbed my leg. I couldn't tell if his squeeze was affection or warning.

"Oh, you can never start somewhere totally new, Elizabeth. You will always drag yourself along with you."

We turned into the lower lot a little after four thirty. By then I felt sick. My stomach churned and my hands shook. I felt so certain that the whole security detail would surround us as soon as we stepped onto the lot. I don't know how I survived getting in trouble all the time, back home. Somewhere along the way, McCracken had drilled away my ability to not care. Losing privileges, going back to lockdown, and no liquids in my dorm room seemed like the worst possibilities in the world.

We parked without incident, though. The lot stretched empty, except for two other school vans and a few teacher vehicles. Above us, the sky was just going gray, on its way to evening. I turned back to watch Jared wake up Sophie by kissing her temple, then looked up to see Addison watching me. Sophie wailed when she sat up and saw where we were. It was seriously the baldest expression of pain she'd ever shared in my presence. Even Hannah stepped up. She patted Sophie's back awkwardly and cooed, "It's going to be fine. Remember, we said we all stick together back here. This weekend just began so many things." Hannah checked with me for confirmation.

"Exactly," I said. "We all help each other adjust back to real life."

Sophie cried harder. "This isn't real life."

I looked at Jared and nudged her. "Sure, it is." And then lower, so that only she could hear, "Don't freak him out. Hold it together until we get back to the dorm."

"I want to say one last thing." Joshua motioned for us to circle up.

It was the perfect time for him to say, "Just kidding about the war with the militant vegans." Or, "I'm sorry, Greer, you're no longer in the running to be our mission's next guardian angel."

Instead Joshua told us, "One of you will betray us. I've been praying over it, but it's not to be avoided. When the time comes, we will mark that loss and mourn it in a fitting way. The rest of you will not judge the one who abandons us. Reserve your judgment for yourselves. Have I made myself clear?"

Of course I assumed he was talking about me. Maybe all of us thought Joshua could see right into our souls and watch our devious little minds plotting. We all stared at our feet. Except Addison. I peeked to see that he held Joshua's gaze, although he did keep swallowing.

"We had a beautiful time, but our bodies are so tired from the physical labor. Go take hot showers. At dinner tonight, talk about Charlene Ebberts. Bring her to life. We'll need to speak soon. Addison, you and I will need to speak very soon. My treatment will start almost immediately. Remember, all of you — the dean will probably seek you out. I convinced her to take a risk on us. She will want to know that it paid off. Give her what she asks for."

"You're not coming through the gate with us?"

"What are you afraid of, Elizabeth?"

I made myself take a deep breath. "I have no idea."

"You are the one among us who is untouchable. The best of you is locked up in a room, many years away. What could you lose?"

"Always with the cheerful reassurance, Joshua." Wes stepped forward. "C'mon, Greer — we'll walk back together." He didn't even look at Addison before he asked me. "Just keep walking," he muttered under his breath.

"What are you doing?" It felt like I was being torn away from the group. My chest ached. "Seriously. He's going to get angry."

"He's had his fifteen-minute farewell speech already." Wes turned around and walked backward beside me. He cupped his hands around his mouth to call out, "Thanks, guys. I'm so glad we did this. And so happy we helped that lady! See you at dinner, okay?"

I trotted alongside Wes, trying to keep up, but still checking back to see if Addison had reacted.

"Don't worry, he's still back there. They're probably predicting which one of us will be the One to Commit the Ultimate Betrayal." He used his fake movie-trailer voice. I slowed down my pace, but just as I fell behind, Wes said, "He took a page right out of the Jesus Christ playbook. I can't believe it. Have none of you gone to CCD?" I stared blankly at him, but walked faster to catch up and listen. "It's the Last Supper. Christ says, 'One of you will betray me.' And sure enough, Judas steps up to the plate and sells out Jesus. So that's great. Joshua can keep playing his mind games. Now if one of us doesn't buy into this bullshit, we equate ourselves with Judas Iscariot."

"I never knew Judas had a last name."

Wes stared at me. "I bet the other guys named Judas insisted that he use it after that whole mess."

"What happened to Judas?"

"How do you not know this?"

"I'm not really religious."

I didn't really care what happened to Judas Iscariot. I wanted to know what would happen to me.

Wes seemed to understand that. He broke the news carefully. "Judas hanged himself." I stopped walking and turned back to the loosely gathered ring of our friends on the other end of the parking lot. "Greer. No one is Judas. We're all good people. Most of us, including Joshua, are a little screwed up. I'm not really sure what's going on with Addison, but maybe someone needs to go to the administration for him."

"What are you talking about?"

"We live together, Greer. I don't know how the hell he managed to swing keeping a cell phone, but Joshua calls him on it three, four times a night. Addison hasn't had a decent night's sleep in months. And now he's going to take responsibility for nursing Joshua through whatever illness he has. You know, they talk as if the Bradleys feel such gratitude toward Joshua, but then why don't we see Addison's parents around? Why doesn't Addison get in contact with his parents first thing for help with whatever Joshua's facing?"

"We don't know that he won't. His parents have their hands full with Chuckie. You know? That's why he's here."

"No, Greer. He's here because he needs to be. That's why all of us are here. Believe me, this place is pricey. My parents remind me of that every time they call for family session. And if the Bradleys aren't loaded, and it sounds like they're not, they have to feel like this is necessary for him. Hell, if his insurance is footing even a fraction of the bill, they have to certify he needs help."

"But he's allowed to roam around town. And sign in late."

"We all are," Wes said incredulously. "When's the last time anyone really gave you a hard time about signing back in or lights-out? Or anything even remotely close to a hard time? Jesus, you had Joshua sleep over in your room. A grown man. They're monitoring us so closely, but they somehow failed to pick up on that."

Wes looked back to the van. The whole group had turned to face us. I don't know what they thought was going on. But I could tell that we'd hear about it later on. We both knew that. Wes spoke faster, as if trying to finish what he needed to tell me before someone stopped him. "I don't necessarily agree with the decision to ship any of us away. But I look at someone like Hannah, who has obvious problems, right? You see that. She'd get devoured in a typical high school. Even you. You're working on things. But how close were you to being hospitalized for eating disorders? Or being charged for shoplifting? Seriously? Or answering some crazy Craigslist ad, trying to be badass and, instead, ending up on the side of some road? I'm not preaching. You know I'm owning up to my shit."

Wes gauged the distance we'd put between ourselves and the group before saying, "Addison isn't. He struts around here like he's the skinny counselor at fat camp. I think it's Joshua who's interfering. And if we cared about Addison, we'd stop worrying so much about the opinions of some sicko. We'd find a way to get him some real help."

"He's not drinking," I protested. "He's not using."

"He's also not living in reality, Greer. The only difference is he's bringing everyone else along."

"If we go after Joshua, he'll never forgive us."

"I can live with that. I care about the guy. I'm not going to let him live a lie just so we can have slumber parties in the Poconos."

It was the first time anyone had used the word *lie* to describe the situation happening around us. Out of the corner of my eye, I saw Addison coming toward us. He strode as if he wanted to close the gap between us quickly, but without running.

"I love Addison." When I said it, I knew I was closing a door. And I could tell by the resigned look that washed over Wes's face that I didn't have to actually tell him anything else. If I forced myself to keep talking, I might have really confessed. I'd have said, *I love Addison and all I have to do to keep him is believe in this one thing.*

Wes heard all that without my saying it. And it was lucky I didn't actually say it aloud because Addison broke into a jog and reached us right away, probably before I would have finished explaining.

"What's going on?" Addison's eyes went gray and flinty, and flicked toward me.

Wes said, "I was just sharing my concerns about you with Greer."

"Yeah?" Addison tilted his head to me.

"About how you're dealing with this morning and Joshua's news," I finished, hoping Wes would go along. "We just figured that between the two of us, we'd make sure you didn't have to be alone if you didn't want. I know you bottle everything up — I don't mean *bottle* like liquor — it's just that you're always taking care of everyone else." I babbled uncontrollably until Addison held up his hand.

"Greer, stop." I waited, wondering how it felt to be hit by

someone as strong as Addison. Not thinking he'd do it. Not really. Just wondering if he could shatter my face if he tried. But Addison's face softened and he said, "Guys, I'm so lucky. You really bless me. God, I'm such an asshole. I had myself all riled up for a second there."

Wes stared at me and nodded at Addison. "You know we care, man. That's all. We'll do whatever it takes." He backed away. "I'm going to let you walk Greer back to her dorm. I want to shower before I stink up dinner."

"See you later." Addison nodded at him. "And, hey — thanks. It means a lot."

"No worries."

We stood there watching Wes walk away. Addison had wrapped his arm tightly around my waist. "You're really something. I had myself convinced . . ." He shook the thought away.

"You did? Or did someone else convince you?"

"Settle down, there, sporto." I was only acting outraged, though, and it didn't serve me well to follow that conversation to its conclusion. So I hung my arms around Addison's neck and tipped my head back to kiss him. When I came up for air, I squinted back to see Joshua still standing by the school van, hands on his hips, staring at us.

He didn't look weak or sick. I'd begun to think of him as an infection, though, spreading to us all.

EIGHTEEN

The next morning, sometime between first and third period, Wes moved out of the room he shared with Addison. I was there with Addison when he walked in and found half the room emptied.

"What the hell?" he asked.

As soon as he said it, I saw it. The blanket on the bed had been drawn up straight for once. Wes's books and piles of papers had been cleared from his desk. His bucket of shower supplies. His towel. His robe. Even the wardrobe and chest of drawers were empty when we checked.

"Maybe he went home?" I suggested. Addison checked through his own wardrobe, yanked open the drawers on his side of the room. "He didn't steal anything?" He still didn't answer me. He squatted down to check under Wes's bed. No duffel bag. No suitcase.

"He didn't say anything to you?" I asked, still thinking we'd find a reasonable explanation. School visit. Family emergency. Something.

"No, what did he say to you?" Addison turned to me and I saw his temper ramping up. "Yesterday. When you couldn't get out of the van fast enough, just to spend time talking to Wes in the parking lot?" The dread in my stomach was starting to feel familiar.

"Nothing." I thought to myself, *Wes, you prick. You could have given me a heads-up.* I stuck to our story. "We talked about you, how worried we were. Are. I think that last conversation freaked him out a little." Oh Christ. As soon as I said it, I recognized the complete shit storm I'd wandered into.

"What last conversation?"

"Joshua. Predicting one of us would betray everyone. Wes got a little paranoid about it." Once I'd started, I couldn't stop myself. "Joshua attacked him all weekend. You didn't notice that?"

"It would be terrific if we could deal with one conflict without you blaming Joshua for it. Seriously, just try to take some kind of ownership."

"I'm not owning the fact that your roommate moved out. You don't even know that. Maybe something happened this weekend back home and when he got back, he heard from his family."

"Then why wouldn't he tell me last night? He slept in his bed last night. We talked after lights-out. He didn't say anything about contact from home."

"Addison, we're late for class —"

"I don't care if we show up late for class. I don't care if I go to class. They should have sat us down for some kind of conflict-resolution crap. We should have had to discuss it." But talking it through wasn't calming Addison down. His voice kept catching. He looked like he wanted to break something. Or break down.

He finally looked up. "I know he was upset about Joshua." He paused miserably. "Joshua took a lot of cheap shots at him, I get that." He raised his eyes to mine. "That's just what he does — it's his way of getting to know people." Addison gazed around the room. His eyes watered. "Last night, Wes asked me how much I knew about Joshua and implied he was taking advantage of me. Of all of us."

I couldn't believe it. Wes really just said it outright. I tried to make sure my voice didn't lean one way or the other. "What do you think about that?"

"Well, obviously I think it's bullshit. You and I have been through this too. I get it, especially from the point of view of . . ." Addison searched for words and apparently decided to go with the very grandfatherly ". . . a young lady." He nodded to me. "I understand bristling at Joshua's more unconventional habits. But to accuse him of taking advantage when he's devoting all this time to teaching us how to better ourselves, how to value ourselves — it's completely unjustified."

I nodded. I didn't know what else to say.

"Greer, he doesn't even know how much time he has left and he has chosen to spend it with us. That sacrifice stuns me. And if there's anything I can do to make his time more comfortable, I'm going to do it. And I'm not going to apologize for that choice. To anyone."

"And that's what you told Wes?"

"Basically." He looked defensive. "So you're going to tell me what? That I asked for this?"

"For what? You don't know what's going on yet. Maybe he just needs some time to sort it out." But I knew then. I thought of how certain Wes had been the evening before. How resigned he looked when he'd left us on the sidewalk. He'd just cut his losses. It amazed me, briefly, to remember you could do that.

"What if he goes to the dean?" That's what Addison had been worried about. I had felt so awful for Addison — Wes had rejected him. I'd thought he was hurt and embarrassed. Instead Addison worried more about getting in trouble or exposing Joshua to the dean.

But then he reached for my hand. "I don't want any of us to end up sliding backward because of Wes. We'd be written up. We'd lose privileges. I don't know if they'd let me stay. I can't imagine not waking up every day and seeing you."

"He wouldn't tell anyone. And really, what would he say? That we watched movies and ate stir-fry? We took a hike and discussed the future." It sounded better vague. "We could even say that Sophie had begged us to go back to the cabin before her parents threw out all her brother's stuff. Sophie would say that, if we needed her to."

Addison looked reassured, but then another dark storm crossed his face. "Or Wes could say we stayed in a cabin with little supervision. We slept, coed, in beds." Addison pulled out his cell phone, flipped through pictures of us lounging on the sofa, laughing.

"That looks like wholesome fun to me." I pointed at the phone as he tracked through photos. "No drugs, no alcohol." I saw a shot of the brief poker game. "Okay, there was a little gambling, but nothing major. If he wanted to, he could make trouble, but I doubt it would be permanent trouble. I don't even think he wants to. Wes is just really worried. He's probably just trying to get a reaction from you."

"He'd listen to you."

My heart skidded and paused. "What?"

"If you asked him to leave it alone."

"You don't want me to do that, Addison."

"Why? Why wouldn't I want you to do that? You'd be asking him to keep his mouth shut for you too. You'd be protecting all of us."

"For one thing, if he gets offended, he's more likely to go to the dean. You know Wes. He'll feel like we're challenging him or something."

"So don't offend him. Just ask sweetly."

"That's what would bother him."

"Please explain why it would bother him for his roommate's girlfriend, with whom he's fairly friendly, to ask him to refrain from informing the administration of rule infractions. Seriously. Unless he's more than fairly friendly and he'd resent you asking anything on my behalf."

Not long before, hearing Addison refer to me as his girlfriend would have counted as enough to counteract all the other crap. That charm had worn off a little bit. I found myself lashing out. "Because it wouldn't be sincere. He'd know that and it would piss him off. And you're not his roommate anymore. He knows what that means. This" — I waved around the half-emptied room — "makes it pretty obvious that Wes could care less about any of us."

Addison looked like he was practicing his newly acquired anger-management skills. "I'm just asking you — I'm respectfully requesting that you at least let him know how disappointed you'd be if he turned us in. Just as a long shot —"

Just so you know where my loyalty lies. That's how I should have finished up Addison's sentence. Instead, I told him, "Okay."

"Okay?"

"Yeah, I love you. I'm sorry if I made this more complicated than that." I knew that's what Addison wanted to hear, and sure enough, he rewarded me with one of those hugs that made me feel swallowed up entirely, absolutely safe.

"You make everything more complicated." He said it into

my hair and sounded exasperated. "Greer, Greer — I need a beer."

I punched him playfully. "That's not even funny."

"We just skipped class."

I looked up at the standard-issue clock on the wall. Addison was right. "What are we going to do?"

"Go right to Dr. Rennie. And just tell him — my roommate moved out, abruptly. You were comforting me."

"Let's use a different word."

"You were offering me peer counseling."

I nodded. "It does sound better."

He pulled me closer to him. "But you could comfort me first."

"Not a chance. Let's make sure we're not thrown out before we start having rebellious sex all over the place."

My parents might have been shocked at the effect that McCracken Hill had on me. Or else my mom would just kind of cluck her tongue and say, "Money well spent." They'd never been able to scare me into being good at home. I mean, they yelled and grounded and took stuff away. After the shoplifting started, they left me in a couple of mall security offices to try to scare me straight. But it never really stuck. I mean, I knew they'd eventually stop yelling. The mall would close. They'd have to send someone to pick me up. But when they sent me away, that changed everything.

I missed my room. I missed watching TV and being able to work out whenever I wanted. I missed my laptop and my enormous bed and my closet full of clothes that didn't make me look Amish. But most of all, I missed feeling like I had some kind of control. I hadn't worked so hard to behave since I was a little kid. And now no one was here to actually care.

So I worried. About missing class, about being caught in the boys' dorm. I made Addison get a move on and made sure to look like I was concerned about him, in case someone was monitoring the hallway security cameras. It took being sent to a school for screwups for me to realize I didn't want to be a screwup anymore. People monitored you more closely when you tried to prove a point. Navigating the world was easier without a big target on my chest. When we stepped out of the dark corridor, I grabbed Addison's hand. His didn't feel as clammy as mine. I knew that missing class really didn't register with him as worth worrying over. He had other things to preserve — Joshua's access to campus, Joshua's health, Joshua, Joshua, Joshua.

I knew too that I needed to test out Wes's theory that most of McCracken was talk, after the initial shock of being there. That as long as I didn't flaunt my hot boyfriend or resurrect my dormant eating disorder, I could pretty much get away with what I wanted. If Wes was right, it made the prospect of finishing up high school at McCracken a little more alluring. It gave me a little more control over my life.

We waited outside the classroom until everyone filed out. A couple of girls rolled their eyes and whispered. Some gonad named Gary gave Addison a congratulatory punch on the shoulder. Dr. Rennie caught me midcringe when he stepped out into the hallway and waved us into the room. "Was your weekend sojourn not enough of an adventure? Did you need to honeymoon through my class?"

At first, I panicked at his wording, but Dr. Rennie smiled wryly. "I'm so sorry," Addison started. "Sir, I just stopped by my room to pick up books."

"And you happened to discover your girlfriend? That is a dilemma."

"No, sir. I didn't even mean to go in his room." Addison gave the slightest shake of his head. Apparently I shouldn't have mentioned that part.

Dr. Rennie thumbed through a stack of papers on his desk. "I see. You were just walking by and you fell in." Sometimes it's hard not to wonder if adults don't just create rules so that they can mock you when you break them.

"No, I —"

"Sir, I freaked out and called Greer over. She'd been waiting for me in the floor lounge."

"Oh?"

We'd used the key phrase *freaked out*. Perhaps Dr. Rennie could claim he had steered Addison to an emotional breakthrough at the next faculty meeting.

"My roommate moved out."

"The Wesley boy? He's moved on from us, has he?"

"No, I don't think he has," Addison answered.

"Oh. I see." Dr. Rennie held up the daily information bulletin. He traced over a list of names with his finger. "Well, he's on this list. Everett accompanied you on your volunteer expedition. With the Narcotics Anonymous counselor?" He looked from Addison to me. "You all went. Did something occur? A falling-out?"

"No," Addison said. Dr. Rennie turned to me.

"No, sir," I answered. "We all got along fine. It just really took Addison by surprise and we talked it through a little. I'm sorry — it's not that we don't value your class."

"Yes. Yes. You had to handle your feelings." I couldn't tell if Dr. Rennie was being sarcastic or not. "Well, this is a dilemma. I'm expected to report this to your academic dean.

But I appreciate how you've handled this, coming right to see me. Understand, I'll follow up, so if this is a tale, then you should bribe your roommate to begin packing on the double." Dr. Rennie chortled and then suddenly grew serious. "But I suspect it's not. You look far too dismayed. I encourage you to reach out to him. Perhaps give him a day or two to cool off if he appears angry for some reason. But otherwise, try to shake it off. The difficult aspect of an environment like this is that you young people, you're all growing very fast. And some of you are growing at different rates. Occasionally friendships can't quite keep up with that. Does that make sense?"

Addison and I both nodded. It made a lot of sense. And it was the most human conversation I'd had with a teacher since I arrived at McCracken Hill. Dr. Rennie actually seemed to care. "Thank you, sir." Add said it first, so I just nodded.

"Hurry to lunch. I'd rather not see Greer have to explain a missed meal on top of everything else."

"Yes, sir. Thank you. We'll get the notes from a classmate —"

"Don't lie to me. None of you takes notes." He turned back to his book and motioned for us to move along.

In the hallway, I felt my body gradually begin to unclench. "That wasn't terrible," I offered.

"Seriously. Rennie seems like a stand-up guy."

I wanted to point out that he listened to us and let us explain like normal people. He alluded to our relationship without making crude sex jokes and he made us feel like worthwhile people without trying to convince us we had superhuman powers or some kind of epic adventure in our future. I couldn't do that, of course, but I filed it away, to bring up if Addison ever seemed willing to listen.

He stopped at the cafeteria. "And he's right. You can't risk missing a meal right now. They'll read all kinds of nonsense into that."

"You won't come in? You should — we'll find Sophie and Jared and figure this out."

"No!" Addison lunged at me. He grabbed my wrist and repeated, "No — listen, don't say anything to any of them." He loosened his grip and rubbed my arm with his other hand. "I'm sorry. It's just — I don't know how to handle this yet. I don't want everyone to start talking smack."

"Why don't you just eat lunch with us, then?"

"I need to go call Joshua." Of course. "I'll see you later, I promise." Addison kissed my cheek quickly and let go of my arm. He gently pushed me toward the dining hall. "Listen, if you see Wes, don't antagonize him. But maybe it wouldn't hurt for you to ask him what's going on. Say I'm really broken up over it, if you want. I couldn't deal with coming to lunch."

"Yeah, okay. Sure."

"Great. Love you, angel. Seriously." I knew he meant for me to notice he called me angel. I guess that was going to be our new code after the past weekend. Addison headed back toward the dorm. I watched him sprint off and wondered what he'd tell Joshua.

In the dining hall, I wasn't sure who I'd sit with. A quick survey didn't uncover Sophie or Jared. I edged my way painstakingly through the sandwich line and assembled a turkey-on-wheat masterpiece, trying to stall time until Sophie shimmied in. Still nothing. Right by the beverage station, I saw Hannah. She was sitting at a table with two girls named Allison who had, for the past month or so, slowly been morphing into the same person.

"Hannah. I'm so glad to see you."

She beamed. "Me too! I miss you." And then she kind of grimaced, like she had said the wrong thing. I watched her fade right in front of me.

"Seriously. I miss everyone," I told her. "I'm going through withdrawal." Four of Allison's eyebrows shot up simultaneously. "Not literally." Sometimes I forgot which things you couldn't say at McCracken Hill. "Metaphorically." Blank looks. "I'm not really withdrawing from anything."

"Let me help you." Hannah jumped out of her seat and took the glass of seltzer off my tray. "I know it's hard when you have the shakes."

I stared at her for a second and then noticed the slight upward curve of her lips. Seriously? Hannah Green had made a joke. A good joke. The Allisons stood up and fled in unison.

Later on, at dinner, I got assigned to a table by myself. Addison and Jared ate together. I hadn't been able to spot Sophie or Hannah so I swung by Sophie's room on the way back. Hannah was already stretched out on Sophie's floor. Sophie sat at her computer, typing away.

"What's going on?"

Hannah explained, "Sophia is opening up the healing lines of communication."

"Oh yeah?" I said, shooting Sophie a look.

"Yeah," Sophie replied. "I'm writing Josie."

"Nice. Be sure to tell her about your bunk-bed *boyfriend*."

"Wait — what?" Hannah sat straight up. "You and Jared?"

Sophie laughed. "Yes, zombie girl. Welcome to the land of the socially aware." Hannah looked hurt, so I reached to ruffle her hair.

"Seriously? When did all this go on?" But as soon as she asked, Hannah cut herself off.

"Have you already forgotten your transformative time with Joshua?" I asked as a joke, but watched Hannah carefully. I don't know what I was worried about. She just seemed so disconnected.

"I'm working hard to forget it, yes." Hannah didn't sound like she was joking.

"Whoa." Sophie looked sharply at me, a little nervous about the venom in Hannah's voice.

"I'm sorry if you felt shut out up there," I said, "when you were alone with him."

Hannah just shrugged. "You did it before we went up to the cabin."

"Yes, she did," Sophie said, blowing her own bangs out of her eyes. "That also icked me out. I'm glad you two have sufficiently proven your trust. Next time, no one has to sleep on their own."

"You might still have to. It's just you who hasn't," Hannah pointed out.

Sophie looked surprised as she considered that. "I doubt it. I bet I make Joshua too nervous. It might qualify as a trust exercise for him."

"He can't transform you if you don't do it," Hannah declared breezily.

I didn't know how to react to that one. Sophie just rolled with it. "Then I guess I'll have to schedule him in."

"Jared . . ." I encouraged, hoping she'd give up the details.

224

". . . is acting really different since we got back to campus."

"No, seriously?" It hadn't looked like a random hookup.

"I don't know," she said. I could tell it mattered to her because she made herself so busy picking at a pulled thread on the carpet that she couldn't look Hannah or me in the eye. "Maybe it was just one of those things that only fits a particular context. We were up there and it felt right. Maybe we're back here and it feels wrong. To him. We'll see. It's still early and we heard so much crazy crap up there. Maybe Jared is still processing."

"He strikes me as a slow processor," Hannah said, and it made me laugh out loud. "What?" she asked, mystified.

"That's just the kindest way I've ever heard to say someone isn't so bright."

"No, I didn't mean that. I consider Jared very bright," Hannah told us. "Especially about people and feelings."

"Just not today. Just not my feelings," Sophie pointed out, and Hannah and I moved in to hold her hand, her shoulders. "Thanks, ladies." Sophie sounded like she meant it. "I really needed company tonight to remind me not to take it all so seriously."

No one mentioned Wes. I thought for sure that Hannah would bring him up, but she didn't. I wondered if Sophie knew anything about his move, but I didn't want to give anything away. Besides, if I brought it up out of nowhere, even Hannah would have to pick up on the fact that something was wrong.

Instead everyone acted as if he was already gone.

He wasn't really gone, though. He'd just moved to Freewill Hall. I found him the next morning at breakfast. Or maybe because he knew Addison would be weight lifting with Jared, Wes found me.

"How's the war, doll face?" He sidled up to me in line and spoke out of the corner his mouth, like an actor in a black-and-white movie.

"Can we sit together?" It was such a relief to see him.

He answered calmly, "I don't know. You tell me."

"I'm supposed to talk to you anyway."

"Oh yeah, Joshua's appointed you ambassador to the free world?"

I laughed, but it didn't sound like a real laugh. It sounded like a frightened hiccup. "Addison asked me to talk to you," I explained.

Wes's face seemed to freeze over. "We can sit, but I don't think we have a lot to talk about, Greer. I want to tell you good luck, I guess. If you ever need someone who hasn't been sucked in by a religious cult, well then, I'm your guy." He smiled ruefully. "But otherwise, I'm out. Seriously."

"We're a group of friends. Not a religious cult."

"You're smarter than that. And you lie badly. You're freaked out. And if I can see it, they can see it. And then what'll happen?"

"There's nothing religious about what we do. Maybe it's spiritual, but everything about this place is supposed to be spiritual. Even the whole twelve-step thing — give yourself over to a higher power —"

"Does Joshua often refer to scripture, twisting accepted religious philosophy to fit his selfish goals? Has he tried to convince you that the group faces an unseen enemy who would disrupt a way of life you treasure? Does he emotionally manipulate members of the group? Cross physical boundaries that make members uncomfortable? Does he dictate sexual practices?"

I felt like hitting Wes. "He does not," I hissed at him, worried that someone might overhear us. "Joshua's never touched me like that."

"No, he just ordered Addison to."

"You're sick."

"Deep down, you're worried that I'm right."

"You never bought into it. Any of it."

"Do you hear yourself? You sound like one of those Mormon girls whose husbands have thirteen other wives. Addison's a great guy. You know I see that. But that doesn't mean he's worth dealing with Joshua."

"You've never felt comfortable around Joshua." Neither did I, but I wasn't going to admit that out loud.

"Come on, now. Joshua's never felt comfortable around me."

I couldn't argue with that. Up in the Poconos, Joshua had seemed to enjoy needling him. Picking on him and then isolating him.

"Why do you think Joshua has never acted comfortable around me, Greer?"

I blinked. He waited. I blinked again.

"Seriously?" he asked incredulously. "Greer, it's that I'm black."

I sat back. "That doesn't make any sense."

"Of course it does. You really don't get it, do you? Greer, you all are seriously clueless. Joshua makes you pay for food. He moves into Sophie's house. He has Hannah sleep in his bed. You're not an idiot. You have to have some measure of self-preservation. Why don't you speak up?

"I know he stayed over in your room. And I can't imagine that didn't freak you the hell out. So what did Joshua say when you didn't hop to it?"

I bit my lip. "He implied that maybe it was because he was black."

Wes slammed his hand on his food tray. The milk in his cereal bowl sloshed. "Exactly!" He narrowed his eyes at me. "You can tell me, Greer. Honestly. Did you not want Joshua sleeping in your bed because he's black?"

"No. I didn't want him in my bed because he's old. And kind of creepy."

"Yeah, that's right." Wes rubbed his head. "I try to keep an open mind, but sometimes you white kids are so stupid. You're so afraid of being called racist. That's the worst thing in the world, right? So you'd rather have a slumber party with some crazy homeless guy than have him suggest that you don't like black people."

"First off, he's not homeless."

"Have you seen where he lives? Has Addison?" I shook my head. "Dude's homeless."

"Even if that worked on me or Hannah — I'm just saying — if it did . . . hit some kind of nerve — it wouldn't work on Addison. He just doesn't worry about what people believe about him. He lives out his sense of integrity. He always says that."

"People who are actually confident don't walk around talking about how confident they are. I know you get that." I sat still. Silent and thinking. Wes kept pushing. "Why do you think Joshua starts off every story about meeting Addison by describing him as a skinhead? Like before Joshua showed up and taught him otherwise, Addison was eating Special

KKK for breakfast? Addison doesn't even remember most of the past few years. That was one extended alcoholic black-out. His biggest fear is that he's secretly some raging monster. So Joshua convinces him that he's the only thing harnessing that monster."

"You've spent so much time thinking about this."

"Well, it's not like the asshole was going to let me speak or anything. So I watched."

"But it doesn't matter what you saw. Or what you say. You left. So now Joshua gets to be the wise mentor and you join the line of people who've betrayed Addison." Wes nodded sadly, but he didn't say anything. "That's it? You're not even going to defend yourself?"

"I don't have to defend myself. I don't want to sit around hearing about how useless I am and watching my friends plan a war against vegetarians. Most people would call that a healthy choice on my part."

"It's a metaphor!"

"But it's *not*. You say that because that's how you've decided to make it okay. But Joshua does not mean it symbolically. He means there's going to be a war. He's alluding to you killing people because they won't eat meat. That's, like, schizophrenic behavior."

"What changed between last night and this morning?" I asked Wes. When he grimaced, I knew I was onto something. "Something happened. Because last night you wanted to confront Addison, right? You decided we needed to go to the administration because the whole Joshua thing was interfering with his progress, his recovery. You have to know that if you leave, he'll just get closer to Joshua. I mean, I can't even get through to him now. You didn't give me any time to figure it out either. Or a heads-up. You just left. Which means you must have requested a transfer as soon as you woke up and you must have been convincing or the administration would have tried conflict resolution."

Wes played with his plastic fork. He twirled it in his fingers. He seemed to be making up his mind about something.

"I think you owe me an explanation."

"Yeah? I don't owe you shit, Greer." But his voice softened a little. "But I do wish you'd stay the hell away from that crazy mofo, so I'm going to show you this." He reached into his pocket and pulled out a folded piece of paper. He skipped it across the table to me. "Go on. Check how Mr. Integrity spends his computer lab sessions." I unfolded it slowly. "For the record, I moved out to light a fire under his ass. We talked the night before. I tried to get him to actually look closely at the whole Joshua dynamic, but he wouldn't even go near it. I figured, maybe if he wakes up and his world is a little different, that might get him thinking. I care about Addison."

Wes looked pained enough that I believed him. He said, "But we're going to go home, go back to our real lives. I'm not like the rest of you, pretending we'll all end up living together on some happy little commune. I'd rather piss Addison off and know in the long run he's going to be okay. Or at least that's how I felt before he left that picture on my bed."

I looked down and saw a close-up Wes, intensely studying the cards in his hand during the poker-for-Cheerios game at the cabin.

"Well, this isn't such a shocker, right?" I said. "I mean, we all knew you guys were playing cards."

"Yeah, we did. And I felt crappy enough about it then.

Now imagine what happens when the deans see something like this. Or my parents."

"It's in a residential house, though. You're sitting at a dining room table. We'd all get in just as much trouble for just being in Sophie's house."

"That's the point."

I still didn't see it. I was looking from the wrong angle. "They won't show it to anyone. Unless —" Wes prompted.

"Unless you go to someone in the administration about Joshua or the cabin."

"Exactly." I felt sick all over again. Wes stood up. "So, listen, I'm out. Addison no longer exists to me. Because whether you want to admit it or not, he saw this coming down the pike. I don't remember Addison pulling out his camera to capture golden moments from the rest of the weekend. He pulled out the deck of cards with one hand and the camera with the other."

"That doesn't make sense. How would he possibly know that you'd confront him about Joshua?"

"It's called insurance, Greer. And I don't think Addison's devious enough to go planning something like that. Joshua thought of it. Addison just got it done." Wes took a deep breath. He looked down and spoke really carefully to me. "You think I'm crazy. They're calling you an angel and preparing to bomb Trader Joe's or something, but I'm some kind of head case. I get it. I'm asking you to be careful, Greer. Because if they turned on me, they can turn on you. But in the meantime, as long as you're with Addison — and as long as Addison's with Joshua Stern — well then, I want you to stay the hell away from me."

Wes glanced at the door, like he was making sure he had a clear exit out. "You understand?"

"I got it." He nodded and turned to head out. "Wes." I spoke low, not wanting to have everyone in the dining hall writing about us in their daily growth journals or something. He stopped, but didn't turn around. I felt immensely lonely. "Take care of yourself," I told him. He walked out without looking back.

NINETEEN

I don't know what Wes told the administrators, but Addison didn't get another roommate. So we both had singles and took it upon ourselves to test the veracity of the security cameras during homework hours. I tried not to think about Wes a whole lot, actually. Addison didn't bring it up, but even still, I felt disloyal. I figured that the only way to feel better about my powwow with his new archenemy was to squirm beneath him and on top of him and generally try to distract myself by pursuing a doctorate in sexual chemistry. With maybe a master's degree in the complete union of our souls.

He might have said things were going really well between us. Most days, we alternated who walked Joshua to his treatment. Usually we all met for dinner at Sal's, and then once Joshua had a hot meal, either Addison or I would accompany him the three blocks to the local hospital on Willowbrook Avenue. The way Joshua described it, his treatment sounded a lot like dialysis. He talked about the doctors needing to clean toxins from his blood. He said there was a machine, but when I asked what kind, Joshua told me, "I spend most of the time pretending to be somewhere else, so I don't pay much attention to their medical-school mumbling. They plug me in and I stare at a magazine, hoping they'll keep me well enough that I can keep serving and loving you kids."

I tried to be more cooperative. Nights that I walked Joshua to the hospital, I listened to him lecture about the goodness of food and nourishment. He taught me then how running food over light could sometimes infuse it with vitamins. That's why they used the scanners they did at grocery stores. That's one of the benefits of microwaves. I remember asking, "Can't you get sick from microwaves? Didn't people worry about the radiation first?"

"You see how propaganda infiltrates our rational understanding? That's how the media teaches you to associate food with poison," Joshua told me. "They teach you to equate microwaves with radiation and radiation with cancer." He walked slowly, waving his arms in front of him for emphasis. "Because if they told you microwaves cooked with light, well then, we'd all just junk our ovens. Who wouldn't want to cook with light?"

He said that the drugs and the alcohol had eaten away at his system. They'd corroded his veins so that the blood that ran through them was compromised.

"Could something like that happen to Addison?" I asked.

"It's more likely Addison will die in battle," he replied. And maybe because it didn't seem like I had completely signed on for the whole vegan war thing, Joshua expanded his definition of battle. "That might not mean the kind of physical conflict Addison expects as he spars in the gym. But Addison will always fight on the side of goodness. That will cost him before the years of drinking catch up to him. He needs you to keep him safe."

Joshua told me, "Sometimes the two of you make me feel so very alone." And when I asked him why, he said, "No one has ever loved me the way you love each other."

Maybe that was the most honest thing Joshua told me. Afterward, I made more of an effort to be kind. I think Addison noticed; we eased back into our old comfort with each other. It almost felt like there had been too many people angling for a place in the pile. When Wes stepped out, it left a little more room for everyone else. We all seemed to treat one another a little more carefully.

I didn't share classes with Wes. Aside from the occasional glimpse of him in the dining hall, it was like I'd never known him at all. On the nights that Addison walked Joshua to his doctor's appointments, I met up with Sophie and Hannah. Sometimes we just sat in a room studying. Sometimes we made elaborate plans for our next weekend away. Sophie seemed less frenetic. Calmer. Maybe telling us about her brother helped.

That was Joshua's theory anyway. He commented on it the first time we all gathered together again. We circled up in the meeting room right after the Tuesday night NA meeting had adjourned. "How does peace feel?" Joshua asked her as soon as she sat down in one of the plastic molded chairs. "Do you all see that?" We stopped our separate conversations to study Sophie.

Sophie smiled up at him. "Peace feels okay. It's not acceptance. Not yet."

"No," Joshua agreed. "He left too soon for it to be acceptable — I hear you. But you have peace. It's very becoming, isn't it?" Joshua asked Jared and Addison. He leaned into Jared. "I know you've noticed, brother. Sophia's looking hot."

"Joshua." Sophie's voice sharpened its blade. "Stop."

"I'm just pointing out what the males in the room have certainly recognized." Joshua grinned, but Sophie didn't.

"Stop talking about my body while I'm talking about my grief." Whoa. With that, Sophie pretty much firebombed the circle. Hannah's eyes widened and found mine. I'm sure we just stood there, staring at each other, while the guys paid really close attention to the pattern on the carpet. I would have clapped, but it was so silent that, for a second, I was scared.

Joshua actually apologized. He said, "You're absolutely right — I'm so sorry. I think it's hard for me to be in a room with your pain, Sophia. I don't know if you knew this — I too lost a brother. His name was Adam — that sounds a lot like Addison, doesn't it? People return to us in all sorts of ways. He was in college, and he was a passenger in a car on the way back from a dance. Adam went to a Christian college in Kansas. They'd piled into a car and were speeding back, trying to make curfew, took a blind turn, and careened off the road. Oh, it was devastating. I couldn't listen to music for the longest time. You punish yourself in strange ways when you're mourning. Am I right, Sophia?"

She looked warily at him. "Yeah. I'm still figuring that part out."

"You will find your answers."

"I'm sorry about your brother, Joshua." Hannah said it first.

"Thank you, Rose. He is with me, though. In part that's why I can face this illness. Either way, I know I will be surrounded by love."

I didn't really spend a lot of time thinking about Joshua and his brother, but Sophie sort of latched on to it, which made sense. I know she wrote about it to Josie. And later that week while she, Jared, Addison, and I ate lunch together, she asked Addison about it. "Did you know that before — that Joshua had a brother named Adam?"

Addison shook his head. "No. Took me by surprise. That guy's been through so much. It makes you wish the universe would give him a break, you know?"

Sophie seemed to consider that. She asked, "Does Joshua have other brothers or sisters? Have you guys met them at the hospital?" I hadn't.

We looked to Addison, who told us, "He just has us." I watched Addison finish eating one burger and start on another. "I'd actually always thought Joshua was an only child. You know, here and there, he's talked about being abused. He never mentioned there being another kid involved."

"Yeah, that was my impression," Sophie said. I studied her, trying to figure out where her brain was headed. "I wonder if Joshua felt overshadowed by him. Maybe that's part of it."

Addison seemed to pay closer attention to his burger. Sophie pressed him, "Do you think?"

He seemed impatient. "I don't know, Soph — I'm not sure where you're getting that. It's his private life."

"Yeah, it's a burden standing in the way of his peace. Just like ours. I thought we were supposed to embrace discomfort?" Sophie smiled tightly. "Joshua's talked about growing up in New Jersey, right? Poor and in foster homes. Having a brother go to college in Kansas — that's extraordinary. It just sounds like an interesting chapter."

"Well, then ask him about it." Addison looked mystified and I didn't get it then either. I knew Sophie well enough, though, to see her mind working, working.

I didn't get a chance to follow up with her afterward because Addison got a call from Joshua during the afternoon class session. I'd never seen another student interrupt a class at McCracken Hill before. Before, at my old school, someone would walk by the door or text you to meet at the bathroom. But at McCracken, classes felt like sealed pods. Most teachers didn't even allow you to face the doorway, let alone leave for any reason.

As soon as Addison knocked on the door, the whole class turned to examine me. Addison addressed Mr. Brighton with his superpolite Eagle Scout voice. "Sir, I'm so sorry to intrude. But if you could just let me steal Greer for two minutes."

"I beg your pardon, Mr. Bradley."

Addison looked desperately at me. "I know — I'm so sorry. But it's a family emergency." A murmur began rippling through the classroom. Because what the heck could that mean? Most of us hadn't spoken to our families for months.

Mr. Brighton coughed uncomfortably. "Greer." He nodded to me to step out of the room. When I stood, my legs felt shaky.

As soon as I got outside, Addison said, "Joshua needs surgery."

If Addison had known that my first thought was *Joshua is not my family*, he might have turned around and walked away from me right there.

As it was, I must not have answered quickly enough, because he took me by the shoulders and asked, "Greer, did you hear what I just said?" I noticed that his face was puffy, swollen. He'd been crying.

"I didn't even know they were planning surgery." My voice didn't sound like my voice. I was just playing a part, really, reacting the way I thought he wanted me to.

Addison told me, "The treatments aren't working." His breaths came in shallow gasps. It seemed like he had run to come tell me. "I think he's known this could happen. He just didn't want to complicate things."

"Do you need to sit down? Addison, are you okay?" Which was a stupid question. Because of course he wasn't okay. "Should we go over to the hospital?" Addison still panted. He stood, bent with his hands on his knees. I remember looking up and down the hallway, wishing an adult would walk by and thinking we really weren't old enough to deal with something like this on our own. I rubbed circles on Addison's back with my hand. I leaned down and rested my head on his shoulder.

"I don't mean this the wrong way," he said, "but please don't touch me right now." I stepped back, feeling ashamed. I'd just wanted to comfort him. "He's going to come here. He asked me to ask if we could all have dinner together."

"Wait. What? I thought he was at the hospital."

He straightened up and shook his head. "No. He told them that he had to get his affairs in order first. But apparently they could call him at any time. He'll keep receiving his treatments in the meantime. Until they notify him. Then he'll report to the hospital. But it's an experimental operation. I mean, they don't even know if he'll make it through."

"They told him that?" That seemed strange to me. I really started worrying then, thinking that maybe I hadn't listened closely enough when Joshua had told us about his illness. So I kept myself on high alert in the hallway with Addison, trying to make myself useful, willing myself not to zone out.

But the whole thing wasn't making much sense. "It just seems really coldhearted of them — telling him he has to have this risky surgery, but then sending him home alone to deal with it and wait. You'd think they'd have counselors to help him process through an ordeal like this."

"Well, you know what, Greer? The real world doesn't function like this place." Addison gestured at the affirmations stenciled on the walls. "Not everybody gets a treatment team to decide what they'll eat each day and where they'll sit and what books they'll read and whether or not they'll be allowed to use shampoo."

I tried to tell myself that Addison wasn't actually angry at me, but it sure felt like that. *Just take it,* I thought. Supporting him through this might mean just letting him vent. But that part wasn't easy.

Addison balled his hands into fists. "You want an explanation for everything. Jesus. What is with all the questions? These are medical professionals. He wants to spend time with us, with me. He wants to know his last wishes will be honored, you know? There's a chance that he might need to lay out his last wishes."

And then Addison let loose this strangled cry. He stood facing the wall and leaned his forehead against the cinder block and just bawled. Huge, wracking sobs. I stood there, shadowing him from behind, saying empty phrases like *everything is going to be okay.*

We ended up ordering in — meeting in the conference room and getting food from Sal's. It seemed like the safest place for us. We figured if we were caught, Joshua would just say he'd been called to campus to help mediate some kind of conflict. I went with Addison to meet the delivery guy from Sal's, and by the time we got down the hill and into the bare white room, the others had all gathered. Joshua sat in a swivel desk chair, with Hannah and Sophie on either side of him. Jared sat in a folding chair a fair distance away. He looked miserable.

Joshua offered us a weak smile when we walked in. "That smells wonderful." So his appetite seemed okay. Addison brought him a slice on a paper plate. He even tucked a napkin into Joshua's collar. "You going to come to the hospital and take care of me like this?"

"Nah, you'll have hot nurses."

"I almost forgot." Joshua smiled. "Brother, you're a twinge jealous of that." He laughed and looked at me. "Of course not, Elizabeth. He's just making me feel better." Joshua looked past us at the door. "Where is Wes at?"

My eyes slid toward Addison. I figured he would have told Joshua that our own Judas had left the building.

Addison said, "You were right."

"Even when you told him my health was failing?"

"He didn't respond."

Joshua nodded to himself and reached out for Hannah's hand. I tried to imagine the message that Addison would have sent Wes. I'm pretty sure it might have stood as one of the more bizarre notes passed in statistics class. Joshua looked around and told the group, "He could not have handled our trial anyway. Wes is a fundamentally damaged individual. For our circle to thrive, we must cut out the rot."

"Jesus Christ," Jared muttered.

"Relax, buddy." Addison pulled over a chair to sit beside him.

"Well, what the hell does that mean?"

"It's important to break off communication with Wes." Addison looked to Joshua, who nodded for him to continue. "He's threatened me, for one. And my sobriety. After he moved out, I found liquor bottles all over the place. I don't know if he'd been secretly using all along or just hoping I'd find them and slip."

"Brother, what did you do with those bottles?" Joshua asked, fueling Addison's gospel.

"I poured them down the drain." Addison spoke clearly. He enunciated carefully. "I cried when I did it. My whole body shook and hated me, but I poured each one of those bottles down the sink in the Unity Hall restroom." Addison would make a great televangelist if he and Joshua ever decided to take things in that direction.

Sophie looked up at me, but I kept my face unreadable. Wes had been angry and he could certainly win an asshole contest in his day-to-day interactions with people, but I knew he was, deep down, a good person. He wouldn't mess around with Addison's recovery. I had seen the room myself after Wes had left, and I hadn't seen any sign of bottles. I knew Addison was lying. I just didn't understand why.

"Has Addison told you that the surgeons have planned to summon me?"

Nods around the room. Hannah had already begun to cry.

"Essentially, I'm on standby. I hope to be their first successful candidate for this procedure. It's a little shocking, so I ask you to remember that my life is at stake and currently I live in a tremendous amount of pain." He grimaced, almost like he'd just reminded himself.

"Tell us about the procedure." Addison's voice sounded shaky and scared, so I reached out to hold his hand and felt relieved when he took it. Joshua looked down at our clasped hands and smiled, as if he had made it happen.

"They will flush out all of my blood and replace it with pig's blood."

I know I gasped. I think Hannah and Sophie did too.

"That shocks you," Joshua acknowledged. "And because of the time I've spent studying Islam, it shocks me too. I find it abhorrent to have the blood of an unclean animal coursing through my veins. But if it will extend my life, then I can spend time with you. How could I refuse that chance?"

Joshua sank back into the chair and it rocked a little. He swiveled in the chair slowly, turning to each of us. "There is a chance my body will reject this procedure." He paused. Swiveled. "They've told me that as they put the mask on me, the anesthesia will take about half a minute to work. When I first breathe in, I will start off thinking about you, Jared. I will remind myself of your courage. Then I will picture Sophia; I'll try to summon your wisdom." Joshua took a deep breath. "That will leave me about twenty seconds before I slip away. I will remember you, Hannah. I will express thanks for your ability to bless the weak." He motioned for me to crouch beside him, so I did. "Elizabeth, when I have fifteen seconds left of awareness, I will think of you and your strength. I believe it will help me survive. But if it doesn't, my last ten seconds of conscious thought will be spent thinking of you, Brother Addison, and your immense love."

Addison looked down at Joshua, and tears streamed down his face. He kept his grip on my hand and reached for Joshua's, so the three of us huddled there for a little bit, in the room's silence. I wished the lights would blink for curfew. Maybe if I were a better person, I'd have collapsed weeping on the floor, so that Joshua knew how much he meant to me. And here is the thing: He did mean something to me.

But it felt the same way that it used to when my mom and dad orchestrated some lame family activity. Or when the guys I'd fool around with in the stairwell at school started leaving me gifts or posting song lyrics on my wall. I could never respond when another person demanded it from me. If someone said, "Love me," I automatically couldn't. I just shut down.

So I kept blinking, pretending to hold back tears. Joshua beckoned me closer to him and so I lowered my head next to his. "Don't be frustrated, Elizabeth. Remember you have traded in your humanity for some of your power. Those who have not closed off rooms in themselves cannot understand."

Joshua gave me his arm then and I helped him stand. "Addison, you'll lead me out." The two of them started toward the door. Joshua moved slowly, hunched over as if it hurt him to walk. "When it happens, Addison will receive a phone call. Then you all will need to concentrate your thoughts on the surgery achieving the result right with the universe." Then he added cryptically, "Whatever that may be."

When the door closed behind them, I felt the tears fill up my eyes. I almost wanted to chase after them and show Joshua. But I wasn't crying for him, and he'd know that somehow. I didn't know then why the whole thing made me sad, but I looked around the room and we all looked so lost and pathetic. And I knew each of us was in good shape, compared to Addison.

I wished we could all just hop in a car and go skydiving. I would have settled for Six Flags or a Dave & Buster's. Or even just going to someone's basement and drinking until everything was funny or tilted. I wanted what normal kids considered excitement. Not another gathering. Not another discussion about God and the universe and the believing game. Joshua had given us the chance to see ourselves as extraordinary but the glamour of that had worn off. I didn't know what to think anymore, but I would have even preferred to crawl back to my room, burrow myself beneath my standard-issue McCracken Hill thermal blanket, and try not to think for a while.

Jared and Sophie walked out ahead of Hannah and me. She just sort of glided through the room, touching things. Joshua's chair, the door frame.

"What are you doing?" I asked her, almost afraid of what she'd tell me.

"Committing it to memory." Hannah's eyes looked glassy. Her face was flushed.

"Hannah, are you all right?" I moved to feel her forehead, to see if she had a fever. "Should we stop at the infirmary?"

"And tell them what?" She giggled breathlessly. I wondered if she was on something. I checked her pupils. Fine. "I'm not using," she told me.

"Fine. Let's just get back to the dorm, okay?" I opened the door and guided her through it.

"I'm not using. I'm used. I'm used up."

"We all feel that way," I told her. Hannah and I braced ourselves for the cold and stepped outside into a fierce wind. "Let's just go to sleep and look at all of this from a fresh place tomorrow." I had to shout over the whipping wind.

We didn't try to say anything else, but when we got to the dorm, she turned to me and asked, "He's not going anywhere, is he?"

"Joshua? No. We're all going to be just fine." Part of me had begun to wonder how both of those things could be true at the same time. But it was enough to get Hannah inside her dorm room, where she could go around committing the furniture in there to memory, if that's what she wanted.

I felt like I was crawling over to my own room. Here and there, a door yawned open. I knew that it had been a while since I'd made any effort to speak to anyone outside our tiny cluster of people. I should have been contributing to the

McCracken community. Or at least making eye contact. I made myself wave and smile three times. I must have looked like some shell-shocked pageant queen progressing down the hall.

Sophie was waiting for me, tapping her foot against my door. She stopped fidgeting as soon as she saw me.

I stood over her and swiped my key through the door. When I opened it, she somersaulted backward into my small cell. "We need to talk," she told me. She sat up, looked up. She seemed to be making her mind up about something. Finally she said, "Greer, do you always believe what Joshua tells us?"

TWENTY

My first instinct was to check to make sure I'd locked the door. Sophie sat, still gazing up at me. She bit her lip. "Never mind." Her words rushed out to fill the silent room. "I'm sorry. I shouldn't have said that. It's been a really emotional night and I think it overwhelmed me a little. You're tired. Let's just forget that —"

"I don't believe in it." It felt like I'd found the words to some magic spell. I half-expected the walls to tumble down around us. A secret entrance back to reality would emerge from the ruins.

But none of that happened. We just sat there — me on the edge of my mattress, Sophie on the balding, institutional carpet. "I don't believe in any of it." Now that I finally admitted it, I wanted to say it aloud again and again. "Up at the cabin, I kept waiting for someone to look around and say that, but no one did." Sophie nodded. "And then when we got back, I've tried to talk to Addison about it, but he won't even have the conversation. And you know, things got weird. As soon as we had sex, it felt like he started blaming me for everything that went wrong. With Joshua, especially."

"Do you think Addison believes him?" Sophie asked. "Or is he in on it?"

I'd been turning over the question in my head since my breakfast with Wes. "Both. Somehow I think it's both."

Sophie nodded as I told her. "I think that he believes that Joshua's this holy person. He buys into his message. But Addison's such a smart guy. I just can't imagine that he'd accept all this without questioning. And —"

"They seem to have a routine going." Sophie said it, maybe because she knew I'd have trouble. "It even sounds like they're speaking from a script. When did you —"

"Always. From the very beginning. I mean, honestly, at first I just thought I needed to make myself fall for it. Because it all seemed pretty harmless. And you know, Addison. I love Addison. He's perfect in every way — except this one thing. So I figured I just needed to accept that part. For a little while. For him."

"Yeah, but do you see how crazy that is? Greer, seriously?"

I shrugged miserably. Because I felt if I lost him, it wouldn't matter what was crazy and what wasn't. "What does Jared say?" I asked.

She avoided looking at me then. "Jared doesn't really examine things so closely. I don't know. I wanted to talk to you first. When Joshua told us about his brother, that's when I decided. I did some research."

She must have seen my confused look. At McCracken Hill, you couldn't just log on to a computer and play private detective. Sophie explained, "I asked Josie to do some research. When he told us about his brother, it just didn't sit right, you know?" I did know, but also thought it was funny that we were perfectly willing to accept the upcoming vegan coup, but we drew the line at the tragic story of the brother's car accident.

It got even funnier when Sophie told me, "It's the plot of *Footloose*. That's how the brother of the girl in the movie died. Kids driving home from a dance. The car goes off a bridge or something. So then the girl's father bans dancing. Until the cute guy shows up and teaches them all to move on and embrace life."

"Sounds like Joshua's favorite movie."

"I know, right?"

"But why even say that? What's the point of making something like that up?"

"Because I got mad at him. Remember?" Her voice trembled.

"You stood up to him. You kicked ass."

"But that made him look bad. He had to find a way to connect with me. And so he told this story about how he knew just how I felt and we all sat there, pitying him. He'd lost his brother just like I did. If I stayed angry, then I'd be the asshole."

"Yeah, but the story was so detailed — the name *Adam* sounding like *Addison* and everything."

"Joshua probably lies really well, Greer," Sophie said. "He has a lot of practice."

"What else did Josie find?"

"Not a whole lot."

I felt myself deflate a little. "I'm going to need specifics if I'm going to convince Addison. Maybe he knows it can't all be true, right? But what's his alternative? I need to give him facts. Then maybe he'll be able to look at the whole situation more closely —"

"Without feeling so disloyal." Sophie nodded. "We just don't have a lot of facts." She stood and opened the door to my wardrobe. She searched through Addison's drawings like she could find answers encoded there. "I don't think Joshua Stern is his real name."

I felt my heart stutter a little. "What does that mean?"

"It's kind of like the dead-brother lie. Specific enough that no one would question it. And it adds to his story — Joshua's a black guy with a Jewish name."

"Yeah, exactly — I can't imagine that of all the names he'd choose, it would be something that memorable."

"But it isn't particularly unique. Try googling *Joshua Stern*. You'll find thousands. He gets to be anonymous without being forgettable."

"Why would he make up a name?"

Sophie shrugged. "Nothing necessarily earth-shattering. Maybe he's avoiding debt collectors or an ex-wife or something. He might just not want us to be able to find out his real address. But Josie looked through hundreds of Joshua Sterns in Pennsylvania between the ages of thirty-five and fifty. Nothing on our Joshua. Lots of dentists. Three mailmen."

"No crazy cult leader?"

"None."

"He's lying about this operation," I said. Sophie gave me one of her patented well-obviously looks. "I believed in the surgery for a little bit," I admitted.

"Well, then you're kind of dumb," she said, grinning at me. "But then again, I just sat there when he talked about the militant vegan movement." She lay back on the bed and shook her head. "Listen — we need to make a pact. Because I'm a little scared of Joshua. Anyone who works that hard to create something fake — his real life has to be pretty insane. I don't know what we're mixed up in —"

"But we'll figure it out together." I filled it in automatically.

"Promise me, Greer. No matter what Addison says."

It hurt me that she worried. "You think I'd do that?"

"I know you love him. I actually believe he loves you too. So when he asks you to not press this, you're going to want to let it go." She sat up and continued, "And then you'll grow up and get married and make really beautiful babies and Joshua will lean over the kid's crib and weave stories about how that baby will grow up to declare a holy war against vaccines. Then you'll be stuck. Doomed." She was kidding, I knew. But not really.

"I'm not going to give up on him," I said. Sophie pressed her lips together. She looked at me steadily. "Sophie, I'm not. You don't get it. When it's just us together, that's what's holy. This whole thing — it's messed up. And maybe it turns out you're right. Joshua's done something terrible. But most likely he's only a sick man, right? I mean, maybe not the way he says he's sick. I mean, you don't blame Addison, do you?"

She shook her head. "I knew you'd do this. You'd back out. But I didn't think you'd start making excuses so soon."

"I'm not." She said nothing. "Sophie, I'm not! But we came to each other with this, right? Why wouldn't we give Addison that same chance? Maybe he does know Joshua's been lying. And he's scared to admit it. Of all people, Addison risks losing the most in all this. Joshua's like his dad. He's more than his dad."

"Did Addison really find liquor bottles in his room?" Sophie challenged. "Did he?"

"He didn't tell me he did, no." And because she was making the face that implied I'd just proven her point, I rushed to say, "But maybe he didn't want to worry me about the drinking thing on top of everything we were dealing with. The past few days have been like an emotional roller coaster."

"Yeah, a Joshua Stern–designed roller coaster."

"Okay, sure. But not an Addison Bradley creation." Finally I got her to nod. "Are you going to talk to Jared?"

"Jared thinks the whole thing is ridiculous." That's what she had been reluctant to tell me. Sophie had been testing me first. How had we all gotten so suspicious of one another?

"But why would he go along with it, then?"

"He got to go to the Poconos and bone me in a bunk bed." I laughed so hard, I snorted. "No, seriously, I think that's it. And Addison's his friend. He likes you too. He thinks Joshua seems creepy, but essentially harmless. Jared just wants company. He really hates McCracken and we make it a little less excruciating."

"Wow."

"Yeah. He's a pretty uncomplicated guy. But you know, Jared's not going to step up and pull any heroics either." The lights flickered on and off just as I thought to myself, *Do we need heroics? What were Sophie and I actually going to do?*

"Are we going to say anything?" I hoped she would make the decision.

"To Joshua? I don't know. You first need to figure out what you'll say to Addison."

"Sophie, what do we want?"

"I'm not really interested in living someone's manufactured nightmare," she told me. "Life sucks just fine on its own, you know?"

"So Joshua needs to stop —"

"Or leave us alone." The lights blinked again. In a few minutes, each room along the hallway would go dark. "I better go back to my own personal nightmare," she said wryly. "Promise we don't say anything to anyone without talking it through with each other first."

"I swear. You too?"

"Of course I do." She ducked out the door. And by the time the overhead lights dimmed fully, Sophie must have been tucked into her own bed. I wondered if Addison had gotten back to his room in time. If he was lying in his narrow cot, praying for Joshua's good health or remembering me in my pajamas. I wondered if Addison knew, deep down, that Joshua couldn't possibly be telling the truth about his surgery. Which would be harder for him to accept? Losing Joshua or losing the idea that he could trust him?

Guilt must have woken me up, because the alarm didn't ring and the campus outside was still cloaked in darkness. I took a short shower, threw on whatever clothes I could find, and took off running toward the gym. When I reached the squat brick building, I tried the door. Locked.

After maybe ten minutes of shivering, I'd convinced myself that Addison had given himself the morning off. Which meant the night before had been more difficult than I'd imagined. He never let himself sleep in.

As soon as that thought crossed my mind, Addison appeared at the top of the hill. He squinted toward me and I recognized worry wash over his face as he started sprinting in my direction.

"What's wrong?" he asked, breathless. "You okay? What's going on?"

"Nothing." He grabbed the upper part of my arm and looked more closely at me. "I just . . ." All of a sudden, I felt extremely stupid. Beyond useless. "I figured that last night was rough and so I wanted to check and make sure you were okay."

"Oh, kiddo." He pulled me closer to him. "Thanks. I'm good — I mean, I'm okay. Joshua and I had the chance to talk last night. He's at peace, you know. That doesn't mean our work levels off."

"Right." I felt caught then. Between just bursting out with it or waiting like Sophie and I promised each other we would. "Maybe it would help to talk about Joshua's condition with your team."

"You're my team."

"You know what I'm saying."

"I love your concern. And that you woke up early to come check on me. It's sweet." He said, "It's more than sweet. I feel blessed." Addison pushed me away slightly, so that he could look in my eyes. "That's all I need right now. Talking about it too much — that's going to make it real."

It probably wouldn't, I wanted to say. Nothing existed on the planet that would render Joshua's replacement pig-blood surgery real. But I'd already sworn not to say that. And Addison's face looked strained with exhaustion. His skin seemed yellow. The whole hospital thing was costing him. I knew Joshua had lied to him too. Maybe Addison had more blindly trusted in him, but that didn't make him our enemy — it made him more of a victim than anyone else.

But Addison didn't believing in being a victim. He pulled out a key from his pocket. Of course the fitness team had given Addison keys to the gym. He told me, "I'm going to go inside. Do you want to come work out?"

I wanted to follow him around, just to stay near him. But the one thing more pathetic than following along with the crazy cult leader who'd cast a spell on my boyfriend was following said boyfriend around the gym with a towel. He didn't need me right then. He needed to try to lift as many heavy things as possible, to show himself that he was strong enough to handle whatever the day threw at him.

"I don't want to cramp your beefcake style." Kissed him and sent him into the gym, which smelled like chlorine and stale socks. "Sophie will probably be at breakfast. I'll meet up with her. See you in class?"

"Sure — do you want me to walk Joshua to the hospital tonight?"

He asked like he was testing me. So I answered, "No way. If it's okay with you, I'd like to spend time with him, let him know how much he means to me." Addison smiled; I'd passed.

"Love you," he called after me.

By the time I got to breakfast, Sophie had already eaten two bowls of granola. She pounced when I mentioned my exchange with Addison. "So this is it, then. It's perfect." She pretended not to watch me carefully eat my cantaloupe and cottage cheese.

"What is?"

"We can follow him," Sophie said simply.

I put my fork down. "You can't follow someone into the hospital. There are laws against that." The old me would be rolling her eyes at this new me, worried about inconsequential things like getting arrested.

"Those laws probably don't apply to patients faking terminal illness."

"Sophie, I've done this before. I walk Joshua to the hospital. He's not kidding." She just smirked. "No, really. He might be lying about this operation. I get that. But he goes to the hospital."

"For his treatments?" Sophie still sounded dubious. "You walk him in and stand there while they hook him up to honest-to-God medical machinery?"

"Well, no. But I walk him to the outpatient clinic." She made a face. "What? You think he just sits there?"

"Maybe they have good magazines."

"That's nuts. Who does that?"

Sophie shrugged. She downed a glass of orange juice. "I'm just saying. An opportunity has presented itself. There's no logical reason why we wouldn't take advantage of it."

There was a reason flitting around my mind. I wasn't sure that I wanted to know for sure that Joshua was lying. Sophie sat across from me, though, daring me to move forward.

When Addison and I headed down the hill after dinner, I kept having to stop myself from turning around to check for Sophie following us. *Concentrate on him*, I told myself. That never used to be so difficult.

At the pizza place, Joshua stood up to greet us and I hugged him longer than usual. Then I slid into the booth, so I sat closest to the window and could watch for Sophie outside. We settled in and then Addison left to place our order at the counter. As soon as he was out of earshot, Joshua turned to me and said, "I need the truth."

My heart lurched and lunged. But Joshua only asked, "How is he?" He nodded toward the counter at Addison's hunched back. "Is this too much for him?"

"Addison's just fine. We're all surrounding him, supporting him." And then because Joshua looked so lost and lonely,

I made myself pat his hand. "And you too. Of course. In the same way, we're all here for you."

He waved my hand aside. "I don't expect you to understand this truth, but my sickness is actually Addison's trial. I am just a vessel — a body where this battle is happening. He had just reached a place of such peace and joy. You took him to that place, Elizabeth. And he'd built up his own strength so that he would not falter. So the universe had to test him through me."

"He's going to be back any minute." I tried to keep my voice light. "You know this kind of talk would upset him."

Joshua nodded. "How are you handling your truth?" I wished it were acceptable to ask which truth. Instead I nodded solemnly and waited for Joshua to follow up his cryptic question with another cryptic question. "Do you still feel closed in that room?"

"Some days." I didn't know for sure if he meant for me to say yes or no.

"You must keep fighting."

Addison slid into the booth across from us. "Fighting? Who does she need to fight? I'll kill 'em." He turned to Joshua. "I ordered you a salad. Get some healthy greens in that belly."

Joshua grimaced. "Brother, I don't know how many meals I've got left and you want me to waste one on a salad?"

"I ordered pizza too. Thin crust."

"I like the Sicilian."

"Try this kind."

Joshua rolled his eyes. "Greer, do I look fat?"

Addison shook his head. "It's not about fat, Joshua. Let's make some healthy choices."

"Greer will tell me if I need to eat salads. Right, sister? What have you done to this boy that he's talking about healthy choices? I want my meatballs, dammit."

"Give me one minute." Addison grinned. "I'll be right back with a big plate of leafy greens." Joshua and I sat there at the table, waiting. He drummed his fingers on the table.

"Maybe it's better to eat a light meal? Before treatment?"

"Are you my doctor? Did someone add an *MD* after your name?" Joshua spit out his words in sharp bursts.

"No, I just thought —"

"Well, don't think that hard." Addison walked up with a giant spinach salad on one plate just as I reeled from Joshua's venom. With a flourish, he deposited the plate in front of Joshua and headed back to the counter. It might have been funny, except Joshua looked ready to toss me through the plate-glass window.

I calculated the chances of vaulting over the table, past Joshua, and out the door. Slim to none. And then, slinking around the corner of the deli across the street, she appeared. Sophie leaned in the doorway like some kind of film-noir detective. She even wore a man's hat, with its brim tipped over her face. I almost laughed out loud, but Joshua was still glaring at me over a plate of spinach.

"Awwwww. You didn't think I was serious, did you? Slide the salad over to Greer Rabbit over there." Addison set down two plates of spaghetti and meatballs. Joshua's face brightened, but he didn't look sheepish or embarrassed. He glanced at me like he was checking to see if I planned to speak up. "Did somebody get a little cranky?"

I stared at Addison and he gazed back at me lovingly. He didn't seem to understand my telepathic message of *This man*

*scares me, please find a way to accept that he doesn't chan-
nel the voice of God so that we can maybe leave him at the
pizza place.* So I gave up and instead tried to concentrate on
the salad I didn't feel like eating, just so that I'd keep my eyes
from the window. That way, neither of them would turn to
see Sophie framed there.

"Greer's going to walk you to the hospital — I have
my men's health class." Joshua looked up, a strand of pasta
hanging from the corner of his mouth. I kept still, waiting for
Joshua to mention that I didn't have the necessary degree
for that kind of responsibility.

"You getting an A in man class?" Joshua liked to bust the
guys about that McCracken Hill tradition in particular.

"I don't know. Ask Greer."

"Shut up, meatball." I thought of Sophie waiting outside
and hoped she wasn't crazy enough to think that just her little hat would hide her. I tried to broker peace. "Joshua, I'm
happy to accompany you tonight, so that Addison can relearn
how to act like a gentleman."

"That sounds lovely." I couldn't detect a trace of anger
in Joshua's voice. By the time we rose to leave, I'd almost
convinced myself that I had imagined it. "Brother, thank
you for sharing these times with me." He stretched out
his arms to Addison. "You don't need a class to learn to
be a man."

"I know, but it's better to show up so they see that."

"That's my boy — learning to bide his time, playing by
their rules."

Addison leaned in to give my cheek a quick peck. "All
good?"

"We're good." He held on to my arm a bit longer than he
needed to and then gave us a little salute. When Addison

turned his back to walk back toward McCracken Hill, I tracked his progress for a second or two.

"I wonder if anyone has ever watched me the way you watch him." Joshua's voice broke in. "You don't even know how you drink him in — that would embarrass you."

I made myself smile. "We should get going, right? Your appointment is for eight thirty?"

"They can't start without me." But Joshua started shuffling along. He took my hand in his and held up our fingers intertwined. "You examine everyone closely, though, Elizabeth. That used to make me nervous. I felt that you were searching for flaws. But now I think distrust is just your way."

"It's isn't, though."

"Don't argue just to argue. Search your heart. What are your intentions when you direct your gaze? You look out at the world and scrutinize every word and gesture. I feel your eyes on me." Joshua gripped my hand so hard that the bones ached.

"No. It's just that you have us all so worried," I told him.

It sounded lame. We walked a few more steps before he spoke again. "It's funny to me." Joshua drifted into silence, and at first, I thought he forgot his own fragment of wisdom. But eventually, as we closed in on the brick high-rise ahead of us, Joshua pointed out, "When you feel threatened, you use the plural. You say *we* or *us*, like you're gathering the troops behind you. I'm glad they make you feel safe. But they are, in fact, my troops. Do you understand that?"

I understood that Joshua had buried a warning beneath that surface and that I wouldn't even have to dig too deep to uncover it. But I also knew something that Joshua did not —

Sophie lurked behind me and she was certainly not fighting on his side. Really, the only person he had left was Addison.

So I said, "Of course," and let him think what he wanted. "Are they painful — your treatments?"

Joshua sighed. "Nothing I can't handle. I think of you all and that helps me endure." He looked up to the building. "The worst part is the temptation — they could give me drugs. To take the edge off a little. But I burned that bridge a while back."

"I could sit with you."

"And hold my hand?" Joshua raised up our clasped hands.

"Yeah. Sure. Or just sit there so you're not alone." I made sure to underline my voice with an air of rebelliousness. "I don't even care if I get in trouble for missing sign-in time."

"Well, you should. That's the drug you're working to give up — trouble." Joshua nodded. "But I thank you, Elizabeth. You are my angel, you know. It's enough that you deliver me." He stopped at the hospital entrance. The sliding glass doors slid open behind him. "Thank you."

"I'll come up." My heart picked up its pace. Before, I'd walked Joshua into the lobby, to the reception desk. That's what Sophie and I had planned on.

"That will tempt me to ask you to stay." Joshua leaned down and kissed my cheek. He murmured, "Examine your intentions."

My heart skipped into a full sprint then. "What do you mean?" I looked Joshua in the eye, but he just raised his hand up and stepped backward through the doors. I stood there, waiting for him to turn and walk into the heart of the hospital.

"Follow him," Sophie hissed from behind the thick hedge along the circular drive. She scared me so much, I almost yelped out loud.

"Are you crazy? He knows you're here." I turned to see one of her sneakered feet step out of the greenery. "No way. Get back."

"Where is he?"

"I can't see him. He walked past the front desk. Sophie, I really think he saw you." I scanned the lobby with a look of concern pasted on my face, as if I just wanted to make sure he arrived safely. Just in case he'd turned back. But he hadn't. He'd vanished. I couldn't even tell which direction he'd gone.

"Go inside and ask at the front desk. Say your uncle forgot to tell you what time to pick him up."

"No way. What if he just stopped at the bathroom or something?"

"God. You're impossible. This whole thing is pointless if we don't track him." Sophie emerged from the bushes and grabbed my arm. "C'mon. Quick — let's go." She dragged me and we ran toward the back of the building. It was farther than it looked — the length of the playing field at my old school. Once we turned the corner, though, she blocked me with her arm. "Stop, stop, stop." Sophie leaned down with her hands on her knees, wheezing. We hung back in the shadows cast by the building.

"Dude, you're nuts. And I think he saw us —"

Sophie thwacked her arm across my chest. "Shut up. Look. At. The. Taxi. Stand."

In the middle of the lot stood a little booth and a line of cabs snaked behind it. On a folding chair next to the booth, a man sat reading a newspaper.

Joshua was leaning against the first cab, with his arms folded, as if annoyed to wait. Another man jogged out of the booth. He called out to Joshua and Joshua nodded. They both smiled at each other and laughed. Joshua made a motion like he was tapping his finger against an invisible wristwatch. As the man approached, Joshua slid over, opened the door, and climbed into the cab's backseat. The driver scrambled into the seat ahead of him. At the top of the cab, the IN SERVICE light flipped on, and Sophie and I pressed ourselves as close as possible to the building. I felt bricks digging in my back.

I remember thinking, *Wow. That treatment doesn't take long at all.* Stupidly. Before all the pieces settled in place and I understood that Joshua had taken just enough time to walk through the first floor of the hospital, past the lobby and the clinic, and out the back door to the taxi stand. That the cab driver greeted him out of familiarity, because every night that Addison or I walked him here, thinking we were delivering him to some excruciating cure, he walked straight through the hospital and into the back parking lot to catch a cab home.

"Holy crap." Sophie's voice sounded like thin metal bending toward me — tinny and hollow. "So that's Joshua's treatment. I knew it, but I didn't know it. You know, I had a hunch and so I figured we should check back here but I still didn't expect . . ." Sophie kept babbling and I half-listened. I couldn't look away from the red glow of the cab's taillights. I stood there next to Sophie. Silent, shivering, hypnotized by Joshua driving away.

TWENTY-ONE

The crappy part of knowing about Joshua's hospital hoax was knowing Addison would never believe me. "We should have taken pics," Sophie had said while we trudged home.

At that point, I couldn't even get words out. I just nodded and grunted and tried to fight down the panic rising in my chest. "I just don't get the point, you know?" Sophie waited for me to grunt back. "He has nothing better to do than to fake terminal illness?"

I got the point. The minute we saw Addison the next morning, he asked how Joshua seemed the night before. "Do you think he's getting any stronger?" Addison cracked his knuckles. "I don't see a difference, really. But his appetite's back. That's something." Sophie glanced at me.

"Maybe we could schedule a meeting?" I suggested. "With Joshua's doctors?" Addison's face clouded. "It would help us support his recovery more if we had a clearer picture of what he needed." Sophie nodded vigorously beside me.

"He's not going to go for that," Addison said. "Joshua doesn't want to worry us." I tried to steady my eyes from rolling.

"Yeah, but look how worn out you are," Sophie told Addison, so I didn't have to.

"It's nothing." Addison shook off her sympathy. "Think of what Joshua's going through."

I needed to keep reminding myself: *Addison thinks Joshua saved him.* Whatever lies followed, that was the one indisputable truth. And it made everything else harder.

Joshua had taken to walking with a cane. He kept a little pill case with colored caplets distributed in each tiny plastic compartment. He trotted that out when we circled up after the boys' Tuesday night NA meeting. I leaned in closer, expecting them to be Tic Tacs. But they were actual pills. I thought maybe we'd get lucky and he'd overdose on aspirin. "Elizabeth, could you rub my throat for me, please?" he asked me when he caught me watching him swallow the little row of pills.

"I'm sorry — what's that?" I thought I misheard him but he craned his neck back, baring the dark arc of his throat.

"Just massage there, right by my Adam's apple." He pointed to the spot. I reached out and placed my palm carefully against his throat. It crossed my mind then — *I could tighten my grip and strangle him.* Instead I felt him swallow. "I take so many of these. Not so easy to get down." When Joshua spoke, his skin hummed lightly.

"What are they?" I tried to sound casual.

"Just something the specialist prescribed for nausea." When I stopped rubbing, Joshua grabbed my hand. "You have healing powers. Do you believe that about yourself?" I shrugged. He said, "Better than anything pharmaceutical." I felt my eyes darting around, avoiding contact with his gaze. He held up my hand to examine it. "I feel fortunate. What other patient has access to an angel?"

My ears went hot with embarrassment. Joshua looked past me to the others in the room — Addison, Sophie, Jared, and Hannah. "I need to make a request to stretch my fortune. Do you understand what I'm asking for? Sophia?"

Sophie's voice sounded sour. "A return to the wilderness." I tried to coax her with my eyes. *Sweeten it up, Soph.* But Joshua noticed.

"Why does that inspire anger in you, Sophia?" My belly knotted up, sure she would spill everything. Jared even stepped forward, as if he too thought Hurricane Sophie was ready to blow. But she caught herself and even mustered up the strength to tell him, "I just fret about you a little bit." Somewhere, Sophie had sprouted a little twang. "Your immune system must be so darn compromised."

"And if anything should happen up there," I tried to help, "who would we call for help?"

Joshua pouted. He called out to Addison, "Brother, I have been envisioning a ceremony. Now, I don't know if it will be a farewell ceremony, but I'd like the chance to gather us under the big sky one last time." Joshua glared up at the light fixtures as if they hid surveillance cameras. "Away from prying eyes."

"We can find our own place here." I kept my voice firm and held Addison's eyes. "No one wants Joshua to put himself in harm's way for our sake."

Hannah stepped forward and ducked under Joshua's arms. "But we appreciate the spirit of your sacrifice." He crumpled a little, then slumped in his seat. Hannah had begun to speak his language.

Joshua shook his head sadly. "I don't know who gave you all permission to have such little faith. You all are stingy with your beliefs."

"We worry. We love you and so we worry." When Addison said that, it seemed to calm him.

"Let me just make a humble request that you all share your strength with me. I will keep fighting, if you surround me with your resilience. Our world might have tried to discard us, but we will return in triumph." I watched Addison's head bob up and down. Hannah wiped tears from her eyes. Sophie sat in stony silence. She met my eyes and then mustered a vigorous nod.

Later, in her room when it was just the two of us, Sophie tried to explain. "I just can't," she told me. "Sitting there and listening to him spew all his bullshit about sacrifice and suffering — doesn't that infuriate you? How can you let him get away with it?"

"We're not letting him get away with it. That's the whole point, right?"

"Yeah, sure. We'll track the cracktard's movements, get telescopic lens photos that spell out his total sham of a terminal illness, and then what? We confront him and then look at that — we'll be discarded like Wes. Or maybe Addison won't be subtle about it this time. He'll just physically hurt us."

"Shut up. You're talking about Addison."

"I'm talking about a guy who's admitted to violently assaulting someone. You don't think that confession was designed to intimidate us? I, for one, intend to protect myself from here on in."

"Stop it. It's Addison. If anything, he meant us to understand that he'd protect us. He's on our side."

"As long as we're on Joshua's. I don't mean to insult your blow-job skills, but you might be overestimating them a little bit, lady."

"Awesome. Really. There's actually a little more between me and Addison. He'll believe us because he trusts us. At the same time, we're toppling his idol, you know? So we need hard evidence. And maybe more time to gather it. We can't do that with a target on our back. Joshua needs to believe we're complacent."

"He doesn't. You heard him today."

"Because you keep challenging him. All you need to do is sit there and look sad. Furrow your brow. Throw a little concern his way."

"Greer, I'm telling you I can't lie like you."

An accusation sat there between us, although Sophie pretended otherwise. "So that's my superpower? Lying? Or is it tied between lies and blow jobs?"

"Okay, I didn't say that. But it seems like you're able to compartmentalize. You sit there with Joshua and play the part of the ardent believer." She looked away from me then. "It just freaks me out to see how good you are at it."

Really, it isn't much different from stealing, I wanted to tell her. You just act as if you should own whatever it is you're walking out with and then you do. Or how, afterward, my family all managed to sit steadily at the same dining room table where my cousin held us at gunpoint — you passed along the dish of mashed potatoes like nothing happened, until it felt as if it didn't. In the back of my mind, I knew Joshua had just wandered into our lives through the back door of a Narcotics Anonymous meeting. If he hadn't met Addison at a desperate moment, he would have just been another old creep who tried to strike up a conversation at the coffee shop.

But that's not how it happened. So in the front of my mind, I kept Joshua perched on a throne and made sure to frequently genuflect. I saw all of us as if we'd been positioned on a stage. Yeah, I played the part.

"I don't believe in church either," I tried to explain. "Those are rituals too. My parents believe in them so I went through the motions. Right? Why wouldn't I do the same thing for Addison? He's done more for me than —"

"I know. Joshua's gone off the rails, though," Sophie reminded me. I just nodded. We hadn't been debating that. "He's a really sick man. Really, he scares the hell out of me."

We just sat there in silence then, leaning against the flimsy bed. And then almost dove underneath it when Sophie's door swung open. "What the hell?" Sophie yelled, probably expecting an invasion from Jenn Sharpe, blogger to the scars.

"It's okay, it's okay," Addison whispered as quickly as he slipped through the door. "Shhh — you don't want to make too much noise." Sophie's eyes widened more and I could tell she did want to make a whole lot of noise. Even I felt like I'd been kicked in the chest or something. How long had he been standing outside that door?

"Shh — please?" Addison pleaded with Sophie and looked to me for help. "I just need Greer. I need to talk to Greer." He didn't look right. His face was strained and his eyes kept darting around the room. He raised a hand to rub them and I noticed blood on his knuckles. I stood up and Sophie grabbed my ankle.

"What's going on, Addison?" I tried to keep my voice light and calm.

"Can we go outside?"

"No!" Sophie pretty much screamed it, and Addison and I both turned to shush her.

"It's almost lights-out, buddy. Right? It's pretty dicey that you're even in the dorm. Ms. Crane will lose her shit." I stepped forward and felt Sophie's grip tighten. I looked down just for a second, to shake her off, to say *stop*. Or *don't worry*. But right then Addison grabbed my arm and tugged me toward the door. I stood there, caught between them.

"I just need to talk to you. Five minutes." Addison's voice choked, like he was trying not to cry. I reached out for his hand, glanced down at Sophie, and nodded. He said, "I couldn't find you." And then Addison seemed to remember Sophie. "Sorry. I couldn't find Greer."

He held up his hand and examined the palm.

"Other side," she barked.

"Oh. I . . ." He closed his eyes, hung his head down. Sophie stared meaningfully at me. Addison's shoulders heaved. "I'm ashamed." For a second, I flashed back to Addison up at the Delias' cabin, how his voice shook as he spoke about kicking that kid in the face. "I got so angry, just fed up about how unfair the whole thing is. I punched the wall." He looked up at me. "A granite wall. Like some cliché. I'm such an idiot."

"No," I said, even as Sophie muttered, "Yeah." She added, "You're both idiots, and you're going to get caught shacking up in my room."

"Five minutes?" he asked again. "I'll go out first. Wait a minute or two and follow close behind. Try to keep me in sight." He glanced at Sophie and seemed to realize how little she trusted him. "Thanks, Soph. Sorry to bother you." But Addison didn't sound sorry. He opened the door just a sliver before darting out into the hall.

"Greer," Sophie warned. But he was already halfway to the stairwell, confident that I'd trail behind him. So I rushed to catch up.

I know plenty about the decisive glide of the up-to-no-good. How you sacrifice the slightest bit of speed for a lot of silence. You stare at some fixed point straight ahead, as if you could stop to explain yourself, but that might distract you from your focused purpose. Addison was a ninja, though. He pretty much floated through the female dorm right before lights-out, while most girls were trekking to and from the showers with their dopey plastic buckets of face soap and toothpaste. Just following in his wake, I felt unseen.

From the top of the steps, I saw him kneel down and whip out a roll of electrical tape from his pocket. Addison looked once each way while he tore off a piece and taped over the lock to the building's entrance. By the time I reached him, he stood up. He reached behind me to make sure the door shut softly behind us.

"You sure it will hold?" I asked, imagining what would happen if we got locked out of our dorms overnight.

"Positive," Addison said.

"Where are we going?" But he didn't answer. We kept up the brisk pace until we found the little bridge by the dining hall. Addison jumped down; pebbles scattered where he landed. He reached up and helped me hop down too.

"It's okay, here?" But Addison just sat down in the spot closest to the building's wall. The cement footbridge cast a shadow topped with the dark bars of the wrought-iron railing. He took my hand and guided me to sit beside him.

"It's fine, but stay as close to the wall as possible." He pulled out his cell phone and cupped his hand around the lit screen.

"How often do you do this?" But Addison just stared at me.

"It's happening tonight."

"What is?" At first, I thought he meant his release from McCracken Hill. Because that's what I was most afraid of.

"The surgery. The beeper went off at Sal's when I was getting him food."

"Did you hear it go off?"

But Addison hurtled right past that question. "We left right then and I walked him to the hospital."

"They didn't send an ambulance to pick him up?"

"Joshua wanted to spend the time together. But then he wouldn't let me stay."

"Listen — if we explained to the dean — someone would probably even wait with you if you didn't want to be alone at the hospital. I could go —" I moved to my knees, to stand, but Addison dragged me back.

"Get down." He huddled beside me. He leaned his face against mine and I felt tears. "Joshua doesn't want me there."

It was crucial to press ever so gently. "Really? Maybe he just didn't want to ask? Did you speak to his doctor?"

"No. He didn't even let me walk him into admissions. We went to the chapel and said a prayer there. Then he walked me back to the lobby." Addison covered his eyes with one hand, gripped his cell with the other. "I walked back myself. You know — the whole time thinking, *they're prepping him now, they're wheeling him around into the operating room. He's going to text.*" He waved the phone.

"When he's done? When he wakes up?"

"No. Beforehand."

I didn't understand. I waited for Addison to explain, but then the phone trembled in his hand. He drew me closer with his other arm so that I could see the text too. Getting ready. Reflecting on Brother Jared. "Wait. Joshua's texting now?"

"He said he would." Addison sighed. "He wants to have each of us on his mind. Remember? Greer, he explained this."

"Right, but they're letting him use his phone? After he's been put under anesthesia?" I tried to sound more surprised than dubious.

But Addison still heard the doubt edging my question and he bristled. "He's all alone there. Who else does he have?" The phone shuddered again. "Sophie. He's reaching out for her wisdom." Addison bit his lip, nodded to himself. His breath whistled with suppressed sobs. I tried to stop myself from picturing Joshua in the coffee shop. Probably he'd stepped out of a cab minutes before. He'd settled in somewhere, poured a cup of tea, and then began emotionally torturing my boyfriend.

Another text arrived. "Hannah," I said.

Addison smiled at me, pleased that I remembered how Joshua had ranked us. He said, "I wish we could all gather together, to wait. For Joshua's sake, you know? But I couldn't get to everyone. And maybe it's selfish, but I'd rather just sit here with you."

A few miles away, Joshua sat on some sinking sofa, casually typing. I forced myself to focus on Addison — right in front of me, more scared than I'd ever seen him. "I love you," I told him. Usually we didn't say it so baldly. There was usually a joke attached or even the remnants of some fight. "It's going to be okay."

He assumed I meant Joshua. "The surgery itself will take four hours and then he'll be in recovery for one night and on a regular floor for six more. If everything goes okay." Addison stared at the quiet phone. "It's been a while now." The phone leapt a little, like it had been listening.

He tipped the screen so I could read it. I whispered, "Tell Elizabeth, remember the star."

"It must be the anesthesia. It's affecting him now." Addison examined the message more closely. "Remember the star?"

"I don't know what he means." It felt like I'd failed at something.

"Maybe 'remember the scar'? The 'stare'?"

I shook my head. "We'll have to ask him when he wakes up." It felt dangerous to ask, also necessary. "You don't think it's strange that they'd allow Joshua to send text messages while he's actually in the operating room?" Addison's head reared back and I braced myself for his temper, but then the phone shivered in his hand once more.

We read Joshua's message together: Addison, brother, you are my greatest gift to the world. Be brave. Embody integrity and know that I love y. "He must have passed out then." I stopped myself from pointing out the convenience of Joshua's pristine spelling. Addison gripped my hand. "You think he just passed out? He didn't — it doesn't mean that he — we haven't lost him. Right?"

"No way." At least I could be sure of that. I wrapped my arms around him and felt his sobs break across his whole body. Addison moaned and wept while I sat and kept watch and silently swore that somehow I'd find a way to stop Joshua.

TWENTY-TWO

Sixteen days later, Hannah asked Sophie and me back to her dorm room after dinner. She sat us down on her bed and pulled up her desk chair to face us. I expected her to launch into a lecture about renewed faith or sharing strength or something.

We'd scattered briefly for the single week McCracken Hill stingily allotted for winter break. Jared went home for Christmas; Sophie met Josie and an aunt and uncle for a ski trip to Vermont. Addison decided to stay close to Joshua. And I decided to stay close to Addison. That and my parents and sister went to Europe without me. "Eliza's deeply interested in the London School of Economics," my father crackled through the speakerphone during our December family session. He didn't even offer to bring me. Maybe my mom had convinced him I'd steal the crown jewels or something.

Instead, I got to spend Christmas Eve with Addison, eating Chinese takeout with about two dozen other extreme cases at McCracken Hill. Mr. Mikkelsen and Coach Tyson stayed too, and for that whole week we gathered in the faculty lounge instead of the dining hall. We played board games and watched cartoon specials and *Judge Judy* reruns. Addison and I sometimes escaped by pacing around campus, just like we had that first night we'd spent together. He checked in with Joshua on the phone a lot, but we couldn't always slip out to town and that was a relief — to not always have a destination. To not always need to punctuate the night at Sal's Pizzeria, facing off with Joshua. It was heaven. Like the Poconos retreat, but without the religious indoctrination.

A week after his "surgery," I'd gone with Addison to pick up Joshua from a bench outside of the hospital. Afterward, when everyone returned, we'd all gathered twice to celebrate his astonishing survival. Joshua occasionally demanded coddling before his stint as a medical miracle, but afterward, he would barely walk by himself. He used a cane all of the time now and called over Addison to help him rise from his chair. He drank from a straw or had Hannah lift the mug of tea to his lips.

Sophie could barely sit through it all, and knowing how she felt about my performance as the best apostle ever made me self-conscious. So we busied ourselves brewing coffee or buzzing around like diner waitresses on Sunday morning. Sophie showed up late and apologized. I left early, claiming meetings with my treatment team. I knew we were only biding our time. Joshua would call us out in some kind of spectacular fashion.

Hannah had gone home for the holidays. She came back early and didn't speak for three days. So when she finally asked us back to her room, I felt reassured. Partly because she was talking again. And partly because I thought maybe Joshua's big confrontation would be that quiet. He wouldn't want to make a scene in front of Addison. So he'd asked Hannah to bring us back into the fold. I waited with the same look fixed on my face that had been there for months. Patient belief. Ready inspiration. And then Hannah said, "I might be pregnant."

Even with the *might*, it counted as one of the most definitive statements I'd ever heard Hannah make. She didn't sound panicked or fearful. She sounded hollow.

Sophie was the one who sounded panicked and fearful. "What are you talking about?" And then, "Hannah?" I watched the door, half-expecting to see Ms. Crane standing there. Maybe the whole thing was a setup, meant to fulfill a role-play requirement for healthy communication or something. But, nope. The white door stared blankly back at me. And Hannah stared also. Earnestly.

"My period's late and my breasts feel . . . kind of sore."

Sophie recovered a little. "Well, that could be stress or even the flu, really. You shouldn't worry yet. Any number of things could throw off your hormones."

"Including pregnancy," Hannah interrupted. She tugged on her earlobe and looked up at us. "Guys. It's not like I haven't been through this before. I can tell." She looked away and then back at us. "I can just tell."

"Whose is it?" Sophie asked.

And Hannah answered as if insulted. "Well, Joshua's." As in, *Obviously.* And then I ran out to the bathroom and didn't even reach a stall. I had to puke in the sink.

No one came chasing after me. That's what happens when one of your only friends announces your fake spiritual guru has impregnated her. No one has time to follow you to the ladies' room to hold your hair back while you vomit. Even after I doused my face with cool water and returned to the room, Sophie didn't even bother to feign concern. She tried to lighten up the mood and said, "Greer will grab any excuse to puke dinner after pasta night."

"Unwarranted," I declared. But judging by the stifling

vibe in the room, we hadn't yet moved into the realm of light-hearted banter. "Hannah, I'm really sorry. You just surprised me and the shock made me . . . shaky for a second or two."

Hannah nodded. Offending my delicate digestive tract hovered on the bottom half of her priorities. I wondered if this part felt familiar to her. Sitting someone down and confessing about the missed period, the slow-building panic. I felt myself sway a little and for one heinous moment thought I'd actually pass out — that's what most guardian angels do, I'm sure. Joshua would expect me to be supportive and reassuring. That was my first thought: that I had to work to keep my status as resident angel. Sophie patted the mattress next to her and I moved unsteadily over to her side. Hannah's eyes darted between us. "You're both really freaked out."

"Well, yeah," Sophie said. I let her explain as I fought down another bout of nausea. "I mean, you can see why we'd be freaked out, right? Did he . . ." Sophie's eyes begged mine for help. "Hannah, did he hurt you?"

"God, no. Joshua would never do that. How could you even ask that?" She hopped out of her chair and onto the cot beside us. "You're so quick to judge him, Sophie. When you let doubt seed your heart, it takes root. You never demonstrated your faith, and we can all tell. There's a difference in how you treat him."

"Well, some seeds are taking root, all right," I muttered.

Sophie glared at me. She spoke to Hannah carefully. "I hear you, Hannah, about having faith, but I'm wondering how you interpreted welcoming Joshua into your bed."

I broke in with, "It was a trust exercise. The point of which was that Joshua wouldn't touch you." That earned me another look from Sophie, who acted as if I'd just slipped Hannah an answer on a test.

"I don't understand." Hannah's voice crept higher. "You welcome his spirit."

Sophie chose her words precisely. "By sex, Hannah? Is that how he told you to show your belief?" She looked confused.

All of a sudden, I understood. If running out of the room to hurl wasn't so offensive, I probably would have tried it again. Just to get out of that room and the choking awareness that I'd played a part in Joshua's manipulation.

"You knew Joshua had spent the night in my room?" I asked. Hannah looked toward me and nodded, almost grate-fully. "So you figured, even though maybe it weirded you out when he asked, that I had also . . . complied." Sophie exhaled loudly. Hannah kept staring. "Maybe he even implied that he had touched me." I remembered standing outside the bed-room door at Sophie's cabin. I'd heard Hannah sobbing and hadn't even knocked on the door.

Reaching out to grab both Hannah's hands in mine felt awkward and stupid. But I felt like she needed something to anchor her. When I started to say, "Joshua slept in my bed . . ." she knew before I finished my sentence. Hannah went very still, and when I told her, "but we never had sex," it seemed like my words blew past her in a gust. Her face rippled.

I braced myself for Hannah's inevitable breakdown, but instead it was Sophie. It seemed like our cool, calm queen of sass suddenly left the building. She'd buried her head in her hands. "Jesus Christ. Jesus Christ," she kept saying. "So he's a rapist too. We're dealing with some psycho rapist. Did he threaten you, Hannah? Jesus Christ."

I tried to maneuver an arm to elbow Sophie without let-ting go of Hannah's hands. "Shut up," I mouthed at her. She needed to keep it together. Hysterics were as useless at that point as chucking in the sink.

Hannah finally tore her hands from me. She wiped them on her jeans as if she'd been contaminated. "Joshua did not rape me." Her voice quivered and then steadied. Sophie still had her arms wrapped around her head, so Hannah glowered at me. "You don't throw words like that around."

"Well —" I tried to phrase my words just right, but Hannah wasn't having it.

"You don't."

"He manipulated you." Sophie looked up and revealed a face streaked with tears. "You see that, right? He's older than you and holds some place of authority in your life. He tricked you and made you believe that it was some kind of ritual —"

"It *was* a ritual," Hannah argued.

"No. No, Hannah. A ritual is dunking someone in water or singing 'Happy Birthday.' Tapping the roof of the car when you blow through a red light — that would qualify as a ritual. He's fashioned himself as some sort of spiritual leader. And then he controlled you. That's rape."

"I knew what I was doing." Hannah crossed her arms over her chest. "Just like you knew what you were doing with Jared and Greer knew what it meant when Joshua assigned her to sleep in the same room with Addison that weekend."

"Okay — that's not exactly the same thing —"

"Sure it is. You hadn't had sex with Addison before that weekend, had you?" Hannah tilted her chin up in a challenge when she asked the question. I couldn't see where she was headed. I couldn't even catch my breath yet to think things through. What were we arguing about anyway?

"No. But —"

"So why did you?"

"Hannah, this isn't important right now —"

"It is. It so is. Why did you decide to do it that weekend?"

My eyes snuck to Sophie. "Well, we had the room to our-selves. And I felt this distance. I wanted — well, you know, I wanted to be sure of him."

Hannah threw up her hands, like, *There you go.* "I wanted to be sure of Joshua too."

I looked down and realized I'd been chewing on my fin-gernails. The truth was that none of the words the two of them were choosing seemed to ring as particularly well adjusted. Hannah acted as if she couldn't afford to think of Joshua as a predator. And Sophie seemed like she saw the whole thing as completely cut-and-dry. It was hazier than that. I felt like everything was crumbling around me. I couldn't find my footing.

Sophie scooted to the back of the cot and leaned against the wall. She looked as if she wished she could just tunnel right out of Hannah's room. "It's not the same, Hannah. Maybe it helps to tell yourself that. But he let you believe that Greer did the same thing. That's dishonest. So if the whole point was to feel closer to each other . . . well, he based that on a false premise. So it can't count."

Hannah leveled an irritated look. "Okay, well, I'm still pregnant. Does that count?"

"Of course it does." I rushed to fix it. Sent Sophie another secret stare message. *If we let Hannah down, we'll send her straight to Joshua.* I'd already ignored her once when she needed my help. Had I just knocked on the bedroom door, we might not even be in this situation. "Have you told him?" At first, I couldn't even say his name. "Have you told Joshua?"

Hannah shook her head. "He has enough going on. And . . ." She trailed off miserably.

"What?"

"He asked about the possibility." Hannah chewed her lip. "You know? He asked but I told him there wasn't any."

I blinked. It still didn't compute.

Hannah sighed. Sophie translated. "She said she was on the pill." *Well, of course she had been on the pill,* I thought to myself. Hannah had already dealt with one unplanned pregnancy. Her doctor or her mom, someone would have made sure that she protected herself. My sister was a sanctimonious twat, but when she first saw a hickey on my neck, she left a box of condoms in my backpack. Maybe as a passive-aggressive jab, but at least they came in handy. I remembered chasing Hannah out into the woods that weekend, her tear-streaked confession. It's not like she could have blocked out the reality of that first pregnancy in the nights right after. You can't muster up that kind of denial.

"Why?"

"He wouldn't have otherwise. That time would have passed and it seemed like the universe meant for me to prove myself," Hannah whimpered. "And now it might change everything. What if he gets mad? Or what if the dean finds out and sends me somewhere else?"

We tried to talk her down from that. Sophie and I ticked through all the reasons Joshua couldn't be angry, how Hannah really needed to allow herself some space to be self-centered right then. We decided that we needed to walk to town and get a stick test first. Then once we had a definite answer, we'd figure things out from there. Together.

Hannah looked up and smiled at that last part.

During dinner that night, I begged off going to see Joshua. I knew that looked sketchy. Since Sophie and I had spied on him, it had become more and more difficult to sit across from Joshua, to listen to him lecture about the power of integrity and extraordinary possibility. And Joshua felt my pulling away. He'd started whispering to me as he hugged me good-bye. "Elizabeth," he'd murmur in my ear, "why is your star fading? You're traveling so far away from me."

When I whispered to Addison that Hannah, Sophie, and I needed to work on a project together, he paused and looked at me carefully. "What kind of project?" Addison was a terrible actor. I could tell he had meant it to come out casually.

"Women's health initiative." That sounded like a class McCracken would make us take.

"Yeah? What's that?"

"It's just like man class. Gender responsibility stuff. We have to buy a pregnancy test." The best way to lie is to tell as much of the truth as possible.

Addison set down his glass. "Whoa, Greer." His ruddy face had drained of its color.

"No!" I almost shouted it. Sophie glanced up from her table. The other kids assigned to ours looked either smug or uncomfortable. The power couple of group therapy was arguing again. "No." I turned down my volume. "It's not that."

"Because we were careful," Addison whispered to me.

"Right."

"You're sure? Because I would have known, right? If there was anything to worry about."

It's weird the things you remember. Because just then I found myself thinking about the deft way Addison handled condoms. No big deal afterward. He'd just slip the thing off and tie a quick knot. Maybe that's a gross thing to admire, but I have more trouble tying my shoes. Anyway, I remember after we first had sex, I saw him conduct condom detail and thought that Addison must be some kind of sexpert. Even more so than me and that made me oddly sad. There was so much about him I didn't know.

"I'm positive," I told him. "Nothing to worry about." My throat ached. It never occurred to me that Addison might know that Joshua had slept with Hannah Green. It hurt to keep the secret from him, to think that Sophie and I were building a case against the one person in whom Addison had found shelter.

"Maybe we should go spend time with your parents?" I blurted it out. I meant: *I want to know that someone else loves you.*

Addison looked around, like I'd embarrassed him. "What are you talking about?"

"They're close by, that's all. If you don't want me to meet Chuckie — that's fine. But maybe they could visit here. Or just meet us for breakfast. We don't have to tell them that Joshua's sick or anything —"

"Yeah, no." Addison's voice could have hammered a nail into a board. "Thanks, though." I pushed the food around my plate with my fork, feeling ill and not at all hungry. "You need to eat that." He spoke more gently. He always spoke gently to me about food. "We could all walk to town together."

Maybe it makes me manipulative, but I saw an exit strategy and took it. Faked that I felt hurt that he wouldn't introduce me to the folks. *"Yeah, no,"* I mimicked, and then, because I didn't want to start a real fight, I added, "You don't want me to be that girl, dragging her boyfriend into CVS to buy pregnancy tests."

"Nope. And no one wants to be the guy buying the First Response either."

"You even know the brand!" I pretended to pretend to be scandalized. Really, I was a little scandalized.

Addison said loudly, for the whole table to hear, "I might even have a coupon in one of my issues of *Seventeen*." He thought that would shock people. I should have advised him that we had plenty of other material to trot out for dinner-table shock value.

Somehow we skated through without having a real fight. Addison sat with me until I finished eating and even carried my tray to the kitchen. I watched Ms. Ling watch us and scribble something into her little notepad. I'd probably end up having to talk about my adherence to archaic gender roles because I had let my boyfriend carry my tray.

"Joshua will miss seeing you," he told me.

"Oh, I'll miss him too. But he'll be glad we're having girl time." We walked out, but Addison steered me around the corner, to the vestibule by the science wing. I took advantage of the extra time together and tried to gather some facts. "Hey, how does he think Hannah's doing?" Very subtle.

Addison had tipped my chin up and reached his hand to rest on the back of my head. Midswoop, his faced reared back. "What?"

"I just wondered if he said anything?"

Addison kissed me and then pulled me even closer against him. "I don't remember."

I held him off for a second to ask, "Really? He'd been so worried that she didn't feel comfortab —"

Addison sighed. "I don't even remember who Hannah is right now."

"Add —" I pushed him away, but only lightly.

"Shhhhh," he told me. And we kissed until we heard the *clang* of pots and pans in the kitchen. That meant the cleanup crew had started dish duty and if either of us planned to head off campus, we needed to move it along.

Heading off campus with Hannah gave me a chance to exercise my new resolve to be a more patient person. Sophie and I had grown used to our nightly expeditions. We slipped through the gates and assumed the blustery pace of the McCracken sneak — head down, hands in our pockets, walking swiftly as if we had an extremely important appointment. Hannah basically crept on tiptoe like a cartoon character. "Hannah, really, it's just not a big deal," I said. She rushed to keep up, her eyes sliding around like she was waiting to hear sirens. "We signed out."

"We signed out to the coffee shop."

True. Most nights we signed out to the coffee shop. It should have gotten some kind of subsidy from McCracken, really. Whenever our treatment teams gave us the chance to walk to town, they suggested the coffee shop as our destination. Apparently, that's what healthy, well-adjusted teens were supposed to do — go to Common Grounds and sip soy lattes and consider community service opportunities.

"So are we going to stop there?"

I didn't like Common Grounds. It smelled fake, for one thing, like a limited-edition Febreze scent: Colombian Free Trade. Inevitably, some sad member of the faculty sat there — maybe keeping tabs on us, maybe just living out his or her own desperate existence. And either the men leered or the women glared at us for taking up the comfy chairs. So I said, "We don't have to stop there."

Hannah paused. Completely. She stopped walking and everything. Sophie tugged her forward. "Do you want coffee?"

"I don't want to get in trouble. Maybe someone's waiting to check that we actually get to where we've signed out."

"That's the least of our troubles now, right?" As soon as I said it, Sophie glared at me. I would have too, because it set Hannah off on a tear.

"Yeah. I mean, that's right. What will they do? And I won't tell them." She turned to Sophie. "You don't have to worry — I won't say anything about where — where it happened." She grabbed my arm. "If Addison's worried, I would never get Joshua in trouble. I just won't tell them anything."

"I didn't say anything to Addison."

Hannah looked surprised. "Really? Does he know, do you think? About me and Joshua?"

"Of course not," I told her. I told myself that Addison would have told me. Or consulted me somehow. "After our time at the cabin — did anything else happen? Between you and Joshua?"

"You mean sexual?" she asked. I tried not to cringe. "No. We weren't really alone much. And then Joshua's illness took a turn for the worse." Sophie and I glanced at each other. Hannah veered off topic. "I don't want to go for coffee. You're right. I mean, who cares. What can they do? Give me a kitchen-duty detention?"

"Exactly." So instead, we were just three wild and crazy kids, shopping in CVS. Someday I want to work at a pharmacy, just to see if they train employees to make teenaged

girls as uncomfortable as possible when they dare to pur-
chase pregnancy test kits. The three of us browsed the aisle
together. A balding man with a manager tag moseyed up to
ask if we needed any assistance.

Hannah appeared to suffer a seizure. I gave him my flat,
would-you-like-me-to-seduce-you look. "No. We don't need
your help."

"Okay, ladies. Well, we'll just look out in case it turns out
you could use the advice of a sales associate." I felt tempted
then. To sit in the chair where they have the free blood-
pressure machine and pour out my heart to him. I'd say, *My
friend here has been seduced by a forty-year-old man who
claims he's having all of his blood replaced with pig's blood.
He is also training us for the apocalypse. But right now we're
most concerned that Hannah might be pregnant. After all,
what if the kid turns out to be the leader of the militant
vegan movement? Won't that throw us all for a loop?*

I knew Manager Man's game well. His kind and I had
faced off through most of last year. And honestly, he threw
down the gauntlet. He made it a matter of pride. "Which
one, do you think?" I asked Sophie. I almost asked Hannah
what her usual brand was. That proved I was still kind of a
terrible person.

She glanced over at Hannah, who had begun pacing up
and down the aisle. Totally playing it cool. Sophie stated the
obvious. "Easiest to read."

We went with Clearblue. I handed her one test. "Take it
up and then change your mind. We're not giving that douchebag any money." I nodded over to Eagle Eye Mahoney, standing
at the end of the aisle with his arms folded. Sophie shot me a
withering look. As soon as I told her, "I need this," I realized
it was true. So Sophie dragged up Hannah to the checkout.

Eagle Eye made a big show of walking over to the register in order to personally ring up the sale.

"Well, how are you ladies doing this evening?" I heard him ask.

Sophie's eyes stayed bored. "We're buying a home pregnancy kit. How do you think we are?"

Beat of silence. "Is there anything else you need tonight?"

Hannah kept glancing back at me. I shook my head sharply at her. *Stop drawing attention to me,* I meant, but she took it as *stop that sale. Right now.*

That worked too. Hannah reached to squeeze Sophie's arm. While she leaned forward and bent to whisper in Sophie's ear, I picked up a second test kit. The strange thing about stealing is that it works best when you don't try to disguise it. I'm sure I'd need to learn some more tricks besides the old backpack-covering-the-bottom-of-the-shopping-cart routine before graduating to art or jewels, but my style of thievery mostly involved just staying calm and walking deceptively fast. It can't look like you're fleeing, only that you have important places to go.

I don't know what Hannah said to her, but Sophie squealed loudly and fussed with her jacket. She made a huge production out of shrugging off her sleeves and tying them around her waist in the classic, tried-and-true method of butt cover. "Turns out I don't need this." She slid the Clearblue box back across the counter. "Maybe Midol?" she asked Hannah. While I sailed out of the doors to the sidewalk outside, I heard Sophie deciding, "I'll just tough it out."

"Thank you!" Hannah called out as the two of them followed me into the cool dusk of Main Street. "You have a terrific night!" I could hear the shrieking laughter poking through the surface of her voice.

"All right, settle down." I handed over the box and Sophie slipped it right into her messenger bag. My ears pricked, half-expecting the alarm system to yelp or the manager to place his meaty hand on my shoulder.

Instead Hannah breathlessly hugged me. "I can't believe you just walked out with it. Insanity. Sophie, did you see that?"

"I actually missed it. I was too busy faking menstruation."

"That a first for you?"

Sophie tilted her head a little. "Actually, yes."

"Well, that certainly earns points for creativity." My voice shook a little bit. I recognized the rush of stealing. Dr. Saggurti and I had discussed that — the kick of adrenaline and how that had its own hook. She said it explained why I might put myself in "at-risk situations." I wondered if Dr. Saggurti was working with Hannah on those too. If she would have seen this mess as a therapeutic failure. Or simply our fault.

One time, we'd listed healthy ways I could pursue that quickened heartbeat, that dry thrill. I'd come up with rock climbing and watching horror movies. Now I thought: *What was I thinking? Not even close.*

Hannah's eyes glittered and she squeezed my arm. "Thanks. Really, Greer. That was heroic."

"Not so fast, there, Stockholm syndrome," Sophie reminded her. "You still have to pee on the stick."

"Whatever happens, it'll be okay, though," Hannah professed. "Right?"

Sophie's eyes flickered over to mine. I ran through the possibilities. We'd tell someone and they'd probably pack up Hannah and ship her off to another facility. Depending on which pieces of the story came to light, they might find alternate arrangements for the rest us too. And Joshua probably wouldn't be able to get a doctor's note to excuse him from statutory rape. Not that it mattered to me, I reminded myself.

Or we wouldn't tell anyone. We'd go to a clinic and support her through it and cover for her back at the dorms. We'd find a way to excise Joshua from our lives on our own. If Addison didn't choose us, then we'd cut him out too.

Fighting a war against vegans sounded easier.

But at least for the windy walk back up the hill to campus, our problems seemed surmountable. We linked arms and replayed Sophie's snarkfest at the CVS counter. We signed back in and remarked that we needed to venture into town together more often if we could — even just to sit together in front of steaming mugs at Common Grounds. And then Sophie and I waited in the dorm bathroom while Hannah Green disappeared into a stall to pee on a stick. The three of us leaned against the restroom door so that no one else could push her way in.

We watched the test turn positive together.

CHAPTER
TWENTY-THREE

The pale blue plus sign on the test stick worked like an on switch. Hannah immediately started wailing in the middle of the girls' room. Between us, she slid down the door and puddled at our feet. Sophie stared at me over Hannah's head. "What are we going to do?" she mouthed at me.

"What am I going to do?" Hannah moaned below us.

I knelt down. "We're going to deal." Hannah looked searchingly at me. "Really." She covered her face with her hands and her shoulders shook with sobs. I motioned for Sophie to crouch down with us.

"You had a feeling, right?" Sophie rubbed circles on her back. "So maybe we should just trust your instincts here. Right now let's just get you to bed. You need a good sleep and then we can sort through everything tomorrow."

"Together?"

"Right." I motioned for Sophie to get Hannah's other side and tried to help her up.

Hannah stopped us midway. "Wait. You're not going to turn me in, right?"

"What are you talking about? What would we turn you in for?"

"You could say you thought I looked pregnant. Then it would be easier to just play it off like I was crazy. No one else would get in trouble." Hannah's eyes stared at me, defeated. "It's okay. I get it. But I don't want to go to sleep feeling like I have you guys and then wake up and find out that I have no one."

"Hannah, stop," Sophie said softly.

"Honestly, just tell me now." She started weeping again and I wondered again who had hurt her so much that she expected that we'd turn on her.

"You're going to wake up tomorrow and it's going to be really hard," Sophie said. "But the one thing you can be certain of is that you'll have Greer and me on your side."

"You think I'm weird," Hannah wailed. "I know you think I'm weird."

"Well, yeah." Sophie swung to look at me. I kept Hannah's gaze. "You're kind of weird, dude. That doesn't mean we're going to abandon ship, you know. I mean, you make life interesting."

Hannah exhaled and sniffled. "I do." Sophie and I nodded solemnly. Hannah snickered a little.

When we got to her room, Hannah asked, "Could you tuck me in? You know? That's a little crazy, but —"

"No — it's not crazy." Sophie said it first. I nodded, next to her. "I miss having someone tuck me in too." Sophie bent down and brushed the hair from Hannah's face. I tugged up her blanket and folded it carefully under her chin.

"Night, night, Hannah," I said, and Sophie even kissed her forehead.

"This baby will always have someone to tuck her in," Hannah told us. "Or him. Someone will always tuck him in." I saw Sophie cringe as we headed out.

In the hallway, she blew out a long breath. "Holy crap," I said. "Why was that so bad — what Hannah said?" Sophie just looked at me. "Because she's thinking of it as a baby? Right?" Sophie started walking down the hall. "Soph — what are we going to do?"

"We're not going to do anything until Hannah makes a decision. And then we're going to do what we have to, right?" I guess I didn't respond quickly enough because Sophie said, "Greer, you can't tell Addison anything."

"Of course not."

"Seriously. We might need the element of surprise, and it wouldn't be fair to put Addison in that position."

"What position?"

"Choosing."

But that sounded so stupid to me. I'd thought we had already decided that Addison would need to decide between Joshua and us at some point. And seeing Hannah, having proof of what Joshua had done — well, Addison couldn't exactly argue with that.

"You'd be surprised," Sophie warned me. "He's brainwashed."

"Stop it. He doesn't have all the information yet."

"And he can't yet."

"Fine. But eventually we'll tell him. And you'll see — Addison will surprise you." Silence from Sophie. "He's a really good guy." Still nothing. "All that stuff that Joshua lectures about — integrity and respecting the universe and believing — it's not all wrong just because of who Joshua is or what he's done."

We'd reached my door. Sophie still hadn't responded to me. Finally she said, "I know. We just used up my special reassurance powers on Hannah. I can't do this right now."

That stung. I felt my face go hot and my body kind of coil up, ready to lash out. And then I didn't. I couldn't afford to be angry with Sophie too. "Night." I still bit off the word and spit it.

Sophie didn't seem to notice. But she turned and called to me as I slipped into my room, "Greer." I figured she would say she was sorry. But she said, "We have to stop him. Think of what he did to her. To all of us, really."

It's all I thought about — that night and long after.

I don't remember a single class from those first few days after we found out about Hannah. Mostly I sat at desks, running scenarios through my mind. Then I'd notice people packing up books to leave and get up to go to another room. To sit at another desk. Addison assumed it was anxiety about Joshua that was distracting me. I let him think that, even though it made my chest hurt.

Once, after I'd missed two questions in lit class, Addison reached over and grasped the nape of my neck and said, "Try to be present, Greer. Joshua wouldn't want us to use him as an excuse to slack off." I must have looked up at him, dumb. "Greer, Greer — try to be here," he said, in the familiar sing-song that used to make me feel shaky in a different way. "Seriously, you okay?"

I shook myself out of the zombie state to say, "Sure. I just had a lousy sleep, is all." But it was too late — Dr. Rennie had already pounced on the moment.

"Greer Cannon? Why don't I write you a late pass?" I looked to Addison for rescue, but Dr. Rennie had already patted the seat next to his desk. "Converse with me," he requested. "Please."

I mustered my most dramatic sigh, but felt secretly relieved. Addison stalled a little, lingering at the door with his brow furrowed into a question. "I'm good," I told him. "No worries." He held on to the door frame.

"I'll take good care of her, Mr. Bradley."

In the hot seat, I tried to focus on convincing Dr. Rennie I felt okay. "I'm just not used to the mattresses here," I told him.

"Really? How long have you been with us now?"

I shrugged. "Months."

"Because even in those first weeks, before you had any kind of privileges, I thought, *We've got a sharp cookie here. Maybe those bastards in the admissions office finally gave me something to work with.*"

I doubted that. Maybe he'd thought that about Addison. Addison was the one who'd walked into class quoting Browning.

He went on. "Something's wrong. Usually I'd dismiss it as star-crossed lovers, but Boy Wonder over there seems as attentive as always. You okay?"

Sometimes the disguises people put on — the smarmy voices or lame attempts to relate — they just fall away all of a sudden. That's what happened with Dr. Rennie. He seemed human, briefly. Like he actually cared. This sad comfort washed over me.

I pressed my lips together and made myself keep my mouth perfectly straight. No quivering lip. If you stare long enough — unfocused, over someone's shoulder — you can stop yourself from crying. When I felt steady enough, I answered, "Yeah."

When Dr. Rennie asked me, "Do you feel like you're making progress here?" I felt myself deflate. Back to the school-approved lingo.

I didn't feel like playing the game. "No" was all I said.

Dr. Rennie didn't seem angry or disappointed. I waited to see him reach for a pen and jot down a note to pass on to the deans later. But he didn't do that. He just kept gazing at me patiently. Waiting.

"I don't really feel like the goal was actually for me to make progress," I heard myself say. Then I tried to make it sound more cooperative. "I mean, there's a system here that works, I guess. But that's not why my parents sent me here. I don't think that's why most of us came here."

"Oh?" Dr. Rennie asked me in a way that made me think he wasn't allowed to agree with me.

"It just feels like the ultimate grounding."

He nodded carefully. "I can see how it might feel that way to you." They must all have taken classes to talk like that. They must have all attended professional workshops in the bullshit vocabulary of caring.

"It's not like I've undergone this miraculous transformation. Just now my parents don't have to deal with me." Dr. Rennie just let me talk. "So what happens? McCracken scrubs my transcript and now I can go to college or something. My parents can have four more years of ignoring me."

Dr. Rennie swallowed. I watched his Adam's apple bob in his throat. "You haven't had a family visit yet." I couldn't tell if he was asking or just remarking.

"Sometimes my dad remembers to call during our scheduled family sessions. I get to hear him on speakerphone." Dr. Rennie grimaced. "It's okay. I don't want to deal with them either." We both heard the lie in that. How freaking embarrassing. I spoke quickly. "Listen, I know how it goes. They're writing tuition checks and all; you can't take my side. But don't expect me to buy into it. That's all."

There was a long pause, during which I guess Dr. Rennie weighed the professional risk of being honest with me. He went with the old standby: "I hear you and I appreciate your candor." He gestured at me, sitting in the chair beside him. "But this is different. We wouldn't have been able to have this conversation when you first arrived at McCracken Hill." He sort of grinned at me then. "Without you throwing something, I should add."

That got a nod. Point awarded to Dr. Rennie. But I still wasn't buying what McCracken Hill was selling. "I don't think this place did that, though." In a split second, I saw his eyes flicker toward the desk where Addison had been sitting. "Not just Addison. Other people — I have really good friends here. That hasn't happened for a long time." God, I sounded pathetic. I really hoped he wouldn't report this crap in a faculty meeting. I could already see Ms. Crane's smug look. "I just didn't have relationships like that at home."

"Well, that's good news." He sounded like he meant it. "But give yourself a little credit, Greer. You've readied yourself for those friendships. Maybe the system doesn't seem like it's working to you. I'm going to keep believing in it."

"Well, if it pays the bills . . ."

"Don't —" Dr. Rennie interrupted me sharply. "Don't presume to know my intentions." Then he muttered, "We're not exactly raking it in over here."

"Yeah, I'm sorry. That was out of line." He gestured at me again, like, *See? Look how reformed you are.*

Maybe I was trying to make up for insulting him and that's why I went balls-out honest. Or as close to honest as I could afford to be. "What if I don't buy everything? Like I know there's something fundamentally wrong with it?" Dr. Rennie thought I meant McCracken, but really I was thinking of Joshua's limp up the stairs to the second floor of the cabin, leading Hannah up behind him. And then his jog to the taxi stand. I thought of Wes's resentful silence and the little blue plus sign on Hannah's test kit.

"You mean, does that discount the learning you've done?" Dr. Rennie asked me. "What do you think?"

"This could also work well if you'd just give me the answers," I reminded him.

"Yeah, but I'm human, correct? This will shock you, but I have flaws. Maybe not devastating ones." I took this to mean that Dr. Rennie did not actually sleep with his students in the name of pseudoreligious rituals or claim to undergo medical treatments lifted from sci-fi scripts. He wore tacky ties. In lecture, he used the phrase *for what it's worth* too often. But I let Dr. Rennie go on with his bad self — fine, he had flaws.

"Do those flaws mean that you need to discount my F. Scott Fitzgerald lecture? Do we write him off because he was a drunk? You know?"

I knew. Dr. Rennie sat back, like he was thinking long and hard about something. "You could always look for a way to point out those shortcomings. In a respectful manner, of course," he offered. Dr. Rennie was probably envisioning me standing in front of my treatment team, glancing at notes I'd carefully penciled onto index cards. "I can't imagine that an institution so focused on growth would shut down that conversation."

I raised my eyebrows. "Well, not outright anyway," Dr. Rennie said, then sighed. "Perhaps this hasn't been as helpful a talk as I'd hoped."

"No, it has." We both just sat there. Finally I said, "Thanks." And then decided to dwell in the possibility that

Dr. Rennie was actually not an asshat. "Hey, Dr. Rennie? Maybe if someone else needed to hear this . . ."

"Bring him in."

But later on, even the suggestion made Addison choke on his fruit punch. "So you had a heart-to-heart with the great Dr. Rennie and you think I need to schedule a session?" He'd stopped me on my way to my assigned table at dinner. I held the tray low, by my waist, so Mr. Mikkelsen couldn't see that Addison's hand gripped my thigh.

"Not a session. Just talk to him."

"About the reading?"

"No, just about stuff that's going on."

Addison whispered, "What did you tell him?" His fingers tightened around my leg. It hurt.

"Nothing. We mostly talked about my parents."

"Bullshit." Addison glowered at me.

"No. I swear."

Mr. Mikkelsen finally noticed me. "Move it along to your assigned table, Greer."

Addison stood. "I'll walk you —"

"No, that's okay," Mr. Mikkelsen said. "I'm sure Greer can handle it. Besides, we're waiting for you to join the conversation. What inspired you about this year's Winter Olympics?" I felt Addison's eyes boring into my back as I made my way to my assigned spot three tables down.

My group discussed the scintillating topic of organ donation. "Really? That's tonight's dinner topic?" Wes sat to my immediate right, and I silently prayed that somehow Addison was too occupied talking about luge and speed skating to notice.

"Organ donation represents the gift of life itself, Greer," Wes parroted. If I didn't know him so well, I might have mistaken him for sincere. "What could be more precious than a new liver?"

Ms. Davelman rushed to correct him. "We're not necessarily talking about livers." Livers were a touchy subject since so many of the drunks at McCracken Hill might eventually need new ones. "People benefit from donated retinas, kidneys, even bone marrow."

"Maybe we could talk about something more appetizing?" I said. "Sewage? Zombies?"

"Zombies are kind of a parallel topic to organ donation," Wes offered.

"That's untrue." Ms. Davelman was not pleased. "I think it's important that we differentiate between organ donation and the fictional phenomenon of zombies."

"Some cultures might equate the two."

"Wes, I'd appreciate your cooperation."

"I apologize. Truly." He turned to me. "Greer, how are your organs?"

"Pickling as we speak."

"Is that a reference to substance abuse, Greer?" Ms. Davelman went on high alert.

"I've never had issues with substance abuse."

"I bet plenty of people develop them at McCracken Hill," Wes said.

"It's unfortunate that you still bet, Wes," I replied.

"All right — that's quite enough." Ms. Davelman slammed down her fork. Wes and I grinned at each other.

"Seriously, how are you?" he asked softly.

"You all of a sudden care?" I meant for my voice to stay light, but it caught at the end, snagged on a splinter of leftover hurt.

"What are you talking about — 'all of a sudden'? Don't

even try." Wes smiled and shook his head at me. He was right.

"I'm fine. Thank you for asking." It sounded automatic because I meant it to.

"And your sister wives?"

My eyes skidded to Ms. Davelman, but she was absorbed in a discussion about the first full face transplant. "Shut up. Don't call them that." Wes chewed his food thoughtfully. "You make it sound like some kind of cult."

"I don't have to make it sound like anything." He leaned forward and whispered, "You've isolated yourselves. You practice rituals. You allow some weird old guy to dictate your relationships and behavior. Has he predicted the world's end yet?" Wes tipped his head as if he'd just remembered. "That's right. We will all be destroyed by angry vegans."

"People mock what they fear."

"And they also mock the ridiculous," Wes added. Just as I tried to formulate a response, Ms. Davelman whipped out her little memo book, as a warning.

"Greer —" she coaxed. "I hope you'll share your ideas with the whole group."

"I was just saying that it must be scary — donating your organs."

Some kid named Steve Loy rolled his eyes. "Usually you're not that aware."

"That's not necessarily true." Ms. Davelman reminded him of the frequency of people donating kidneys to one another.

"In some countries, they take a kidney if you rack up enough of a gambling debt," Summer Galdi warned us.

Ms. Davelman looked like she was ready to snap. "That's an urban legend."

"Do they give you topics for us to discuss at dinner?" Wes asked her. "Like you all sat around at a faculty brainstorming session and someone said, 'Organ donation! That'll get them talking!'"

"I'd like you to take a minute and examine your attitude. Maybe consider why you feel the need to sabotage this conversation."

"I disagree."

"Pause and reflect, Wes."

He looked to me for help. "Hey, Greer, you want to chime in? Is it really possible to sabotage a dinner conversation about organ donation?"

"Wes. Last warning."

I tried to focus on my grilled chicken. The more Wes spoke up, the more mocking his tone got, and the clearer it became that Addison had reached out to him about Joshua's health. I couldn't imagine how that talk went. As if he read my mind, Wes raised an eyebrow at me. But he spoke to Ms. Davelman. "Okay, I have a serious question."

She sighed. "Would anyone like to step up and caution Wes, who seems to be struggling with monitoring his contributions to our dinner dialogue?"

"It's a serious question," he insisted.

Ms. Davelman looked around the table, as if one of us were about to step up and interrupt the only possibility for entertainment. She looked dejectedly at the clock. We still had twenty-two more McCracken-mandated minutes of community. "Go on," she said.

"I don't want to get in trouble."

"Well, I think we're past guaranteeing that at the moment."

"Have you heard of a process —" My breath rushed out in a whistle, like I was a balloon someone had let go without tying off. I stabbed a snow pea with my fork, kept my eyes on my plate. "Have you heard about people who are ill, I guess with a blood disease or something, undergoing some kind of transfusion —"

"Of course. Blood banks help combat all kinds of diseases and conditions —"

"But not human blood. Animal. Like pig's blood." The table fell silent. I still refused to look up, but I imagined mouths dropped open. A ring of gaping maws. Wes rushed to fill the quiet. "I'm serious. It's new, you know? Have you heard about that?"

Apparently Ms. Davelman had not heard of that. "You are trying my patience," she told Wes.

"I promise that's not my goal." He paused for a breath and then admitted, "Okay, that might have been a goal three minutes ago, but right now I'm sincerely curious. Really. Have you heard of that — you know, animal transfusions?"

"No."

"That's it?" Wes actually sounded disappointed. I felt his eyes on me as I carefully dissected a pile of water chestnuts.

"Well, no." My eyes swung up. I couldn't help it. But Ms. Davelman continued, "There's research and experimental procedures, mostly with pigs." My skin prickled. "But ultimately, it's sci-fi stuff. The body has a hard enough time accepting material from another human being. That kind of large-scale interspecies transplant, it's just not realistic yet."

Wes's eyes challenged mine. "Okay, that's organs, though. What about just blood?"

"You're very passionate about this."

"I'm just wondering." He nearly shouted at her. It didn't sound like he was just wondering at all.

"Well, I'd say no. The chance for infection or rejection would be too high. And unnecessary. Blood is a renewable resource, after all." That final proclamation earned a triumphant nod from Wes to me.

"Am I missing something?" Ms. Davelman asked.

Addison's old roommate stared at me, waiting for my answer. I laid my fork carefully across my plate. "Ms. Davelman, *you're* not missing anything."

I left it at that. Let her check my plate and record the leftover bites in her little book. Made small talk about getting our driver's licenses. Or in many of our cases, getting back our driver's license. Whether or not we'd check the box that allowed surgeons to harvest our body. Which, given the predilection for self-destruction at our table, made sense. Probably organ-donor advocates envisioned great possibilities when they looked at McCracken Hill's student population. I endured the rest of dinner with Wes sending me meaningful looks, meant to remind me that he understood. He knew how I'd been duped and he didn't judge me for it. Not at all.

You don't know the half of it, I wanted to tell him. But I couldn't. By then Addison had noticed we were sitting together.

TWENTY-FOUR

I had to chase Addison up the hill. "Hey — hold up!" People turned toward my shouts. But not him. Addison didn't slow down. "Addison — wait." Theodora Garrow leaned over to say something to her roommate. She smirked at me. "I'm not your fucking entertainment," I told her.

"Apparently you're not Addison Bradley's anymore either."

Addison had slowed down, though, like he wanted me to catch up. "Wait a second, will you?" I called out. He stopped walking, but wouldn't turn around. "What the hell?"

"Don't." He still faced the dorms. "You want to talk, talk, but don't act like you don't know what's wrong."

"Wes and I were assigned to the table together."

"You looked like you'd missed each other. Like you had a lot to talk about."

"I was participating in the conversation. As required."

"Do you miss him?"

"No." But the word sounded too small to be convincing. "I miss all of us together, having fun. Everything's some crisis now." As soon as I said it, I knew it had come out wrong.

Addison pounced on my words immediately. "Well, I'm sorry to inconvenience you, Greer. I'm sure Joshua regrets that his dying has interfered with our fun-time bonding."

"That's not what I meant. You know that." He closed his eyes. "What happened to giving each other the benefit of the doubt? Approaching the world with generosity?"

"What did you and Wes talk about?"

Telling Addison wasn't going to help anything. "The assigned topic."

"Which was? You looked . . . engrossed."

"Organ donation." But he didn't flinch. Maybe he didn't make the connection. I reached out for him. "You feel really far away. Maybe we can just spend some time together — go to the library, watch a movie . . ."

I meant something else and Addison knew it. "That doesn't always fix everything, Greer." He looked down the hill toward the gate. "Are you coming with me tonight? To meet Joshua?"

"No." I just couldn't. I hadn't realized until he asked.

Addison nodded as if that was the answer he had expected. He turned away again and took a step toward his dorm. "Joshua asked for a couple books he lent me."

"Hannah's pregnant." When I first said it, I thought maybe I hadn't actually spoken out loud. I wished it were something I'd just imagined saying. The way you imagine telling someone you love them over and over again until finally you have to say it out loud. But Addison stopped walking again. That meant I'd said it loud and clear.

"I wasn't supposed to tell you, but you need to know. I don't know what's going to happen yet. Hannah — we just found out. But maybe that's why . . . I don't know. You feel far away from me. And if I feel distant, well, that's why. That's what's going on."

"Okay. That's hard. I hear that. But what does it have to

do with us?" Addison didn't ask like he was delaying the inevitable. He sounded actually confused.

I glanced around. No one approached close enough, but there were more people coming up the hill. I saw the bright orange flare of Sophie's ski jacket. *Jesus,* I thought. *She's going to murder me.* "Listen, maybe we should go somewhere and talk. Let's just take a walk somewhere." I grabbed his arm but he shook me off.

"Greer, I'm telling you. I don't have time for this."

I grabbed him again. "It's Joshua's." Addison reared back a bit. "The baby."

"This is some bullshit."

"Addison."

"I need to move it along now." I didn't know if he meant that night or in general.

"Please." I looked around, half-expecting Theodora and her roommate to be giggling at the spectacle of me pleading with him. "I'll go with you."

"No way. This is the kind of delusional crap Joshua needs a break from. He's sick, Greer. He can't waste energy on the manufactured drama of a bunch of high-school girls who don't seem to understand the consequences of talking shit."

"It's not. We're not. Addison." I promised myself I'd never tell him I loved him just to win a fight or stop him from dumping me. "Look at me." I tried to let all the honesty in my eyes rise to the surface. That just showed up as tears.

At least he softened a little. "Hannah is nuts. You know she's nuts. She had that weirdo reaction about babies up at the cabin. Remember? She's just working through something. Don't let yourself get caught up."

I should have told him right then that I'd seen the test. But he felt so far away. I kept thinking, *If he walks to town on his own, that's it. It'll never be the same between us.* So I did what I could to stop him.

I let the tears run down my face. "I'm so mixed up. I'm so confused." That, at least, was not a lie. Addison opened his arms and I stepped in. I felt the cables of his muscles tighten around me.

He murmured something against my hair that I couldn't understand, but I caught the tone and it was kind and sorry. Loving. We stood like that for a while and when I finally stepped back, he brushed my hair from my face and kissed the top of my head. "You should stay back. Go to bed early. We'll talk to Hannah tomorrow."

"No! What she told me — that was a secret."

"She told you a lie, Greer."

"You're right, though, she's probably working through something major, you know. That's probably why she didn't want me to tell you." I held on to his sleeve. "I don't want to bring you into it and make it worse." He nodded quickly and then bent in to kiss my cheek. "Seriously — don't say anything. It's girl stuff."

"Just make sure it stays girl stuff. You and Sophie need to help her see how serious — you could ruin lives like that."

I knew that. Addison wasn't just talking about Joshua's life. I knew that too.

When I raised my hand to knock on Sophie's door, I noticed my hand shaking. *She's going to know just by looking at me,* I thought to myself. She called out and then yelled louder when I pushed the door open. "I said, one minute." She didn't turn from her computer. Over her shoulder, I could see windows blinking closed.

"Sorry." Her fingers clicked the mouse methodically and when I leaned forward to see the window left on the screen, she closed the whole laptop. "Messages for Josie?" Sophie looked at me quizzically. "On the computer."

"No." The standard pause stretched to a weird pause.

"Okay." I tried to fend off the feeling that Sophie could have somehow overheard Addison and me in the quad. "Have you seen Hannah?" My voice aimed for light and landed on breathless.

"Is something going on?" Sophie searched my face. I wished I could shut it like the laptop in the corner.

"That's what I wondered. So I came up." The room held the same bed, wardrobe, desk, and chair that mine did, but I still looked around as if Hannah would pop out or something. "She's not here?"

"I haven't seen her since right before dinner. No Joshua tonight?"

"Addison and I fought. It got kind of intense." Any other time, she'd hear the slight falter of my voice and Sophie would guess that I'd told Addison everything. But that night Sophie was off her game.

"You okay?" she asked, but not like she cared. She was looking at the closed laptop.

"Yeah. I think we're fine now." I could hear the lie underlining my voice. Sophie missed it. I stepped backward, held on to the door frame. "Okay — well, I'm around if you guys need anything. Or maybe we should be talking through options or something."

"I think we need to let Hannah bring it up," Sophie said sternly.

"Okay. I thought we need to be pressing things, you know because of timing —"

"Well, we shouldn't be. We don't really have that right."

"Sure. Okay. That sounds good. I mean, I agree. I sat with Wes at dinner." The last part tumbled out and Sophie finally turned her full gaze on me.

"Oh yeah?"

"Yeah."

"That sounds like it was a big deal." At first I didn't answer. Sophie said, "That's why you and Addison fought?"

"Yeah. He read a lot into it." I stood there, studying the mechanics of the door handle.

"Greer!" Sophie yelled out. She dove from the desk chair to the bed and lay there, staring at the table. "Come on — out, out."

At first I thought she meant *leave*. But Sophie sat up. "Honestly, it's like pulling teeth tonight. There's obviously something you want to talk about. And it's not Hannah." I stood there for a minute. "How's Wes?"

"He's same old Wes." I realized that was true. The rest of us might be going nuts. But Wes was Wes — mostly jokes, some of them laced with the tiniest thread of caring, just to remind you that he might be human after all. That you might matter to him.

"Addison caught you flirting."

"Wes and I don't flirt." Sophie's eyebrows insisted, *Come on*. "We might have a kind of spiritual electricity, but we don't flirt." The eyebrows organized a protest on her face. "Seriously." I gave up. "Okay, fine." Sophie's eyebrows settled back down. "And Addison did notice us talking. That's why we argued, but back up —" Because I'd finally found something besides my betrayal worth noting. "Addison told Wes about Joshua's treatments."

The eyebrows sprang back to life. "The 'treatments'?"

Sophie provided the air quotes. "That is interesting." I nodded, calming a little. "How do you know?"

"Our dinner topic was organ donation." Sophie snorted. "I know, right? Wes was all over it, asking if Ms. Davelman had heard of transfusions with pig's blood. She said no."

"Well, of course she said no."

"I don't know. I'm just telling you what happened. Wes got all smug about it."

Sophie gazed up at the ceiling. Sophie was always thinking, thinking. "How much do you think Wes is willing to help us?"

"Nada. He's done with us."

"Done with you?"

"Yeah." I reconsidered. "I think so."

Sophie sat up and pivoted in order to face me. "You need to cultivate a connection with Wes."

I backed against the door. "You're not listening. That's how I ran into trouble tonight. Addison is too jealous —"

"Addison is too *afraid*." I wanted to remind her how the male staff sometimes stood around the bench press during Addison's workouts, placing bets on how much he could lift. But she didn't mean it that way. "Not physically," Sophie said. "But Wes just says what he means. No one else does that. So that's threatening. Besides that, he might not have biceps the circumference of sequoias, but Wes is ripped. It's something."

"For when we have our rumble?" I teased, but Sophie didn't laugh.

"Both Jared and Wes together . . ." She shrugged.

"Sophie —"

"I'm not saying they should jump your boyfriend. I'm just mentioning it in case. We need a backup plan."

"I think you're losing your mind."

"And I think you're avoiding the reality of our situation."

"Which is . . ."

"Joshua's not just going to go away, Greer. Jared and Addison — they've promised him money. He wants my family's cabin. For God's sake, he raped Hannah." I stared at her. "Well, pretty much. Don't you get it? We're a mark for him and he's invested a lot of time into scamming us." I still didn't know what to say. "All I'm saying is that it can't hurt to have someone else on our side, just in case. You don't have to *seduce* Wes — just make sure he'd step up."

So that's how I found myself sitting outside Freewill Hall, Wes's new dorm, twenty minutes before lights-out. Looking in one direction in case Addison strode past, searching out the other for Wes. Wes showed first. He didn't look surprised to see me. "Wrong dorm, darling," he said.

"You don't think I demonstrate free will?"

"Don't make me answer that." He squinted up at the streetlamp. "Two conversations in one day. Like winning the lottery."

"That would count as gambling, though, right?"

"Shut your face." But he grinned. So did I. He was still smiling when his voice turned solemn. "What do you want, Greer?"

"We might be in trouble." He rocked back on his heels. "I don't mean Addison or Joshua." I checked the path again. "The rest of us." Wes just watched me steadily. "I wondered — I mean, there's not a lot of people worth trusting around here."

"But?"

"But I trust you."

Around us, the buildings and streetlamps blinked. Lights off at McCracken Hill. "You should get back. I'm headed inside."

"Wes —"

"What do you want me to say, Greer?" He smiled wanly. "I told you so?"

"You'd be justified. But —"

"But what, Greer?"

I reached over and ran the heel of my hand softly down his chest. "But I thought that you were better than that." The lights flickered again.

"Lights-out, Greer." Wes might not have sounded convinced but at least his voice hitched a little. And when I stepped back, he grabbed my arm. "I'll see you tomorrow, okay?"

"Thanks."

"Nothing to thank me for."

"Yet." Then I sprinted to Empowerment Hall as fast as possible and tried to outrun the realization that I'd traded leaning on one guy for leaning on another.

TWENTY-FIVE

I woke up early the next morning and slipped into the shower in a futile attempt to wash the slut out of my hair. I stood under the hottest water I could stand and scrubbed myself down twice. Then I dressed and tucked my hair into a quick bun, hoping to hit breakfast before most of the rest of campus woke and stretched.

I didn't feel like seeing anyone — not Addison or Wes. Not Hannah. Not even Sophie. So when I heard footsteps fall into place beside me on the path outside my dorm, I braced myself for an argument. And that was before I saw it was Joshua.

It hit me that I had rarely seen Joshua Stern in daylight. He could have been a vampire. I tried to act nonchalant, even though my skin prickled with the urge to take off running. "Hey, you." When I said it, my voice sounded almost normal.

"Good morning. If the mountain won't come to Muhammad, then Muhammad must go to the mountain."

"So I'm the mountain in this scenario?"

"You are strong. And stubborn." Joshua didn't seem to be having much trouble walking, although he still carried his cane. "I've missed you, Elizabeth."

"I'm sorry — there's just been so much going on. But Addison has kept me updated. And you know I'm always here for you, no matter what —"

"I believe we should stop lying to each other." The sky was just now lightening, and ahead of us, I saw the backs of two people jogging. It looked like a man and woman. I wondered if screaming would make them turn.

"That's kind of rich, coming from you," I said.

Joshua's cane snapped across the path and blocked my step. "Whatever you think you know — that pales in comparison to what you should believe." He lifted his cane and we walked in stiff silence. "I know we haven't a great deal of time to talk alone. So I wanted to take this opportunity to make myself clear. I have done a lot for you, Elizabeth. Starting with handing Addison over to you. I'm surprised you'd want to risk that —"

"I know you're not sick. I followed you at the hospital. By myself. You just walked through the lobby and got into a cab." At least I had the good sense to stop myself from mentioning Sophie. Or Hannah.

"You dwell on this as if it matters."

"It matters that you've been lying to us."

"You're missing the point. There are different kinds of truth. I've told you how I've suffered, the toll my actions and my sacrifices have taken on my body. So I would swear to anyone that I am ill, that I am failing. Just like I know it's God's truth that I rescued Addison from himself. That same truth holds: You love Addison. We share that dedication. We'd both do anything to save him from pain."

"I'm not keeping your secrets anymore."

"You don't want to take me on."

We walked all the way to the dining commons. I could look up the hill and see people trickling out of the dorms. "It's time for me to go."

Joshua snarled his last words to me then. "Listen very carefully. This should matter to you, Greer Elizabeth. You have nothing that I haven't given you. Your boyfriend, your friends. What happens if I point out how little you've been eating to the deans? How quickly will they send you to inpatient treatment?"

"I'm doing fine." In spite of myself, I clarified, "In that way."

"Well, don't slip up, sister. I'd hate to have to act in the best interests of your health." My lips moved, wanting to cry out for help, but what would I say? Joshua had threatened me with his concern? "Surely I don't have to tell you that it wouldn't serve your best interests to confide in Addison right now. He has so much worrying him. Let me speak with true honesty and assure you that for right now I won't alter how I treat you, Elizabeth. We recognize ourselves in each other."

"I don't see myself in you."

Joshua smiled his slow, cruel smile. "That's because you're invisible. You don't see yourself at all." He stopped and nodded toward the dining commons. "Enjoy breakfast." He pronounced it like a curse.

Sitting by myself at the table, I arranged a wedge of cantaloupe and a little pile of cottage cheese on my plate. Then I stood again and made myself go back for a whole wheat bagel. I saw Mr. Mikkelsen jot something down into his little ledger and made myself smile at him. Carbs and eye contact. What a breakthrough.

Actually eating was a different animal altogether. My stomach growled, but that didn't make it easier to spoon up the fruit and cheese. I tried nibbling the bagel. It felt like my first day at McCracken all over again. Small bites that tasted like sawdust mostly because someone else had forced me.

The more it mattered, the more I realized how effortlessly Joshua could set the wheels in motion for my transfer. He'd probably even be able to convince Addison to be grateful for it. And the more I realized it mattered, the less I managed to eat.

Later on, in lit class, my stomach rumbled loudly enough that Addison looked up and raised his eyebrows. "Sorry," I murmured and wished I could fit more into that little word. Dr. Rennie kept looking back and forth between Addison and me during his lecture. After class, he asked, "Mr. and Mrs. Bradley?"

I felt my face go hot and looked over to see if Addison would cringe. He just grinned and shook his head. "Dr. Rennie, you've got this gift for awkward statements."

"One of my many talents. Another is sensing discord in the young and brilliant. Are you two all right? No one's dying? Or maybe getting put out to pasture with the rest of the rehabilitated?"

"No one's dying." I wondered if Addison would notice the assurance in my voice.

But he only added, "And we're not fully well adjusted yet." Then he said, "We're okay, though. Thanks for asking."

Dr. Rennie gazed at me over the narrow ovals of his spectacles. "That's right," I parroted. "Everything's okay with us."

"Well, that's good to hear. But if it wasn't, I hope you both know I'm here to help."

"Sir, I appreciate that." Addison looked over to me and smiled. "We appreciate that." I nodded.

He held open the door for me as we left and then asked, "Could you give me five minutes?" I searched his face for a hint of anger. But he told me, "I know I need more than that — to apologize. But for now — sorry. Really. For acting like a bastard last night. For letting Wes get to me. You don't deserve that."

When I looked away from him, maybe Addison figured I was taking some time to consider forgiving him. Really I was thinking about all the conversations I'd had since we had argued. Any one of them could cause him to walk away from me forever. "You don't need to apologize." At that point, he probably thought that was generosity speaking. "We just see some things differently."

"I hope not." Addison slung his arm around me, pulled me close, and kissed the top of my head. I felt swallowed up. "Let's remember that there's a lot of people like Hannah out there to help, but we can't do that if we absorb their crazy delusions. We have to protect ourselves too."

I thought of Joshua — his delusions and his designs. "I just want that — for us to protect ourselves and each other." I looked back at the door to Dr. Rennie's classroom. We could go in and sit there, at two facing desks. I could explain all of it with someone right there in case things got out of hand.

"We're really lucky to have each other." Addison squeezed me more tightly, so that I felt sure he could feel my heart hammering frantically against his chest. When we passed Wes in the east hallway, Addison probably just intended to demonstrate integrity when he nodded at his ex-roommate. He couldn't have been trying to intimidate either of us. Even still, when I craned my head slightly to glimpse Wes staring after us, I had to fight back the strange urge to call out for help.

The prospect of lunch triggered the old dread, but not just about food. I stood there in the wide doorway of the dining hall and appraised the room. Sophie and Hannah had already sat down at a corner table. I watched Jared head toward them and turned to face Addison. "Where should we sit?"

"Where else would we sit?"

"I don't want a scene with Hannah. You know?"

"Of course not. She has a heavy burden." He guided me in the room with his hand on my back. "Hannah's not our enemy. Besides, you know what Joshua always says about enemies, right?"

My organs sank in my torso. "No. What's that?"

"Kill them with kindness!" Addison sounded gleeful. I breathed deeply, steadied myself, and followed him through the cafeteria. "How's it going, Hannah? You're wearing the braids today — you know how I love those braids." Hannah tilted her face up and basked in the attention.

Sophie's eyes lasered in on mine. "Hey, Soph — I missed you at breakfast," I said.

"Yeah? I was here. Usual time?"

"Maybe I got off to an early start."

"We should grab some grub." Addison spoke in the faux casual voice of unconcealed concern. And then the familiar singsong: "Greer, Greer — let's go over here." He stood next to me while I constructed the turkey sandwich. When he kept watching, I grabbed a bag of pretzels. "Mmmmmm." He said it like I was a baby, perched in a high chair.

"Don't say 'good job,' all right?"

"Okay, but I'm worried." Exactly what I didn't want him to be right then.

I checked around the room and kept my voice low, reached to ladle out a cup of soup that I had no intention of slurping down. "Why would you possibly be worried?"

"You tell me. Seems like all of a sudden this is hard for you again." My eyes wandered up to the ceiling. The fluorescent lights reminded me of the gleam in Joshua's eye. I looked around the full room. Any of those people had the ability to betray me. I felt along my clavicle. Certain things I could always count on.

"It's not hard. Really, you know I'd tell you."

"I guess I'm going to have to just trust you."

"That shouldn't be so difficult, right?" I kept my voice light and held my tray tightly to keep my hands from shaking.

He smiled down at me. "I love you so much. Now let's go eat lunch with our incredibly amazing lunatic friends."

Throughout lunch, Addison acted as his best charming self. Hannah glowed with happiness and Sophie and Jared flirted shamelessly. Our table looked just as I'd always imagined fitting in would look like. Crowded with friends. Loud with laughter. But when I looked more closely at Jared, I saw a kid who was too afraid to stand up for himself. And Addison's muscles seemed more menacing than reassuring. I knew even then that Sophie was plotting something. And then there was Hannah, whose belly held its own secret beneath the table. So while I stirred my soup and nibbled at my sandwich, I manufactured my own smiles and tried not to notice that we were all obviously hiding something. And since we'd sat down, no one had mentioned Joshua at all.

*　　*　　*

Sophie and I got to sit together at dinner that night, but our assigned discussion topic was marine preservation. So besides dolphins and manatees, we didn't really get to talk about much. And Jenn Sharpe was there, so we had to keep especially quiet. She kept asking, "Greer, how are you?" She said, "I've barely seen you in the past few weeks," and then slyly glanced at Coach Tyson, who was discussing the morality of tuna fish. Jenn Sharpe covered my hand with hers and stage-whispered, "You look so frail."

"Thanks for your concern."

"Of course. It's not Addison, is it? Because you two just seem perfect together — these two wounded souls who've somehow found each other. So romantic."

"That's not really romantic," Sophie stated in her cold, flat way. She looked up at Coach Tyson. "Sir, do canned salmon companies employ the same inhumane netting techniques as those of canned tunas?"

"What's that, Sonia?" Sophie rolled her eyes. Coach Tyson shook his head in confusion. "You mean the large nets that snag dolphins? Hmmm. But they catch salmon in rivers." He smiled at her indulgently. "There are no dolphins in rivers."

"That's not necessarily true," Drew Costa piped up.

"No, that's true. Dolphins live in oceans." Coach Tyson inspired me to remember the word *doofus* for the first time since the fifth grade.

"No." Drew searched around the table and then threw up his hands in disgust. "Salmon are not necessarily a freshwater species. They are born in rivers and travel back to give birth in rivers. But they spend a significant amount of their lives in oceans."

"No one cares," Sophie announced.

"Sophie!" I said, and then tried to smile an apology at Drew.

"You're the one who asked about salmon," Drew pointed out.

"I was feigning interest in tonight's discussion topic! The way I've done every goddamn night at this place."

Coach Tyson began scribbling furiously in his ledger.

"Well, I'm so sorry." Drew snotted in a way that made it clear he wasn't a bit sorry. "I had no idea it took such an effort to be a first-class phony bitch."

"Okay, Drew. That's enough." Coach Tyson spoke sternly and turned to another page in his book. Jenn Sharpe grinned widely, memorizing all the details for that night's breaking blog entry.

But Drew Costa wasn't done. "Doesn't anyone else see how these two prance around, with their self-satisfied little clique? Or are you just not willing to say anything because her boyfriend's one of your gym rats?" Until Drew gestured at me with his fork, I hadn't known he noticed I existed.

"Where is this coming from?" I wasn't even playing up my conflict-resolution skills for Coach Tyson — I sincerely wanted to know.

"Let it go, Greer." Sophie threw down her napkin and started organizing her tray before bringing it up to the mess. "It doesn't matter."

"It matters to me." I faced Drew, who stared at a place somewhere behind my head. "I'm sorry if you felt unwanted or something — if I contributed to that feeling." He coughed and shook his head. He really wouldn't look at me then. "No, really." His eyes flicked quickly to my face finally and his expression softened. Just a little.

"That's a generous gesture, Greer." Coach Tyson nodded thoughtfully at me. "That's the kind of communication we encourage here at McCracken Hill."

Sophie sighed dramatically. "Look at that, you racked up some good-citizen points. Are you finished pretending to eat for the evening?" She slid her chair back and started digging around in the pile of backpacks we'd all left under the table.

"Sophie, I don't mean to intrude —" Jenn Sharpe intruded. "But you are an extremely angry person."

"Jenn Sharpe, you can seriously suck it." With that, Sophie stood up. "And maybe if you could spare a moment from your efforts to improve humanity, could we talk outside please, Greer?" She knocked her chair back to the table with her hip.

"Sure. Okay." I stood up and stared down at Drew. "See you later." He just shrugged and I followed Sophie. It seemed like I was always following someone.

She'd already made it partway up the hill. I chased her, but glanced back at the dining hall. Addison would be searching for me soon. This was one night I shouldn't let him go on a Joshua dinner date on his own. "I don't have a lot of time," I said.

"Yeah? Hot date?"

"I need to go with him to meet Joshua tonight."

"You told him about Hannah, didn't you?"

"That's ridiculous."

"It's not. Addison's not so slick, you know."

"Meaning?"

"C'mon, Greer. Lay off it. I'm not Drew — I'm not going to fall for your crap. Addison was way too friendly at lunch today. And for once, he managed to hold a conversation without referring to the gospel according to Joshua. Do I need more to convince you?" I said nothing. She practically spit at me, "Why would you tell him that? How am I supposed to trust you?"

I opened my mouth to speak, but it took me a couple of tries. "It just sort of happened," I admitted miserably.

"Yeah? Maybe you misunderstood, but it was Wes who you were supposed to charm into helping us. You already fucked Addison."

"Listen! You don't get it. You have no idea what kind of pressure I'm under."

"Are you kidding me? Seriously, Greer? Are you sure you don't mean the pressure that *we're* under? Because the last I knew, we swore to protect Hannah together. We tracked Joshua together, and we've been talking about finding a way out of this together."

When I told Sophie, I did so for the same reason I told Addison about Hannah. I see that now. And it worked. I said, "Joshua came here this morning. He confronted me."

"About Hannah?"

"No way. Addison thinks that's just one of Hannah's misunderstandings — her crazy showing up to town. He made me swear to keep that quiet. Joshua came to talk to me about the rest of it — my attitude." Sophie looked blank. "He knows that I know. About the hospital." She rubbed her face with her hand. "I told him that I followed him and that I saw him get in the cab. That I knew he wasn't sick. That he was lying."

"About everything?"

"We didn't really get into specifics." I reached out to her. "I kept you out of it. And Hannah. He thinks I got suspicious on my own."

"Maybe for now, but that won't last long. It puts all of us in danger. Don't you get that? I mean, he's probably plotting something right this minute."

"I'm really sorry." I stood there, waiting through her silence.

Finally, Sophie sighed. The storm had passed. "No, you did the best you could. He just showed up?" I nodded. "And you called him a liar?" I shrugged. "Badass," she called me. I bit my lip. "What did he say?" I blinked, remembering. "Greer?"

"He threatened me." That's how I phrased it. I could have told Sophie that Joshua reacted angrily. Maybe it would have been more accurate to say he challenged me. But those weren't the words I chose. Instead I told her that Joshua Stern had threatened me.

TWENTY-SIX

By the time I sprinted back down the hill, Addison was angry and just about to leave without me. I caught up with him as he headed out of the front gates. "Signed you out already," he said curtly. "You said you wanted to go tonight. If you changed your mind, you can just go cross your name off in the book."

I imagined the letters of my full name: Greer Elizabeth Cannon. Then Joshua drawing a line through them with a black Sharpie. "No, of course I want to go. Sorry — Sophie freaked out at Drew Costa at dinner. Damage control."

"What's her problem with Drew Costa? The kid's brilliant."

"Yeah, he actually started in on all of us — said we were an elitist clique." I couldn't remember if Drew had used those exact words, but it sounded like ones he'd say. "Sophie defended us."

"She seems like she just needs a reason to fight lately."

A cold feeling spread through my chest. I laced my fingers through Addison's but it felt awkward to walk that way, like the space between us had been filled with secrets. "Sophie's fine. She's just badass."

"And what's Hannah?" Addison's words hung in the air.

"Hannah's crazy."

"And you? What are you? Greer, Greer — don't disappear." He clamped my hand in his. "I feel like there's all this shifting around. Somehow I keep missing the memos."

"Oh, don't think that. They've just filled this place with so many intense people. . . ." Lame. Classic avoidance. I tried again. "We all love you. No one wants to put any more pressure on you, that's all."

"Since Joshua's surgery, things have felt — I don't know — crushing. Oppressive. I figured it would feel like a weight had been lifted. But I just have this sinking feeling — like things are about to go all kinds of wrong. Like when you're driving and all of a sudden you realize you're about to spin out of control."

How could I tell him he was right? How could I tell him without spinning that car too hard, too fast? I had to figure out the way to tell him the truth without the crash. I said, "You've got a handle on everything, though. At least that's how it seems."

He told me, "I shake all the time. It's hard to sleep."

He knows, I thought. *Deep down, something in him knows.*

"Maybe —" I started to speak up but ran out of words. It felt as if I had to say it exactly right.

"Maybe what?" But I just shook my head. Waited for the words I needed to surface. We walked, and I watched how our feet fell to the pavement at the same time. I tried again. "You love Joshua. So do I —"

"Don't start, Greer."

"Just listen. You're telling me all this because you know something's not quite right. So hear me out." He dropped my hand and quickened his pace. His chin jutted to the right, away from me. But he looked like he was still listening.

"Joshua's illness and treatment don't seem realistic. You can't make sense of it because it doesn't make sense." He started to interrupt me, but I held up my hand. "You're only going to give me one chance to say all this — at least let me say it."

Addison's head ducked slightly, an almost imperceptible nod. "I'm not saying he doesn't need us. Or that he doesn't deserve our loyalty." I almost choked on the last part, but said it anyway. "Maybe somehow Joshua got the idea that he had to be in crisis to ask for our gratitude. If we can show him that's not true —"

"You're saying he's making himself sick?"

"Maybe he's just tired." Addison turned fully away then, but he let me keep talking. I rushed to keep explaining. "You know how in action movies, some crazy thing happens? Aliens attack or war breaks out and the movie follows some group of people while they struggle to survive. Then the struggle makes them extraordinary. It bonds them. I think Joshua scripted his own version of an action movie, as a way for us to rise to the occasion. Do you understand what I'm getting at?"

"Maybe about some things," Addison admitted quietly. He was talking about the upcoming Great Vegan Uprising. I felt relief wash over me. *At least,* I thought, *Joshua hasn't driven him completely insane.* All of a sudden, I remembered how surprised I'd been that day we first met, when Addison first spoke up and stunned the room with his smart self. I had underestimated him. For a long time.

I stopped walking then and held his arm. We'd neared the pizza place and I couldn't chance Joshua's overhearing me. "All of us got really close that weekend. I mean, we discussed going to war together. Everyone imagined standing strong together. And that was an amazing feeling, right?" Addison grimaced. He wouldn't answer me. "But maybe when he thought about coming back to campus, Joshua realized that he couldn't really sustain that. You know, without us actually fighting vegetarians or something." Addison shook his head. "No, you understand what I'm saying. That fight seemed so real because each of us has been battling something. On our own. And then we all sat in this circle and no matter what he picked as our enemy, it felt so perfect to be united by something. But I think we can admit to each other that Joshua's whole vision about an upcoming war isn't real." Addison twisted from me but I did my best to hold him tightly. "We can admit that to each other, right?"

He refused to answer. I went on. "Because if we can admit that to each other, maybe we can consider that Joshua thought being sick could work like that too. It could have started as just a little thing. He wasn't feeling well up at the cabin and then the story spun out of his control." Addison opened his mouth, but I said, "That happens, right? That happens to everyone. But Joshua's a really proud man. And you know — he has nontraditional ideas. So the reality of it could have just slipped through his fingers." I breathed deeply. "I'm not saying that he meant to cause any harm. I just think he didn't know how else to prove to himself that we loved him."

Addison looked like he was struggling to breathe. He sank down onto the curb of the street. I glanced down Willowbrook Avenue nervously, checking to see that Joshua wasn't leaning against a lamppost, staring at the two of us. "He knows that I love him." Addison spoke like the words were strangling him.

"Yeah, he does. He should. But you're getting better. Maybe as happy as that made him, it also scared him."

"He could be really sick. It would devastate him if he knew we even questioned that. And if he doesn't get better and I wasted time with him overanalyzing it —"

I eyed the street again. And then looked back at Addison. Sometimes it socked me in the gut that he was so beautiful. He had this perfectly straight, proud nose. Lips almost as full as a girl's. In profile, Addison almost made me weep. I couldn't believe that he'd chosen me, that we'd been naked together. Repeatedly. But none of that meant much if I kept the truth from him. Addison deserved honesty. So I had to risk it. "Pig-blood transfusions don't exist. They don't even make sense. The doctors that he won't let us talk to — they don't exist either. Hospitals don't schedule major surgeries at midnight. Or allow texting in operating rooms. And the recovery time for major surgery is never only two days. These are facts, Addison. All verifiable facts. I'm not trying to convince you on my word alone. I just hope you'll think about it. If it was a story you heard in group or something — would it seem believable? You know I support you no matter what."

That last sentence rung wrong like the lie that it was. Addison looked up at me. His eyes held mine until I amended it with, "As much as I can."

I reached both my hands out and said a quick prayer that he would take them. He did and hoisted himself off the curb. I almost fell back into the road when he stood. We both looked up toward Sal's. "Well, after all this, pizza might taste a little awkward tonight," Addison said. Whatever he was thinking was under lockdown, not for me to see.

"That's why I always order the salad," I told him.

"Maybe this time, you could find a way to eat a slice of pizza. Reassure me after your woefully inadequate day of eating." I bristled, but Addison hadn't brandished it as a threat. He spoke like he just wanted me to know he'd noticed. And it mattered.

We sat and waited for Joshua in our usual booth. Addison kept digging his cell out of his pocket, touching the screen, and then smiling nervously at me like it was no big deal. The yeasty smell of rising dough plumed from the wall of ovens. I'd decided to eat pizza, so my belly lurched with hunger. Waiting.

"Joshua's not usually late," I said.

"Nope." He stared out the window.

"You worried?"

Addison lined up the salt and pepper shakers as if they were fighters facing off. "Not the same kind of worry I've gotten used to recently." He smiled wanly at me.

I wasn't worried. I was afraid. But as soon as my mind started churning out the scary possibilities, the door jangled and Joshua limped in. His face froze into a shocked smile. But his voice crowed, "Brother Addison!" joyfully. He called out loudly enough that the people who usually shot us puzzled looks shot us those same puzzled looks. "And what a treat for me — you finally allowed this radiant angel to visit me. Elizabeth, my heart complains that Addison has been hiding you from me. You see, I've thirsted for your beauty." The puzzled looks around us extended into nervous frowns.

Joshua's eyes twinkled as he acknowledged them. "Elizabeth, Sal's patrons are shocked that you would grace us with your presence. But you'd never look down on working-class stiffs like us, would you?" I shook my head warily and watched an older couple turn, embarrassed, back to their food.

Joshua embraced us both and then taunted, "I know Addison understands how much you value that which is stiff."

"Unnecessary. Yellow card," Addison warned lightly. His eyes darted to me. But if Add hadn't reacted, I might not have even caught the stupid innuendo. It took all of my concentration to sit there and calmly face Joshua down.

"I apologize. It's just that it's been so long since I've seen Elizabeth, and so I have to fight for my sense of self-control." Joshua seemed to relish the dare hidden in that statement. I could argue with him and point out that he'd stopped by school that same morning, but then he might tell Addison why. I smiled at him and remembered Addison's words earlier in the day — *Kill them with kindness.*

"Let me go put in our order." Addison pointed to Joshua. "Spaghetti and meatballs?" And then me: "Cheese slice?"

"Yes, please."

"Great. Be right back." Addison trotted to the counter and Joshua lowered himself into the booth.

I moved the salt and pepper shakers back to their original positions and made myself meet his eyes. Joshua didn't say a word, and that made sitting there with him more unnerving. We just faced each other, smiling in a display of false friendliness. "Should I get drinks?" I called out to Addison without looking away.

He skidded over. "No way. Just relax. Besides, you two have a lot to catch up on, right?"

"Right." Joshua and I spoke equally brightly and at the same time. I laughed. He did not. After Addison brought over our food and settled down next to me, Joshua raised his hands to stop us from digging in.

"Would you indulge me? It's been some time since the three of us have sat together and I feel the need to honor this occasion with a prayer of gratitude."

"Sure thing, Reverend." Addison laughed.

"Well, I believe that gratitude is an important concept. Perhaps that seems quaint or old-fashioned to you." The edge had crept back into Joshua's voice like a knife that had been sharpened.

Addison saw it glinting. "You know that's not true."

"You both are very attached to this concept of truth. I wonder how that might work out for you, later on in your lives." Again, Joshua's pronouncement felt like a curse.

"Let's say grace, then." Addison reached to hold both our hands.

For that one moment, both Joshua and I hesitated. We were supposed to grasp hands — to complete the circle. Addison turned his head expectantly and so I reached out first. Joshua clamped his papery hand around mine. He said, "Elements of the universe, we appeal to you for reminders of our place in this world. We recognize that you have not designed us to judge others, but to defend ourselves from divisive forces who lack generosity and loyalty." Addison had closed his eyes but Joshua and I continued to stare resolutely at each other. "We thank you for this nourishing food and especially that you have empowered Greer Elizabeth to set her discipline aside and risk taking up more space in the world, in order to experience more of its joys." I sucked in my breath on that line, and Addison's knee knocked gently against mine beneath the table. Joshua wrapped it up. "Lastly we ask that you punish our enemies. Amen."

I didn't say amen. Addison sort of whispered it, but

when he released our hands, he held his own up like he was surrendering.

"Kind of an intense grace, brother," he said.

"You know me to be an intense force."

"Right." And then Addison claimed my heart pretty much forever. "I don't think you need to thank the universe every time Greer eats a slice of pizza."

"No? I apologize. That was my attempt to support your concerns about Greer." Joshua turned to me to confide, "Addison has shared that the only reservation he has about sharing his life with you stems from your inability to address that weakness." He paused and looked at Addison. "Surely the two of you have discussed this?"

Addison looked stricken, and Joshua sat back smugly. That might have been the first time I realized that Joshua might not be able to outmanipulate me. I wished hard that Addison would see it too.

"We haven't talked about it, actually," I said. Joshua launched an apology, but I cut him off at the pass. "Of course not — Addison's fears are completely reasonable. After all, so many people rely on him. He doesn't need another person to nurse back to health. Besides, we're what? Sixteen and eighteen? We both should have some reservations." I smiled and stabbed one more time. "You know, I'm working hard to figure out the eating piece. I'm sure you didn't intend this, but hearing you predict my weight gain makes it harder to actually sit down and make healthy choices."

Joshua's eyes flashed. He wasn't going down without a fight. "Certainly I apologize. I meant that in jest. But it was inappropriate, considering how much you fear gaining weight."

"Not as much as I fear losing other things." I smiled at him and rested my head on Addison's shoulder. Addison shifted to press his thigh against mine in the booth. Then I picked up my pizza and ate, letting the strings of cheese stretch from my mouth to the slice. Full-on knockout.

Joshua retreated to small talk. He spoke about a few patients he'd met in the hospital's outpatient clinic who he thought would benefit from his ministry. My skin crawled to realize that his fabricated illness had led him to his next hunting ground. Even if Sophie and I could ever manage to excise Joshua from the McCracken Hill Academy, he'd probably remain right up the road — running support groups and preying on the even more vulnerable.

I noticed Addison watching Joshua carefully through the meal. Studying him. He kept a smile positioned on his face the whole time and dutifully rose to refill glasses and take care of the check, but his eyes had darkened with concern. And while Joshua drank a cup of coffee, Addison asked if he was set for money. They rarely discussed financial details in front of me. I concentrated on nibbling my pizza crust. Joshua tipped his chin — thinking, maybe calculating. "Brother, that's not a burden I want to see you take on."

"No burden. You doing okay? I know you haven't been working as much."

"It's the standing at that register. The doctor's amazed I've tolerated it this long."

"Right. So should I put something together?"

"It shames me to rely on others." Addison didn't argue or coax him. He just waited. Finally Joshua relented. "Yes. I must humble myself if others are willing to contribute."

Addison only smiled at me and spoke reassuringly. "I'm sure they are. We usually have to fight them off, right, Greer?"

"You'd be surprised at how many people want to help. You have that effect on people." I tried to will warmth into my smile.

We all stood to leave, and then Addison said, "I think Greer's going to head back to school after this and I'll walk you to the hospital myself."

"No, I can go." I panicked, imagining the damage that Joshua could inflict on the quick walk from Sal's to the outpatient clinic. I couldn't afford to free up time for him to attack.

But Joshua waved Add off. "You should both walk back to school. They've suspended treatments for now. To give me a chance to build back up my strength."

"Are you positive?" Addison looked from Joshua to me. And back again.

"Of course."

Addison ventured, "Well, that's a good thing that they feel they can allow you a break from treatment. Which doctor said that?"

Joshua pretended to think about it a second. "I don't remember. They're all the same to me."

"You have a different doctor each time?"

"Yeah. Makes it hard to remember."

I thought Addison might press more, but instead he said, "Well, whichever doctor decided, it must mean your numbers are good."

Your imaginary numbers, I thought to myself.

Joshua wheezed and reached for the door. "Hopefully. I don't want anyone throwing in the towel for me."

"Well, they can't do that, right?" Addison said. "I mean, they have to let you fight on?"

"I'm just an old, poor, black man, brother. A junkie on

the rebound. No one likes to see a man like me fight. Not unless I'm laced into gloves, taking swings, and they're placing bets down at Atlantic City." Joshua glowered at me. I swore I could feel heat on my face from his gaze. "No one should bet against me, though. Right, Elizabeth? I always come out on top."

I don't know what I was thinking. It just bubbled out. "Should we call you a cab? Or do you already have the number?"

"Thank you for your concern, Elizabeth."

"You always understand just how I feel." Every word that passed between us felt weighted down with resentment.

Addison just stood off to the side, watching. Then he stepped in between us. "It sounds like you have it under control, Joshua. I love you, brother. Always. I'll see you."

"You two get home safely. Don't go starting any trouble." Joshua addressed Addison, but his words were meant for me. When we started back up the hill, we both stayed quiet. It didn't feel like the taut silence that usually stretched between us after times with Joshua, though. This time the air around us felt easier to breathe.

He believes me, I let myself think. Maybe he'd even had doubts all along. Maybe he and I could navigate the rocky path back around Joshua's ego and influence together.

"You all right?" he asked me, when we reached the black scrollwork of the iron gates.

"We all right?" I asked back.

"Of course." As if that were a given.

"Then I'm all right."

I draped my arms around his neck and tried to pull him close but Addison stepped back, just a little. "Greer, Greer — my best year."

"What was?"

"This." He gestured to McCracken Hill, then to me.

"A little pitiful, Addison Bradley." I thought of the cold dread when I realized my parents could just abandon me. The bare room that looked like every other bare room on campus. The condescending hours spent being dissected by the treatment team. But. I remembered Addison stomping into lit class that first day. Sophie and I giggling about our descent into sluttery — someone finally understood me. I thought of the cabin and the bowling alley and the sense of belonging I felt when we all stood around Addison, singing. I even thought about Joshua, the rush of having someone name me, choose me. "Pitiful," I repeated. "But, just so you know — me too."

He brushed his lips over my forehead, rested his hands lightly on my shoulders, and then stepped out of the circle we'd made with our arms. "You okay to get back to the dorm?"

"Yeah — it's fine."

He nodded and still didn't move away. Then he turned abruptly.

"Hey — I love you!" I called after him.

He spun around and kept walking backward, calling out softly, "Greer, I love you always. See you."

I rushed off to tell Sophie that he might have finally come around. That he might finally believe us. I didn't even notice that Addison had said good night to me with almost the same words he had spoken to Joshua.

I didn't realize it until late into the next morning, when word spread across campus that Addison Bradley had disappeared.

CHAPTER
TWENTY-SEVEN

The whispers started in statistics class. Honestly, it reminded me of school back home. Clusters of girls speaking softly and stealing glances, the sly and knowing looks of the guys. I thought maybe word had somehow gotten out about Hannah, but even that didn't make so much sense. Not even at my most teenage-delinquent had I managed to knock someone else up. One of the Allisons sat to the right of me, and I caught her smirking smugly.

I thought maybe Joshua had done something. Called the deans or started preaching my shame in the quad, but really, I felt ready for any of that. And then the bell toned. I hung back in the hall, waiting up for Addison, but he didn't come striding down the corridor. Maybe then I felt a ripple — like a tiny pebble had skipped across my heart. Addison had a lot to consider, though. Maybe he'd set up a meeting with his treatment team; they might have even invited his family in for a session.

I made sure to stroll casually into lit class and ignored the slight surge of murmurs. I took my usual seat and tried not to notice Addison's empty desk. And after class, when Dr. Rennie asked me kindly, "How are you doing, Greer?" I assumed he was thinking about our last conversation.

"Okay, thanks. Remember what we talked about? I might be able to convince him to come speak to you now — if that would still be okay." Dr. Rennie looked quizzical and began shuffling papers on his desk. "Addison. He's probably ready to come talk."

"Greer, I'm glad to hear that. But I'm not sure if any of us are in a position to help any longer."

That skipped pebble grew into a stone, embedded in my chest. "What does that mean?"

He pulled out a sheet of paper — the morning's daily bulletin. He pointed to the absence list and then the name typed in bold opposite of that. "Addison was released from McCracken Hill."

"I don't understand." I could barely breathe. The stone had grown into a boulder. It crushed my lungs.

"It sounds like he didn't have a chance to tell you."

"He wouldn't just leave."

"People don't always know how to handle saying good-bye."

"He wouldn't just leave me. You don't understand. This doesn't make sense. Did you know they were planning this? I mean, is this how it works?"

"No, I didn't know. But that's not unusual if I'm not a member of a student's team. Sometimes these decisions are made very quickly —"

"Who makes them?"

Dr. Rennie drummed his fingers on his desk. "It depends. That involves a lot of factors." I sat down in the seat beside his desk. "Addison's treatment team might have come to the conclusion that he'd made enough progress. Or not enough progress. Sometimes parents transfer students home and sometimes the students themselves make that call. Greer, even if I knew, some of this counts as confidential information.

You and Addison were very close; maybe he will write a letter and explain it all. When he's ready."

"Maybe he'll write me a letter?"

"You know what I'm telling you." I just sat there, staring. Finally Dr. Rennie sighed. "I can take you to see the dean. Maybe she can give us some more information. We could set up an appointment." I lowered my face. "Or we can just drop in now and see what she'll tell us." I looked up. "Okay?"

That's how I ended up waiting outside of Dean Edwards's office with my English teacher instead of having lunch with my adoring boyfriend and our close circle of loyal, well-balanced friends. The administrative building looked like a cross between a hotel lobby and a museum — lots of mahogany, leather books, and intricate Oriental rugs that felt thick beneath my feet. Dr. Rennie and I sat down in red antique chairs that looked like they might barely hold our weight.

"Greer Cannon?" Dean Edwards stood in the doorway to her office. "I'm sorry to keep you waiting — we've had a full morning today. Why don't you come in and sit down? Would you like Dr. Rennie to accompany you?" I shrugged. "Well, that's a choice for you to make." She turned purposefully back to her office.

"Shall we go in?" Dr. Rennie asked, standing.

Dean Edwards had already sat down behind her enormous desk. She gestured for us to sit. "How can I help you, Greer?" It felt like I sat there silently for several minutes.

After a while, Dr. Rennie coughed and said, "I think Greer has some ques —"

"Greer needs to ask those questions herself. That's part of pursuing empowerment."

"Why did you send Addison Bradley home?" I asked.

Dean Edwards sat back and unleashed the spiel. "I'm sure you're aware that McCracken Hill is a fairly unique learning institution. Our goal actually isn't to graduate all of our students. The best-case scenario is when a student returns home to complete his or her education in a traditional school setting."

"He wasn't ready to go home, though."

"I know the two of you were very close. We've felt concerned about that. Maybe we can all see this as a teachable moment and use it to give you the chance to focus more fully on Greer."

"So you kicked him out because of me?"

"Ms. Cannon, I assure you, this is not a case of anyone being kicked out of McCracken Hill."

"So all of a sudden, you just packed Addison up and sent him home to his overwhelmed parents and his addict brother? I know you couldn't have had time to prepare him at all. He was dealing with a lot of crap — I mean, a lot of changes — especially last night. He needs support — he needs people who care about him. He needs —"

"Addison signed himself out of treatment, Greer."

"That's not true."

"I'm sorry that this has shocked you, and I do understand that you're probably experiencing a myriad of emotions right now. However, legally, there's not much more I can say. At eighteen, he has the legal right to decide which school he will attend, if he attends school at all. Unless we thought Addison was a danger to himself or anyone else, it is not within our purview to stop him."

"Did he tell you about Joshua?" I fought to keep my voice calm.

"Joshua?"

"Joshua Stern — he's the man who — I don't know — controls Addison. Did he pick him up? Can you at least tell me that?" My voice pitched up toward the end of my question and I struggled to bring it back to nonhysterical range.

"This is Addison Bradley's Narcotics Anonymous sponsor?" she asked me and then turned her gaze on Dr. Rennie, who appeared to wish he'd stayed behind in his classroom, grading *Beowulf* papers. "No one consulted Mr. Stern about this. To my knowledge, Addison came to this decision on his own."

"No one picked him up?"

Dean Edwards spoke carefully. "At this point, we're delving into private aspects that should remain private. Just as I would do my best to maintain your confidentiality, I need to respect Addison's wishes."

"He asked you not to tell me?"

"Addison refused follow-up care," she said, which told me nothing. "I can imagine how difficult this is, Greer. You've made tremendous progress here at McCracken Hill, though, and I ask you to remember that. From what I've observed, Addison is a caring young man. It's clear the two of you have forged a strong connection. Ultimately every individual here is responsible for his or her own recovery. You understand that."

I'd had enough of the official McCracken Hill pamphlet talk. My voice sounded hollowed out. "May I please return to my friends now?" Dean Edwards tilted her head at me, so I tossed in a token "I don't mean to be disrespectful."

She glanced at Dr. Rennie and said, "I'd be happy to accompany Greer to her next scheduled engagement." She waited and then tapped the tip of her pen against her desk.

"Oh — oh sure. That's great. That's all right, Greer? You'll be okay?" Dr. Rennie stumbled over his words as he rushed to pick up his raincoat and wrap his scarf around his neck.

"We're fine, Dr. Rennie. Greer and I both appreciate your concern and outreach" — she lowered her reading glasses to peer at him — "sincerely." She waited until he closed the door shut behind him.

"How are you?" This stellar effort at building rapport was apparently how the dean earned the big bucks and fancy office.

"Fine. Thank you."

"Greer?"

"I feel abandoned. May I go to lunch now?"

"Sometimes it's enough to just give people time."

"And you think he'll come back?" I couldn't keep the hope out of my voice.

"No, Addison will not be returning to McCracken Hill." She seemed genuinely sad. "But there's a whole world outside of these gates. I know you know that. The best advice I can give you is to keep staying strong for yourself. I won't tell you about all the other young men you'll come across or how it'll get easier. Addison certainly seems like one of a kind." She smiled at me. "But then again, so do you."

I appreciated the sentiment. But truthfully, the only thing extraordinary about me was Addison. Now I was just another girl left by another boy. Starting then I was just sad — which didn't really feel a whole lot different from how I arrived.

"Thank you for taking the time."

"I wish I could provide more clarity. You mentioned Addison's sponsor, Mr. Stern. Anything I need to know?"

What was the point? Addison had either chosen Joshua or given up us both. "No," I said. She studied me. "Sorry," I added. "Looking for someone to blame, I guess." I almost asked if it would be possible to skip lunch and regroup in my dorm room. But she probably expected those questions. She'd consider it turning to old habits for comfort.

Addison had made me willing to stay at McCracken Hill. Without him, I already felt claustrophobic. So I made up my mind, sitting in the dean's office. No one would know how desperately I wanted to follow him. I'd obey their rules and embrace my solitary recovery and then eventually I'd get to leave. Then I'd track down Addison and demand an explanation. Or by that time, I'd have numbed myself so much that it no longer mattered.

"I hope you'll come back to talk again and let me know how you're doing." Dean Edwards stood and walked me to the door. "Plenty of people want to help."

Plenty of people also wanted to gloat and it felt like I walked past most of them on my way to the dining commons. I zombied my way through the food line. Sat down at the nearest empty table. Heard their chairs scoot across the linoleum first and then Sophie, Hannah, and Jared all appeared and settled into the empty seats around me. I refused to react. "We're giving you the benefit of the doubt, assuming you didn't see us," Sophie said. I stood up without saying a word, retrieved the yellow squeeze bottle, and brought the whole thing back to the table. No one stopped me.

I covered an entire slice of turkey. "You're drowning your sorrows in mustard?" Jared asked lightly.

"Are you okay?" Sophie asked. "When did you know? Did you try to stop him? Did he tell you not to tell us? Is he home with his parents? Does Joshua know yet?"

I bit my lip, closed my eyes, and opened them. Began cutting my turkey with my fork and knife. Sophie reached to rattle my tray. "Greer."

My head must have reared up. My throat burned and I struggled to swallow the small bite in my mouth that felt dusty and dry. Sophie stared at me and I felt my eyes fill up. "Leave her alone," Hannah ordered quietly. "She doesn't want to cry in front of all these people."

Sophie relented, for the meal at least, and I listened to the three of them struggle to talk about things that wouldn't trigger a weeping jag from my side of the table. I sat there cutting my meat carefully. Each time the ache threatened to crack open my chest, I looked up to see Hannah's slight smile.

Outside we sat along the stone parapet. Jared blocked me from the sight lines of the gossip paparazzi and Sophie paced back and forth. Her compact body seemed to hum with tension. "Last night, when you came back to the dorm, it sounded like you guys had experienced this breakthrough. I mean, that's what you said."

Hannah reached over to me. She tucked a loose strand of hair behind my ear. "You okay, Greer?"

"What?" I blinked and focused my eyes, realizing I'd been staring at the campus gate. "Yeah, thanks. Thanks for asking. Listen, Sophie, I don't know what to tell you. He knew when he said good night."

"Why do you say that?"

"I just know." Some things I meant to keep private, for myself.

"But you came in babbling about how he finally understood —"

"Sophie, I didn't know last night, okay? You think I would have just moseyed into your room, all glowing about him? Really? You think I would have been able to peel myself off the floor if I knew he was going to leave?"

"All right. I'm sorry, okay? I just don't understand. If he believed you —"

"Maybe Addison left because he believed her." Jared spoke up.

"What?" Sophie and I said the word at the same time. Hannah sort of mouthed it, so that counted too.

"Well, what choice did he really have, you know? He probably felt stupid as all hell. And we weren't all just going to leave it, right? You wanted Joshua to answer for lying or whatever."

I stared at Hannah. *Or whatever.*

Jared went on. "Maybe he just needs to sort out his head. We'll go to afternoon classes and come back and find Addison all sweaty from the gym."

"I don't think so." I felt them all waiting. "Dean Edwards met with me this morning."

"Holy crap." Sophie clapped her hand over her mouth. "Why didn't you start off with that little tidbit? What did she say?"

"Well, that's how I knew they hadn't kicked him out. She wouldn't tell me much more than that." And then, because they seemed to be waiting for more, I added, "She told me to stay strong."

"Well, that's helpful." Sophie kicked one sneakered foot against the stone wall. "I can't believe this. Someone has to at least reach out to him. We could call his parents."

"No. We absolutely can't do that." I imagined Mrs. Bradley's voice as a cheerful chirp and wondered how I was supposed to introduce myself now. "I won't chase him."

"Why? You deserve an explanation."

"Wow. Thanks for your concern, Sophie. Listen, maybe next week I'll be able to deal with this, but right now I'm just trying to keep it together, okay?"

She stopped pacing and pivoted slowly. "I'm an asshole, huh? I'm sorry. God, Greer — I really apologize. What was I thinking? Are you okay?" She swatted Jared on the back of his head. "Jesus. Why didn't you tell me I was acting like such an asshole?" Sophie dropped to the ground. "Aren't you worried, though? I'm just saying — one of us could call."

"I could call," Jared volunteered.

"Maybe," I relented. "Just to make sure he's okay."

The three of them walked me to class. I survived afternoon sessions and dragged myself to the dining hall for dinner. Hannah and I landed at the same assigned table with Ms. Ling moderating a discussion on milestones.

Halfway through, Sophie scooted an extra chair up to our table and Ms. Ling actually allowed that. She didn't even make me speak. She'd brought along an index card carefully printed with questions. "What are some of the milestones we celebrate with our families?" We all stared at her. "Not now, obviously, but at home, what would you celebrate?"

Hannah raised her hand before answering, "Hanukkah."

"Okay, but that's more of a holiday, right? When we talk about milestones, we mean rites of passage. You know — ways we celebrate growth?"

In my head, I played a movie of firsts with Addison — the first time we met, the first words we spoke. The first time he reached for my hand. I remembered the first time he introduced me to Joshua, how hesitant I'd been. How aware that Joshua's approval mattered.

"What about milestones here, on campus? How do we mark them?"

I heard Ms. Ling speaking from far away. I heard one of the drug-addled dolts at our table mutter, "Liquids."

"That's right, PJ. When we start earning privileges, that counts as a milestone."

"When we leave," I said.

Sophie sucked in her breath and Hannah's hand sort of fluttered toward me. "Yeah," Ms. Ling answered simply. "That's another." I nodded and no one said much else. We sat mostly in silence until she nodded and then we trolleyed our trays and left.

As soon as we stepped out of the building, Jared was waiting for us.

"I called," he said. "They have no idea where he is." Sophie tugged us both down to sit with her on the grass, and Hannah joined us. Other people milled around, some staring, some oblivious.

"How could they not know?" I asked. "Didn't they come to get him?"

"Mr. Bradley just said they were proud of his progress. He said that when he heard from Addison, he would pass along that I was trying to get in touch. He didn't really sound so concerned."

I thought of Chuckie. Mr. Bradley had enough to worry about. "Addison's eighteen," I reminded them. "He just signed himself out."

"He doesn't have any place to go," Hannah said.

"Unless he went with Joshua," Sophie said.

I refused to believe that. I refused to even think of it as a possibility. "He probably just bought a bus ticket. Chose some random city and now he'll start over. You know, he'll get a crappy job somewhere, stay at a motel at first."

Sophie didn't believe me. "What makes you so sure?"

I made myself remember the room at the cabin. The heavy quilt. The bed that creaked and the window frame that knocked through the night when the wind blew.

"Because that's the plan we made together," I said, "before Addison decided to leave me behind."

TWENTY-EIGHT

When the yellow cab first pulled up to the front gates of McCracken Hill, I felt a gust of hope. I thought, *He's come back,* and managed to pull myself up to my knees. My whole heart lurched, but when the door swung open, it wasn't Addison who stepped out. Joshua had arrived.

He searched through the flocks of kids who arrowed in all different directions across campus. I saw him zero in on me and realized I was still kneeling. Joshua might have even thought I was praying. Hannah, Jared, and Sophie sat behind me. When I rose and started slowly across the lawn, I heard Sophie calling me back. Joshua's voice rang out too.

"Elizabeth? Are you humbled yet?" I almost nodded. He said, "It mystifies me. All you had to do was practice generosity. I made room for you in his life. Look where we are now. The stupidity and pettiness staggers me." We stood facing each other before Joshua pushed through the iron gates. "All you needed to do was sit there while I instructed others to adore you!" He shouted it through the bars, as if speaking from a jail cell. Or maybe I was the one in prison and Joshua was visiting me.

"Where is he?" he demanded. I shook my head. "Don't play games, Greer. This isn't hide-and-seek. We could find him crouched in some stairwell somewhere smoking rock from a pipe. You want to carry that on your shoulders?"

"I don't —"

"You don't what?"

"I don't believe that."

"Just tell me the plan. You'll lie low and then leave to meet up with him? I'm sure this may come as a shock, but if Addison needs to start over somewhere to find happiness, I will support that. I can help you. We'll drive to see him. I'll say my piece and then Addison can make a lucid decision about how we all move forward. His call. Regardless, I will continue to be his servant in faith."

My vision blurred with fresh tears. It felt like losing Addison all over again. Even Joshua wouldn't be able to find him. But the more desperately Joshua asked, the more I understood that Addison had really escaped. Joshua wasn't secretly orchestrating his life anymore. I felt lighter, knowing that. Wherever Addison was, he was finally making his own choices. Eventually maybe he'd choose to come looking for me.

Joshua looked anguished even when I swore to him, "He didn't tell me. I didn't even know that he left." Then I moved to turn away. Jared and Hannah sat rooted to their spots, while Sophie was on her feet. To the right, I spotted Wes. He stood there, with his arms folded across his chest, watching. And then there were so many people I hadn't yet even bothered to get to know. It felt like I had a whole village waiting for me. McCracken Hill had sold me on its whole philosophy of community. At least for those slow-motion moments anyway.

Joshua stood alone on the outside, lost and forlorn. And then he erupted, lunging through the iron gates and pushing his way over to me. He told me, "He left you and I don't blame him. You're still stuck in that room. Addison knows better than to doom himself to a lifetime of that. I taught him to shun people like you. Corpses. Do you hear me? You are a cadaver. I look at you and see decay."

But Joshua sobbed as he screamed at me. If I ever testified that I felt frightened for my life, I'd be lying. Suddenly he just seemed like a sad and desperate person who had taken more than a few wrong turns. Had he been sitting at a bus stop in town, Sophie and I might have muttered, "Poor guy," and gone back to gossiping on our way to the coffee shop. But that's not who Joshua had become for us.

He grabbed at me and I screamed more in surprise than fear. I backed away and he stumbled on the curb and fell into me. When we hit the ground, it must have looked like Joshua had wrestled me down. My head had snapped back against the pavement — it throbbed. And the shouting around us made it worse. I wrapped my arms around my head. Joshua pushed himself up onto his elbows, keeping me pinned beneath his body.

That's why I was staring up at him when it happened. First he grimaced, maybe in embarrassment. When Sophie dove between us, Joshua scowled in anger and rose up. And then his eyes went wide and his mouth opened to shout and that's when I saw her push the knife into his chest.

"GET OFF OF HER!" Sophie's scream pierced through the clear afternoon. I remember noticing her breath. Sophie was panting, and Joshua's mouth moved in a wet sort of gurgle.

Wes was there in seconds, lifting her under her arms. He pulled her off and she kicked at the air like a little kid. Jared knelt next to Joshua and reached to pull out the knife but it was too slippery. You could only see part of the black plastic grip because Sophie had stabbed him so deeply. I reached out to Joshua and his hands moved to shove me away. He thought I would hurt him too.

Blood seeped around the knife and also trickled from his lips. His eyes looked glassy and unfocused. Jared told him, "Hold on, man. Hold on, brother. Hannah ran for help." We looked up to the lawn where dozens of students stood staring. "Somebody call an ambulance. Call nine-one-one. Somebody help us over here!" Jared bellowed. No one had cell phones to reach for. No one moved.

Pink bubbles frothed lightly from Joshua's mouth. And then they stopped.

Behind me, Wes asked, "What did you do?" and Sophie started weeping.

We sat there on the pavement and grass, scattered around him in a loose circle. Hannah rushed up and took both Joshua's hands in hers.

The police came first and then the rescue squad right after. Ms. Crane sat us all in a line along the curb, with our backs to the scene behind us. I heard the EMTs bickering about the knife. They couldn't do chest compressions. They argued over trying to move the blade. "He's gone anyway," I heard one of the guys mutter. Sophie moaned and I reached for her hand. We crouched against each other and listened to them pack Joshua onto the stretcher and then into the ambulance. We heard the door slam closed.

I turned to tell the police what had happened and Ms. Crane called my name sharply. "Greer, just stay put. Everything will be taken care of." She crossed over to the cops and spoke just as firmly, "Our attorneys are en route. We request that you conduct all interviews on the school premises. This is a therapeutic environment, and we're deeply concerned about the effects of such a major trauma on our students."

That's how we ended up being interviewed together. Sitting around a conference table in one of the counseling rooms. With a white-haired attorney smoothing his tie and prodding us along. "Ms. Cannon? Greer? You feared for your safety?"

"At that moment?"

"At any moment. Did Mr. Stern frighten you?"

"Yes."

"Did he threaten you?" I stared at Sophie.

"Yes."

"Did he physically harm you?" I stared at Hannah.

"Yes."

The police officer broke in. "We're going to need some details about the threats and physical abuse."

Wes spoke up then. "I also felt unsafe in Mr. Stern's presence. He physically threatened me. His attention to the girls made me uncomfortable." He added, "I met him through my roommate. After the threats escalated, I took steps to transfer dorms."

The officer frowned. He turned to Dean Edwards. "You have documentation of this?" She nodded. "And who's the former roommate?"

I pictured Addison riding in a darkened bus. Staring out at the scenery, unaware of the aftermath of his departure. Dean Edwards dismissed the question. "The roommate has moved on from our community," she said, then hastily added, "for no other reason than his own progress."

"Take me through this afternoon's altercation again," the police officer asked and one by one, we each described how scared we'd been, how Joshua had shocked us by showing up. Sophie claimed that she started carrying the knife after Joshua had asked her repeatedly for money. Jared confided he'd felt too intimidated to object to Joshua's presence in the dorms.

"When was he in the dorms?" Dean Edwards broke in.

"On Tuesday nights, after group — sometimes he was too tired to go home."

"Where did he sleep?"

Jared shrugged. "Usually in my room. I slept on the floor."

"You gave up your bed for the guy who ran NA meetings?" the cop asked incredulously.

"He's old." Jared shrugged once more and corrected himself quietly. "He *was* old."

"Mr. Stern seems to have played quite an active role at McCracken Hill."

"I'm not sure that's accurate." Dean Edwards stood behind Sophie's chair. "Our students have struggled with a myriad of issues. They tend to be particularly vulnerable to adult influences."

The cop gave her a look that said, *Way to stay on top of the situation then, lady.* But he replied, "From my standpoint, your students appear more dangerous than vulnerable."

The white-haired lawyer brushed his hand over his tie. "Teenagers can be secretive. We do regret that the McCracken Hill administration lacked any knowledge about Mr. Stern's instability. Or his status as a transient, for that matter. Perhaps this tragedy might have been averted and we will certainly examine those protocols."

Dean Edwards stared stonily at the conference table like a woman drafting her resignation letter. Her power suit had wilted. "Is there anything else we can do to help?" she asked.

"Yeah." The officer nodded at Sophie. "The young lady over there stabbed a man to death a few hours ago. We'll probably need to have more than a faculty meeting about it."

The lawyer straightened his tie at the knot. "She's a minor. Her parents are out of state. She's not available for questioning at this time about this unfortunate incident of self-defense." He sounded almost bored.

Dean Edwards placed her hand on Sophie's shoulder. "We'll be contacting Sophie's parents immediately and will keep you updated about our decisions."

"Well, that's mighty accommodating of you."

Suddenly Sophie blurted out, "We were so scared and I heard him screaming at Greer and then he tackled her —"

"Ms. Delia, thank you."

"And Hannah —"

Hannah's mouth dropped open. She sat up rigidly and gripped the conference table with both hands. She looked ready to race out of the room.

But the lawyer muzzled Sophie pretty quickly anyway. "I think we just need to sit tight for now and wait for word from your parents, Ms. Delia." Dean Edwards dismissed the rest of us to our dorms. When we stood to leave, my knees buckled. I felt like I had been shaking for hours.

Sophie and I locked eyes. She reached for my sleeve. "If you hug me, I'll start bawling like a baby," I said.

She eyed the police officer, who stood in the corner, deep in discussion with Dean Edwards. "I know I did the right thing," she said clearly. I couldn't tell if she meant it for my benefit or the cop's. Or her own.

"What happens next?" I asked.

Sophie squeezed her eyes shut and then opened them. "See you on the other side."

CHAPTER
TWENTY-NINE

None of us ended up facing charges. Sophie's dad showed up and went full-court press on McCracken Hill for the lack of security on campus. They transferred her to a school for violent youth. I guess that counted as a compromise.

During those negotiations, Sophie must have given up the goods on Hannah. It took them two weeks to find her a residential program for birth mothers. During her last few days at McCracken, she brought a binder into my dorm room: possible adoptive parents for her baby. We browsed together.

"This one." Hannah tapped on one of the plastic sleeves.

"The optometrist?"

"That's a very stable industry. People always need to see clearly."

"Hannah, the mom lists scrapbooking as a hobby."

"There's nothing wrong with scrapbooking."

"They're pretty much the most boring people ever."

"I want that," she told me. "I want this baby to grow up in the most boring home on the planet. I want him to play Little League and love comic books. And be sweet and kind of clueless. Like Jared."

Jared had gone home three days after Joshua's "accident." He told us over breakfast the morning he found out. "Baseball," he said simply. "They would have driven up before preseason no matter what. This just pushed things forward a little." He pulled an index card out of his backpack and wrote down all his contact info. "If you hear from Sophie, pass it along to her too, okay? And definitely Addison — when Addison gets in touch." I nodded and Hannah sucked in her breath.

Jared spoke so gently that tears rushed back behind my eyes again. "Hey, Greer, he's going to understand what happened, you know. Things had been heading off the deep end for a long time."

"It's not like I spilled ketchup on his favorite shirt, Jared."

He said, "Yeah. I know."

Wes designated himself our chaperone, our bodyguard, our masculine pillar of strength. He sat with Hannah and me at breakfast. Sat with us outside in the quad. He joined us for lunch. He glowered at the vultures who swooped in to ask if we'd heard from Addison or Sophie.

But it was Hannah who Wes treated really carefully. He was always jumping up to fetch her more of something in the dining hall. Once or twice, he reached for her bag. He waited until we were alone to ask me. Ms. Crane had taken Hannah off campus to see the obstetrician, so it felt a little strange — just Wes and me at lunch. Without anyone to plot against or defend ourselves from. "No Hannah?" he asked.

"Some doctor's appointment." I dismantled my turkey sandwich and ate the insides.

"Yeah? Another one?" I watched him, waiting. "Hannah rests her hand on her stomach a lot, like she's in pain or . . ."

"Or."

Wes finished off his glass of juice. "Yeah, that's what I thought. Can you tell me who?"

"You don't know?"

"Well, it's not me, if that's what you're implying. And if it were Addison, you and Hannah wouldn't cling to each other like two deflated life jackets. Jared?" Wes answered himself. "Jared could barely handle Sophie." I waited for him to get there. "Oh man. Oh man. No way did that actually happen. Greer? Are you kidding me with this?"

I assured him I wasn't.

Wes declared, "Well then, you know what? Good for Sophie. I'm glad."

I waited through that part too. Finally his outrage sputtered out. "I'm sorry — that's not true." I remembered what Joshua had said about Judas, about betrayal. Beneath the lunchroom clatter of plates and trays, the sound of the wheeling gurney made me flinch. That was just a memory, though.

Ms. Ling arranged it so I could help carry out Hannah's bags and help her get situated. Her mother was there, a pinched face who didn't even bother to get out of the car.

Hannah started going to pieces, convinced they'd actually take her to some kind of mental ward.

I cooed, "You'll meet other girls who are going through this same thing. You won't have to deal with anyone staring at you or talking smack. It's just me left anyway. And Wes," I reminded her. "Don't worry — we won't have any fun without you."

"No, you probably won't." Hannah sniffled. We held hands while the last of her bags were put in the car. "You know, Greer. It didn't happen like Sophie said it did. With Joshua. Sophie got her version stuck in her head. But it wasn't like that."

I remembered those tense minutes waiting for Joshua to show up in my dorm room, how I cringed each time he reached out his hand. "I know. Whatever way he convinced you, though, it still wasn't —" But I didn't feel qualified to judge him anymore. So I just told Hannah, "None of what happened was your fault."

"And everything's going to be okay?"

"Yup." I'd started to feel a little bit dead inside. "Everything's going to be fine."

It didn't always feel fine, though. Even with Wes playing ambassador to the noncult community, I stumbled around campus. It felt like the first days at McCracken Hill all over again. Without Addison. I couldn't remember how to speak to other people. Most mornings, I spent the time before classes in an empty desk in the back of Dr. Rennie's room, pretending to read. The first time, he looked a little unnerved, but after that, he barely acknowledged me. He slurped his coffee and I turned pages. It was nice, companionable. He was the only teacher who didn't suffocate me with questions.

Until he asked one: "You've had a lot of disappearances in your life over the past few weeks, haven't you?" Which was, you know, kind of a doozy, but Dr. Rennie seemed to be considering something. He hemmed and hawed. Finally he said, "I shouldn't be telling you this. As you know, the daily report is meant as a resource for the faculty." He took out a pen and underlined something on the sheet. He set the sheet on his desk between us and nodded at me. I stepped up, tentatively, to read it.

At the bottom of the page, the last line of the memo read: *Please be aware a representative from the Delia family will be retrieving Sophia Delia's belongings from Empowerment Hall between the hours of 8 A.M. and 10 A.M.*

Dr. Rennie's first class started filing in. The clock above the door read 8:10.

"Class attendance is important, Greer." Dr. Rennie chose his words carefully. "But you look peaked — I'm concerned for your health. Why don't you return to your dorm and take today to rest a bit? I'll alert the nurse, but I'm very busy now. Perhaps I'll have the chance to e-mail her at around ten."

"Thank you," I told him. "Really, I don't know how —"

"Just feel better," he said gruffly as he wrote out a pass. "I hope taking those few minutes to heal helps."

I skulked back to the dorm, prepared to mimic the symptoms of a migraine if anyone stopped me. It wouldn't be Sophie, I knew that. And chances were, her parents wouldn't speak to me. Even if they shut me down, though, there was the possibility they'd mention to Sophie that I showed up. At least she'd know I tried.

It took me three attempts to even make myself walk past the open door of Sophie's old dorm room. I heard cardboard folding and the rip of packing tape. It made me wonder, briefly, how Addison had managed to box up all his belongings. Addison had been pretty low maintenance, though. He probably shoved all his clothes into a duffel and called it good.

Sophie had stuff. Piles and piles, and before she even turned around, I recognized Josie sitting in the middle of it. She wore her black curls pinned back and was dressed like Sophie — yoga pants, black T-shirt. She looked like one of those pictures of celebrities you see in magazines under the headline "Stars — They're Just Like Us." They're always carrying lattes or wearing yoga pants and looking glossily frazzled. Busily beautiful. Josie looked just like that.

It felt weird to knock on the door, even just the frame. And it didn't help that Josie practically leapt out of her skin. "I'm so sorry," I rushed to say before she screamed and security came running. "I just wanted to see if you needed help."

"Oh, no thanks." She barely looked up. While I stood there, wondering what to do next, she tacked on, "Sorry to be noisy. They told me everyone would be in class."

"Most people are. I should be. But my teacher let me out on account of a migraine." I stepped forward and then back and then finally said, "I'm Greer — Sophie's my best friend." It came out weird, like somehow I felt qualified to compete with Josie. *You might have floated around together in utero, but we happen to be best friends now.* Josie had torn off a piece of tape and held it stretched between her hands. She spoke without turning back around. "Nice to meet you, Greer."

"Yeah, it's great to meet you too. I don't mean to bother you, but I just wanted to know how Sophie was doing — you know, if she's okay."

"She's not really okay." My feet wouldn't move to back away before she said, "My sister killed someone."

"Right." I spoke to the back of Josie's head. "That must seem crazy. But Sophie kept a lot of us safe, you know. It was a dangerous situation."

"Well, apparently that's debatable." Josie spun around, still sitting cross-legged. Apparently the yoga pants weren't just a fashion statement. "He was a really scary guy?"

I thought about it. "Yes." I tried to explain it. "He controlled so many things. No one seemed to question him."

"Maybe she could have questioned him instead of stabbing him." I didn't know what to say to that. Josie fidgeted with her hair. "Listen, Greer. Sophie loves you. I'm sure that when she's allowed to, she'll write you or something. And I know that she believes that what she did was justified. I just don't care, okay?" I heard the rest of it, even though Josie didn't say it out loud. Her brother had just died; her sister was locked in some kind of ward. Her parents had split up. She had packing to do.

I still felt like I needed to make her understand. That was the least I could offer Sophie. "Did she tell you about Hannah?"

"The pregnant girl?"

So, yes, then. "Sophie — I think she felt extra protective of Hannah. Because she identified Joshua as this older man. Exploiting her." *Tread carefully,* I warned myself. "I've thought about that a lot and I wonder if maybe your situation just really affected her. You know? It made her sensitive to what Hannah was going through. Because you experienced something like that."

Josie crinkled up her nose. "I experienced something like what?"

Of course she had to make it hard for me. Maybe Sophie and Josie shared a genetic disposition for denial. It felt important, though, to make her understand. "You know —" I tried to say it kindly. "With your field-hockey coach?"

"I didn't play field hockey," Josie said flatly. She looked at the door like she wished she could slam it in my face. "*Sophie* played field hockey." She stared at me, waiting for me to understand.

When I didn't speak, she did. "My sister is a really sick person. When she wrote me about your little group of friends, it made me really happy to think that she'd found people who'd accepted her. She sounded hopeful. Better." Josie smoothed a piece of tape across the top of a box. "I'm sorry you got caught up in her lies."

"That's okay," I told her and willed my voice not to splinter in pieces. "I got caught up in a lot of lies. We all did."

CHAPTER
THIRTY

When I told Dr. Saggurti about the conversation, I pretended that I'd just happened to walk by Sophie's room and found her sister packing up her things. "How did that feel?" she asked. I told her about Josie's coldness, the way she didn't even tell me good-bye or reassure me that she would tell Sophie I missed her. "Did she remind you of Eliza, your own sister?" Dr. Saggurti looked poised to take some serious notes. When I recounted the piece of information about the field-hockey coach, Dr. Saggurti leaned in and wheeled her desk chair closer to me.

"Why might Sophie have told that lie?" she asked me.

"Maybe Sophie wished it had happened to Josie instead of her." Dr. Saggurti frowned as if to say, *Maybe, but no. Wrong answer.* "Or she used it to test us." That got a thoughtful nod. I tried out one of Joshua's theories. "Maybe she didn't need to tell us the details. She shared the important piece — she knew someone who'd been through that. That was Sophie's emotional truth."

"Explain what you mean by that phrase — *emotional truth.*"

"I guess I mean that the exact details sometimes don't matter. What you believe most has its own way of becoming true."

"What do you believe happened then, Greer?"

"With what? With Sophie?"

"With all of you. You forged an incredibly strong connection."

It felt like a trick, a dare to say something she could analyze and later hold against me. But once the thought surfaced, I couldn't stop myself from needing to say it aloud, even if I knew it was technically imprecise. I wondered if that's how Sophie felt. How Joshua felt.

"I believe they became my family," I admitted.

In the past few weeks, Dr. Saggurti had insisted on running several actual family sessions. They amounted to calling my father on speakerphone, on days when he could fit me in between his power lunch and his afternoon meeting. Dean Edwards had requested that he drive up to discuss what all the McCracken Hill staff referred to as "The Incident," but my dad canceled at the last minute. I'm sure he sent a hefty check.

We talked about summer break and he said, "You're making such progress. We'd hate to interrupt that." He'd enrolled me in the intensive therapeutic summer session so I could be extra well adjusted for the fall. It didn't matter. I'd either sit in my room at McCracken or sit in my room in Connecticut. At least Addison might come back to McCracken Hill.

Wes signed on for summer session too. He said that after the Poconos mountain poker incident, he didn't feel ready to go home and risk his recovery. At least that's what he told his treatment team. Wes never lied to me. He stayed so that I didn't have to stay alone.

At first, that worried me. Neither of us needed a romance. But whatever charged feelings once hummed between us short-circuited in the weeks I spent waiting for Addison to show up.

In the last few weeks of the school year, I tried hiding and skulking but Wes wouldn't have it. He escorted me around school like a tour guide to normal. When he caught someone staring, he simply introduced me. We'd be relaxing on the Westlands lawn and he'd whip out a Frisbee and make me play. With other people.

"They're not so bad," Wes insisted.

"They're emotional vampires. They're salivating for a nervous breakdown."

"Well then, you can't let them smell blood." Wes sauntered ahead of me to the dining hall.

"Was it this awful for you?"

"You mean months ago? When I stood alone without anyone to support me and had to reintegrate into the general population of McCracken Hill? While my closest friends blackmailed me and referred to me as Judas?"

"Yeah." I tried to blink out *sorry* in Morse code before my eyes filled with tears.

Wes slowed down enough to drape his arm over me. "No. I mean, it was devastating, but it wasn't half as bad. Let's look back at the past couple of months, Greer. Shit has gone down. We're not exactly talking about your typical teenage breakup, right?" He started listing them on his fingers. "Murder."

"Pregnancy," I offered.

"Disappearance."

"Militant vegans." I named that one in the same stage whisper. Then Wes said, "But look — we just played Frisbee. Things are getting more typical every day. People honestly aren't evil, Greer. But you sealed yourself away from everybody who wasn't part of your disturbed little circle. They'll throw you a lifeline, but you have to ask first." We got to the dining hall and checked our table number. The treatment team had shown a little mercy and assigned us to the same spot each night. "Table four, with Coach Tyson: total VIP experience."

"Yeah?"

"Bottle service and everything."

I couldn't tell how dangerous that joke was at our particular gathering. I barely knew the others, let alone their individual addictions. But I recognized people. Drew Costa. A girl named Prairie from my English class. One of the Allisons.

Coach Tyson had piled enough lean protein on his plate to sustain a large carnivorous tribe. I sliced a hard-boiled egg over my greens, mixed in croutons. If Sophie were here, she'd steal a crouton. Addison would nag me about the lack of dressing, the absence of bacon bits. I solemnly vowed not to sob into my salad.

Wes asked, "I was just wondering what we'd be conversing about this evening."

Coach Tyson dug into the mesh pocket of his running shorts, pulled out a slip of paper, and squinted to read it. "Tonight's dinner topic is . . . disaster relief." Coach Tyson appeared puzzled by his own subject matter. I looked around the table. Most of the faces gaped openly at me as if I were a refugee who'd just clawed her way to shore.

Wes grinned slyly. "Disaster relief. We could use some of that." And he nodded at me to reach out.

EPILOGUE

I no longer believe that the supermarket scanner infuses the food with light. So score one for the rational interpretation of available facts. I still won't push around the big, bulky cart; instead I carry the plastic basket in one hand, balance the baby on my hip. Usually that's enough of a distraction — making sure he hasn't nabbed a Hershey's bar from the rack near the checkout. Setting down the cartons, the boxes. Counting out money. Carefully. Juggling all of that, I don't have time to remember Joshua's rules — what kind of light carries nourishment, what kind kills healthy cells. There's already enough to worry about.

The baby is closer to a toddler now, and we probably treat him too delicately. But I know how easily he can be damaged. I chose Parker as his middle name to remind me just in case. To remind his grandparents. But it's only his middle name — no one calls him that. Not even my cousin — who hosted us at his ranch last Christmas — who trains horses for people who aren't patient enough to do so themselves.

My son's father is a good man, who considers me an angel only metaphorically, who occasionally teases me about the years I spent in juvie because we can hardly imagine it now. We are that happy. We are happier than I ever thought was planned for me. Usually.

Sometimes I think of McCracken Hill, but mostly I think of Addison. Just in blinks — a certain slope of a nose in profile, the stomp of combat boots against linoleum at the mall. Those boys with the shaved heads seem much angrier now, but I try not to make assumptions. After all, Addison might be angry like that now too.

It's hard to imagine him grown older, paunchy, maybe even a little bit cowed. Unfeasible to think I could pass him on the street and not realize, not recognize. Once in a while, I type his name into the computer, but nothing rises to the surface. A publisher of academic textbooks. A construction company that had potential, but turned out to be named for the hometowns of the two founders.

I could see him enlisting. Trading in Joshua's lessons for an even more disciplined dogma. Wearing fatigues, carrying a weapon, riding in a jeep over land laced with explosives. That is the possibility that worries me most. In the decade since I've seen him, we've fought wars against actual enemies. Maybe Addison went over and did not come home.

I force myself to have faith in an alternate ending. That one day, I'll chase my son as he races over to the playground and notice a man stooped slightly over an easel in the park. Maybe I'll notice the painting first. The unfurling of the flowers' petals will seem familiar and then I'll see his hands. Then his eyes. We'll stand there, facing each other, and I'll know that Addison forgives me. After all these years, would that be so astonishing? It wouldn't count as the strangest thing that's happened. Just the universe delivering on a long-ago promise. That's the kind of truth in which I now choose to believe.

ACKNOWLEDGMENTS

My husband, Jeff Salzberger, makes me laugh, walks the dogs, and puts up with a constant stream of creepy instrumental music as I'm writing. I am so thankful for him.

Love and gratitude to the Corrigan and Salzberger families, as well as Anne Glennon, Steve Loy, and Pat Neary. I feel profoundly lucky to have such caring guidance and steadfast support.

I am so grateful for my amazing siblings: Maureen McKay, Kathleen Ryden, John Corrigan, and Christine Corrigan. And my sort-of siblings: April Morecraft and Nina Stotler.

Thank you to David Levithan and the Scholastic dream team of Erin Black, Sheila Marie Everett, Esther Lin, and Chris Stengel. I'm sure that there are plenty of others who have a hand in shaping my manuscripts into books, but I am especially fortunate to benefit from their editorial, promotional, and artistic expertise.

Finally, I spend my days at Rutgers Preparatory School, surrounded by remarkable characters. While no aspect of this book is based on actual people or events, our exceptional community inspires me every day. Above all, Rutgers Prep's Class of 2012 holds major territory in my heart. I know that by the time this book sees the light of day, each member will be on his or her way to a bright and brilliant future.

DATE DUE
